Steampunk Reloaded

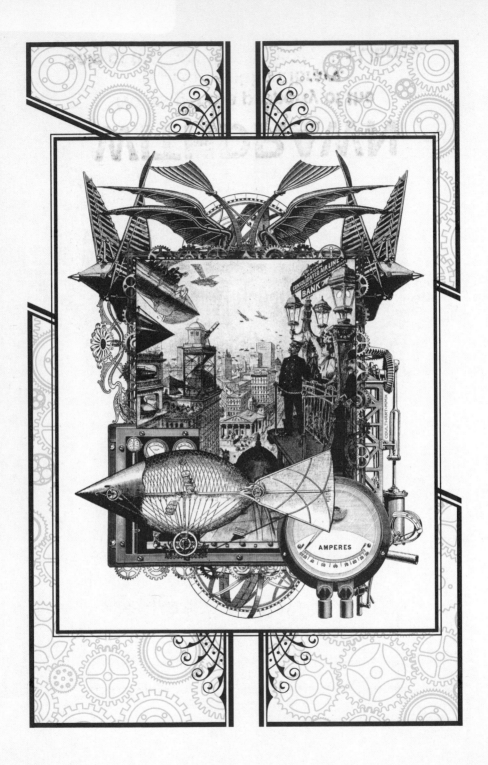

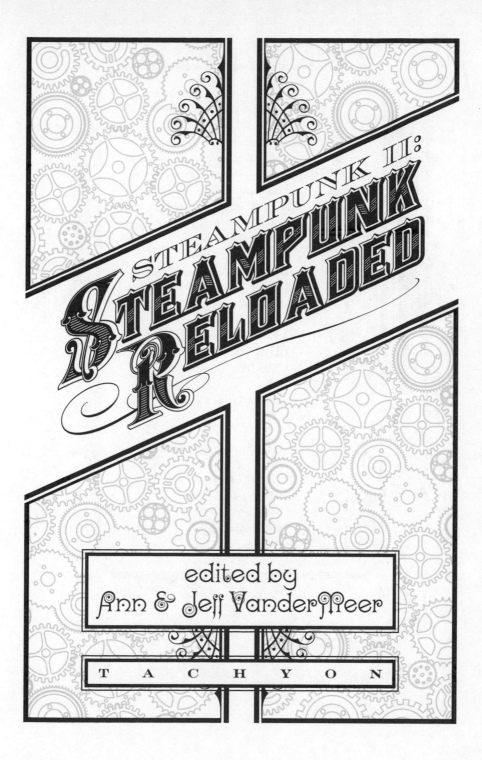

STEAMPUNK II:

STEAMPUNK
RELOADED

edited by
Ann & Jeff VanderMeer

TACHYON

Cover design by Ann Monn
Cover image © 2010 by Dan Jones / Tinkerbots
Interior design by John Coulthart

Tachyon Publications
1459 18ᵀᴴ Street #139
San Francisco, CA 94110

Series Editor: Jacob Weisman
Project Editor: Jill Roberts

Printed in the United States by Worzalla

ISBN 13: 978-1-61696-001-8
ISBN 10: 1-161696-001-9

First Edition: 2010
9 8 7 6 5 4 3 2 1

❈[Art by Eric Orchard]❈

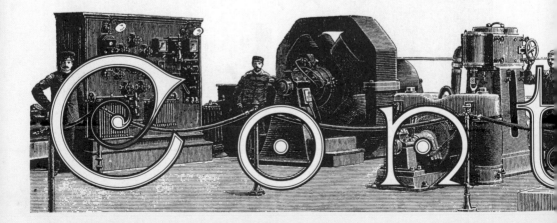

Nonfiction

☞ *Transition art & text by Ramona Szczerba*

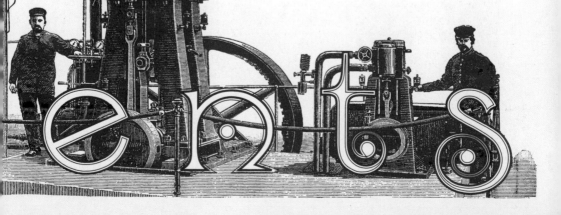

INTRODUCTION

What Is Steampunk?
Ann & Jeff VanderMeer

B Y NOW, "STEAMPUNK" has become a somewhat ubiquitous term in the media. Every week, it's the subject of Internet debates. Is steampunk "in" or "out," in good health or staggering toward the junkyard? Is steampunk progressive or reactionary, a movement or "just" an aesthetic tool kit used by a variety of creators in different media? Every week, too, writers for websites and blogs grapple with defining the term, often armed with second- or third-hand knowledge of the facts or the history.

Here are those facts, and that history. Modern steampunk fiction derives at least in part from works by Jules Verne and H. G. Wells in the 1800s and early twentieth century that featured steam-powered inventions, airships, and (sometimes) mad inventors. These books tended to be somewhat cautionary in nature, with a healthy unwillingness to accept "progress" as always inevitable and good. Some scholars, like Jess Nevins, also believe that the American Edisonades of the 1800s can be viewed as a form of proto-steampunk, although it's unlikely that modern steampunk writers are much influenced by these long-out-of-print works, which used steam inventions as a way of visualizing Manifest Destiny through simplistic, optimistic "cowboys-versus-indians" adventures. These adventures often contained the racist overtones common to the times and have not dated well.

How long did it take proto-steampunk to become "steampunk"? Despite several Verne or Wells homages, it wasn't until the 1970s that a true Godfather of modern steampunk would emerge: Michael Moorcock, who wrote his Nomads of the Air series over a period from 1971 to 1981. These books feature amazing battles between opposing fleets of airships, along with complex political and military intrigue. The novels were, Moorcock says, "intended as an intervention, if you like, into certain Edwardian views of Empire... They were intended to show that there was no such thing as a benign empire and that even if it seemed benign it wasn't. The stories were as much addressed to an emergent American empire as to the declining British." In a political sense, then, Moorcock's novels supported Verne's cautionary posture toward the role of technology in the world. They were also intensely progressive, a blistering critique of Victorian Imperialism, and hugely sympathetic to those peoples subjugated by the British.

However, the term "steampunk" was not invented until 1987, when K. W. Jeter coined it to describe his new novel *Infernal Devices* and previous novel *Morlock Nights*. In the pages of *Locus* magazine (#315, April 1987), Jeter wrote, with no little amount of mischief in his tone, "I think Victorian fantasies are going to be the next big thing, as long as we can come up with a fitting collective term...like 'steampunks,' perhaps." Jeter along with fellow writers Tim Powers (*The Anubis Gates*) and James Blaylock (the novella "Lord Kelvin's Machine," featured in our first anthology) spearheaded the steampunk literary movement.

Three years after Jeter's letter to the editor, William Gibson and Bruce Sterling published *The Difference Engine* (1990), which is most often cited as the seminal steampunk novel. It also had more in common with Moorcock's work, in terms of its undisguised insertion of social and political commentary, than novels by Powers, Blaylock, and Jeter. Set primarily in 1855, *The Difference Engine* posits an alternate reality in which Charles Babbage successfully built a mechanical computer, thus ushering in the Information Age at the same time as the Industrial Revolution. Juxtaposing Lord Byron, airships, and commentary on the unsavory aspects of the Victorian era, the novel's many steampunk pleasures include a vast and somewhat clunky mechanical AI housed in a fake Egyptian pyramid. Sterling and Gibson, like Moorcock, also comment on the role of technology in building empires.

Although other steampunk works were written during this time, the "movement," such as it was, died out or became part of the mainstream of science fiction. Throughout the 1990s and early parts of the aughts, steampunk mostly took the form of comics and movies (for a discussion of such works, refer to the essays in volume one)—and found expression through the nascent steampunk subculture. The subculture riffed off of those movies and comics, the works of Verne and Wells, and the Victorian era itself to create a vibrant fashion, arts, maker, and DIY community. While parts of this community might pay too little attention to the dark underpinnings of true Victorian society, in general it is progressive, inquisitive, and inclusive.

Mostly because of the spark and inspiration provided by the existence of this subculture, more and more writers are once again writing steampunk fiction. However, it's very different from what came before. The books that form the core of the canon from the first wave of steampunk—Moorcock, Jeter, Powers, Sterling, Gibson—are generally a small part of the influence on this next wave of steampunk. This next wave is also largely dominated by women, including Gail Carriger, Cherie Priest, Karin Lowachee and Ekaterina Sedia, and has begun to move away from being purely Victorian or English in setting or culture. In another generation, the true energy behind steampunk may have moved away from Anglo settings and perspectives altogether.

More importantly for the health of this anthology, perhaps, much more steampunk *short* fiction is being written than ever before in the history of the subgenre. Inspiration for this fiction is as likely to include the novels of manners as Verne and the growing influence of non-Western cultures. The influence of the maker movement is also apparent in what we would call a burgeoning of "steampunk tinker" stories that speak to the themes of self-sufficiency and DIY aesthetics that permeate the subculture. In short, steampunk has indeed become an aesthetic toolbox useful for a range of approaches.

Within this anthology, you'll find a rich sampling of that toolbox, from the mixing of Indian legend and the maker movement in Shweta Narayan's "The Mechanical Aviary of Emperor Jalal-ud-din Muhammad Akbar" to G. D. Falksen's use of steampunk to satirize our current fixation on the Internet, from Margo Lanagan's brilliant feminist take on automatons, "Machine Maid," to Samantha Henderson's original mash-up of faery and trickster stories in "Wild Copper."

We've also been careful to provide some historically relevant material from before the last decade, including Marc Laidlaw's cautionary tale about the beginnings of photography and "The Gernsback Continuum," the story by William Gibson that not only presaged the steampunk maker movement but also inspired the steampunk offshoot of "Raygun Gothic." (From Wikipedia: "a visual style that incorporates various aspects of the Googie, Streamline Moderne and Art Deco architectural styles when applied to retro-futuristic science fiction environments.")

Adding additional context to all of these great stories is a delightful and unexpected find: Vilhelm Bergsøe's "Flying Fish," translated here for the first time from the original Danish. "Flying Fish" isn't just an interesting story in its own right, but a great example of proto-steampunk from Verne's day and, in its generally progressive politics, an antidote to the reactionary approaches taken by the Edisonades of that time period.

"Flying Fish" isn't the only original material included herein—there's the 17,000-word "A Secret History of Steampunk" featuring contributions from the likes of Rikki Ducornet, Angela Slatter, L. L. Hannett, Fábio Fernandes, and Felix Gilman. We're also proud to present new fiction from rising star Ramsey Shehadeh and multiple World Fantasy Award winner Jeffrey Ford.

Finally, essays in the back of the book by Gail Carriger and Jake von Slatt provide more context on the steampunk subculture, with a "The Future of Steampunk" roundtable interview giving some glimpse of what steampunk might be like in the next decade.

In short, steampunk is alive and well and manifesting in a myriad of ways. We feel that this anthology provides an essential snapshot of that variety and that energy. Enjoy!

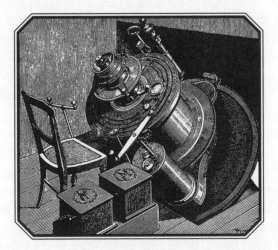

FICTION

ASYLUM FOR THE INSANE

Obadiah Theremin MD

"Obadiah Theremin, MD": Say what you will about Dr. Theremin, but there can be no question that the man was a dedicated clinician. Most psychiatrists rely on pills and talk to treat their patients, but since Obadiah saw the most hopeless of cases, he saw no harm in going that extra mile. Postulating that disturbed thoughts, like hot air, tend to rise only to precipitate misery upon their hosts, the good Dr. Theremin fitted himself with a device of his own invention that funneled the offending thoughts through a mysterious centrifuge and directly into his own cerebral cortex where he could process them thoroughly with his own unimpeachable sanity. Offending byproducts would pass harmlessly, he theorized, out of the handy faucet he implanted in his left ear, or could be simply exhaled with his pipe smoke—simple! In addition, those plagued by tortuous indecision could present their quandary to him at which point one or the other side of his forked beard would curl slightly at the tip, providing the querent with a definitive response. Meanwhile, his patented Mood-O-Meter hummed eerily on his desk, its needle spinning wildly to indicate his patient's current state. Okay, it's true that he was eventually committed himself, the protective goggles he swore by notwithstanding, but among the seriously deranged, he remains a legendary favorite.

Art & text by Ramona Szczerba.

The Gernsback Continuum

William Gibson

WILLIAM GIBSON is the author of several iconic works of fiction, including the novel *Neuromancer* and the short story collection *Burning Chrome*. He also co-authored the classic steampunk novel *The Difference Engine* with Bruce Sterling. More recent works include *Pattern Recognition*, *Spook Country*, and *Zero History*. "The Gernsback Continuum" first appeared in *Universe 11* in 1981. Gibson's use of the term "raygun gothic" has been used to describe an offshoot of the steampunk aesthetic exemplified by such movies as *Sky Captain and the World of Tomorrow* and Tim Burton's *Mars Attacks!* The term has also been used by maker Sean Orlando and his crew, creators of the Steampunk Treehouse, to describe their latest installation, a retro-futuristic rocketship.

MERCIFULLY, THE WHOLE thing is starting to fade, to become an episode. When I do still catch the odd glimpse, it's peripheral; mere fragments of mad-doctor chrome, confining themselves to the corner of the eye. There was that flying-wing liner over San Francisco last week, but it was almost translucent. And the shark-fin roadsters have gotten scarcer, and freeways discreetly avoid unfolding themselves into the gleaming eighty-lane monsters I was forced to drive last month in my rented Toyota. And I know that none of it will follow me to New York; my vision is narrowing to a single wavelength of probability. I've worked hard for that. Television helped a lot.

I suppose it started in London, in that bogus Greek taverna in Battersea Park Road, with lunch on Cohen's corporate tab. Dead steam-table food and it took them thirty minutes to find an ice bucket for the retsina. Cohen works for Barris-Watford, who publish big, trendy "trade" paperbacks: illustrated histories of the neon sign, the pinball machine, the windup toys of Occupied Japan. I'd gone over to shoot a series of shoe ads; California girls with tanned legs and frisky Day-Glo jogging shoes had capered for me down the escalators of St. John's Wood and across the platforms of Tooting Bec. A lean and hungry young agency had decided that the mystery of London Transport would sell waffle-tread nylon runners.

They decide; I shoot. And Cohen, whom I knew vaguely from the old days in New York, had invited me to lunch the day before I was due out of Heathrow. He brought along a very fashionably dressed young woman named Dialta Downes, who was virtually chinless and evidently a noted pop-art historian. In retrospect, I see her walking in beside Cohen under a floating neon sign that flashes THIS WAY LIES MADNESS in huge sans-serif capitals.

Cohen introduced us and explained that Dialta was the prime mover behind the latest Barris-Watford project, an illustrated history of what she called "American Streamlined Moderne." Cohen called it "raygun Gothic." Their working title was *The Airstream Futuropolis: The Tomorrow That Never Was.*

There's a British obsession with the more baroque elements of American pop culture, something like the weird cowboys-and-Indians fetish of the West Germans or the aberrant French hunger for old Jerry Lewis films. In Dialta Downes this manifested itself in a mania for a uniquely American form of architecture that most Americans are scarcely aware of. At first I wasn't sure what she was talking about, but gradually it began to dawn on me. I found myself remembering Sunday morning television in the Fifties.

Sometimes they'd run old eroded newsreels as filler on the local station. You'd sit there with a peanut butter sandwich and a glass of milk, and a static-ridden Hollywood baritone would tell you that there was A Flying Car in Your Future. And three Detroit engineers would putter around with this big old Nash with wings, and you'd see it rumbling furiously down some deserted Michigan runway. You never actually saw it take off, but it flew away to Dialta Downes's never-never land, true home of a generation of completely uninhibited technophiles. She was talking about those odds and ends of "futuristic" Thirties and Forties architecture you pass daily in American cities without noticing: the movie marquees ribbed to radiate some mysterious energy, the dime stores faced with fluted aluminum, the chrome-tube chairs gathering dust in the lobbies of transient hotels. She saw these things as segments of a dreamworld, abandoned in the uncaring present; she wanted me to photograph them for her.

The Thirties had seen the first generation of American industrial designers; until the Thirties, all pencil sharpeners had looked like pencil sharpeners—your basic Victorian mechanism, perhaps with a curlicue of decorative trim. After the advent of the designers, some pencil sharpeners looked as though they'd been put together in wind tunnels. For the most part, the change was only skin-deep; under the streamlined chrome shell, you'd find the same Victorian mechanism. Which made a certain kind of sense, because the most successful American designers had been recruited from the ranks of Broadway theater designers. It was all a stage set, a series of elaborate props for playing at living in the future.

Over coffee, Cohen produced a fat manila envelope full of glossies. I saw the winged statues that guard the Hoover Dam, forty-foot concrete hood ornaments leaning steadfastly into an imaginary hurricane. I saw a dozen shots of Frank Lloyd Wright's Johnson Wax Building, juxtaposed with the covers of old *Amazing Stories* pulps, by an artist named Frank R. Paul; the employees of Johnson Wax must have felt as though they were walking into one of Paul's spray-paint pulp Utopias. Wright's building looked as though it had been designed for people who wore white togas and Lucite sandals. I hesitated over one sketch of a particularly grandiose prop-driven airliner, all wing, like a fat, symmetrical boomerang with windows in unlikely places. Labeled arrows indicated the locations of the grand ballroom and two squash courts. It was dated 1936.

"This thing couldn't have flown…?" I looked at Dialta Downes.

"Oh, no, quite impossible, even with those twelve giant props; but they loved the look, don't you see? New York to London in less than two days, first-class dining rooms, private cabins, sun decks, dancing to jazz in the evening…. The designers were populists, you see; they were trying to give the public what it wanted. What the public wanted was the future."

I'd been in Burbank for three days, trying to suffuse a really dull-looking rocker with charisma, when I got the package from Cohen. It is possible to photograph what isn't there; it's damned hard to do, and consequently a very marketable talent. While I'm not bad at it, I'm not exactly the best, either, and this poor guy strained my Nikon's credibility. I got out depressed because I do like to do a good job, but not totally depressed, because I did make sure I'd gotten the check for the job, and I decided to restore myself with the sublime artiness of the Barris-Watford assignment. Cohen had sent me some books on Thirties design, more photos of streamlined buildings, and a list of Dialta Downes's fifty favorite examples of the style in California.

Architectural photography can involve a lot of waiting; the building becomes a kind of sundial, while you wait for a shadow to crawl away from a detail you want, or for the mass and balance of the structure to reveal itself in a certain way. While I was waiting, I thought of myself in Dialta Downes's America. When I isolated a few of the factory buildings on the ground glass of the Hasselblad, they came across with a kind of sinister totalitarian dignity, like the stadiums Albert Speer built for Hitler. But the rest of it was relentlessly tacky; ephemeral stuff extruded by the collective American subconscious of the Thirties, tending mostly to survive along depressing strips lined with dusty motels, mattress wholesalers, and small used-car lots. I went for the gas stations in a big way.

During the high point of the Downes Age, they put Ming the Merciless in charge of designing California gas stations. Favoring the architecture of his native Mongo, he cruised up and down the coast erecting raygun emplacements in white stucco. Lots of them featured superfluous central towers ringed with those strange radiator flanges that were a signature motif of the style and which made them look as though they might generate potent bursts of raw technological enthusiasm if you could only find the switch that turned them on. I shot one in San Jose an hour before the bulldozers arrived and drove right through the structural truth of plaster and lathing and cheap concrete.

"Think of it," Dialta Downes had said, "as a kind of alternate America: a 1980 that never happened. An architecture of broken dreams."

And that was my frame of mind as I made the stations of her convoluted socioarchitectural cross in my red Toyota—as I gradually tuned in to her image of a shadowy America-that-wasn't, of Coca-Cola plants like beached submarines, and fifth-run movie houses like the temples of some lost sect that had worshiped blue mirrors and geometry. And as I moved among these secret ruins, I found myself wondering what the inhabitants of that lost future would think of the world I lived in. The Thirties dreamed white marble and slipstream chrome, immortal crystal and burnished bronze, but the rockets on the covers of the Gernsback pulps had fallen on London in the dead of night, screaming. After the war, everyone had a car—no wings for it—and the promised superhighway to drive it down, so that the sky itself darkened, and the fumes ate the marble and pitted the miracle crystal…

And one day, on the outskirts of Bolinas, when I was setting up to shoot a particularly lavish example of Ming's martial architecture, I penetrated a fine membrane, a membrane of probability…

Ever so gently, I went over the Edge—

And looked up to see a twelve-engined thing like a bloated boomerang, all wing, thrumming its way east with an elephantine grace, so low that I could count the rivets in its dull silver skin, and hear—maybe—the echo of jazz.

I took it to Kihn. Merv Kihn, freelance journalist with an extensive line in Texas pterodactyls, redneck UFO contactees, bush-league Loch Ness monsters, and the Top Ten conspiracy theories in the loonier reaches of the American mass mind.

"It's good," said Kihn, polishing his yellow Polaroid shooting glasses on the hem of his Hawaiian shirt, "but it's not *mental;* lacks the true quill."

"But I saw it, Mervyn." We were seated poolside in brilliant Arizona sunlight. He was in Tucson waiting for a group of retired Las Vegas civil servants whose leader received messages from Them on her microwave oven. I'd driven all night and was feeling it.

"Of course you did. Of course you saw it. You've read my stuff; haven't you grasped my blanket solution to the UFO problem? It's simple, plain and country simple: people"—he settled the glasses carefully on his long hawk nose and fixed me with his best basilisk glare—"*see*...things. People see these things. Nothing's there, but people *see* them anyway. Because they need to, probably. You've read Jung, you should know the score.... In your case, it's so obvious: You admit you were thinking about this crackpot architecture, having fantasies.... Look, I'm sure you've taken your share of drugs, right? How many people survived the Sixties in California without having the odd hallucination? All those nights when you discovered that whole armies of Disney technicians had been employed to weave animated holograms of Egyptian hieroglyphs into the fabric of your jeans, say, or the times when—"

"But it wasn't like that."

"Of course not. It wasn't like that at all; it was 'in a setting of clear reality,' right? Everything normal, and then there's the monster, the mandala, the neon cigar. In your case, a giant Tom Swift airplane. It happens *all the time.* You aren't even crazy. You know that, don't you?" He fished a beer out of the battered foam cooler beside his deck chair.

"Last week I was in Virginia. Grayson County. I interviewed a sixteen-year-old girl who'd been assaulted by a *bar hade.*"

"A what?"

"A bear head. The severed head of a bear. This *bar hade,* see, was floating around on its own little flying saucer, looked kind of like the hubcaps on cousin Wayne's vintage Caddy. Had red, glowing eyes like two cigar stubs and telescoping chrome antennas poking up behind its ears." He burped.

"It assaulted her? How?"

"You don't want to know; you're obviously impressionable. 'It was cold'"—he lapsed into his bad Southern accent—"'and metallic.' It made electronic noises. Now that is the real thing, the straight goods from the mass unconscious, friend; that little girl is a witch. There's no place for her to function in this society. She'd have seen the devil if she hadn't been brought up on *The Bionic Woman* and all those *Star Trek* reruns. She is clued into the main vein. And she knows that it happened to her. I got out ten minutes before the heavy UFO boys showed up with the polygraph."

I must have looked pained, because he set his beer down carefully beside the cooler and sat up.

"If you want a classier explanation, I'd say you saw a semiotic ghost. All these contactee stories, for instance, are framed in a kind of sci-fi imagery that permeates our culture. I could buy aliens, but not aliens that look like Fifties' comic art. They're semiotic phantoms, bits of deep cultural imagery that have split off and taken on a life of their own, like the Jules Verne airships that those old Kansas farmers were always seeing. But you saw a different kind of ghost, that's all. That plane was part of the mass unconscious, once. You picked up on that, somehow. The important thing is not to worry about it."

I did worry about it, though.

Kihn combed his thinning blond hair and went off to hear what They had had to say over the radar range lately, and I drew the curtains in my room and lay down in air-conditioned darkness to worry about it. I was still worrying about it when I woke up. Kihn had left a note on my door; he was flying up north in a chartered plane to check out a cattle-mutilation rumor ("muties," he called them; another of his journalistic specialties).

I had a meal, showered, took a crumbling diet pill that had been kicking around in the bottom of my shaving kit for three years, and headed back to Los Angeles.

The speed limited my vision to the tunnel of the Toyota's headlights. The body could drive, I told myself, while the mind maintained. Maintained and stayed away from the weird peripheral window dressing of amphetamine and exhaustion, the spectral, luminous vegetation that grows out of the corners of the mind's eye along late-night highways. But the mind had its own ideas, and Kihn's opinion of what I was already thinking of as my "sighting" rattled endlessly through my head in a tight, lopsided orbit. Semiotic ghosts. Fragments of the Mass Dream, whirling past in the wind of my passage. Somehow this feedback-loop aggravated the diet pill, and the speed-vegetation along the road began to assume the colors of infrared satellite images, glowing shreds blown apart in the Toyota's slipstream.

I pulled over, then, and a half-dozen aluminum beer cans winked goodnight as I killed the headlights. I wondered what time it was in London, and tried to imagine Dialta Downes having breakfast in her Hampstead flat, surrounded by streamlined chrome figurines and books on American culture.

Desert nights in that country are enormous; the moon is closer. I watched the moon for a long time and decided that Kihn was right. The main thing was not to worry. All across the continent, daily, people who were more normal than I'd ever aspired to be saw giant birds, Bigfeet, flying oil refineries; they kept Kihn busy and solvent. Why should I be upset by a glimpse of the 1930s pop imagination loose over Bolinas? I decided to go to sleep, with nothing worse to worry about than rattlesnakes and cannibal hippies, safe amid the friendly roadside garbage of my own familiar continuum. In the morning I'd drive down to Nogales and photograph the old brothels, something I'd intended to do for years. The diet pill had given up.

The light woke me, and then the voices. The light came from somewhere behind me and threw shifting shadows inside the car. The voices were calm, indistinct, male and female, engaged in conversation.

My neck was stiff and my eyeballs felt gritty in their sockets. My leg had gone to sleep, pressed against the steering wheel. I fumbled for my glasses in the pocket of my work shirt and finally got them on.

Then I looked behind me and saw the city.

The books on Thirties design were in the trunk; one of them contained sketches of an idealized city that drew on *Metropolis* and *Things to Come*, but squared everything, soaring up through an architect's perfect clouds to zeppelin docks and mad neon spires. That city was a scale model of the one that rose behind me. Spire stood on spire in gleaming ziggurat steps that climbed to a central golden temple tower ringed with the crazy radiator flanges of the Mongo gas stations. You could hide the Empire State Building in the smallest of those towers. Roads of crystal soared between the spires, crossed and recrossed by smooth silver shapes like beads of running mercury. The air was thick with ships: giant wing-liners, little darting silver things (sometimes one of the quicksilver shapes from the sky bridges rose gracefully into the air and flew up to join the dance), mile-long blimps, hovering dragonfly things that were gyrocopters...

I closed my eyes tight and swung around in the seat. When I opened them, I willed myself to see the mileage meter, the pale road dust on the black plastic dashboard, the overflowing ashtray.

"Amphetamine psychosis," I said. I opened my eyes. The dash was still there, the dust, the crushed filter tips. Very carefully, without moving my head, I turned the headlights on.

And saw them.

They were blond. They were standing beside their car, an aluminum avocado with a central shark-fin rudder jutting up from its spine and smooth black tires like a child's toy. He had his arm around her waist and was gesturing toward the city. They were both in white: loose clothing, bare legs, spotless white sun shoes. Neither of them seemed aware of the beams of my headlights. He was saying something wise and strong, and she was nodding, and suddenly I was frightened, frightened in an entirely different way. Sanity had ceased to be an issue; I knew, somehow, that the city behind me was Tucson—a dream Tucson thrown up out of the collective yearning of an era. That it was real, entirely real. But the couple in front of me lived in it, and they frightened me.

They were the children of Dialta Downes's '80-that-wasn't; they were Heirs to the Dream. They were white, blond, and they probably had blue eyes. They were American. Dialta had said that the Future had come to America first, but had finally passed it by. But not here, in the heart of the Dream. Here, we'd gone on and on, in a dream logic that knew nothing of pollution, the finite bounds of fossil fuel, or foreign wars it was possible to lose. They were smug, happy, and utterly content with themselves and their world. And in the Dream, it was *their* world.

Behind me, the illuminated city: Searchlights swept the sky for the sheer joy of it. I imagined them thronging the plazas of white marble, orderly and alert, their bright eyes shining with enthusiasm for their floodlit avenues and silver cars.

It had all the sinister fruitiness of Hitler Youth propaganda.

I put the car in gear and drove forward slowly, until the bumper was within three feet of them. They still hadn't seen me. I rolled the window down and listened to what the man was saying. His words were bright and hollow as the pitch in some chamber of commerce brochure, and I knew that he believed in them absolutely.

"John," I heard the woman say, "we've forgotten to take our food pills." She clicked two bright wafers from a thing on her belt and passed one to him. I backed onto the highway and headed for Los Angeles, wincing and shaking my head.

I phoned Kihn from a gas station. A new one, in bad Spanish Modern. He was back from his expedition and didn't seem to mind the call.

"Yeah, that is a weird one. Did you try to get any pictures? Not that they ever come out, but it adds an interesting *frisson* to your story, not having the pictures turn out…"

But what should I do?

"Watch lots of television, particularly game shows and soaps. Go to porn movies. Ever see *Nazi Love Motel*? They've got it on cable, here. Really awful. Just what you need."

What was he talking about?

"Quit yelling and listen to me. I'm letting you in on a trade secret: Really bad media can exorcise your semiotic ghosts. If it keeps the saucer people off my back, it can keep these Art Deco futuroids off yours. Try it. What have you got to lose?"

Then he begged off, pleading an early-morning date with the Elect.

"The who?"

"These oldsters from Vegas; the ones with the microwaves."

I considered putting a collect call through to London, getting Cohen at Barris-Watford and telling him his photographer was checked out for a protracted season in the Twilight Zone. In the end, I let a machine mix me a really impossible cup of black coffee and climbed back into the Toyota for the haul to Los Angeles.

Los Angeles was a bad idea, and I spent two weeks there. It was prime Downes country; too much of the Dream there, and too many fragments of the Dream waiting to snare me. I nearly wrecked the car on a stretch of overpass near Disneyland when the road fanned out like an origami trick and left me swerving through a dozen minilanes of whizzing chrome teardrops with shark fins. Even worse, Hollywood was full of people who looked too much like the couple I'd seen in Arizona. I hired an Italian director who was making ends meet doing darkroom work and installing patio decks around swimming pools until his ship came in; he made prints of all the negatives I'd accumulated on the Downes job. I didn't want to look at the stuff myself. It didn't seem to bother Leonardo, though, and when he was finished I checked the prints, riffling through them like a deck of cards, sealed them up, and sent them air freight to London. Then I took a taxi to a theater that was showing *Nazi Love Motel* and kept my eyes shut all the way.

Cohen's congratulatory wire was forwarded to me in San Francisco a week later. Dialta had loved the pictures. He admired the way I'd "really gotten into it," and looked forward to working with me again. That afternoon I spotted a flying wing over Castro Street, but there was something tenuous about it, as if it were only half there. I rushed to the nearest newsstand and gathered up as much as I could find on the petroleum crisis and the nuclear energy hazard. I'd just decided to buy a plane ticket for New York.

"Hell of a world we live in, huh?" The proprietor was a thin black man with bad teeth and an obvious wig. I nodded, fishing in my jeans for change, anxious to find a park bench where I could submerge myself in hard evidence of the human near-dystopia we live in. "But it could be worse, huh?"

"That's right," I said, "or even worse, it could be perfect."

He watched me as I headed down the street with my little bundle of condensed catastrophe.

Great Breakthroughs in Darkness

(BEING, EARLY ENTRIES FROM *The Secret Encyclopaedia of Photography*)

AUTHORIZED BY

Marc Laidlaw

CHIEF SECRETARY OF THE MINISTRY OF
PHOTOGRAPHIC ARCANA, CORRESPONDENT OF NO
FEW ACADEMIES, DEVOTED HUSBAND, &C.

After publishing half a dozen novels, MARC LAIDLAW (WWW.MARCLAIDLAW.COM), jaded by the demanding glamour of life as a full-time legal secretary, joined the fledgling Valve Software to help create and write the bestselling *Half-Life* series of videogames. He remains at Valve, refining his Pacific Northwest pallor, playing games, and dabbling in the occasional short story. His novels have been finalists for the Philip K. Dick Award and the World Fantasy Award, while his so-far-penultimate novel, *The 37th Mandala*, received the International Horror Guild Award for Best Novel. Of his story, Laidlaw writes, "Photography has been a sporadic serial obsession of mine, culminating in the construction of a working darkroom which I assembled just in time for the birth of our first child, after which I never used it again. As with most writers, my obsessions tend to both fuel and justify the creation of fiction about them."

"Alas! That this speculation is somewhat too refined to be introduced into a modern novel or romance; for what a *denouement* we should have, if we could suppose the secrets of the darkened chamber to be revealed by the testimony of the imprinted paper!" —William Henry Fox Talbot

-A-

AANSCHULTZ, CONREID
(c. 1820–October 12, 1888)

Inventor of the praxiscope technology (*which see*), Professor Aanschultz believed that close observation of physiology and similar superficial phenomena could lead to direct revelation of the inner or secret processes of nature. Apparent proof of this now discredited theory was offered by his psychopraxiscope, which purported to offer instantaneous viewing of any subject's thoughts. (Later researchers demonstrated that the device "functioned" by creating interference patterns in the inner eye of the observer, triggering phosphene splash and lucid dreaming.) Aanschultz's theories collapsed, and the Professor himself died in a Parisian lunatic asylum, after his notorious macropraxiscope failed to extract any particular meaning from the contours of the Belgian countryside near Waterloo. Some say he was already unstable from abuse of his autopsychopraxiscope, thought to be particularly dangerous because of autophagous feedback patterns generated in its operator's brain. However, there is evidence that Aanschultz was quite mad already, owing to the trauma of an earlier research disaster.

AANSCHULTZ LENS
The key lens used in Aanschultz's notorious psychopraxiscope, designed to capture and focus abaxial rays reflecting from a subject's eye.

ABAT-JOUR
A skylight or aperture for admitting light to a studio, or an arrangement for securing the same end by reflection. In the days when studios for portraiture were generally found at the tops of buildings not originally erected for that purpose, and perhaps in narrow thoroughfares or with a high obstruction adjacent, I found myself climbing a narrow, ill-lit flight of stairs, away from the sound of wagon wheels rattling on cobblestones, the common foetor of a busy city street, and toward a more rarified and addictive stench compounded of chemicals that would one day be known to have contributed directly to society's (and my own) madness and disease. It was necessary to obtain all available top light in the choked alleys, and Aanschultz had done everything he could in a city whose sky was blackly draped with burning sperm.

I came out into a dazzling light compounded of sunlight and acetylene, between walls yellowed by iodine vapor, covering my nose at the stench of mercury fumes, the reek of sulphur. My own fingertips were blackened from such stuff; and eczema procurata, symptomatic of a metal allergy, had sent a prurient rash all up the sensitive skin of my inner arms, which, though so bound in bandages that I could scarcely scratch them through my heavy woollen sleeves, were a constant seeping agony. At night I wore a woman's long kid gloves coated with coal tar, and each morning dressed my wounds with an ointment of mercuric nitrate (*60 g*), carbolic acid (*10 ccs*), zinc oxide (*30 g*) and lanoline (*480*

"), which I had learned to mix myself when the chemist professed a groundless horror of contagion. I had feared at first that the rash might spread over my body, down my flanks, invading the delicate skin of my thighs and those organs between them, softer by far. I dreaded walking like a crab, legs bowed far apart, experiencing excruciating pain at micturition and intercourse (at least syphilis is painless; even when it chews away one's face, I am told, there is a pleasant numbness)—but so far this nightmare had not developed. Still, I held my tender arms slightly spread away from my sides, seeming always on the verge of drawing the twin Janssen photographic revolvers which I carried in holsters slung around my waist, popular hand-held versions of that amazing "gun" which first captured the transit of Venus across the face of our local star.

The laboratory, I say, was a fury of painfully brilliant light and sharp, membrane-searing smells. Despite my admiration for the Professor's efficiency, I found it not well-suited for artistic purposes, a side light being usually preferable instead of the glare of a thousand suns that came down through the cruelly contrived abat-jour. But Aanschultz, being of a scientific bent, saw in twilight landscapes only some great treasure to be prised forth with all necessary force. He would have disemboweled the earth itself if he thought an empirical secret were lodged just out of reach in its craw. I had suggested a more oblique light, but the Professor would not hear of it.

"That is for your prissy studios—for your fussy bourgeois sitters!" he would rage at my "aesthetic" suggestions. "I am a man of science. My subjects come not for flattering portraits, but for insight—I observe the whole man here." To which I replied: "And yet you have not *captured* him. You have not impressed a single supposition on so much as one thin sheet of tin or silver or albumen glass. The fleeting things you see cannot be captured. Which is less than I can say of even the poorest photograph, however superficial." And here he always scoffed at me and turned away, pacing, so that I knew my jibes had cut to the core of his own doubts, and that he was still, with relentless logic, stalking a way to fix the visions viewed so briefly (however engrossingly) in his praxiscope.

He needed lasting records of his studies—some substance the equivalent of photographic paper that might hold the scope's pictures in place for all to see, for all time. It was this magical medium which he now sought. I thought it must be something of a "Deep" paper—a sheet of more than three dimensions, into which thoughts might be imprinted in all their complexity, a sort of mind-freezing mirror. When he shared his own ideas, I quickly became lost, and if I made any comment it soon led to vicious argument. I could not follow Aanschultz's arguments on any subject; even our discussions of what or where to eat for lunch, what beer went best with bratwurst, could become incomprehensible. Only another genius could follow where Aanschultz went in his thoughts. With time I had even stopped looking in his eyes—with or without a psychopraxiscope.

"I am nearly there," he told me today, as I reached the top of the stairs with a celebratory bottle in hand.

"You've found a way to fix the psychic images?"

"No—something new. My life's work. This will live long after me."

He said the same of every current preoccupation. His assistants were everywhere, adjusting the huge rack of movable mirrors that conducted light down from the rooftops, in from the street, over from the alleyway, wherever there happened to be a stray unreaped ray of it. Their calls rang out through the laboratory, echoing down through pipes like those in great ships, whereby the captain barks orders to the engine room. In the center of the chamber stood the solar navigator with his vast charts and compass and astrolabes scattered around him, constantly shouting into any one of the dozen pipes that coiled down from the ceiling like dangling vines, dispatching orders to those who stood in clearer sight of the sun but with a less complete foreknowledge of its motion; and as he shouted, the mirrors canted this way and that, and the huge collectors on the roof purred in their oiled bearings and the entire building creaked under the shifting weight and the laboratory burned like a furnace, although cleverly, without any heat. There was a watery luminescence in the air, a constant distorted rippling that sent wavelets lapping over the walls and tables and charts and retorts and tarnished boxes, turning the iodine stains a lurid green; this was the result of light pouring through racks of blue glass vials, old glass that had run and blistered with age, stoppered bottles full of copper sulphate which also swivelled and tilted according to the instructions of another assistant who stood very near the navigator. I had to raise my own bottle and drink very deeply before any of this made much sense to me, or until I could approach a state of focused distraction more like that of my friend and mentor, the great Professor Conreid Aanschultz, who now came at me and snatched the bottle from my hands and helped himself. He courteously polished every curve of the flask with a fresh chamois before handing it back, eradicating his last fingerprint as the bottle left his fingers, so that the now nearly empty vessel gleamed as brightly as those blue ones. I finished it off and dropped it in a half-assembled filter rack, where it would find a useful life even empty. The Professor made use of all *Things*.

"This way," he said, leading me past a huge hissing copperclad acetylene generator of the dreadnought variety, attended by several anxious-looking children in the act of releasing quantities of gas through a purifier. The proximity of this somewhat dangerous operation to the racks of burning Bray 00000 lamps made me uncomfortable, and I was grateful to move over a light-baffling threshold into darkness. Here, a different sort of chaos reigned, but it was, if anything, even more intense and busy. I sensed, even before my eyes had adjusted to the weak and eerie working light, that these assistants were closer to Aanschultz's actual current work, and that this work must be very near to completion, for they had that weary, pacified air of slaves who have been whipped to the very limits of human endurance and then suspended beyond that point for days on end. I doubted any had slept or rested for nearly as long as Aanschultz, who was possessed of superhuman reserves. I myself, of quite contrary disposition, had risen late that morning, feasted on a huge lunch (which even now was producing unexpected gases like my own internal rumbling dreadnought), and, feeling benevolent, had decided to answer my friend's urgent message of the previous day, which had hinted that his fever pitch of work was about to bear fruit—a pronouncement he always made long in advance of the actual climax, thus giving me plenty of my own slow time to come around. For poor Aanschultz, time was compressed from line to point. His was a world of constant Discovery.

I bumped into nearly everything and everyone in the darkened chamber before my eyes adjusted, when finally I found myself bathed in a deep, rich violet light, decanted through yet another rack of bottles, although of a correspondingly darker hue. Blood or burgundy, they seemed at first; and reminded me of the liquid edge of clouds one sometimes sees at sunset, when all form seems to buzz and crackle as it melts into the coming night, and the eye tingles in anticipation of discovering unsuspected hues. My skin now hummed with this same subtle optical electricity. Things in the room seemed to glow with an inner light.

"Here we are," he said. "This will make everything possible. This is my—"

ABAT-NUIT

By this name Aanschultz referred to a bevelled opening he had cut into an odd corner of the room, a tight and complex angle formed between the floor and the brick abutment of a chimney shaft from the floors below. I could not see how he had managed to collect any light from this darkest of corners, but I quickly saw my error. For it was not light he bothered to collect in this way, but darkness.

Darkness was somehow channeled into the room and then filtered through those racks of purple bottles, in some of which I now thought to see floating specks and slowly tumbling shapes that might have been wine lees or bloodclots. I even speculated that I saw the fingers of a deformed, pickled foetus clutching at the rays that passed through its glass cell, playing inverse shadow-shapes on the walls of the dark room, casting its enlarged and gloomy spell over all us awed and frightened older children.

Unfiltered, the darkness was much harder to characterize; when I tried to peer into it, Aanschultz pulled me away, muttering, "Useless for our purposes."

"Our?" I repeated, as if I had anything to do with this. For even then it seemed an evil power my friend had harnessed, something best left to its own devices—something which, in collaboration with human genius, could only lead to the worsening of an already precarious situation.

"This is my greatest work yet," he confided, but I could see that his assistants thought otherwise. The shadows already darkening Europe seemed thickest in this corner of the room. I felt that the strangely beveled opening with its canted mirror inside a silvery-black throat, reflecting darkness from an impossible angle, was in fact the source of all unease to be found in the streets and in the marketplace. It was as if everyone had always known about this webby corner, and feared that it might eventually be prised open by the violent levering of a powerful mind.

I comforted myself with the notion that this was a discovery, not an invention, and therefore for all purposes inevitable. Given a mind as focused as Aanschultz's, this corner was bound to be routed out and put to some use. However, I already suspected that the eventual use would not be that which Aanschultz expected.

I watched a thin girl with badly bruised arms weakly pulling a lever alongside the abat-nuit to admit more darkness through the purple bottles, and the deepening darkness seemed to penetrate her skin as well as the jars, pouring through the webs of her fingers, the meat of her arms, so that the shadows of bone and cartilage glowed within them, flesh flensed away in the revealing black radiance. It was little consolation to think that the discovery was implicit in the fact of this corner, this source of darkness built into the universe, embedded in creation like an aberration in a lens and therefore unavoidable. It had taken merely a mind possessed of an equal or complementary aberration to uncover it. I only hoped Aanschultz possessed the power to compensate for the darkness's distortion, much as chromatic aberration may be compensated or avoided entirely by the use of an apochromatic lens. But I had little hope for this in my friend's case. Have I mentioned it was his cruelty which chiefly attracted me?

ABAXIAL

Away from the axis. A term applied to the oblique or marginal rays passing through a lens. Thus the light of our story is inevitably deflected from its most straightforward path by the medium of the *Encyclopaedia* itself, and this entry in particular. Would that it were otherwise, and this a perfect world. Some go so far as to state that the entirety of Creation is itself an

ABERRATION

A functional result of optical law. Yet I felt that this matter might be considered Aanschultz's fault, despite my unwillingness to think any ill of my friend. In my professional capacity, I was surrounded constantly by the fat and the beautiful; the lazy, plump and pretty. They flocked to my studio in hordes, in droves, in carriages and cars, in swan-necked paddle boats; and their laughter flowed up and down the three flights of stairs to my studios and galleries, where my polite assistants bade them sit and wait until *Monsieur Artiste* might be available. Sometimes Monsieur failed to appear at all, and they were forced with much complaining to be photographed by a mere apprentice, at a reduced rate, although I always kept on hand plenty of pre-signed plates so that they might take away an original and be as impressive as their friends. I flirted with the ladies; was indulgent with the children; I spoke to the gentlemen as if I had always been one of them, concerned with the state of trade, rates of exchange, the crisis in labor, the inevitable collapse of economies. I was in short a chameleon, softer than any of them, lazier and more variable, yet prouder. They meant nothing to me; they were all so easy and pretty and (I thought then) expendable.

Yet there was only one Aanschultz. On the first and only day he came to sit for me (he had decided to require all his staff to wear tintype badges for security reasons and himself set the first example), I knew I had never met his like. He looked hopelessly out of place in my waiting chambers, awkward on the steep stairs, white and etiolated in the diffuse cuprous light of my abat-jour. Yet his eyes were livid; he had violet pupils, and I wished—not for the first time—that there were some way of capturing color with all my clever lenses and cameras. None of my staff colorists could hope to duplicate that hue. The fat pleasant women flocking the studios grew thin and uncomfortable at the sight of him, covering their mouths with handkerchiefs, exuding sharp perfumes of fear that neutralized their ambergris and artificial scents. He did not leer or bare his teeth or rub his hands and cackle; these obvious melodramatic motions would only have cheapened and blunted the sense one had of his refined cruelty.

Perhaps "cruel" is the wrong word. It was a severity in his nature—an unwillingness to tolerate any thought, sensation, or companion duller than a razor's edge. I felt instantly stimulated by his presence, as if I had at last found someone against whom I could gauge myself, not as opponent or enemy, but as a student who forever tries and tests himself against the model of his mentor. In my youth I had known instinctively that it is always better to stay near those I considered my superiors; for then I could never let my own skills diminish, but must constantly be polishing and practicing them. With age and success, I had nearly forgotten that crucial lesson, having sheltered too long in the cozy nests and parlors of Society. Aanschultz's laboratory proved to be their perfect antidote.

We two could not have been less alike. As I have said, I had no clear understanding of, and only slightly more interest in, the natural sciences. Art was All, to me. It had been my passion and my livelihood for so long now that I had nearly forgotten there was any other way of life. Aanschultz reintroduced me to the concepts of hard speculation and experimentation, a lively curriculum which soon showed welcome results in my own artistic practices. For in the city, certain competitors had mastered my methods and now offered similar services at lower prices, lacking only the fame of my name to beat me out of business. In the coltish marketplace, where economies trembled beneath the rasping tongue of forces so bleak they seemed the product of one's own fears, with no objective source in the universe, it began to seem less than essential to possess an extraordinary signature on an otherwise ordinary photograph; why spend all that money for a Name when just down the street, for two-thirds the price, one could have a photograph of equivalent quality, lacking only my florid famous autograph (of which, after all, there was already a glut)? So you see, I was in danger already when I met Aanschultz, without yet suspecting its encroachment. With his aid I was soon able to improve the quality of my product far beyond the reach of my competitors. Once more my name reclaimed its rightful magic potency, not for empty reasons, not through mere force of advertising, but because I was indeed superior.

To all of Paris I might have been a great man, an artistic genius, but in Aanschultz's presence I felt like a young and stupid child. The scraps I scavenged from his workshop floors were not even the shavings of his important work. He hardly knew the good he did me, for although an immediate bond developed between us, at times he hardly seemed aware of my presence. I would begin to think that he had forgotten me completely; weeks might pass when I heard not a word from him; and then, suddenly, my faith in our friendship would be reaffirmed, for out of all the people he might have told—his scientific peers, politicians, the wealthy—he would come to me first with news of his latest breakthrough, as if my opinion were of greatest importance to him. I fancied that he looked to me for artistic inspiration (no matter how much he might belittle the impulse) just as I came to him for his scientific rigor.

It was this rigor which at times bordered on cruelty—though only when emotion was somehow caught in the slow, ineluctably turning gears of his logic. He would not scruple to destroy a scrap of human fancy with diamond drills and acid blasts in order to discover some irreducible atom of hard fact (+10 on the Mohs scale) at its core. This meant, unfortunately, that each of his advances had left a trail of crushed "victims," not all of whom had thrown themselves willingly before the juggernaut. I sensed that this poor girl would soon be one of them.

ABRASION MARKS

of a curious sort covered her arms, something like a cross between bruises, burns and blistering. Due to my own eczema, I felt a sympathic pang as she backed away from the levers of the abat-nuit, Aanschultz brushing her off angrily to make the final adjustments himself. She looked very young to be working such long hours in the darkness, so near the source of those strange black rays, but when I mentioned this to my friend he merely swept a hand in the direction of another part of the room, where a thin woman lay stretched out on a stained pallet, her arm thrown over her eyes, head back, mouth gaping; at first she appeared as dead as the drowned poseur Hippolyte Bayard, but I saw her breast rising and falling raggedly. The girl at the lever moved slowly, painfully, over to this woman and knelt down beside her, then very tenderly laid her head on the barely moving breast, so that I knew they were mother and child. Leaving Aanschultz for the moment, I sank down beside them, stroking the girl's frayed black hair gently as I asked if there were anything I could do for them.

"Who's there?" the woman said hoarsely.

I gave my name, but she appeared not to recognize it. She didn't need illustrious visitors now, I knew.

"He's with the Professor," the child said, scratching vigorously at her arms though it obviously worsened them. I could see red, oozing meat through the scratches her fingernails left.

"You should bandage those arms," I said. "I have sterile cloth and ointment in my carriage if you'd like me to do it."

"Bandages and ointment, he says," said the woman. "As if there's any healing it. Leave her alone now—she's done what she could where I had to leave off. You'll just get the doctor mad at both of us."

"I'm sure he'd understand if I—"

"Leave us be!" the woman howled, sitting up now, propped on both hands so that her eyes came uncovered, to my horror; for across her cheeks, forehead and nose was an advanced variety of the same damage her daughter suffered; her eyesockets held little heaps of charred ash that, as she thrust her face forward in anger, poured like black salt from between her withered lids and sifted softly onto the floor, reminding me unavoidably of that other and most excellent abrading powder which may be rubbed on dried negatives to provide a "tooth" for the penciller's art, consisting of one part powdered resin and two parts cuttle-fish bone, the whole being sifted through silk. I suspected this powder would do just as well, were I crass enough to gather it in my kerchief. She fell back choking and coughing on the black dust, beating at the air, while her daughter moved away from me in tears, and jumped when she heard Aanschultz's sharp command.

I turned to see my friend beckoning with one crooked finger for the girl to come and hold the levers just so while he screwed down a clamp.

"My God, Aanschultz," I said, without much hope of a satisfactory answer. "Don't you see what your darkness has done to these wretches?"

He muttered from the side of his mouth: "It's not a problem any longer. A short soak in a bath of potassium iodide and iodine will protect the surface from abrasion."

"A print surface, perhaps, but these are people!"

"It works on me," he said, thrusting at me a bare arm that showed scarcely any scarring. "Now either let the girl do her work, or do it for her."

I backed away quickly, wishing things were otherwise; but in those days Aanschultz and his peers needed fear no distracting investigations from the occupational safety officials. He could with impunity remain oblivious to everything but the work that absorbed him.

ABSORPTION

This term is used in a chemical, an optical, and an esoteric sense. In the first case it designates the taking up of one substance by another, just as a sponge absorbs or sucks up water, with hardly any chemical but merely a physical change involved; this is by far the least esoteric meaning, roughly akin to those surface phenomena which Aanschultz hoped to strip aside. Optically, absorption is applied to the suppression of light, and to it are due all color effects, including the dense dark stippling of the pores of Aanschultz's face, ravaged by the pox in early years, and the weird violet aura—the same color as his eyes, as if it had bled out of them—that limned his profile as he bent closer to that weirdly angled aperture into artificial darkness.

My friend, with unexpected consideration for my lack of expertise, now said: "According to Draper's law, only those rays which are absorbed by a substance act chemically on it; when not absorbed, light is converted into some other form of energy. This dark beam converts matter in ways heretofore unsuspected, and is itself transformed into a new substance. Give me my phantospectroscope."

This last command was meant for the girl, who hurriedly retrieved a well-worn astrolabe-like device from a concealed cabinet and pressed it into her master's hands.

"The spectrum is like nothing ever seen on this earth," he said, pulling aside the rack of filter bottles and bending toward his abat-nuit with the phantospectroscope at his eye, like a sorcerer stooping to divine the future in the embers of a hearth where some sacrifice has just done charring. I could not bear the cold heat of that unshielded black fire. I took several quick steps back.

"I would show you," he went on, "but it would mean nothing to you. This is my real triumph, this phantospectroscope; it will be the foundation of a new science. Until now, visual methods of spectral inspection have been confined to the visible portion of the spectrum; the ultraviolet and infrared regions gave way before slow photographic methods; and there we came to a halt. But I have gone beyond that now. Ha! Yes!"

He thrust the phantospectroscope back into the burned hands of his assistant and made a final adjustment to the levers that controlled the angle and intensity of rays conducted through the abat-nuit. As the darkness deepened in that clinical space, it dawned on me that the third and deepest meaning of absorption was something like worship, and not completely dissimilar to terror.

ACCELERATOR!

my friend shouted, and I sensed rather than saw the girl moving toward him, but too slowly. Common accelerators are sodium carbonate, washing soda, ammonia, potassium carbonate, sodium hydrate (caustic soda), and potassium hydrate (caustic potash), none of which suited Aanschultz. He screamed again, and now there was a rush of bodies, a crush of them in the small corner of the room. An accelerator shortens the duration of development and brings out an image more quickly, but the images he sought to capture required special attention. As is written in the *Encyclopaedia of Photography* (1911, exoteric edition), "Accelerators cannot be used as fancy dictates." I threw myself back, fearful that otherwise I would be shoved through the gaping abat-nuit and myself dissolve into that negative essence. I heard the girl mewing at my feet, trod on by her fellows, and I leaned to help her up. But at that moment there was a quickening in the evil corner, and I put my hands to a more instinctive use.

ACCOMMODATION OF THE EYE

The darkness cupped inside my palms seemed welcoming by comparison to the anti-light that had emptied the room of all meaning. With both eyes covered, I felt I was beyond harm. I could not immediately understand the source of the noises and commotion I heard around me, nor did I wish to. (*See also*, "Axial Accommodation.")

ACCUMULATOR

Apparently (and this I worked out afterward in hospital beside Aanschultz) the room had absorbed its fill of the neutralizing light. All things threatened to split at their seams. Matter itself, the atmosphere, Aanschultz's assistants, bare thought, creaking metaphor—these things and others were stuffed to the bursting point. My own mind was a peaking crest of images and insights, a wave about to break. Aanschultz screamed incomprehensible commands as he realized the sudden danger; but there must have been no one who still retained the necessary self-control to obey him. My friend himself leapt to reverse the charge, to shut down the opening, sliding the rack of filtering jars back in place—but even he was too late to prevent one small, significant rupture.

I heard the inexplicable popping of corks, accompanied by a simultaneous metallic grating, followed by the shattering of glass. Aanschultz later whispered of what he had glimpsed out of the edges of his eyes, and by no means can I—nor would I—discredit him.

It was the bottles and jars in the filter rack that burst. Or rather, some burst, curved glass shards and gelatinous contents flying, spewing, dripping, clotting the floor and ceiling, spitting backward into the bolt-hole of night. Other receptacles opened with more deliberation. Aanschultz later blushed when he described, with perfect objectivity, the sight of certain jar lids unscrewing themselves from within. The dripping and splashes and soft wet steps I heard, he said, bore an actual correspondence in physical reality, but he refused ever to go into further detail on exactly what manner of things, curdled there and quickened in those jars by the action of that deep black light, leapt forth to scatter through the laboratory, slipping between the feet of his assistants, scurrying for the shadows, bleeding away between the planks of the floor and the cracks of our minds, seeping out into the world. My own memory is somewhat more distorted by emotion, for I felt the girl clutching at my ankles and heard her terrible cries. I forced myself to tear my hands away from my face—while still keeping my eyes pressed tight shut—and leaned down to offer help. No sooner had I taken hold of her fingers than she began to scream more desperately. Fearing that I was aggravating her wounds, I relaxed my hands to ease her pain; but she clung even more tightly to my hands and her screams intensified. It was as if something were pulling her away from me, as if I were her final anchor. As soon as I realized this, as soon as I tried to get a better hold on her, she slipped away. I heard her mother calling. The girl's cries were smothered. Across the floor rushed a liquid seething, as of a sudden flood draining from the room and down the abat-nuit and out of the laboratory entirely.

My first impulse was to follow, but I could no longer see a thing, even with my eyes wide open.

"A light!" I shouted, and Aanschultz overlapped my own words with his own: "No!"

But too late. The need for fire was instinctive, beyond Aanschultz's ability to quell by force or reason. A match was struck, a lantern lit and instantly in panic dropped; and as we fled onrushing flames, in that instant of total exposure, Aanschultz's most ambitious and momentous experiment reached its climax…although the denouement for the rest of Europe and the world would be a painful and protracted one.

ACETALDEHYDE
(*See* "Aldehyde.")

ACETIC ACID
The oldest of acids, with many uses in photography, in early days as a constituent of the developer for wet plates, later for clearing iron from bromide prints, to assist in uranium toning, and as a restrainer. It is extremely volatile and should be kept in a glass-stoppered bottle and in a cool place.

ACETIC ETHER
Synonym, ethyl acetate. A light, volatile, colorless liquid with pleasant acetous smell, sometimes used in making collodion. It should be kept in well-stoppered bottles away from fire, as the vapor is very inflammable.

ACETONE
A colorless volatile liquid of peculiar and characteristic odor, with two separate and distinct uses in photography, as an addition to developers and in varnish making. As the vapor is highly inflammable, the liquid should be kept in a bottle with a close-fitting cork or glass stopper.

ACETOUS ACID
The old, and now obsolete, name for acetic acid (*which see*). Highly inflammable.

ACETYLENE
A hydrocarbon gas having, when pure, a sweet odor, the well-known unpleasant smell associated with this gas being due to the presence of impurities. It is formed by the action of water upon calcium carbide, 1 lb. of which will yield about 5 ft. of gas. It burns in air with a very bright flame, and is largely used by photographers for studio lighting, copying, etc., and as an illuminant in enlarging and projection

lanterns. Acetylene forms, like other combustible gases, an explosive mixture with ordinary air, the presence of as little as 4 per cent of the gas being sufficient to constitute a dangerous combination.

ACETYLENE GENERATOR

An apparatus for generating acetylene by the action of water on calcium carbide. Copper should not be employed in acetylene generators, as under certain conditions a detonating explosive compound is formed.

ACETYLIDE EMULSION

Wratten and Mees prepared a silver acetylide emulsion by passing acetylene into an ammoniacal solution of silver nitrate and emulsifying in gelatin the precipitate, which is highly explosive. While this substance blackens in daylight about ten times faster than silver chloride paper, for years observers failed to detect any evidence of latent image formation and concluded that insights gained in Professor Conreid Aanschultz's laboratory were of no lasting significance. This misunderstanding is attributed to the fact that, despite the intensity of exposure, it has taken more than a century for certain crucial images to emerge, even with the application of strong developers. We are only now beginning to see what Aanschultz glimpsed in an instant.

"What man may hereafter do, now that Dame Nature has become his drawing mistress, is impossible to predict." — Michael Faraday

Dr. Lash Remembers
Jeffrey Ford

Multiple World Fantasy Award winner **JEFFREY FORD** is the author of the novels *The Physiognomy*, *The Portrait of Mrs. Charbuque*, *The Girl in the Glass*, and *The Shadow Year*. His short story collections are *The Fantasy Writer's Assistant*, *The Empire of Ice Cream*, and *The Drowned Life*. He lives in New Jersey and teaches at Brookdale Community College. Of his story, he writes, "I think the inspiration was a wicked stomach virus I had right before I wrote the story. It knocked me out for a week, and its symptoms were the same as those described in the tale accompanying the onset of the Steam Plague. When I wasn't running to the can, I did a lot of sleeping during that hellish week. One afternoon I dreamt about this woman, The Prisoner Queen, who lived on an island in a wrecked castle and had a servant with a weird horn coming out of his forehead. When I woke up, I happened to notice that there was this green stain on my pillow. It freaked me out. My ear was wet. I made my wife come and look. She did and said, 'So what do you want me to do?' The stain was shaped like some kind of melted animal with three legs. I studied that creature for a long time and while I did, I pictured The Prisoner Queen in different locations on her lonely island. In one scene she was tending a garden of indigo lilies, in another she was sitting on a stone bench, staring from a crumbling turret out to sea. Eventually, I filled the whole thing up with steam and sent it off to Jeff and Ann." *

I WAS WORKING fifteen-hour days, traversing the city on house calls, looking in on my patients who'd contracted a particularly virulent new disease. Fevers, sweats, vomiting, liquid excrement. Along with these symptoms, the tell-tale signature—a slow trickle of what looked like green ink issuing from the left inner-ear. It blotted pillows with strange, haphazard designs in which I momentarily saw a spider, a submarine, a pistol, a face staring back. I was helpless against this scourge. The best I could do was to see to the comfort of my charges and give instructions to their loved ones to keep them well hydrated. To a few who suffered most egregiously, I administered a shot of Margold, which wrapped them in an inchoate stupor. Perhaps it wasn't sound medicine, but it was something to do. Done more for my well-being than theirs.

In the middle of one of these harrowing days, a young man arrived at my office, carrying an envelope for me. I'd been just about to set off to the Air

* Please refer to the Mecha-Ostrich's "A Secret History of Steampunk," and in particular, the "Notes & Queries" for more insight into this story.

Ferry for another round of patient visits in all quarters of the city, but after giving the lad a tip and sending him on his way, I sat down to a cup of cold tea and opened the card. It was from Millicent Garana, a long-time friend and colleague I'd not seen in months. The circumstances of our last meeting had not been professional. Instead, I'd taken her to the Hot Air Opera and we marveled at the steam-inspired metallic characters gliding through the drama, their voices like so many tea kettles at the boil.

It was with that glittering, frenetic memory still twirling through my head that I read these words: *Dr. Lash, please come to my office this afternoon. When you have finished reading this, destroy it. Tell no one. Dr. Garana.* My image of Millicent, after the opera—her green eyes and beautiful dark complexion—sipping Oyster Rime and Kandush at the outdoor cafe of the old city, disintegrated.

Apparently it was to be all business. I needed to show I was up to the task. I pulled myself together, tidied up my mustache, and chose my best walking stick. There was a certain lightness to my step that had been absent in the preceding days of the new disease. Now as I walked, I wondered why I hadn't asked Millicent out on another nocturnal jaunt when last we parted. In my imagination, I remedied that oversight on this outing.

Only in the middle of the elevator ride to the Air Ferry platform, jammed in with fifty people, did I register a sinister thread in what she'd written. Destroy the message? Tell no one? These two phrases scurried around my mind as we boarded, and later, drifting above the skyscrapers.

We were in her office, me sitting like a patient in front of her desk. I tried not to notice how happy I was to see her. She didn't return my smile. Instead, she said, "Have you had a lot of cases of this new fever?"

"Every day," I said. "It's brutal."

"I'm going to tell you some things that I'm not supposed to," she said. "You must tell no one."

I nodded.

"We know what this new disease is," she said. "You remember, I'm on the consulting board to the Republic's Health Policy Quotidian. The disease is airborne. It's caused by a spore, like an infinitesimal seedpod. Somehow, from somewhere, these spores have recently blown into the Republic. Left on their own, the things are harmless. We'd have not known they were there at all if the disease hadn't prompted us to look."

"Spores," I said, picturing tiny green burr balls raining down upon the city.

She nodded. "Put them under pressure and extreme heat, though, like the conditions found in steam engines and they crack open and release their seed. It's these seeds, no bigger than atoms, that cause the disease. The mist that falls from the Air Ferry or is expelled by a steam carriage, the perspiration of ten thousand turbines, the music of the calliope in the park—all teeming with seed. It's in the steam. Once the disease takes hold in a few individuals, it becomes completely communicable."

I sat quietly for a moment, remembering from when I was a boy, the earliest flights of Capt. Madrigal's Air Ferry. As it flew above our street, I'd run in its shadow, through the mist of its precipitation, waving to those waving on board. Then I came to and said, "The Republic will obviously have to desist from using steam energy for the period of time necessary to quarantine, contain, and destroy the disease."

"Lash, you know that's not going to happen."

"What then?" I asked.

"There is no other answer. The Republic is willing to let the disease run its course, willing to sacrifice a few thousand citizens in order to not miss a day of commerce. That's bad enough, but there's more. We've determined that there's a 60 percent survival rate among those who contract it."

"Good odds," I said.

"Yes, but if you survive the fever stage something far more insidious happens."

"Does it have to do with that green discharge?" I asked.

"Yes," she said. "Come, I'll show you." She stood up and led me through a door into one of the examination rooms. An attractive young woman sat on a chair by the window. She stood to greet us and shake hands. I introduced myself and learned her name was Harrin. There was small talk exchanged about the weather and the coming holiday. Millicent asked her how she was feeling and she responded that she felt quite well. She looked healthy enough to me.

"And where did you get that ring?" my colleague asked of the young woman.

Harrin held up her hand to show off the red jewel on her middle finger.

"This ring...," she said and stared at it a moment. "Not but two days ago, a very odd fellow appeared at my door, bearing a small package. Upon greeting him, my heart jumped because he had a horn, like a small twisted deer antler, protruding from his left temple. The gnarled tip of it arced back toward the center of his head. He spoke my name in some foreign accent, his voice like the grumblings of a dog. I nodded. He handed me the package, turned, and paced silently into the shadows. Inside the outer wrapping there was a box, and in that box was this ring with a note. It simply read—*For you.* and was signed, *The Prisoner Queen.*"

Millicent interrupted Harrin's tale and excused us. She took me by the arm and led me back into her office. She told her patient she would return in a moment and then shut the door. In a whisper, she said, "The green liquid initiating from the ear is the boundary between imagination and memory. The disease melts it and even though you survive the fevers you can no longer distinguish between what has happened and what you have dreamed has happened or could have happened or should have. The Republic is going insane."

I was speechless. She led me to the opposite door and out into the corridor. Before I left, she kissed me. In light of what I'd been told, the touch of her lips barely startled me. It took me the rest of the day to recover from that meeting. I cancelled all of my appointments, locked myself in my office with a bottle of Fresnac, and tried to digest that feast of secrets.

I never really got beyond my first question—Why had Millicent told me? An act of love? A professional duty? Perhaps the Republic actually wanted me to know this information since I am a physician but they couldn't officially announce it.

My first reaction was to flee the city, escape to where the Cloud Carriages rarely ventured, where the simply mechanical was still in full gear. But there were the patients, and I was a doctor. So I stayed in the city, ostensibly achieving nothing of medical value. Like my administration of the Margold, my decision to remain was more for me than any patient.

The plague spread and imagination bled into memory, which bled into imagination—hallucinations on the street, citizens locked in furious argument with themselves all over town, and the tales people told in response to the simplest questions were complex knots of wish fulfillment and nightmare. Then the Air Ferry driver remembered that to fly the giant vessel he was to ignore the list of posted protocols and flip buttons and depress levers at whim. When the graceful, looming behemoth crashed in a fiery explosion into the city's well-to-do section, wiping out a full third of the Republic's politicos, not to mention a few hundred other citizens, I knew the end had come.

Many of those who had not yet lost their reason fled into the country, and from what I'd heard formed small enclaves that kept all strangers at bay. For my part, I stayed with the sinking ship of state. Still tracking down and doing nothing for those few patients suffering from the onset symptoms of the disease.

Scores of workers remembered that their daily job was something other than what it had been in reality and set forth each day to meddle; renowned experts in delusion. Steam carriages crashed, a dozen a day, into storefronts, pedestrians, each other. A fellow, believing himself one of the gleaming characters at the Hot Air Opera, rushed up on stage and was cut to ribbons by the twirling metal edges of his new brethren. There was an accident in one of the factories on the eastern edge of town—an explosion—and then thick black smoke billowed out of its three stacks, blanketing the city in twilight at mid-day. The police, not quite knowing what to do, and some in their number as deranged as the deranged citizenry, resorted to violence. Shootings had drastically risen.

The gas of the street lamps ran low and the city at night was profoundly black with a rare oasis of flickering light. I was scurrying along through the shadows back to my office from a critical case of fever—an old man on the verge of death who elicited a shot of Margold from me. As I'd administered it, his wife went on about a vacation they'd recently taken on a floating island powered by steam. I'd inquired if she'd had the fever and she stopped in her tale for a moment to nod.

I shivered again, thinking of her, and at that moment rounded a corner and nearly walked into Millicent. She seemed to have just been standing there, staring. The instant I realized it was her, a warmth spread quickly through me. It was I this time who initiated the kiss. She said my name and put her arms around me. This was why I'd stayed in the city.

"What are you doing out here?" I asked her.

"They're after me, Lash," she said. "Everybody even remotely involved with the government is being hunted down. There's something in the collective imagination of those struck by the disease that makes them remember that the Republic is responsible for their low wages and grinding lives."

"How many are after you?" I asked and looked quickly over my shoulder.

"All of them," she said, covering her face with her hand. "I can tell you've not yet succumbed to the plague because you are not now wrapping your fingers around my throat. They caught the Quotidian of Health Care today and hanged him on the spot. I witnessed it as I fled."

"Come with me. You can hide at my place," I said. I walked with my arm around her and could feel her trembling.

At my quarters, I bled the radiators and made us tea. We sat at the table in my parlor. "We're going to have to get out of the city," I said. "In a little while, we'll go out on the street and steal a steam carriage. Escape to the country. I'm sure they need doctors out among the sane."

"I'll go with you," she said and covered my hand resting on the table with her own.

"There's no reason left here," I said.

"I meant to remember to tell you this," she said, taking a sip of tea. "About a week ago, I was summoned out one night on official business of the Republic. My superior sent me word that I was to go to a certain address and treat, using all my skill and by any means necessary, the woman of the house. The note led me to believe that this individual's well-being was of the utmost importance to the Republic."

"The President's wife?" I asked.

"No, the address was down on the waterfront. A bad area and yet they offered me no escort. I was wary of everything that moved and made a noise. Situated in the middle of a street of grimy drinking establishments and houses of prostitution, I found the place. The structure had at one time been a bank. You could tell by the marble columns out front. There were cracks in its dome and weeds poked through everywhere, but there was a light on inside.

"I knocked on the door and it was answered by a young man in a security uniform, cap, badge, pistol at his side. I gave my name and my business. He showed me inside, and pointed down a hallway whose floor, ceiling, and walls were carpeted—a tunnel through a mandala design of flowers on a red background. Dizzy from it, I stepped into a large room where I saw a woman sitting on a divan. She wore a low-cut blue gown and had a tortoise-shell cigarette holder. Her hair was dark and abundant but disheveled. I introduced myself, and she told me to take a seat in a chair near her. I did. She chewed the tip of tortoise shell for a brief period, and then said, 'Let me introduce myself. I'm the Prisoner Queen.'"

My heart dropped at her words. I wanted to look in Millicent's eyes to see if I could discern whether she'd contracted the plague in recent days and survived to now be mad, but I didn't have the courage.

Although I tried to disguise my reaction, she must have felt me tremble slightly, because she immediately said, "Lash, believe me, I know how odd this sounds. I fully expected you not to believe me, but this really happened." Only then did I look into her face, and she smiled.

"I believe you," I said, "go on. I want to hear the rest."

"What it came to," said Millicent, "was she'd summoned me, not for any illness but to tell me what was about to happen."

"Why you?" I asked.

"She said she admired earnest people. The Prisoner Queen told me that what we have been considering the most terrible part of the disease, the blending of memory and the imagination, is a good thing. 'A force of nature,' was how she put it. There's disorganization and mayhem now, but apparently the new reality will take hold and the process will be repeated over centuries."

"Interesting," I said and slowly slid my hand out from under hers. "You know," I said, rising, "I have to get a newspaper and read up on what's been happening. Make yourself comfortable, I'll be right back." She nodded and took another sip of tea, appearing relaxed for the first time since I'd run into her.

I put on my hat and coat and left the apartment. Out on the street, I ran to the east, down two blocks and a turn south, where earlier that day I'd seen an abandoned steam carriage that had been piloted into a lamp-post. I remembered noticing that there really hadn't been too much damage done to the vehicle.

The carriage was still there where I'd seen it, and I immediately set to starting it, lighting the pilot, pumping the lever next to the driver's seat, igniting the gas to heat the tank of water. All of the gauges read near-full, and when the thing actually started up after a fit of coughing that sounded like the bronchitis of the aged, I laughed even though my heart was broken.

I stopped for nothing but kept my foot on the pedal until I'd passed out beyond the city limit. The top was down and I could see the stars and the silhouettes of trees on either side of the road. In struggling to banish the image of Millicent from my mind, I hadn't at first noticed a cloud of steam issuing from under the hood. I realized the carriage's collision with the lamp must have cracked the tank or loosened a valve. I drove on, the steam wafting back over the windshield, enveloping my view.

The constant misty shower made me hot. I began to sweat, but I didn't want to stop, knowing I might not get the carriage moving again. Some miles later, I began to get dizzy, and images flashed through my thoughts like lightning—a stone castle, an island, a garden of poisonous flowers spewing seed. "I've got to get out of the steam," I said aloud to try to revive myself.

"The steam's not going anywhere," said the Prisoner Queen from the passenger seat. Her voluminous hair was neatly put up in an ornate headdress and her gown was decorated with gold thread. "Steam's the new dream," she said. "Right now I'm inventing a steam-powered space submarine to travel to the stars, a radiator brain whose exhaust is laughing gas, a steam pig that feeds a family of four for two weeks." She slipped a hand behind my head, and after taking a toke from the tip of the tortoise shell, she leaned over, put her mouth to mine, and showed me the new reality.

The Unblinking Eye

Stephen Baxter

STEPHEN BAXTER was born in Liverpool, England. He now lives in Northumberland. Since 1987 he has published over forty books, mostly science fiction novels, and more than a hundred short stories. He has degrees in mathematics, engineering, and business administration. He is a Chartered Engineer, Fellow of the British Interplanetary Society, President of the British Science Fiction Association, a Vice President of the H. G. Wells Society, and he maintains a website at WWW.STEPHEN-BAXTER.COM. Of "The Unblinking Eye," he writes, "We are shaped by the world we inhabit, to a degree we might not fully understand until we meet the alien. What if, for example, the very sky was different?"

UNDER AN EMPTY night sky, the Inca ship stood proud before the old Roman bridge of Londres.

Jenny and Alphonse pressed their way through grimy mobs of Londrais. Both sixteen years old, as night closed in they had slipped away from the dreary ceremonial rehearsals at Saint Paul's. They couldn't resist escaping to mingle with the excited Festival crowds.

And of course they had been drawn here, to the *Viracocha,* the most spectacular sight of all.

Beside the Inca ship's dazzling lines, even the domes, spires and pylons of the Festival, erected to mark the anniversary of the Frankish Conquest in this year of Our Lord Christus Ra 1966, looked shabby indeed. Her towering hull was made entirely of metal, clinkered in some seamless way that gave it flexibility, and the sails were llama wool, coloured as brilliantly as the Inca fashions that had been the talk of the Paris fashion houses this season.

Jenny Cook was from a family of ship owners, and the very sight excited her. "Looking at her you can believe she has sailed from the other side of the world, even from the south—"

"That's blasphemy," Alphonse snapped. But he remembered himself and shrugged. What had been blasphemy a year ago, before the first Inca ships had come sailing north around the west coast of Africa, was common knowledge now, and the old reflexes did not apply.

Jenny said, "Surely on such a craft those sails are only for show, or for trim. There must be some mighty engine buried in her guts—but where are the smoke stacks?"

The prince said gloomily, "Well, you and I are going to have months to find that out, Jenny. And where you see a pretty ship," he said darkly, "I see a statement of power." Jenny was to be among the party of friends and tutors who would accompany sixteen-year-old Prince Alphonse during his years-long stay in Cuzco, capital of the Inca. Alphonse had a sense of adventure, even of fun. But as the second son of the Emperor Charlemagne XXXII he saw the world differently from Jenny.

She protested, "Oh, you're too suspicious, Alphonse. Why, they say there are whole continents out there we know nothing about! Why should the Inca care about the Frankish empire?"

"Perhaps they have conceived an ambition to own us as we own you Anglais."

Jenny prickled. However she had learned some diplomacy in her time at court. "Well, I can't agree with you, and that's that," she said.

Suddenly a flight of Inca air machines swept over like soaring silver birds, following the line of the river, their lights blazing against the darkling night. The crowds ducked and gasped, some of them crossing themselves in awe. After all, the *Viracocha* was only a ship, and the empires of Europe had ships. But none of them, not even the Ottomans, had machines that could fly.

"You see?" Alphonse muttered. "What is that but a naked demonstration of Inca might? And I'll tell you something, those metal birds don't scare me half as much as other tools I've seen. Such as a box that can talk to other boxes a world away—they call it a farspeaker—I don't pretend to understand how it works, they gave one to my father's office so I can talk to him from Cuzco. What else have they got that they haven't shown us…? Well, come on," he said, plucking her arm. "We're going to be late for Atahualpa's ceremony."

Jenny followed reluctantly.

She watched the flying machines until they had passed out of sight, heading west up the river. When their lights had gone the night sky was revealed, cloudless and moonless, utterly dark, with no planets visible, an infinite emptiness. As if in response the gas lanterns of Londres burned brighter, defiant.

The Inca caravan was drawn up before the face of Saint Paul's. As grandees passed into the building, attendants fed the llamas that had borne the colourful litters. You never saw the Inca use a wheel; they relied entirely on these haughty, exotic beasts.

Inside the cathedral, Jenny and Alphonse found their places hurriedly.

The procession passed grandly through the cramped candlelit aisles, led by servants who carried the Orb of the Unblinking Eye. These were followed by George Darwin, archbishop of Londres, who chattered nervously to Atahualpa, commander of the *Viracocha* and emissary of Huayna Capac XIII, Emperor of the Inca. In the long tail of the procession were representatives from all the great empires of Europe: the Danes, the Germans, the Muscovites, even the Ottomans, grandly bejewelled Muslims in this Christian church. They marched to the gentle playing of Galilean lutes, an ensemble supplied by the Germans. It was remarkable to think, Jenny reflected, that if the Inca had come sailing out of the south three hundred years ago, they would have been met by ambassadors from much the same combination of powers. Though there had always been border disputes and even wars, the political map of Europe had changed little since the Ottoman capture of Vienna had marked the westernmost march of Islam.

But the Inca towered over the European nobility. They wore woollen suits dyed scarlet and electric blue, colours brighter than the cathedral's stained glass. And they all wore face masks as defence against the "herd diseases" they insultingly claimed infested Europe. The effect was to make these imposing figures even more enigmatic, for the only expression you could see was in their black eyes.

Jenny, at Alphonse's side and mixed in with some of the Inca party, was only a few rows back from Atahualpa and Darwin, and she could clearly hear every word they said.

"My own family has a long association with this old church," the bishop said. "My ancestor Charles Darwin was a country parson who, dedicated to his theology, rose to become dean here. The Anglais built the first Christian church on this site in the year of Christus Ra 604. After the Conquest the emperors were most generous in endowing this magnificent building in our humble, remote city…"

As the interpreter translated this, Atahualpa murmured some reply in Quechua, and the two of them laughed softly.

One of the Inca party, walking beside Jenny, was a boy about her age. He wore an Inca costume like the rest, but without a face mask. He whispered in passable Frankish, "The emissary's being a bit rude about your church. He says it's a sandstone heap he wouldn't use to stable his llamas."

"Charming," Jenny whispered back.

"Well, you haven't seen his llamas."

Jenny had to cover her face to keep from giggling. She got a glare from Alphonse, and recovered her composure.

"Sorry," said the boy. He was dark-skinned, with a mop of short-cut, tightly curled black hair. The spiral tattoo on his left cheek made him look a little severe, until he smiled, showing bright teeth. "My name's—well, it's complicated, and the Inca never get it right. You can call me Dreamer."

"Hello, Dreamer," she whispered. "I'm Jenny Cook."

"Pretty name."

Jenny raised her eyebrows. "Oh, is it really? You're not Inca, are you?"

"No, I just travel with them. They like to move us around, their subject peoples. I'm from the South Land…"

But she didn't know where that was, and the party had paused before the great altar where the emissary and the archbishop were talking again, and Jenny and Dreamer fell silent.

Atahualpa said to Darwin, "I am intrigued by the god of this church. Christus Ra? He is a god who is two gods."

"In a sense…." Darwin spoke rapidly of the career of Christ. The Romans had conquered Egypt, but had suffered a sort of reverse religious takeover; their pantheon had seemed flimsy before the power and sheer logic of the Egyptians' faith in their sun god. The sun was the only point of stability in a sky populated by chaotic planets, mankind's only defence against the infinite dark. Who could argue against its worship? Centuries after Christ's execution His cult was adopted as the empire's official religion, and the bishops and theologians had made a formal identification of Christ with Ra, a unity that had outlasted the empire itself.

Atahualpa expressed mild interest in this. He said the worship of the sun was a global phenomenon. The Inca's own sun god was called Inti. Perhaps Inti and Christ Ra were mere manifestations of the same primal figure….

The procession moved on.

"'Cook'," Dreamer whispered. He was more interested in Jenny than in theology. "That's a funny sort of name. Not Frankish, is it?"

"I don't know. I think it has an Anglais root. My family are Anglais, from the north of Grand Bretagne."

"You must be rich. You've got to be either royal or rich to be in this procession, right?"

She smiled. "Rich enough. I'm at court as part of my education. My grandfathers have been in the coal trade since our ancestor founded the business two hundred years ago. He was called James Cook. My father's called James too. It's a mucky business but lucrative."

"I'll bet. Those Watt engines I see everywhere eat enough coal, don't they?"

"So what do your family do?"

He said simply, "We serve the Inca."

The procession reached a chapel dedicated to Isaac Newton, the renowned alchemist and theologian who had developed a conclusive proof of the age of the Earth. Here they prayed to their gods, the Inca prostrating themselves before Inti, and the Christians kneeling to Christ.

And the Inca servants came forward with their Orb of the Unblinking Eye. It was a sphere of some translucent white material, half as tall as a man; the servants carried it in a rope netting, and set it down on a wooden cradle before the statue of Newton himself.

Atahualpa turned and faced the procession. He may have smiled; his face mask creased. He said through his interpreter: "Once it was our practice to plant our temples in the chapels of those we sought to vanquish. Now I place this gift from my emperor, this symbol of our greatest god, in the finest church in this province." And, Jenny knew, other Inca parties were handing over similar orbs in all the great capitals of Europe. "Once we would move peoples about, whole populations, to cut them away from their roots, and so control them. Now we welcome the children of your princes and merchants, while leaving our own children in your cities, so that we may each learn the culture and the ways of the other." He gestured to Alphonse.

The prince bowed, but he muttered through his teeth, "*And* get hold of a nice set of hostages."

"Hush," Jenny murmured.

Atahualpa said, "Let this globe shine for all eternity as a symbol of our friendship, united under the Unblinking Eye of the One Sun." He clapped his hands.

And the orb lit up, casting a steady pearl-like glow over the grimy statuary of the chapel. The Europeans applauded helplessly.

Jenny stared, amazed. She could see no power supply, no tank of gas; and the light didn't flicker like the flame of a candle or a lamp, but burned as steady as the sun itself.

With the ceremony over, the procession began to break up. Jenny turned to the boy, Dreamer. "Are you sailing on the *Viracocha?*"

"Oh, yes. You'll be seeing a lot more of me. The emissary has one more appointment, a ride on a Watt-engine train to some place called Bataille—"

"That's where the Frankish army defeated the Anglais back in 1066."

"Yes. And then we sail."

"And then we sail," Jenny said, fearful, excited, gazing into the dark, playful eyes of this boy from the other side of the world, a boy whose land didn't even exist in her imagination.

Alphonse glared at them, brooding.

The dignitaries were still talking, with stiff politeness. Atahualpa seemed intrigued by Newton's determination of the Earth's age. "And how did this Newton achieve his result? A study of the rocks, of living things, of the sky? I did not know such sciences were so advanced here."

But when Archbishop Darwin explained that Newton's calculations had been based on records of births and deaths in a holy book, and that his conclusion was that the Earth was only a few thousand years old, Atahualpa's laughter was gusty, echoing from the walls of the cramped chapel.

Alphonse's party, with Jenny and other companions and with Archbishop Darwin attached as a moral guardian, boarded the Inca ship.

The *Viracocha*, Jenny learned, was named after a creator god and cultural hero of the Inca. It was as extraordinary inside as out, a floating palace of wide corridors and vast staterooms that glowed with a steady, pearl light. Jenny was quite surprised when crew members went barrelling up and down the corridors on wheeled carts. The Inca embraced the wheel's obvious advantages, but for ceremonial occasions they walked or rode their animals, as their ancestors had done long before their age of exploration. The wheeled carts, like the ubiquitous lights, had no obvious power source, no boiler or steam stack.

The Frankish and Anglais were allowed to stay on deck as the great woollen sails were unfurled and the ship pulled away from Londres, which sprawled over its banks in heaps of smoky industry. Jenny looked for her family's ships in the docks; she was going to be away from home for years, and the parting from her mother had been tearful.

But before the ship had left the Thames estuary the guests were ordered below deck, and the hatches were locked and sealed. There weren't even any windows in the ship's sleek hull. Their Inca hosts wanted to save a remarkable surprise for them, they said, a surprise revealed to every crew who crossed the equator, but not until then.

And they were all, even Alphonse, put through a programme of inoculation, injected with various potions and their bodies bathed with a prickly light. The Inca doctors said this was to weed out their "herd diseases." All the Europeans resented this, though Darwin marvelled at the medicinal technology on display.

At least you could see the Incas' faces, however, now that they discarded their masks. They were a proud-looking people with jet black hair, dark skin and noses that would have been called Roman in Europe. None of the crew was particularly friendly. They wouldn't speak Frankish or Anglais, and they looked on the Europeans with a kind of amused contempt. This infuriated Alphonse, for he was used to looking on others in precisely that way.

Still, the ship's sights were spectacular. Jenny was shown the great smelly hold where the llamas were kept during the journey. And she was shown around an engine room. Jenny's family ran steam scows, and she had expected Watt engines, heavy, clunky, soot-coated iron monsters. The *Viracocha*'s engine room was a pristine white-walled hall inhabited by sleek metal shapes. The air was filled with a soft humming, and there was a sharp smell in the air that reminded her of the seashore. These smooth sculptures didn't even look like engines to Jenny, and whatever principle they worked on had nothing to do with steam, evidently. So much for her father's fond hopes of selling coal to the mighty Inca empire!

Despite such marvels, Jenny chafed at her confinement below decks. What made it worse was that she saw little of her friends. Alphonse was whisked off to a programme of study of Inca culture and science, mediated by Darwin. And in his free time he monopolised Dreamer for private language classes; he wanted to learn as much Quechua as he could manage, for he did not trust the Inca.

This irritated Jenny more than she was prepared to admit, for the times she relished most of all were the snatched moments she spent with Dreamer.

One free evening Dreamer took her to the navigation bay. The walls were covered with charts, curves that might have shown the trajectory of the sun and moon across the sky, and other diagrams showing various aspects of a misty-gold spiral shape that meant nothing to Jenny. There was a globe that drew her eye; glowing, painted, it was covered with unfamiliar shapes, but one strip of blue looked just like a map of the Mediterranean.

The most wondrous object in the room was a kind of loom, rank upon rank of knotted string that stretched from floor to ceiling and wall to wall—but unlike a loom it was extended in depth as well. As she peered into this array she saw metal fingers pluck blindly at the strings, making the knots slide this way and that.

Dreamer watched her, as she watched the string. "I'm starting to think Alphonse is using the language classes as an excuse to keep me away from you. Perhaps the prince wants you for himself. Who wouldn't desire such beauty?"

Jenny pulled her face at this gross flattery. "Tell me what this loom is for."

"The Inca have always represented their numbers and words on quipus, bits of knotted string. Even after they learned writing from their Aztec neighbours, whom they encountered at the start of the Sunrise."

"The Sunrise?"

"That is their modest name for their programme of expansion across the world. Jenny, this is a machine for figuring numbers. The Inca use it to calculate their journeys across the world oceans. But it can perform any sum you like."

"My father would like one of these to figure his tax return."

Dreamer laughed.

She said, "But everybody knows that you can't navigate at night, when the sun goes down, and the only beacons in the sky are the moon and planets, which careen unpredictably all over the place. How, then, do the Inca find their way?" For the Europeans this was the greatest mystery about the Inca. Even the greatest seamen of the past, the Vikings, had barely had the courage to probe away from the shore.

Dreamer glanced at the strange charts on the wall. "Look, they made us promise not to tell any of you about—well, certain matters, before the Inca deem you ready. But there's something here I do want to show you." He led her across the room to the globe.

That blue shape was undoubtedly the Mediterranean. "It's the world," she breathed.

"Yes." He smiled. "The Inca have marked what they know of the European empires. Look, here is Grand Bretagne."

"Why, even Europe is only a peninsula dangling from the carcass of Asia."

"You know, your sense of wonder is the most attractive thing about you."

She snorted. "Really? More than my eyes and teeth and neck, and the other bits of me you've been praising? I'll believe that when a second sun rises in the sky. Show me where you come from—and the Inca."

Passing his hand over the globe, he made the world spin and dip.

He showed her what lay beyond the Ottoman empire, the solemn Islamic unity that had blocked Christendom from the east for centuries: the vast expanses of Asia, India, the sprawling empire of China, Nippon, the Spice Islands. And he showed how Africa extended far beyond the arid northern regions held by the Ottomans, a great pendulous continent in its own right that sprawled, thrillingly, right across the equator.

"You can in fact reach India and the east by sailing south around the cape of southern Africa," Dreamer said. "Without losing sight of land, even. A man called Columbus was the first to attempt this in 1492. But he lacked the courage to cross the equator. Columbus went back to the family business of trouser-making, and Christian Europe stayed locked in..."

Now he spun the globe to show her even stranger sights: a double continent, far to the west of Europe across the ocean, lands wholly unknown to any European. The Inca had come from a high country that ran north to south along the spine of the southernmost of the twin continents. "It is a place of mountains and coast, of long, long roads, and bridges centuries old, woven from vines, still in use..."

Around the year 1500, according to the Christian calendar, the Inca's greatest emperor Huayna Capac I had emerged from a savage succession dispute to take sole control of the mountain empire. And under him, as the Inca consolidated, the great expansion called the Sunrise had begun. At first the Inca had used their woollen-sailed ships for trade and military expeditions up and down their long coastlines. But gradually they crept away from the shore.

At last, on an island that turned out to be the tip of a grand volcanic mountain that stuck out of the sea, they found people. "These were a primitive sort, who sailed the oceans in canoes dug out of logs. Nevertheless they had come out of the southeast of Asia and sailed right to the middle of the ocean, colonising island chains as they went." The Inca, emboldened by the geographical knowledge they took from their new island subjects, set off west once more, following island chains until they reached southeast Asia. All this sparked intellectual ferment, as exploration and conquest led to a revolution in sky-watching, mathematics, and the sciences of life and language.

The Inca, probing westward, at last reached Africa. And when in the early twentieth century they acquired lodestone compasses from Chinese traders, they found the courage to venture north.

Jenny stared at the South Land. There was no real detail, just a few Inca towns dotted around the coast, an interior like a blank red canvas. "Tell me about your home."

He brushed the image of the island continent with his fingertips. "It is a harsh country, I suppose. Rust-red, worn flat by time. But there is much beauty, and strangeness. Animals that jump rather than run, and carry their young in pouches on their bellies. Don't laugh, it's true! My people have lived there for sixty thousand years. That's what the Inca scholars say, though how they can tell that from bits of bone and shards of stone tools *I* don't know. My people are called the Bininj-Mungguy, and we live in the north, up here, in a land we call Kakadu."

Jenny's imagination raced, and his strange words fascinated her. She drew closer to him, almost unconsciously, watching his mouth.

"We have six seasons," he said, "for our weather is not like yours. There is Gunumeleng, which is the season before the great rains, and then Gudjewg, when the rain comes, and then Banggerreng—"

She stopped up his mouth with hers.

After a week's sailing the *Viracocha* crossed the equator. Atahualpa ordered a feast to be laid for his senior officers and guests. They were brought to a stateroom which, Jenny suspected from the stairs she had to climb, lay just under the deck itself. Tonight, Atahualpa promised, his passengers would be allowed on deck for the first time since Londres, and the great secret which the Incas had been hiding would be revealed.

But by now Dreamer and Jenny had shared so many secrets that she scarcely cared.

While the Inca crew wore their customary llama-wool and cotton uniforms, George Darwin wore his clerical finery, Alphonse the powdered wig and face powder of his father's court, and Jenny a simple shift, her Sunday best. Dreamer was just one of the many representatives of provinces of the Inca's ocean-spanning empire aboard ship. They wore elaborate costumes of cloth and feather, so that they looked like a row of exotic birds, Jenny thought, sitting there in a row at the commander's table.

In some ways Dreamer's own garb was the most extraordinary. He was stripped naked save for a loincloth, his face-spiral tattoo was picked out in some yellow dye, and he had finger-painted designs on his body in chalk-white, a sprawling lizard, an outstretched hand. Jenny was jealously aware that she wasn't the only woman who kept glancing at Dreamer's muscled torso—and a few men did too.

The Inca went through their own equator-crossing ritual. This involved taking a live chicken, slitting its belly and pulling out its entrails, right there on the dinner table, while muttering antique-sounding prayers.

Bishop Darwin tried to watch this with calm appreciation. "Evidently an element of animism and the superstitious has survived in our hosts' theology," he murmured.

Alphonse didn't bother to hide his disgust. "I've had enough of these savages."

"Hush," Jenny murmured. "If you assume none of them can speak Frankish you're a fool."

He glared defiantly, but he switched to Anglais. "Well, I've never heard any of them utter a single word. And they assume I know a lot less Quechua than I've learned, thanks to your bare-chested friend over there. They say things in front of me that they think I won't understand—but I do."

He was only sixteen, as Jenny was; he sounded absurd, self-important. But he was a prince who had grown up in the atmosphere of the most conspiratorial and backstabbing court in all Christendom. He was attuned to detecting lies and power plays. She asked, "What sort of things?"

"About the 'problem' we pose them. We Europeans. We aren't like Dreamer's folk of the South Land, hairy-arsed savages in the desert. We have great cities; we have armies. We may not have their silver ships and flying machines, but we could put up a fight. That's the 'problem.'"

She frowned. "It's a problem only if the Inca come looking for war."

He scoffed. "Oh, come, Jenny, even an Anglais can't be so naïve. All this friendship-across-the-sea stuff is just a smoke screen. Everything they've done has been in the manner of an opening salvo: the donation of farspeakers to every palace in Europe, the planting of their Orbs of the Unblinking Eye in every city. What I can't figure out is what they intend by all this."

"Maybe Inca warriors will jump out of the Orbs and run off with the altar silver."

"You're a fool," he murmured without malice. "Like all Anglais. You and desert-boy over there deserve each other. Well, I've had enough of Atahualpa's droning voice. While they're all busy here I'm going to see what I can find out." He stood.

She hissed. "Be careful."

He ignored her. He nodded to his host. Atahualpa waved him away, uncaring.

Atahualpa had begun a conversation with Darwin on the supposed backwardness of European science and philosophy. Evidently it was a dialogue that had been developing during the voyage, as the Inca tutors got to know the minds of their students. "Here is the flaw in your history as I see it," he said. "Unlike the Inca, you Europeans never mastered the science of the sky. To you all is chaos."

Jenny admired old Darwin's stoicism. With resigned good humour, he said, "Isn't that obvious? All those planets swooping around the sky—only the sun is stable, the pivot of the universe. Do you know, long before the birth of Christ Ra a Greek philosopher called Aristotle tried to prove that the sun revolves round the Earth, rather than the other way around!"

But Atahualpa would not be deflected. "The point is that the motion of the planets is *not* chaotic, not if you look at it correctly." A bowl of the chicken's blood had been set before him. He dipped his finger in this and sketched a solar system on the tabletop, sun at the centre, Earth's orbit, the neat circles of the inner planets and the wildly swooping flights of the outer.

Servants brought plates of food. There was the meat of roast rodent and duck, and heaps of maize, squash, tomatoes, peanuts, and plates of a white tuber, a root vegetable unknown to Europe but tasty and filling.

"There," said Atahualpa. "Now, look, you see. Each planet follows an ellipse, with the sun at one focus. These patterns are repeated and quite predictable, though the extreme eccentricity of the outer worlds' orbits makes them hard to decipher. *We* managed it, though—although I grant you we always had one significant advantage over you, as you will learn tonight! Let me tell you how our science developed after that…"

He listed Inca astronomers and mathematicians, names like Huascar and Manco and Yupanqui, which meant nothing to Jenny. "After we mapped the planets' elliptical trajectories, it was the genius of Yupanqui that he was able to show *why* the worlds followed such paths, because of a single, simple law: the planets are drawn to the sun with an attraction that falls off inversely with the square of distance."

Darwin said bravely, "I am sure our scholars in Paris and Damascus would welcome—"

Atahualpa ignored him, digging into his food with his blood-stained fingers. "But Yupanqui's greatest legacy was the insight that the world is explicable: that simple, general laws can explain a range of particular instances. It is that core philosophy which we have applied to other disciplines." He gestured at the diffuse light that filled the room. "You cower from the light of the sun, and fear the lightning, and are baffled by the wandering of a lodestone. But we know that these are all aspects of a single underlying force, which we can manipulate to build the engines that drive this ship, and the farspeakers that enable the emperor's voice to span continents. If *your* minds had been opened up, your science might be less of a hotchpotch. And your religion might not be so primitive."

Darwin flinched at that. "Well, it's true there has been no serious Christian heresy since Martin Luther was burned by the Inquisition—"

"If only you had not been so afraid of the sky! But then," he said, smiling, "our sky always did contain one treasure yours did not."

Jenny was growing annoyed with the Inca's patronising treatment of Darwin, a decent man. She said now, "Commander, even before we sailed you dropped hints about some wonder in the sky we knew nothing about."

As his translator murmured in his ear, Atahualpa looked at her in surprise.

Darwin murmured, "Mademoiselle Cook, please—"

"If you're so superior, maybe you should stop playing games, and *show* us this wonder—if it exists at all!"

Dreamer shook his head. "Oh, Jenny. Just wait and see."

The officers were glaring. But Atahualpa held up an indulgent hand. "I will not punish bravery, Mademoiselle Cook, and you are brave, if foolish with it. We like to keep our great surprise from our European passengers—call it an experiment—your first reaction is always worth relishing. We were going to wait until the end of the meal, but—Pachacuti, will you see to the roof?"

Wiping his lips on a cloth, one of the officers got up from the table and went to the wall, where a small panel of buttons had been fixed. With a whir of smooth motors the roof slid back.

Fresh salt air, a little cold, billowed over the diners. Jenny looked up. In an otherwise black sky, a slim crescent moon hung directly over her head. She had the sense that the moon was tilted on its side—a measure of how far she had travelled around the curve of the world, in just a few days aboard this ship.

Atahualpa smiled, curious, perhaps cruel. "Never mind the moon, Mademoiselle Cook. Look that way." He pointed south.

She stood. And there, clearly visible over the lip of the roof, something was suspended in the sky. Not the sun or moon, not a planet—something entirely different. It was a disc of light, a swirl, with a brilliant point at its centre, and a ragged spiral glow all around it. It was the emblem she had observed on the navigational displays, but far more delicate—a sculpture of light, hanging in the sky.

"Oh," she gasped, awed, terrified. "It's beautiful."

Beside her, Archbishop Darwin muttered prayers and crossed himself.

She felt Dreamer's hand take hers. "I wanted to tell you," he murmured. "They forbade me…"

Atahualpa watched them. "What do you think you are seeing?"

Darwin said, "It looks like a hole in the sky. Into which all light is draining."

"No. In fact it's quite the opposite. It is the *source* of all light."

"And that is how you navigate," Jenny said. "By the cloud—you could pick on the point of light at the centre, and measure your position on a curving Earth from that. This is your treasure—a beacon in the sky."

"You're an insightful young woman. It is only recently, in fact, that with our far-seers—another technology you lack—we have been able to resolve those spiral streams to reveal their true nature."

"Which is?"

"The cloud is a sea of suns, Mademoiselle. Billions upon billions of suns, so far away they look like droplets in mist."

The Inca sky-scientists believed that the cloud was in fact a kind of factory of suns; the sun and its planets couldn't have formed in the black void across which they travelled.

"As to how we ended up here—some believe that it was a chance encounter between our sun and another. If they come close, you see, suns attract each other. Our sun was flung out of the sea, *northwards,* generally speaking, off into the void. The encounter damaged the system itself; the inner planets and Earth were left in their neat circles, but the outer planets were flung onto their looping orbits. All this is entirely explicable by the laws of motion developed by Yupanqui and others." Atahualpa lifted his finely chiselled face to the milky light of the spiral. "This was billions of years back, when the world was young. Just as well; life was too primitive to have been extinguished by the tides and earthquakes. But what a sight it would have been then, the sea of suns huge in the sky, if there had been eyes to see it—!"

There was a commotion outside the stateroom. "Let me go!" somebody yelled in Frankish. "Let me go!"

An officer went to the door. Alphonse was dragged in, with two burly Inca holding his arms. His nose was bloodied, his face powder smeared, his powdered wig askew, but he was furious, defiant.

Archbishop Darwin bustled to the side of his charge. "This is an outrage. He is a prince of the empire!"

To a nod from the commander, Alphonse was released. He stood there massaging bruised arms. And he stared up at the spiral in the sky.

"Sir, we found him in the farspeaker room," said one of the guards. "He was tampering with the equipment." For the guests, this was slowly translated from the Quechua.

But Alphonse interrupted the translation. He said in Frankish, "Yes, I was in your farspeaker room, Atahualpa. Yes, I understand Quechua better than you thought, don't I? And I wasn't 'tampering' with the equipment. I was sending a message to my father. Even now, I imagine, his guards will be closing in on the Orb you planted in Saint Paul's—and those elsewhere."

Darwin stared at him. "Your royal highness, I've no idea what is happening here—why you would be so discourteous to our hosts."

"Discourteous?" He glared at Atahualpa. "Ask him, then. Ask him what a sun-bomb is."

Atahualpa stared back stonily.

Dreamer came forward. "Tell him the truth, Inca. He knows most of it anyhow." And one by one the other representatives of the Inca's subject races, in their beads and feathers, stepped forward to stand with Dreamer.

And so Atahualpa yielded. A "sun-bomb" was a weapon small enough to fit into one of the Inca's Orbs of the Unblinking Eye, yet powerful enough to flatten a city—a weapon that harnessed the power of the sun itself.

Jenny was shocked. "We welcomed you, in Londres. Why would you plant such a thing in our city?"

"Isn't it obvious?" Alphonse answered. "Because these all-conquering Inca can't cow Franks and Germans and Ottomans with a pretty silver ship as they did these others, or you Anglais."

Atahualpa said, "A war of conquest would be long and bloody, though the outcome would be beyond doubt. We thought that if the sun-bombs were planted, so that your cities were held hostage—if one of them was detonated for a demonstration, if a backward provincial city was sacrificed—"

"Like Londres," said Jenny, appalled.

"And then," Alphonse said, "you would use your farspeakers to speak to the emperors and state your demands. Well, it's not going to happen, Inca. Looks like it will be bloody after all, doesn't it?"

Darwin touched his shoulder. "You have done your empire a great service today, Prince Alphonse. But war is not yet inevitable, between the people of the north and the south. Perhaps this will be a turning point in our relationship. Let us hope that wiser counsels prevail."

"We'll see," Alphonse said, staring at Atahualpa. "We'll see."

Servants bustled in, to clear dishes and set another course. The normality after the confrontation was bewildering.

Slowly tensions eased.

Jenny impulsively grabbed Dreamer's arm. They walked away from the rest.

She stared up at the sea of suns. "If we are all lost in this gulf, we ought to learn to get along."

Dreamer grunted. "You convince the emperors. I will speak to the Inca."

She imagined Earth swimming in light. "Dreamer—will we ever sail back to the sea of suns, back to where we came from?"

"Well, you never know," he said. "But the sea is further away than you imagine, I think. I don't think you and I will live to see it."

Jenny said impulsively, "Our children might."

"Yes. Our children might. Come on. Let's get this wretched dinner over with."

The stateroom roof slid closed, hiding the sea of suns from their sight.

The Steam Dancer (1896)

Caitlín R. Kiernan

Caitlín R. Kiernan is the award-winning author of nine novels, including *Silk*, *Threshold*, *Low Red Moon*, *Murder of Angels*, *Daughter of Hounds*, and, most recently, *The Red Tree*. She is a prolific short-fiction writer, and her stories have been collected in *Tales of Pain and Wonder*, *From Weird and Distant Shores*, *Wrongs Things*, *To Charles Fort, With Love*, *Alabaster*, *A Is for Alien*, and *The Ammonite Violin & Others*. She lives in Providence, Rhode Island. Of her story, she writes, "I'm honestly not sure what, exactly, served as the primary inspiration for 'The Steam Dancer (1896).' It's easier for me to see the influences at work here than to recall what triggered the story. It was written during June 2007, and was the first of the stories I've set in my alternate-history Denver, Colorado, which I've named Cherry Creek. I know I was wanting to write a story that would work as science fiction and also as a western. It's one of those rare instances where the title occurred to me before I began work on the piece, which is always nice."

I

MISSOURI BANKS LIVES in the great smoky city at the edge of the mountains, here where the endless yellow prairie laps gently with grassy waves and locust tides at the exposed bones of the world jutting suddenly up towards the western sky. She was not born here, but came to the city long ago, when she was still only a small child and her father traveled from town to town in one of Edison's electric wagons selling his herbs and medicinals, his stinking poultices and elixirs. This is the city where her mother grew suddenly ill with miner's fever and where all her father's liniments and ministrations could not restore his wife's failing health or spare her life. In his grief, he drank a vial of either antimony or arsenic a few days after the funeral, leaving his only daughter and only child to fend for herself. And so, she grew up here, an orphan, one of a thousand or so dispossessed urchins with sooty bare feet and sooty faces, filching coal with sooty hands to stay warm in winter, clothed in rags, and eating what could be found in trash barrels and what could be begged or stolen.

But these things are only her past, and she has a bit of paper torn from a lending-library book of old plays which reads *What's past is prologue*, which she tacked up on the wall near her dressing mirror in the room she shares with the mechanic. Whenever the weight of Missouri's past begins to press in upon her, she reads those words aloud to herself, once or twice or however many times is required, and usually it makes her feel at least a little better. It has been years since she was alone and on the streets. She has the mechanic, and he loves her, and most of the time she believes that she loves him, as well.

He found her when she was nineteen, living in a shanty on the edge of the colliers' slum, hiding away in among the spoil piles and the rusting ruin of junked steam shovels and hydraulic pumps and bent bore-drill heads. He was out looking for salvage, and salvage is what he found, finding her when he lifted a broad sheet of corrugated tin, uncovering the squalid burrow where she lay slowly dying on a filthy mattress. She'd been badly bitten during a swarm of red-bellied bloatflies, and now the hungry white maggots were doing their work. It was not an uncommon fate for the likes of Missouri Banks, those caught out in the open during the spring swarms, those without safe houses to hide inside until the voracious flies had come and gone, moving on to bedevil other towns and cities and farms. By the time the mechanic chanced upon her, Missouri's left leg, along with her right hand and forearm, was gangrenous, seething with the larvae. Her left eye was a pulpy, painful boil, and he carried her to the charity hospital on Arapahoe where he paid the surgeons who meticulously picked out the parasites and sliced away the rotten flesh and finally performed the necessary amputations. Afterwards, the mechanic nursed her back to health, and when she was well enough, he fashioned for her a new leg and a new arm. The eye was entirely beyond his expertise, but he knew a Chinaman in San Francisco who did nothing but eyes and ears, and it happened that the Chinaman owed the mechanic a favour. And in this way was Missouri Banks made whole again, after a fashion, and the mechanic took her as his lover and then as his wife, and they found a better, roomier room in an upscale boardinghouse near the Seventh Avenue irrigation works.

And today, which is the seventh day of July, she settles onto the little bench in front of the dressing-table mirror and reads aloud to herself the shred of paper.

"What's past is prologue," she says, and then sits looking at her face and the artificial eye and listening to the oppressive drone of cicadas outside the open window. The mechanic has promised that someday he will read her *The Tempest* by William Shakespeare, which he says is where the line was taken from. She can read it herself, she's told him, because she isn't illiterate. But the truth is she'd much prefer to hear him read, breathing out the words in his rough, soothing voice, and often he does read to her in the evenings.

She thinks that she has grown to be a very beautiful woman, and sometimes she believes the parts she wasn't born with have only served to make her that much more so and not any the less. Missouri smiles and gazes back at her reflection, admiring the high cheekbones and full lips (which were her mother's before her), the glistening beads of sweat on her chin and forehead and upper lip, the way her left eye pulses with a soft turquoise radiance. Afternoon light glints off the galvanized plating of her mechanical arm, the sculpted steel rods and struts, the well-oiled wheels and cogs, all the rivets and welds and perfectly fitted joints. For now, it hangs heavy and limp at her side, because she hasn't yet cranked its tiny double-acting Trevithick engine. There's only the noise of the cicadas and the traffic down on the street and the faint, familiar, comforting chug of her leg.

Other women are only whole, she thinks. Other women are only born, not made. I have been crafted.

With her living left hand, Missouri wipes some of the sweat from her face and then turns towards the small electric fan perched on the chifforobe. It hardly does more than stir the muggy summer air about, and she thinks how good it would be to go back to bed. How good to spend the whole damned day lying naked on cool sheets, dozing and dreaming and waiting for the mechanic to come home from the foundry. But she dances at Madam Ling's place four days a week, and today is one of those days, so soon she'll have to get dressed and start her arm, then make her way to the trolley and on down to the Asian Quarter. The mechanic didn't want her to work, but she told him she owed him a great debt and it would be far kinder of him to allow her to repay it. And, being kind, he knew she was telling the truth. Sometimes, he even comes down to see, to sit among the Coolies and the pungent clouds of opium smoke and watch her on the stage.

2

The shrewd old woman known in the city only as Madam Ling made the long crossing to America sometime in 1861, shortly after the end of the Second Opium War. Missouri has heard that she garnered a tidy fortune from smuggling and piracy, and maybe a bit of murder, too, but that she found Hong Kong considerably less amenable to her business ventures after the treaty that ended the war and legalized the import of opium to China. She came ashore in San Francisco and followed the railroads and airships east across the Rockies,

and when she reached the city at the edge of the prairie, she went no farther. She opened a saloon and whorehouse, the Nine Dragons, on a muddy,
unnamed thoroughfare, and the mechanic has explained to Missouri that in
China nine is considered a very lucky number. The Nine Dragons is wedged in
between a hotel and a gambling house, and no matter the time of day or night
seems always just as busy. Madam Ling never wants for trade.

Missouri always undresses behind the curtain, before she takes the stage,
and so presents herself to the sleepy-eyed men wearing only a fringed shawl of
vermilion silk, her corset and sheer muslin shift, her white linen pantalettes.
The shawl was a gift from Madam Ling, who told her in broken English that
it came all the way from Beijing. Madam Ling of the Nine Dragons is not
renowned for her generosity towards white women, or much of anyone else,
and Missouri knows the gift was a reward for the men who come here just to
watch her. She does not have many belongings, but she treasures the shawl as
one of her most prized possessions and keeps it safe in a cedar chest at the foot
of the bed she shares with the mechanic, and it always smells of the camphor-
soaked cotton balls she uses to keep the moths at bay.

There is no applause, but she knows that most eyes have turned her way
now. She stands sweating in the flickering gaslight glow, the open flames that
ring the small stage, and listens to the men muttering in Mandarin amongst
themselves and laying down mahjong tiles and sucking at their pipes. And
then her music begins, the negro piano player and the woman who plucks so
proficiently at a guzheng's twenty-five strings, the thin man at his xiao flute,
and the burly Irishman who keeps the beat on a goatskin bodhran and always
takes his pay in Chinese whores. The smoky air fills with a peculiar, jangling
rendition of the final aria of Verdi's *La Traviata*, because Madam Ling is a great
admirer of Italian opera. The four musicians huddle together, occupying the
space that has been set aside especially for them, crammed between the bar and
the stage, and Missouri breathes in deeply, taking her cues as much from the
reliable metronome rhythms of the engines that drive her metal leg and arm as
from the music.

This is her time, her moment as truly as any moment will ever belong to
Missouri Banks.

And her dance is not what men might see in the white saloons and dance halls
and brothels strung out along Broadway and Lawrence, not the schottisches and
waltzes of the ladies of the line, the uptown sporting women in their fine ruffled

skirts made in New York and Chicago. No one has ever taught Missouri how to dance, and these are only the moves that come naturally to her, that she finds for herself. This is the interplay and synthesis of her body and the mechanic's handiwork, of the music and her own secret dreams. Her clothes fall away in gentle, inevitable drifts, like the first snows of October. Steel toe to flesh-and-bone heel, the graceful arch of an iron calf and the clockwork motion of porcelain and nickel fingers across her sweaty belly and thighs. She spins and sways and dips, as lissome and sure of herself as anything that was ever only born of Nature. And there is such joy in the dance that she might almost offer prayers of thanks to her suicide father and the bloatfly maggots that took her leg and arm and eye. There is such joy in the dancing, it might almost match the delight and peace she's found in the arms of the mechanic. There is such joy, and she thinks this is why some men and women turn to drink and laudanum, tinctures of morphine and Madam Ling's black tar, because they cannot dance.

The music rises and falls, like the seas of grass rustling to themselves out beyond the edges of the city, and the delicate mechanisms of her prosthetics clank and hum and whine. And Missouri weaves herself through this land-scape of sound with the easy dexterity of pronghorn antelope and deer fleeing the jaws of wolves or the hunters' rifles, the long haunches and fleet paws of jackrabbits running out before a wildfire. For this moment, she is lost, and, for this moment, she wishes never to be found again. Soon, the air has begun to smell of the steam leaking from the exhaust ports in her leg and arm, an oily, hot sort of aroma that is as sweet to Missouri Banks as rosewater or honeysuckle blossoms. She closes her eyes—the one she was born with and the one from San Francisco—and feels no shame whatsoever at the lazy stares of the opium smokers. The piston rods in her left leg pump something more alive than blood, and the flywheels turn on their axles. She is muscle and skin, steel and artifice. She is the woman who was once a filthy, ragged guttersnipe, and she is Madam Ling's special attraction, a wondrous child of Terpsichore and Industry. Once she overheard the piano player whispering to the Irishman, and he said, "You'd think she emerged outta her momma's womb like that," and then there was a joke about screwing automata. But, however it might have been meant, she took it as praise and confirmation.

Too soon the music ends, leaving her gasping and breathless, dripping sweat and an iridescent sheen of lubricant onto the boards, and she must sit in her room backstage and wait out another hour before her next dance.

3

And after the mechanic has washed away the day's share of grime and they're finished with their modest supper of apple pie and beans with thick slices of bacon, after his evening cigar and her cup of strong black Indian tea, after all the little habits and rituals of their nights together are done, he follows her to bed. The mechanic sits down and the springs squeak like stepped-on mice; he leans back against the tarnished brass headboard, smiling his easy, disarming smile while she undresses. When she slips the stocking off her right leg, he sees the gauze bandage wrapped about her knee, and his smile fades to concern.

"Here," he says. "What's that? What happened there?" and he points at her leg.

"It's nothing," she tells him. "It's nothing much."

"That seems an awful lot of dressing for nothing much. Did you fall?"

"I didn't fall," she replies. "I never fall."

"Of course not," he says. "Only us mere mortal folk fall. Of course you didn't fall. So what is it? It ain't the latest goddamn fashion."

Missouri drapes her stocking across the footboard, which is also brass, and turns her head to frown at him over her shoulder.

"A burn," she says, "that's all. One of Madam Ling's girls patched it for me. It's nothing to worry over."

"How bad a burn?"

"I said it's nothing, didn't I?"

"You did," says the mechanic and nods his head, looking not the least bit convinced. "But that secondary sliding valve's leaking again, and that's what did it. Am I right?"

Missouri turns back to her bandaged knee, wishing that there'd been some way to hide it from him, because she doesn't feel like him fussing over her tonight. "It doesn't hurt much at all. Madam Ling had a salve—"

"Haven't I been telling you that seal needs to be replaced?"

"I know you have."

"Well, you just stay in tomorrow, and I'll take that leg with me to the shop, get it fixed up tip-top again. Have it back before you know it."

"It's *fine*. I already patched it. It'll hold."

"Until the *next* time," he says, and she knows well enough from the tone of his voice that he doesn't want to argue with her about this, that he's losing patience. "You go and let that valve blow out, and you'll be needing a good deal more doctoring than a chink whore can provide. There's a lot of pressure builds up inside those pistons. You know that, Missouri."

"Yeah, I know that," she says.

"Sometimes you don't *act* like you know it."

"I can't stay in tomorrow. But I'll let you take it the next day, I swear. I'll stay in Thursday, and you can take my leg then."

"Thursday," the mechanic grumbles. "And so I just gotta keep my fingers crossed until then?"

"It'll be fine," she tells him again, trying to sound reassuring and reasonable, trying not to let the bright rind of panic show in her voice. "I won't push so hard. I'll stick to the slow dances."

And then a long and disagreeable sort of silence settles over the room, and for a time she sits there at the edge of the bed, staring at both her legs, at injured meat and treacherous, unreliable metal. *Machines break down,* she thinks, *and the flesh is weak. Ain't nothing yet conjured by God nor man won't go and turn against you, sooner or later.* Missouri sighs and lightly presses a porcelain thumb to the artificial leg's green release switch; there's a series of dull clicks and pops as it comes free of the bolts set directly into her pelvic bones.

"I'll stay in tomorrow," she says and sets her left leg into its stand near the foot of their bed. "I'll send word to Madam Ling. She'll understand."

When the mechanic doesn't tell her that it's really for the best, when he doesn't say anything at all, she looks and sees he's dozed off sitting up, still wearing his trousers and suspenders and undershirt. "You," she says quietly, then reaches for the release switch on her right arm.

4

When she feels his hands on her, Missouri thinks at first that this is only some new direction her dream has taken, the rambling dream of her father's medicine wagon and of buffalo, of rutted roads and a flaxen Nebraska sky filled with flocks of automatic birds chirping arias from *La Traviata*. But there's something substantial about the pale light of the waxing moon falling though the open window and the way the curtains move in the midnight breeze that convinces her she's awake. Then he kisses her, and one hand wanders down across her breasts and stomach and lingers in the unruly thatch of hair between her legs.

"Unless maybe you got something better to be doing," he mutters in her ear.

"Well, now that you mention it, I *was* dreaming," she tells him, "before you woke me up," and the mechanic laughs.

"Then maybe I should let you get back to it." But when he starts to take his hand away from her privy parts, she takes hold of it and rubs his fingertips across her labia.

"So, what exactly were you dreaming about that's got you in such a cooperative mood, Miss Missouri Banks?" he asks, and kisses her again, the dark stubble on his cheeks scratching at her face.

"Wouldn't you like to know," she says.

"I figure that's likely why I inquired."

His face is washed in the soft blue-green glow of her San Francisco eye, which switched on as soon as she awoke, and times like this it's hard not to imagine all the ways her life might have gone but didn't, how very unlikely that it went this way, instead. And she starts to tell him the truth, her dream of being a little girl and all the manufactured birds, the shaggy herds of bison, and how her father kept insisting he should give up peddling his herbs and remedies and settle down somewhere. But at the last, and for no particular reason, she changes her mind, and Missouri tells him another dream, just something she makes up off the top of her sleep-blurred head.

"You might not like it," she says.

"Might not," he agrees. "Then again, you never know," and the first joint of an index finger slips inside her.

"Then again," she whispers, and so she tells him a dream she's never dreamt. How there was a terrible fire and before it was over and done with, the flames had claimed half the city, there where the grass ends and the mountains start. And at first, she tells him, it was an awful, awful dream, because she was trapped in the boardinghouse when it burned, and she could see him down on the street, calling for her, but, try as they may, they could not reach each other.

"Why you want to go and have a dream like that for?" he asks.

"You wanted to hear it. Now shut up and listen."

So he does as he's bidden, and she describes to him seeing an enormous airship hovering above the flames, spewing its load of water and sand into the ravenous inferno.

"There might have been a dragon," she says. "Or it might have only been started by lightning."

"A dragon," he replies, working his finger in a little deeper. "Yes, I think it must definitely have been a dragon. They're so ill-tempered this time of year."

"Shut up. This is my dream," she tells him, even though it isn't. "I almost died, so much of me got burned away, and they had me scattered about in pieces in the Charity Hospital. But you went right to work, putting me back together again. You worked night and day at the shop, making me a pretty metal face and a tin heart, and you built my breasts—"

"—from sterling silver," he says. "And your nipples I fashioned from out of pure gold."

"And just how the sam hell did you know *that*?" she grins. Then Missouri reaches down and moves his hand, slowly pulling his finger out of her. Before he can protest, she's laid his palm over the four bare bolts where her leg fits on. He smiles and licks at her nipples, then grips one of the bolts and gives it a very slight tug.

"Well, while you were sleeping," he says, "I made a small window in your skull, only just large enough that I can see inside. So, no more secrets. But don't you fret. I expect your hair will hide it quite completely. Madam Ling will never even notice, and nary a Chinaman will steal a glimpse of your sweet, darling brain."

"Why, I never even felt a thing."

"I was very careful not to wake you."

"Until you did."

And then the talk is done, without either of them acknowledging that the time has come, and there's no more of her fiery, undreamt dreams or his glib comebacks. There's only the mechanic's busy, eager hands upon her, only her belly pressed against his, the grind of their hips after he has entered her, his fingertips lingering at the sensitive bolts where her prosthetics attach. She likes that best of all, that faint electric tingle, and she knows *he* knows, though she has never had to tell him so. Outside and far away, she thinks she hears an owl, but there are no owls in the city.

5

And when she wakes again, the boardinghouse room is filled with the dusty light of a summer morning. The mechanic is gone, and he's taken her leg with him. Her crutches are leaned against the wall near her side of the bed. She stares at them for a while, wondering how long it has been since the last time she had to use them, then deciding it doesn't really matter, because however long it's been, it hasn't been long enough. There's a note, too, on her night-stand, and the mechanic says not to worry about Madam Ling, that he'll send one of the boys from the foundry down to the Asian Quarter with the news. Take it easy, he says. Let that burn heal. Burns can be bad. Burns can scar, if you don't look after them.

When the clanging steeple bells of St. Margaret of Castello's have rung nine o'clock, she shuts her eyes and thinks about going back to sleep. St. Margaret, she recalls, is a patron saint of the crippled, an Italian woman who was born blind and hunchbacked, lame and malformed. Missouri envies the men and women who take comfort in those bells, who find in their tolling more than the time of day. She has never believed in the Catholic god or any other sort, unless perhaps it was some capricious heathen deity assigned to watch over starving, maggot-ridden guttersnipes. She imagines what form that god might assume, and it is a far more fearsome thing than any hunchbacked crone. A wolf, she thinks. Yes, an enormous black wolf—or coyote, perhaps—all ribs and mange and a distended, empty belly, crooked ivory fangs, and burning eyes like smoldering embers glimpsed through a cast-iron grate. *That* would be her god, if ever she'd had been blessed with such a thing. Her mother had come from Presbyterian stock somewhere back in Virginia, but her father believed in nothing more powerful than the hand of man, and he was not about to have his child's head filled up with Protestant superstition and nonsense, not in a Modern age of science and enlightenment.

Missouri opens her eyes again, her green eye—all cornea and iris, aqueous and vitreous humours—and the ersatz one designed for her in San Francisco. The crutches are still right there, near enough that she could reach out and touch them. They have good sheepskin padding and the vulcanized rubber tips have pivots and are filled with some shock-absorbing gelatinous substance, the name of which she has been told and cannot recall. The mechanic ordered them for her special from a company in some faraway Prussian city, and she knows they cost more than he could rightly afford, but she hates them anyway. And lying on the sweat-damp sheets, smelling the hazy morning air rustling the gingham curtains, she wonders if she built a little shrine to the wolf god of all collier guttersnipes, if maybe he would come in the night and take the crutches away so she would never have to see them again.

"It's not that simple, Missouri," she says aloud, and she thinks that those could have been her father's words, if the theosophists are right and the dead might ever speak through the mouths of the living.

"Leave me alone, old man" she says and sits up. "Go back to the grave you yearned for, and leave me be."

Her arm is waiting for her at the foot of the bed, right where she left it the night before, reclining in its cradle, next to the empty space her leg *ought* to occupy. And the hot breeze through the window, the street- and coal-smoke-scented breeze, causes the scrap of paper tacked up by her vanity mirror to flutter against the wall. Her proverb, her precious stolen scrap of Shakespeare. *What's past is prologue.*

Missouri Banks considers how she can keep herself busy until the mechanic comes back to her—a torn shirt sleeve that needs mending, and she's no slouch with a needle and thread. Her good stockings could use a rinsing. The dressing on her leg should be changed, and Madam Ling saw to it she had a small tin of the pungent salve to reapply when Missouri changed the bandages. Easily half a dozen such mundane tasks, any woman's work, any woman who is not a dancer, and nothing that won't wait until the bells of St. Margaret's ring ten or eleven. And so she watches the window, the sunlight and flapping gingham, and it isn't difficult to call up with almost perfect clarity the piano and the guzheng and the Irishman thumping his bodhran, the exotic, festive trill of the xiao. And with the music swelling loudly inside her skull, she can then recall the dance. And she is not a cripple in need of patron saints or a guttersnipe praying to black wolf gods, but Madam Ling's specialty, the steam- and blood-powered gem of the Nine Dragons. She moves across the boards, and men watch her with dark and drowsy eyes as she pirouettes and prances through grey opium clouds.

The Cast-Iron Kid

Andrew Knighton

ANDREW KNIGHTON lives and occasionally writes in Stockport, England. He's had a couple dozen stories published in magazines such as *Murky Depths*, *Dark Horizons*, and *Jupiter*. He occasionally scrawls down thoughts and details of his latest stories at ANDREWKNIGHTON.WORDPRESS.COM. He writes, "This story comes from a childhood watching westerns with my dad. I loved the sights and sounds of the imagined west. The hats. The spurs. The steely gazes. The tense silence breaking into sudden violence. But most of all, I was drawn to the code of the West. The sense that there were rules at play here, rules totally different to those around me. As a kid, I wanted to understand those rules. As an adult, I want to understand what happens when you break them."

JOHNNY HAD LIVED his whole twelve years in Dirtville, but even he knew it for a useless dustbowl of a place, like a dried-out patch of prairie grass clinging to the thin, lifeless soil. The fields were all but barren, livestock too scrawny to be worth the effort of eating. Only one shop was still open and its shelves were mostly filled with air. Since the railroad had changed route, taking the trains and travellers with it, half the buildings had been torn down for trade or firewood, or just to get at the prairie dogs nested underneath.

Johnny watched as Dog-Valley Dan slowly paced the main street of Dirtville, his strides weighty with resolve. Thirty-seven cartridge cases glinted on a thong round Dan's neck, one for every man who'd dared face him in a shoot-out. Thirty-seven corpses, rotting in dusty frontier graveyards.

Dan was an infamous outlaw, wanted in seven states for his exploits on the gunfighting circuit. The last man who'd stopped in Dirtville, a salesman named Hicky, had brought a stack of newspapers and penny dreadfuls describing the exploits of these men, and Johnny had mastered just enough of his letters to read those stories. Like the rest of the townspeople he trembled in anticipation at Dan's arrival.

As Dan stalked the wide, sandy street folks peered nervously out through flimsy wooden shop-fronts. A small child, running into the open, was whisked away by his mother, a shrew-faced woman in a faded bonnet. The only sounds were the clink of Dan's spurs and the creaking of the general store sign. Johnny held his breath and gripped his catapult tight to his chest.

A figure in a wide black Stetson emerged from the rickety saloon. Behind him the barkeep, Mr. Kent, peered hawk-nosed over the top of the still-swinging doors with their peeling paint. The man in the hat turned to face Dan, fat gloved hand dangling below his holster.

"You the Cast-Iron Kid?" Dan asked, his words echoing down the empty street.

The figure in the Stetson nodded, steam rising from his wide shoulders in the midday heat.

"I hear tell you're a coward, boy," Dan drawled his usual lazy provocation. "Gonna prove me wrong?"

The Cast-Iron Kid's face was wrapped in impassive shadow. With a hiss he strode into the middle of the street and turned to face Dan. The silence stretched out, long and tense, as dust blew against the boarded-up storefronts and a tumbleweed rolled down the road.

"Draw." The Kid's voice emerged, low and scratchy.

Before the words could hit the floor Dan's pistol was in his hand, bucking and roaring, chambers spinning as he let fly. Six sharp clangs rang out as bullets hit the Kid and ricocheted off into the distance. Dan stared, slack-jawed, as for the first time in his brutal life an opponent failed to fall beneath a hail of lead.

Slowly, the Kid's coat slid to the ground, revealing a wide chest of gleaming grey, six shallow dents where the bloodstains should have been. He doffed his hat and a cylindrical head reflected the sun's rays, ridged and flat-topped like an old tin can with dark, gaping holes for a mouth and eyes. Steam emerged from a short smokestack on his back, and every movement was accompanied by a hiss of oiled pistons or whir of hidden gears.

"My turn," came the crackling gramophone voice as the Kid's hinged fingers reached for his gun.

Sooner or later, every gunslinger and fist-fighter came to Dirtville, drawn by the reputation of the Cast-Iron Kid. Word was the Kid had never been beat, and for the fast-draw fanatics of the Western Territory, that sounded an awful lot like a challenge. Johnny figured no other boy saw so many famous faces, not even the sons of politicians in Washington or rich business folks up in New York. From the stoop of Elmer Klief's porch he watched the Kid take on Desolation Sal and Wilson Payne, Gettysburg Phil and Running Hammer, leaving each one cold in the dirt. One time, the sheriff of neighbouring Harper's Fall raised a posse of a dozen men and rode them into Dirtville to bring justice for those the Kid had killed. They lynched the metal man out by the old well, hanging him from an oak so dry and shrivelled it barely even bent beneath Cast-Iron's weight. But he soon got bored of swinging, tore the improvised gallows clean out of the earth and beat the posse into a rich dark smear. That fall, crops grew round the old well for the first time in years.

Some fights took it out of the Kid, but he always got patched back up. If Johnny kept quiet he got to sit in the smithy while the town's elders, like old Mr. Moore the watchmaker and Heinrich Altman the railroad engineer, tinkered with the Kid's innards to keep him in shape. They cleaned pipes and calibrated gears while Jim Roe's wife, Ellen, who everyone knew was the real strength at the smithy, beat the dents out of that shining carapace. As the years passed Johnny got older and the adults a little greyer, but old Cast-Iron stayed just the same.

The Stranger rode into town on a white horse named Ghost, past the derelict station and the tiny, cramped graveyard. There was little soil to be dug this side of the mountains, and most of it had to be kept for the malnourished crops. But that didn't stop folks dying, so the gravedigger had taken to planting the deceased vertically, feet first in deep, narrow tunnels. The bleached crosses clustered tight on Boot Hill.

Johnny sat by the side of the road, stretching out the cord on his home-made catapult. As The Stranger approached Johnny let fly, shattering one of the old bottles perched on a nearby fence. Then he reached down into the dry dirt, fingers seeking another good-sized pebble.

"That's mighty fine shooting," The Stranger said. "Reckon you must be the best shot this side of Tombstone."

Johnny loosed a sharp flint which clattered ineffectively off the fence. He shook his head.

"Try these," The Stranger said, pulling a handful of ball-bearings from his bag and placing them beside the boy. Johnny picked one up, feeling the cold lead weight in his palm.

"What're they for?" he asked.

The Stranger shrugged.

"Engine stuff," he said. "I had a buddy used to work the railroads, gave me them for luck."

"Don't you need 'em?" Johnny asked.

The Stranger looked round at the barren valley full of pale, weather-beaten buildings with cracked windows and loose tiles.

"Not as much as you, I reckon," he said.

"You here for Cast-Iron?" Johnny asked.

The Stranger nodded and pulled two dimes from the pocket of his vest. "What can you tell me about him?"

The boy pursed his lips, sucking thoughtfully.

"He's real iron," he said, accepting the coins. "Ma says the menfolk built him to draw folks in, on account of the railroad don't run through here no more, and there ain't no other way to make a living round these parts."

He poked a finger through a hole in his oversized shirt.

"This here came off of Oklahoma Slim. Mr. Klief got his pants, on account of his old breeches didn't have no backside left to 'em, and Sally Altman got his jacket to keep her warm in winter. He had a whole bag of gold too. The mayor took it to the traders at Harper's Fall, got us all manner of grain and tinned food. When we heard you was coming Ma said we'd eat well this winter."

The Stranger rose slowly to his feet and stood gazing at the distant hills. The wind blew long, dark curls of hair across his stern face. There was a long silence, broken only by the rusty creaking of the general store sign.

"What's your name, boy?" The Stranger said at last.

"Johnny," the boy replied.

"Thanks, Johnny," The Stranger said and raised his hat before turning back towards his horse.

Johnny plucked one of the lead balls from the dirt, rolled it around in his grubby fingers. He glanced nervously up the street into town, but nothing moved except the tumbleweeds. Still clutching the ball-bearing he ran after The Stranger and whispered conspiratorially in his ear.

"Bullets bounce off of him."

The Stranger nodded, tethered his horse, and strode up the long street into town. Stopping outside the general store he rolled up his sleeves, unhooked his spurs from his boots, and plucked a two-by-four from the barrel by the door.

With a calm, quiet tread he stepped into the shadow of the saloon and placed himself next to the creaking door, back pressed up against the wall, plank raised firmly in two calloused hands. There he waited.

After twenty minutes Johnny heard the rattle of the bar door followed by a whirring of gears. The Stranger hefted the plank up to his shoulder and, as the Kid's looming shadow passed, swung out with all his might. There was a clang like a cathedral bell and the gleaming barrel head flew away, leaving steam pouring from between shiny shoulders. The Stranger struck again and again, splinters flying as he battered the Kid with his improvised club, sending the dented body reeling back into the street, dust spurting beneath each heavy footfall. With a thud that echoed down the whole valley Cast-Iron's gleaming shell crashed to the ground, a lone gearwheel tumbling out of the gaping neck-hole and rolling to a halt at Johnny's feet.

The Stranger cast aside the splintered remnants of his club and leaned down over the heap of dusty metal, sweat dribbling down his face in the noonday heat.

"That's for my buddy Dan," The Stranger said, mouth finally lifting in the hollow image of a smile. But his grin turned to a grimace as the headless body stirred, rising from the packed ochre earth and reaching out towards him. Cold steel hands clamped round The Stranger's throat, tightening and twisting with ruthless mechanical might. The man's eyes bulged, foam fringing his mouth, and even though Johnny looked away he could not escape those desperate rasping breaths or the final sickening snap.

Johnny took one last look at the graveyard, thinking of all the wanderers and lawmen he'd seen dropped into its pits as he grew up. Sure, some of them had been mean, and more had been villains of the West's worst sort, but that didn't make it right. In one hand he clutched his catapult, a sturdy frame of wood-scraps and rat-glue, an object of his own making, not scavenged from some poor sap sleeping on Boot Hill. In the other he hefted the thing he'd gone to Tombstone for, trading in his fifteenth birthday hat. Sheriff Peterson's hat, still smelling of hair-cream and blood.

He stood outside the saloon and called for the Cast-Iron Kid, called him every dark curse-name ever muttered and more he'd dreamed up on the long lonely journey back to Dirtville. At last the doors parted and the Kid strode into the street, piston innards hissing.

"What is it, little Johnny?" the gramophone voice asked.

"It's my turn," Johnny declared. "I'm calling you out, like those other folks did."

The Kid let out a long, mirthless laugh.

"This how you get to become a man, is it?" he asked. "Well, little Johnny, let's see what make of man you are."

Johnny pulled back on the sling, rubber straining, scrap-wood creaking, the smells of sweat and rat-glue cutting through his fear. The Kid started to laugh again, the sound circling and repeating. Then he fell silent as something struck his chest with a clang, a wide iron bar marked "N" and "S" at either end. Gears froze as the magnet's power flowed through them, sticking each one to the next. The street was filled with tinkling and whirring as delicate springs and ratchets caught fast and snapped. The Cast-Iron Kid stood motionless, joints stuck in place, steam seeping through the gaps. His firebox backed up and choked on its own fumes, sending clouds of soot-black smoke pouring from his mouth and eyes. Fingers spasmed, stretched back on themselves and burst apart in a hail of tiny articulated plates. Then with a thud that echoed back from the mountains the Kid fell forwards, showering Johnny with dry, lifeless desert dust.

There was no space left in the graveyard for the Cast-Iron Kid, so they melted him down and sold him as engine parts. Years later, folks passing through Harper's Fall would tell of the sheriff there who sat on his stoop running two ball-bearings round his hand, one of worn lead, the other of cold cast iron.

Machine Maid

Margo Lanagan

MARGO LANAGAN's most recent novel, *Tender Morsels,* was a Printz Honor Book and won the World Fantasy Award for Best Novel. Her collection of speculative fiction short stories, *Black Juice,* was also widely acclaimed; won two World Fantasy Awards, two Ditmar, and two Aurealis awards; was shortlisted for the *Los Angeles Times* Book Prize; and also won a Printz Honor. Her collection *Red Spikes* was a CBCA Book of the Year and was shortlisted for the Commonwealth Writers Prize and longlisted for the Frank O'Connor International Short Story Award. Margo lives in Sydney, Australia, and maintains a blog at AMONGAMIDWHILE.BLOGSPOT.COM. Of "Machine Maid," she writes, "For this story I did a bit of research about automatons, which along with dolls and clowns have to be some of the creepiest things people have invented. The woman isolated on a bush property is an oft-used character in Australian fiction; I just decided to give her the intellectual curiosity and the means to fight back against her situation."

WE CAME TO Cuttajunga through the goldfields; Mr. Goverman was most eager to show me the sites of his successes.

They were impressive only in being so very unprepossessing. How could such dusty earth, such quantities of it piled up discarded by the road and all up and down the disembowelled hills, have yielded anything of value? How did this devastated place have any connection with the metal of crowns and rings and chains of office, and with the palaces and halls where such things were worn and wielded, on the far side of the globe?

Well, it must, I said to myself, as I stood obediently at the roadside, feeling the dust stain my hems and spoil the shine of my Pattison's shoes. See how much attention is being paid it, by this over-layer of dusty men shoveling, crawling, winching up buckets or baskets of broken rock, or simply standing, at rest from their labours as they watch one of their number return, proof in his carriage and the cut of his coat that they are not toiling here for nothing. There must be something of value here.

"This hill is fairly well dug out," said Mr. Goverman, "and there was only ever wash-gold from ancient watercourses here in any case. 'Tis good for nobody but Chinamen now." And indeed I saw several of the creatures, in their smockish clothing and their umbrella-ish hats, each with his long pigtail, earnestly working at a pile of tailings in the gully that ran by the road.

The town was hardly worthy of the name, it was such a collection of sordid drinking-palaces, fragile houses and luckless miners lounging about the lanes. Bowling alleys there were, and a theatre, and stew-houses offering meals for so little, one wondered how the keepers turned a profit. And all blazed and fluttered and showed its patches and cracks in the unrelenting sunlight.

The only woman I saw leaned above the street on a balcony railing that looked set to give way beneath her generous arms. She was dressed with profound tastelessness and she smoked a pipe, as a gypsy or a man would, surveying the street below and having no care that it saw her so clearly. I guessed her to be Mrs. Bawden, there being a painted canvas sign strung between the veranda posts beneath her feet: "MRS. HUBERT BAWDEN/Companions Live and Electric." Her gaze went over us as my husband drew my attention to how far one could see across the wretched diggings from this elevation. I felt as if the creature had raked me into disarray with her nails. *She* would know exactly the humiliations Mr. Goverman had visited on me in the night; she would be smiling to herself at my prim and upright demeanour now, at the thought of what had been pushed at these firm-closed lips while the animal that was my husband pleaded and panted above.

On we went, thank goodness, and soon we were viewing a panorama similar to that of the dug-out hill, only the work here involved larger machinery than the human body. Parties of men trooped in and out of several caverns dug into the hillside, pushing roughly made trucks along rails between the mines and the precarious, thundering houses where the stamping-machines punished the gold from the obdurate quartz. My husband had launched into a disquisition on the geological feature that resulted in this hill's having borne him so much fruit, and if truth be told it gave me some pleasure to imagine the forces he described at their work in their unpeopled age, heaving and pressing, breaking and slicing and finally resting, their uppermost layers washed and smoothed by rains, while the quartz-seam underneath, split away and forced upward from its initial deposition, held secret in its cracks and crevices its gleamless measure of gold.

But we must move on, to reach our new home before dark. The country grew ever more desolate, dry as a whisper and grey, grey under cover of this grey, disorderly forest. Unearthly birds the size of men stalked among the ragged tree-trunks, and others, lurid, shrieking, flocked to the boughs. In places the trees were cut down and their bodies piled into great windrows; set alight, and with an estate's new house rising half-built from the hill or field beyond, they presented a scene more suggestive of devastation by war than of the hopefulness and ambition of a youthful colony.

Cuttajunga when we reached it was not of such uncomfortable newness; Mr. Goverman had bought it from a gentleman pastoralist who had tamed and tended his allotment of this harsh land, but in the end had not loved it enough to be buried in it, and had returned to Sussex to live out his last years. The house had a settled look, and ivy, even, covered the shady side; the garden was a miracle of home plants watered by an ingenious system of runnels brought up by electric pump from the stream, and the fields on which our fortune grazed in the form of fat black cattle were free of the stumps and wreckage that marked other properties as having so recently been torn from the primeval bush.

"I hope you will be very happy here," said my husband, handing me down from the sulky.

The smile I returned him felt very wan from within, for now there would be nothing in the way of society or culture to diminish, or to compensate me for, the ghastly rituals of married life, now there would only be Mr. Goverman and me, marooned on this island of wealth and comfort, amid the fields and cattle, bordered on all sides by the tattered wilderness.

Cuttajunga was all as he had described it to me during the long grey miles: the kitchen anchored by its weighty stove and ornamented with shining pans, the orchard and the vegetable garden, which Mr. Goverman immediately set the electric yard-man watering, for they were parched after his short absence. There was a farm manager, Mr. Fredericks, who appeared not to know how to greet and converse with such a foreign creature as a woman, but instead droned to my husband about stock movements and water and feed until I thought he must be some kind of lunatic. The housekeeper, Mrs. Sanford, was a blowsy, bobbing, distractible woman who behaved as if she were accustomed to being slapped or shouted into line rather than reasoned with. The maid, Sarah Poplin, was of the poorest material. "She has some native blood in her," Mr. Goverman told me *sotto voce* when she had flounced away from his introductions. "You will be a marvellously civilising influence on her, I am sure."

"I can but try to be," I murmured. I had been forewarned, by Melbourne matrons as well as by Mr. Goverman himself, of the difficulty of finding and retaining staff, what with the goldfields promising any man or woman an independent fortune, should they happen to kick over the right pebble "up north," or "out west."

The other maid, the mechanical one Mr. Goverman had promised me, lived seated in a little cabinet attached to a charging chamber under the back stairs. Her name was Clarissa—I did not like to call such creatures by real names, but she would not recognise commands without their being prefaced by that combination of guttural and sibilant. She was of unnervingly fine quality, and beautiful with it; except for the rigidity of her face I would say she was undoubtedly more comely than I was. Her eyes were the most realistic I had seen, blue-irised and glossy between thickly lashed lids; her hair sprang dark from her clear brow without the clumping that usually characterises an electric servant's hair; each strand must be set individually. She would have cost a great deal, both to craft and to import from her native France; I had never seen so close a simulacrum of a real person, myself.

Mr. Goverman, seeing how impressed I was, insisted on commanding Clarissa upright and showing me her interior workings. I hardly knew where to rest my eyes as my husband's hands unlaced the automaton's dress behind with such practised motions, but once he had removed the panels from her back and head, the intricate machine-scape that gleamed and whirred within as Clarissa enacted his simple commands so fascinated me that I was able to forget the womanliness of this figure and the maleness of my man as he explained how this impeller drove this shaft to turn this cam and translate into the lifting of Clarissa's heavy, strong arms *this* way, and the bowing of her body *that* way, all the movements smooth, balanced and, again, the subtlest and most realistic I had witnessed in one of these creatures.

"Does she speak, then?" I said, peering into the back of her head.

"No, no," he said. "There is not sufficient room with all her other functions to allow for speaking."

"Why then are her mouth-parts so carefully made?" I moved my own head to allow more window-light into Clarissa's head-workings; the red silk-covered cavity that was the doll's mouth enlivened the brass and steel scenery, and I could discern some system of rings around it, their inner edges clothed with india-rubber, which seemed purpose-built for producing the movements of speech.

"Oh, she once spoke," said my husband. "She once sang. She is adapted from her usage as an entertainer on the Paris stage. I was impressed by the authenticity of her movements. But, alas, my dear, if you are to have your carpets beaten you must forgo her lovely singing."

He fixed her head-panel back into place. "She interests you," he said. "Have I taken an engineer for a wife?" He spoke in an amused tone, but I heard the edge in it of my mother's anxiety, felt the vacancy in my hands where she had snatched away the treatise on artificial movement I had taken from my brother Artie's bookshelf. *So unbecoming, for a girl to know such things.* She clutched the book to herself and looked me up and down as if *I* were some kind of electrically powered creature, and malfunctioning into the bargain. *For your pretty head to be full of...of cog-wheels and machine-oil,* she said disgustedly. *I will find you some more suitable reading.* My husband officiously buttoning the doll dress; my mother sweeping from the parlour with the fascinating book—I recognised this dreary feeling. As soon as I evinced a budding interest in some area of worldly affairs, people inevitably began working to keep it from blossoming. I was meant to be vapid and colourless like my mother, a silent helpmeet in the shadows of Father and my brothers; I was not to engage with the world myself, but only to witness and encourage the men's engagement, to be a decorative background to it, like the parlour wallpaper, like the draped window against which my mother smiled and sat mute as Father discoursed to our dinner-guests, the window that was obscured by impressive velvet at night, that in daytime prettified the world outside with its cascade of lace foliage.

I had barely had time to accustom myself to my new role as mistress of Cuttajunga when Mr. Goverman informed me that he would be absent for a period of weeks, riding the boundaries of his estate and perhaps venturing farther up-country in the company of his distant neighbour Captain Jollyon and some of that gentleman's stockmen and tamed natives.

"Perhaps you will appreciate my leaving you," he said, the night before he left, as he withdrew himself from me after having completed the marriage act. "You need not endure the crudeness of my touching you, for a little while."

My face was locked aside, stiff as a doll's on the pillow, and my entire body was motionless with revulsion, with humiliation. Still I did feel relief, firstly that he was done, and would not require to emit himself at my face or onto my bosom, and secondly, yes, that the nightmare of our congress would not recur for at least two full weeks and possibly more. I turned from him, and waited—not long—for his breathing to deepen and lengthen into sleep, before I rose to wash the slime of him, the smell of him, from my person.

After the riding-party left, my staff waited a day or two before deserting me. Sarah Poplin disappeared in the night, without a word. The following afternoon, as I was contemplating which of her tasks I should next instruct Mrs. Sanford to take up, that woman came into my parlour and announced that she and Mr. Fredericks had married and now intended to leave my service, Mr. Fredericks to try his luck on the western goldfields. Direct upon her quitting the room, she said, she would be quitting the house for the wider world.

"But Mrs. Sanf—Mrs. Fredericks," I said. "You leave me quite solitary and helpless. Whatever shall I do?"

"You have that machine-woman, at least, I tell myself. She's the strength of two of me."

"But no intelligence," I said. "She cannot accomplish half the tasks you can, with a quarter the subtlety. But you are right, she will never leave me, at least. She will stay out of stupidity, if not loyalty."

At the sound of that awkward word "loyalty" the new Mrs. Fredericks blushed, and soon despite my protestations she was gone, walking off without a backward glance along the western road. Her *inamorata* walked beside her, curved like a wilting grass-stalk over her stout figure, droning who knew what passionate promises into that pitiless ear. The house, meaningless, unattended around me, echoed with the fact that I was not the kind of woman servants felt compelled either to obey or to protect. Not under these conditions, at any rate, so remote from society and opinion.

I stood watching her go, keeping myself motionless rather than striding up and down as I wished to in my distress; should either of them turn, I did not want them to see the state of terror to which they had reduced me.

I was alone. My nearest respectable neighbour was Captain Jollyon's wife, a pretty, native-born chatterer with a house-party of Melbourne friends currently gathered around her, a day's ride from here. I could not abide the thought of throwing myself on the mercies of so inconsequential a person.

And I was not quite alone, was I? I was not quite helpless. I had electric servants—the yard-man and Clarissa. And I had…I pressed my hands to my waist and sat rather heavily in a woven cane chair, heedless for the moment of the afternoon sun shafting in under the veranda roof. I was almost certain by now that I carried Cuttajunga's heir in my womb. All my washing, all my shrinking from my husband's advances, had not been sufficient to stop his seed taking root in me. He had "covered" me as a stallion covers a mare, and in time I would bring forth a Master Goverman, who would complete my banishment into utter obscurity behind my family of menfolk.

But for now—I straightened in the creaking, ticking chair, focusing again on the two diminishing figures as they flickered along the shade-dappled road between the bowing, bleeding, bark-shedding eucalypt trees—for now, I had Master Goverman tucked away neatly inside me, all his needs met, much as Clarissa's and the yard-man's were by their respective electrification chambers. He required no more action from me than that I merely continue, and sustain His Little Lordship by sustaining my own self.

I did not ride to Captain Jollyon's; I did not take the sulky into the town to send the police after my disloyal servants, or to hire any replacements for them. I decided that I would manage, with Clarissa and the yard-man. I had more than three months' stores; I had a thriving vegetable garden; and I did not long for human company so strongly that stupid company would suffice, or uncivilised. If the truth be told, the more I considered my situation, the greater I felt it suited me, and the more relieved I was to have been abandoned by that sly Poplin girl, by Mr. Droning Fredericks and his resentful-seeming wife. I felt, indeed, that I was well rid of them, that I might enjoy this short season where I prevailed, solitary, in this gigantic landscape, before life and my husband returned, crowding around me, bidding me this way and that, interfering with my body, and my mind, and my reputation, in ways I could neither control nor rebuff.

And so I lived a few days proudly independent, calling my mechanical servants out, the yard-man from his charging shed and Clarissa from her cupboard under the stairs, only when I required them to undertake the more tedious and strenuous tasks of watering, or sweeping, or stirring the copper. And I returned them thence when those were completed; I kept neither of them sitting about the place to give the illusion of a resident population. I was quite comfortable walking from room to empty room, and striding or riding about my husband's empty property unaccompanied.

After several days, despite fully occupying myself as my own housekeeper and chambermaid, I began to feel restless when evening came and it was time to retire to my parlour and occupy myself with ladylike pursuits. Needlework of the decorative kind had always infuriated me; nothing in my new house was sufficiently worn to require mending yet; I had never sung well, or played the piano or the violin as my cousins did and my brother James; I could sketch, but if the choice was between reproducing the drear landscapes I moved in by day, and stretching my heartstrings by re-creating remembered scenes of London and the surrounding countryside, I felt disinclined to exercise that talent. My husband had bought me a library, but I found it to contain nothing but fashionable novels, most of which gave me the same sense of irritation, of having my mind and my being confined to meaningless matters, as conversation with that gentleman did, or with women such as Mrs. Jollyon, and it was a great freedom to cease attempting to occupy my time with them.

Then, one afternoon, I set Clarissa to sweeping the paved paths around the house, and I sat myself at a corner of the veranda ready to redirect her when she reached me. I was labouring on a letter to Mother—a daughterly letter, full of lies and optimism, telling the news of my own impending motherhood as if it were wonderful, as if it were ordinary. I looked up from my duties at the automaton as she trundled and swept, thorough and inhumanly regular and pauseless in her sweeping. My disinclination to continue my letter, and the glimpse I had had of Clarissa's workings through the opening of her back combined with the frag-mented memory of a diagram I had examined in Artie's treatise—which I had borrowed many times in secret after Mother had forbidden it me, which I had wrestled to understand. In something like a stroke of mental lightning I saw the full chain of causes and effects that produced one movement, her turning from the left side to the right at the limit of her sweeping. I could not have described it; I could not even recall it fully, a moment later. But the flash was sufficient to make me forget my letter, my mother. Intently I watched Clarissa progress down the path, hoping for another such insight. None came, and she reached me, and I turned her with a command to the right so that she would sweep the path down to the hedge, and still I watched her, as dutifully she went on. And then, in the bottom half of my written page, I drew some lines, the shape of one of the cams I had seen, that had something of a duck-bill-like projection from its edge, a length of thin cable coming up to a pulley. The marks were hardly more than traces of idle movements; they were barely identifiable as mechanical parts, but as they streaked and ghosted up out of the paper I knew that I had found myself an oc-cupation for my long and lonely days. It was more purposeless than embroidery; it would produce nothing of beauty; it would not make me a better daughter, wife, or mother, but it would satisfy me utterly.

She never failed to unnerve me, smiling out in her vague way when I opened the door of the cabinet under the stairs. Her toes would move in her shoes, her fingers splay and crook and enact the last other movements of the lubrication sequence. Her beautiful mouth, too, pursed and stretched and made moues, subtle and unnatural. Un-mouthlike sounds came from behind the india-rubber lips, inside the busy mechanical head. Her ears were cupped themselves slightly for the sound of my commands.

"Clarissa: Stand," I would say, and step back to make room for her.

She would bend forward and push herself upright, using her hands on the rim of the cabinet.

"Clarissa: Forward. Two steps," I would command, and she would perform them.

Now I could see the loosened back of the garment, the wheels and work-ings coming to a stop inside her. I left them visible now, unless I was putting her to work outside, so that I would not have the same troubles over and over, removing the panel from her back. I brought the lamp nearer, my gaze already on the parts I had been mis-drawing in my tiredness at the end of the day before. I would already be absorbed in her labyrinthine structure; even as I followed her to the study I would be checking her insides against the fistful of drawings I had made—the "translations," as I liked to think of them. She was a marvellous thing, which I was intent on reducing to mere mechanics; by the end of my project it would no longer disturb me to lock her away in her cabinet as into a coffin; I would know her seeming aliveness for the illusion it was; I would have diagrammed all the person-ness, all her apparent human-ity, out of her. She would unnerve me no longer; I would know her for exactly what she was.

By the time Mr. Goverman returned home I had discovered much more than I wished to. I made my first unwelcome finding one breathlessly hot afternoon perhaps three days before he arrived, when I had brought Clarissa to the study, commanded her to kneel and opened the back of her head, and was busy drawing what I could see of her mouth-parts behind the chutes and membrane-discs and tuning-forks of her hearing apparatus. Soft gusts of hot wind ventured in through the window from time to time, the gentlest buffetings, which did nothing to refresh me, but only moved my looser hair or vaguely rippled the buttoned edge of Clarissa's gown.

It was frustrating, attempting to draw this mouth. I do not know what exclamation I loosed in my annoyance, but it must have included a guttural and a sibilant at some point and further sounds the doll mistook for a command, for suddenly, smoothly, expensively, she lifted her arms from her sides where she knelt, manipulated her lovely fingers, her beautifully engineered elbow and shoulder joints, and drew her loosened bodice down from her shoulders, so that her bosom, so unbodily and yet so naked-seeming, was exposed to the hot study air. I heard in the momentarily still air the muted clicks and slidings within her head—I saw, indistinctly in the shadows, partly behind other workings, the movements of her mouth readying itself for something.

I rose and stood before her; she remained kneeling, straight-backed and shameless, presenting her shining breasts, gazing without embarrassment or any other emotion at my belly. The seam of her lips glistened a little with exuded oil, and the shiftings in her weighty head ceased.

I crouched before her awful readiness. I knew how tall my husband was; I knew what this doll was about. Like one girl confiding in another, like a tiny child in play with its mother or nurse, I reached out and touched Clarissa's lower lip. It yielded—not exactly as if it welcomed my touch and expectations, but with a bland absence of resistance, an emotionless acceptance that I knew I could not muster in my own marriage-bed.

I pushed my forefinger against the meeting-place of the automaton's lips. They gave, a little; they allowed my fingertip to push them apart. Slowly my finger sank in, touching the porcelain teeth. They too moved aside, following pad and joint of my finger as if learning its shape as it intruded.

Her tongue—what cloth was it, so slippery smooth? And how so wet? I pulled out my finger and rubbed the wetness with my thumb; it was a clear kind of oil or gel; I could not quite say what it was. It smelled of nothing, not perfumed, not bodily, not as machine-oil should. It must be very refined.

I put the finger back in, all the way to the knuckle. I thought I might be able to reach to the back of the cavity as I had seen it from within, the clothy, closed-off throat with its elaborate mechanical corsetry. Inside her felt disconcertingly like a real mouth; I expected the doll at any moment to release my finger and ask, with this tongue, with this palate and throat and teeth, what I thought I was about. But she only held to my finger, closely all around like living tissue, living muscle.

And then some response was triggered in her, by the very tip of my finger in her throat. Her lips clasped my knuckle somewhat tighter, and her mouth moved against the rest of my finger. Oh, it was strange! It reminded me of a caterpillar, the concertina-like way they convey themselves across a leaf, along a branch; the rippling. Back and forth along my finger the ripples ran, combining the movements of her resisting my intrusive finger with those of attempting to milk it, massaging it root to tip with a firm and varied persuasiveness. How was such seeming randomness generated? I must translate that, I must account for it in my drawings. Yet at the same time I wanted to know nothing of it; there was something in the sensations that made my own throat clench, my stomach rebel, and every part of me below the waist solidify in a kind of horror.

What horrified me worst was that I knew, as a married woman, how to put an end to the rippling. Yet the notion of doing so, and in that way imitating the most repellent, the most beast-like movements of my husband, when, blinded, stupid with his lust he…emptied himself into me, as if I were a spittoon or the pit of a privy, stilled my hand amid the awful mouth-movements. I was on the point of spasm myself, spasms of revulsion, near-vomiting. Before they should overtake me I jabbed the automaton several times in her lubricious silken throat, my knuckle easily pushing her lips and teeth aside, my finger inside her mouth-workings cold, and bonily slender, and passionless—unless curiosity is a passion, unless disgust is.

Clarissa clamped that cold finger tightly, and some workings braced her neck against what should follow upon such prodding: my husband's convulsions in his ecstasy. It was as if the man was in the room with us, I imagined his exclamations so clearly. I shuddered there myself, a shudder so rich with feeling that my own eyes were sightless with it a moment. Then the doll relaxed her grip on me, and my arm's weight drew my forefinger from her mouth, slack as my husband's member would be slack, gleaming as that would gleam with her lubricants. Quietly, dutifully, she began a mouthish process; her lips parted slightly to allow the stuff of him, the mess of him, the man-spittle, to flow forth, to fall to her bosom. Some of her oil welled out eventually onto her pillowy, rosy lower lip. I watched the whole sequence with a stony attentiveness. When the oil dripped to her shining décolletage, such pity afflicted me at what this doll had been created to undergo that I stood and, using my own handkerchief bordered with Irish lace, cleaned the poor creature's bosom, wiped her mouth as a nurse wipes a child's, and when I was certain no further oils would come forth I restored her the modesty of her bodice; I raised her from her kneeling and took her, I hardly knew why, to sit in her cabinet. I did not close her in, then—I only stood, awkward, regarding her serene face. I felt as if I ought to say something—to apologise, perhaps; perhaps to accuse. Then—and I moved with such certainty that I must have noticed-without-noticing this before—my hand went to a pleat of the velvet lining of the lid of the cabinet, and a dry *pop* sounded under my fingertips, and I drew forth a folded slip of creamy writing paper, which matched that on which Clarissa's domestic commands were written. I opened and glanced down it, the encoded list of Clarissa's tortures, the list of my own.

Revulsion attacked me then, and hurriedly I refolded and replaced the paper, and shut the doll away, and went and stood at the study window gazing out over the green lawn and the dark hedge to the near-featureless landscape beyond, the green-gold fields a-glare in the unforgiving sunlight.

Clarissa's other activities—I began to study and translate them next morning—were more obviously, comically, hideously calculated to meet a man's needs. She could be made to suffer two ways, lying like an upturned frog with her legs and her arms crooked around her torturer—without an actual man within them they contracted tightly enough to hold a very slight man indeed—or propped on all fours like any number of other beasts. In both positions she maintained continuous subtle rotations and rockings of her hips, and I could hear within her similar silky-wet movements to those her mouth had made about my finger, working studiedly upon my husband's intangible member.

To prevent her drawers becoming soaked with the lubricant oil and betraying to Mr. Goverman that I had discovered his unfaithfulness with the doll, I was forced to remove them. When I exposed her marriage parts my whole body flushed hot with mortification, and this heat afflicted me periodically throughout the course of her demonstration. Studiously applying myself to my drawing, and to the intellectual effort of translating the doll's mechanisms into her movements, was all I could do to cool myself.

If they had not been what they were, one would have considered her underparts fine examples of the seamstress's craft, or perhaps the upholsterer's. A softly heart-shaped area of wiry dark hairs formed something of a welcome or an announcement that this was no child's doll, with all such private features erased and denied. Then such padded folds, cream-velvety without, red-purple and beaded with moisture within, eventuated behind these hairs, between these heavy legs, that I shook and burned examining them. My own such parts I had no more than washed with haste and efficiency; my husband's incursions within them had been utterly surprising to me, that I should be shaped so, and for such abominable usages. Now I could see them, and on another, one constructed never to feel a whisper of embarrassment. That I should be so curious, so fascinated, disgusted me; I told myself this was all in the spirit of scientific enquiry, this was all to assist in a complete translation of the doll's movements, but the sensations that gripped me—the hot shame; the excruciating awareness, as I examined her fore and aft, of the corresponding places on my own body; the sudden exquisite sensitivity of my fingertips to her softness and her slickness and the differing textures of the fleshy doors into her; the stiffness in my neck and jaw from my rage and repugnance—these were anything but scientific.

In a shaking voice I commanded her, from the secret list. The room's atmosphere was now entirely strange, and I shivered to picture some person walking in, and I made Clarissa pause in her clasping, in her undulations, several times, so that I could circle the house and reassure myself that the country around was as deserted as ever. For what was anyone to make of the scene, of the half-clothed automaton whirring and squirming in her mechanical pleasure, of the cold-faced human seated on the ottoman watching, of the list dropped to the floor so as not to be crumpled in those tight-clenched fists?

Mr. Goverman's return woke me from the state I had plunged into by the end of the week, wherein I barely ate and did not bother to dress, but at first light went in my night-dress to the study where Clarissa stood, and all day drew, surely and intricately and in a blistering cold rage, the working innards of the doll. Something warned me—some far distant jingle of harness carried to my ears on the breeze, some hoofstrike beyond the hills echoing through the earth and up through the foundations of the homestead and into my pillow—and I rose and bathed and clothed myself properly and hid my translations away and was well engaged in housekeeperly activities by the time my husband's party approached across the fields.

Then duties crowded in on me: to be hostess, to cook and prepare rooms; to apologise for the makeshiftness of our hospitality, and the absence of servants; to inform Mr. Goverman of the presence of his heir; to submit to his embraces that night. My season of solitude vanished like a frightened bird, and the days filled up so fully with words and work, with negotiations and the maintaining of various appearances, that I scarcely had time to recall how I had occupied myself before, let alone determine any particular action to take arising from my discoveries.

Days and then weeks and then months passed, and little Master Goverman began at last to be evident to the point where I was forced to withdraw again from society, such as it was. And I was also forced—because my husband conceived a sudden dislike of visiting the vestibule of his son's little palace—to endure close visitings at my face and bosom of the most grotesque parts of Mr. Goverman's anatomy, during which he would seem to lose the powers of articulate speech and even, sometimes, of rational thought. His early reticence and acceptance of my refusals to have him near in that way were transformed now; he no longer apologised, but seemed to delight in my resistance, to take extra pleasure in grasping my head and restraining me in his chosen position, to exult, almost, in his final befoulment of me. I would watch him with our guests, or conferring with Mr. Brightwell, the new manager, and marvel at this well-dressed man of manners. Could he have any connection with the lamplit or moonlit assortment of limbs and hairiness and animal odours that assaulted me in the nights? I hardly knew which I hated worst, his savagery then or his expertise in disguising it now. What a sleight-of-hand marriage was, how fraudulent the social world! I despised every matron that she did not complain, every new bride as she sank from the glow and glory of betrothal and wedding to invisible compliant wifeliness, every man that he took these concealments and these changes as his due, that he took what he took, in exchange for what he gave a woman, which we called—fools that we were!—respectability.

By the time Mr. Goverman left for the city in the sixth month of my pregnancy, I will concede that I was no longer quite myself. Only a thin layer of propriety concealed my rage at my imprisonment—in this savage land, in this brute institution, in this swelling body dominated by the needs and nudgings of my little master within. I will plead, if ever I am called to account, that it was insanity kept me up during those nights, at first studying my translations (What certain hand had drawn these? Why, they looked almost authentic, almost the work of an engineer!) and then (What leap into the darkness was this?) re-translating them, some of them, into new drawings, devising how this part could be substituted for that, or a spring from the mantel-clock in a spare room could be added here, how a rusted saw-blade could be thinned and polished and given an edge and inserted there, out of sight within existing mechanisms, how this cam could be pared away a little there, and this whole arm of the apparatus adjusted higher to allow for the fact that I could not resort to actual metal casting for my lunatic enterprise.

Once the plans were before me, and Mr. Goverman still away arranging the terms of his investment in the mining consortium, to the accompaniment, no doubt, of a great deal of roast meat and brandy, cigars, and theatre attendances, there remained no more for me to do—lamplit, lumbering, discreet in the sounds I made, undisturbed through the nights—but piece by piece to dismantle and reassemble Clarissa's head according to those sure-handed drawings. I went about in the days like a thief, collecting a tool here, something that could be fashioned into a component there. I tested, I adjusted, I perfected. I was very happy. And then one early morning Lilty Meddows, my maid, knocked uncertainly at the study door to offer me tea and porridge, and there I was, as brightly cheerful as if I had only just risen from my sleep, stirring the just-burnt ashes of my translations, and with Clarissa demure in the armchair opposite, sealed up and fully clothed, betraying nothing of what I had accomplished on her.

Life, I discovered, is always more complex than it seems. The ground on which one bases one's beliefs, and actions arising from those beliefs, is sand, is quicksand, or reveals itself instead to be water. Circumstances change; madnesses end, or lessen, or begin inexorable transformations into new madnesses.

Mr. Goverman returned. I greeted him warmly. I was very frightened of what I had done, at the same time as, with the influx of normality that came with his return, with the bolstering of the sense of people watching me, so that I could not behave oddly or poorly, often I found my own actions impossible to credit. I only knew that each morning I greeted my husband more cordially; each night that I accepted him into my bed I did so with less dread and even with a species of amiable curiosity; I attended very much more closely to what he enjoyed in the marriage bed, and he in turn, in his surprise, in his ignorance, ventured to try and discover ways by which I might perhaps experience pleasures approaching the intensity of his own.

My impending maternity ended these experiments before they had progressed very far, however, and I left Cuttajunga for Melbourne and Holmegrange, a large, pleasant house by the wintry sea, where wealthy country ladies were sent by their solicitous husbands to await the birth of the colony's heirs and learn the arts and rituals of motherhood.

There I surprised myself very much by giving birth to a daughter, and there Mr. Goverman surprised me when very soon upon the birth he visited, by being more than delighted to welcome little Mary Grace into the world.

"She is *exactly* her mother," he said, looking up from the bundle of her in his arms, and I was astonished to see the glisten of tears in his eyes. Did he love me, then? Was this what love was? Was this, then, also affection, that I felt in return, this tortuous knot of puzzlements and awareness somewhere in my chest, somewhere above and behind my head? Had I birthed more than a child during that long day and night?

Certainly I loved Mary Grace—complete and unqualified, my love surprised me with its certainty when the rest of me was so awash with conflicting emotions, like an iron stanchion standing firm in a rushing current. I had only to look on her puzzling wakefulness, her innocent sleep, to know that region of my own heart clearly. And perhaps a little of my enchantment with my daughter puffed out—like wattle blossom!—and gilded Mr. Goverman too. Was that how it went, then, that wifely attachment grew from motherly? Why had my own mother not told me, when I had not the wit to ask her myself?

Mr. Goverman returned to Cuttajunga to ready it for Her Little Ladyship, and in his absence, through the milky, babe-ruled days of my lying-in, I wondered and I floundered and I feared, in all the doubt that surrounded my one iron-hard, iron-firm attachment in the world. I did not have leisure or privacy to draw, but in my mind I resurrected the drawings I had burnt in the study at the homestead, and laboured on the adjustments that would be necessary to restore Clarissa to her former state, or near it. If only he loved me and was loyal to me enough; if only he could control his urges until I returned.

Lilty was at my side; Mary Grace was in my arms; train-smoke and train-steam, all around, warmed us momentarily before delivering us up to the winter air, to the view of the ravaged country that was to be my daughter's home.

"Where is he?" said Lilty. "I cannot see him. I thought he would be here."

"Of course he will be." I strode forward through the smoke.

Four tall men, in long black coats, stood by the station gate, watching me in solemnity and some fear, I thought. Captain Jollyon stepped out from among them, but his customary jauntiness had quite deserted him. There was a man who by his headgear must be a policeman; a collared man, a reverend; and Dr.

Stone, my husband's physician. I did not know what to think, or feel. I must not turn and run; that was all I knew.

The train, which had been such a comforting, noisome, busy wall behind me, slid away, leaving a vastness out there, with Lilty twittering against it, senseless. The gentlemen ushered me, expected me to move with them. They made Lilty take Mary Grace from me. They made me sit, in the station waiting room, and then they sat either side of me, and Captain Jollyon sat on one heel before me, and they delivered their tidings.

It is easy to look bewildered when you have killed a man and are not suspected. It is easy to seem innocent, when all believe you to be so.

It must have been the maid Abigail, they said, from the blood in the kitchen, and the fact that she had disappeared. Mrs. Hodds, the housekeeper? She was at Cuttajunga now, but she had been at the Captain's, visiting her cousin Esther on their night off, when the deed was done. Mrs. Hodds it was who had found the master in the morning, bled to death in his bed, lying just as if asleep. She had called Dr. Stone here, who had discovered the dreadful crime.

I went with them, silent, stunned that it all had happened just as I wished. The sky opened up so widely above the carriage, I feared we would fall out into it, these four black-coated crows of men and me lace-petticoated among them, like a bit of cloud, like a puff of train-steam disappearing. Now that they had cluttered up my clear knowledge with their stories, they respected my silence; only the reverend, who could not be suspected of impropriety, occasionally glanced at my stiff face and patted my gloved hand.

At Cuttajunga Mrs. Hodds ran at me weeping, and Mr. Brightwell turned his hat in his hands and covered it with muttered condolences. Then that was over, and Mrs. Hodds did more cluttering, more exclaiming, and told me what she had had to clean, until one of the black coats sharply interrupted her laundry listing: "Mrs. Goverman hardly wants to hear this, woman."

I did not require sedating; I had not become hysterical; I had not shed a tear. But then Mary Grace became fretful, and I took her and Lilty into the study—"But you must not say a word, Lilty, not a *word*," I told her. And as I fed my little daughter, there looking down into her soft face, her mouth working so busy and greedily, her eyes closed in supreme confidence that the milk would continue, forever if it were required—that was when the immense loneliness of my situation hollowed out around me, and of my pitiable husband's, who had retired to the room now above us, and in his horror—for he must have realised what I had done, and who I therefore was—felt his lifeblood ebb away.

Still I did not weep, but my throat and my chest hardened with occluded tears, and I thought—I welcomed the thought—that my heart might stop from the strain of containing them.

Abigail, Abigail: the name kept flying from people's mouths like an insect, distracting me from my thoughts. The pursuit of Abigail preoccupied everyone. I let it, for it prevented them asking other questions; it prevented them seeing through my grief to my guilt.

In the night I rose from my bed. Lilty was asleep on the bedchamber couch, on the doctor's advice and the reverend's, in case I should need her in the state of confusion into which my sudden widowhood had plunged me. I took the candle downstairs, and along the hall to the back of the house.

I should have brought a rag, I thought. A damp rag. But in any case, she will be so bloodied, her bodice, her skirts—it will have all run down. Did he leave the piece in her mouth? I wondered. Will I find it there? Or did he retrieve it and have it with him, in his handkerchief, or in his bed, bound against him with the wrappings nearer where it belonged? It was not a question one could ask Captain Jollyon, or even Dr. Stone.

I opened the door of the charging chamber. There was no smudge or spot on or near the cabinet door that I could see on close examination by candle-light.

I opened the cabinet. "Clarissa?" I said in my surprise, and she began her initiation-lubrication sequence, almost as if in pleasure at seeing me and be-ing greeted, almost the way Mary Grace's limbs came alive when she heard my voice, her smoky-grey eyes seeking my face above her cradle. The chamber buzzed and crawled with the sounds of the doll's coming to life, and I could identify each one, as you recognise the gait of a familiar, or the cough he gives before knocking on your parlour door, or his cry to the stable boy as he rides up out of the afternoon, after weeks away.

"Clarissa: Stand," I said, and I made her turn, a full circle so that I could assure myself that not a single drop of blood was on any part of her clothing; then, that her garments had not been washed, for there was the tea-drop I had spilt upon her bodice myself during my studies. I might have unbuttoned her;

I might have brought the candle close to scrutinise her breasts, her teeth, for blood not quite cleansed away, but I was prevented, for here came Lilty down the stairs, rubbing her sleepy eyes.

"Oh, ma'am! I was frightened for you! Come, you'd only to wake me, ma'am. You've no need to resort to mechanical people. What is it you were wanting? She's no good warming milk for you, that one—you know that."

And on she scolded, so fierce and gentle in the midnight, so comforting to my confusion—which was genuine now, albeit not sourced where she thought, not where any of them thought—that I allowed her to put the doll away, to lead me to the kitchen, to murmur over me as she warmed and honeyed me some milk.

"The girl Abigail," I said when I was calmer, into the steam above the cup. "Is there any news of her?"

"Don't you worry, Mrs. Goverman." Lilty clashed the pot into the wash basin, slopped some water in. Then she sat opposite me, her jaw set, her fists red and white on the table in front of her. "They will find that Abigail. There is only so many people in this country yet that she can hide among. And most of them would sell their mothers for a penny or a half-pint. Don't you worry." She leaned across and squeezed my cold hand with her hot, damp one. "They will track that girl down. They will bring her to justice."

The Unbecoming of Virgil Smythe

Ramsey Shehadeh

RAMSEY SHEHADEH writes software by day and short stories by night. His fiction has appeared in *Weird Tales* and *Fantasy & Science Fiction*. He lives near Washington D.C., and blogs at www.DOODLEPLEX.COM. Of this story, he writes, "Some time ago, I became obsessed with Agatha Christie's *Murder on the Orient Express*, and decided that what I needed to do was write an updated version of that story. It would take place on a similar train, with similar characters working their way through a similar mystery, and contain only a bare minimum of interstellar monsters. It didn't quite work out the way I'd planned: the train survived, but my Edwardian characters shaded inexorably Victorian, the monsters gained a voice and a cause, and the simple mystery morphed into a fractured tale of causality subverted. All of which seems, in retrospect, entirely appropriate."

1: The Lady on the Platform

THE CLOCK ON the platform struck eleven, and Philip George Herbert's head, sinking slowly down the front of his body, shot back up to its summit and spun around to regard the clockface. "Oh, felicitous tidings, m'lady!" he said. "The train will arrive at any moment. Your gentle patience is rewarded at last!"

"Yes, thank you, Philip," said Chloe, stiffly. "I too can read the time."

"It is my pleasure, m'lady." He trundled into her field of vision, and smiled up at her. She *thought* it was a smile, at any rate. It was often difficult to tell. Dromedons did not have *mouthes*, as such: rather cunning arrangements of flesh and orifice that suited the purpose. Ragged ochre fins ran down the sides of his head, and flecks of purple mica swam in the greys of his eyes. "May I fetch you a stool, m'lady? You must be weary indeed."

"Thank you, no."

"It would give Mademoiselle's humble servant great pleasure."

"No," she snapped. And then, in a more moderate tone: "Thank you."

Her patience, in point of fact, was wearing thin. She'd spent six weary months in the company of Philip George Herbert. He was obsequious to the point of mockery: always shuffling underfoot, offering to carry this, or fetch that, or brush arrant flakes of dandruff off of her shoulders. Always pointing out puddles whose "upsplash might soil the hem of m'lady's vestments," or prowling ahead when she went out to take the air, exhorting the crowds of dromedons she inevitably encountered to make way for the auspicious lady. Chloe had instructed him on many occasions not to refer to her in that manner, but Philip George Herbert persisted; and so she often found herself striding mortified through throngs of parted dromedons, feeling keenly the dull resentment burning in their dull eyes.

She'd arrived in Hampshire Bubble six months ago, at the behest of its Viceroy, and her father, Lord Peter Gammen. She was to be his helpmeet and social factotum, arranging dinners at the manse, standing in at ribbon-cutting ceremonies, and generally serving as the ornament at his side. Despite appearances, it was difficult work. One had to be beautiful at all times, and lively, and skilled at that species of conversation wherein wit obscured the necessary banality. All very exciting, at first, but when the novelty waned her days became first a chore, and then a torment.

It wasn't just the dromedons. Nor was it the constant crush of duty, or the tedium, or the tiresome provinciality of the colonials. All of these annoyances played their part, of course, but she was principally put out by the shocking impertinence of time. She'd lived her entire life in the sequential world, where one could expect events to occur in some sort of order. Out here in the between, events had a much more liberal view of their responsibilities.

To be fair, the causality bubble that surrounded Hampshire colony was generally quite successful in enforcing the natural order of cause and effect. Even so, Chloe sometimes found herself arriving at market before she'd left the house, or finishing afternoon tea before she'd poured it. Once, she glanced at the hall mirror and saw an old crone staring back at her, poached skin and age spots and thin hair and sunken eyes, tendons standing out in her neck like hawsers. The image was gone as quickly as it appeared, but it occasioned the first of many tearful appeals to her father: send me home.

Lord Gammen was, for all his vices, a doting and considerate father, who could not bear the sight of his daughter's unhappiness. And so, in due course, her entreaties had the desired effect: her passage back into the coherent universe was booked on the Taurus Express. In a first-class berth, of course.

The sound of a whistle clove the murmuring silence of the platform. She turned, with all the others, to study the mouth of the tunnel. It was a simple, unadorned brick archway, a hemisphere of darkness embedded in the side of the mountain that towered over the station. The track that issued from its mouth was real, as was the archway's intricate brickwork, but all of the rest—the mountain, the cottonball clouds floating in the bright blue sky, the sky itself—was illusory, an anti-chaos simulacrum manufactured by frightfully complex machinery sunk into the weft of the bubblewall. It was a convincing illusion, and Chloe often found it possible to forget the insanity that it concealed.

Presently, a rush of steam blurted out of the tunnel, and hung roiling before the wall. There was something faintly disquieting in the way the steam moved, something slick and undulant, a species of incorporeal serpentry. Chloe pursed her lips in distaste, but did not look away.

And then, with a deafening blast of its whistle, the train burst through the steam and lanced into the station, rippling the hem of her skirts and upsetting her hat. She put a steadying hand on its crown and watched the cars blow by: engine, lounges, dining cars, sleepers, caboose—all gleaming black metal, red and green striping, brass fittings.

"Goodness," she whispered. "What a lovely sight."

"Not so lovely as m'lady," said the dromedon, each word sodden with the usual unctuous flattery. Chloe rounded on him, her patience spent at last.

And froze.

For where the dromedon had been there was now a space of grey primordial nothingness, and in that nullity she saw the whole span of the universe, past, present, and future, compressed into a space both absent and infinite.

She went mad.

2: The Conductor in First Class

Virgil Smythe was hurrying down the length of the sleeper car, peeking round the teetering stack of linens in his arms, when he heard the scream. He bent and peered out the window, at the platform, where a lady of quality lay writhing on the ground, scrabbling frantically at her person. A ring of gawkers was already forming.

Virgil did not recognize the woman. In fact, he was quite sure that he'd never met her: not in this life, nor the previous one. Nevertheless, he knew her. Further: he knew her intimately.

This made no sense, but he had no time to puzzle through these imponderables. He turned around, braced the linens against the wall, and knocked on Mr. Renault's door.

It opened, and Mr. Renault peered out, a round, aged faced ringed in a faintly angelic aureole of sparse white hair. "Ah, Terrence," he said. "You have come."

"Forgive the delay, Mr. Renault. I had some difficulty locating the items you requested. Will these serve?"

Mr. Renault opened his door all the way and studied the linens. "They are not quite the shade of green I'd hoped for, Terrence. They have a faint aquamarine quality to them, do they not? I believe I requested something in the chartreuse family."

"Indeed you did, sir. But I'm afraid we have nothing in that vein. The only other shade I could find was a dark forest green."

Mr. Renault backed away and put his hands up in horror. "Oh good lord, no," he said. "I could never sleep on a forest green. Simply *loathsome* color. *Much* worse than the ecru horrors that clothe my bed at present."

"May I make up your room then, sir?"

Mr. Renault chewed on his lower lip, considering. "I suppose so," he said. "I shall probably manage an uneasy slumber, though this aquamarine will likely make a mash of my bowels. Which are, as you know, extraordinarily sensitive to the slightest upset, Terrence."

"Indeed, sir," said Virgil. Bells were ringing up and down the length of the car. Virgil was by now devoting all of his energies to masking his impatience, a skill at which he excelled. He'd spent this life catering to the odd whims of the unreasonably wealthy, and embracing their eccentric obsessions as his own. And he'd spent his previous life indulging in these selfsame whims and obsessions. There was a time when he'd stood on the opposite end of these sorts of colloquies, making irrational demands with the blithe insouciance of a monarch dropping edicts.

That was before the catastrophe, of course.

Virgil Smythe unbecame himself in a dingy apartment in Yorkshire Bubble, in the year of our Lord 2503.

It began—as all such tragedies begin—with ambition. From the beginning, Virgil knew that it was his destiny to become a concert pianist. He taught himself how to play at age eight, and had mastered Rachmaninov's Third by age ten, Mozart's piano concertos by twelve, Beethoven's entire canon by thirteen.

All of which would seem to presage a brilliant career, save for one unfortunate impediment: his monstrous lack of talent. All of the music he played, he played very, very badly. Indeed, the last of his teachers, a nasty old German with sallow breath and Promethean eyebrows, suggested that Virgil wouldn't recognize talent if it tapped him on the shoulder and introduced itself.

But Virgil was wealthy, impatient, and obsessed. At eighteen, he decided that if his destiny refused to come to him, he would simply have to hunt it down.

And so he left his home and ventured into the realm of fungible reality known as the bubbleworlds, seeking a chaos wizard named Angstrom Jones, who—it was said—could mine the nether-region of unattached causality between the bubbles, and reshape desire into reality. Jones was something of a mythical figure in the sequential universe, and many of the stories surrounding him were plainly farcical. But if even a tenth of the powers ascribed to him were real, he would be able to grant Virgil his dreams.

He found Angstrom after many months of fruitless searching, in a tenement in Yorkshire Bubble. Or rather, he found a drunken and disheveled old man who had once been Angstrom, but was now a broken-down derelict with no prospects and only a tenuous attachment to life. Virgil spent many weeks nursing him back into some semblance of health and sobriety, and many weeks more convincing him to perform the service he required.

The transformation took place in Mr. Angstrom's filthy apartment. They sat on the floor, cross-legged, while the wizard chanted himself into some sort of trance. When he opened his eyes, he seemed a different person: preternaturally calm, supremely confident. He curled his hand into a claw and tore a slit in the world and withdrew from it a small dancing something. It was golden or leaden or silver, liquid or solid, brilliant or dull. It was an orb, or it was a rod, or it was a box. Or it was all of these things. Or none of them.

Virgil could not look at it for very long. It made his mind hurt.

"This ore," said Angstrom, "is a distillate of pure, unassigned potential. It is reality so primitive and unformed that it can be shaped into anything. How am I to shape yours?"

"Into the best pianist that humanity has ever known," said Virgil.

"This is difficult."

"Nevertheless," said Virgil.

Angstrom nodded, gravely, and began to do something complex with his hands. The ore warped and shuddered, flashed and rumbled. Virgil looked away again, but the room about him began to change too: it melted and reformed, it slid into and out of existence, it guttered. When the wizard spoke again, his voice was small, distant, and frightened. "Oh dear," he said.

And then the world broke into a billion pieces, and skittered away on ticking spiderlegs.

Virgil awoke on a tiny bed in a tiny apartment in Calcutta Bubble, feeling very strange indeed. He rose, ran a hand through his hair, and then studied himself in the mirror that hung over a small dresser near the door. The face that looked back at him was not his. It was narrow and hungry and a little haggard. Eyes that should have been blue were brown. His finely sculpted aquiline nose was puggish now, his blonde hair brown.

He turned back to his bed and saw his wife stirring under the sheets. He looked at his infant child, sleeping fitfully in her crib. It occurred to him that he did not have a wife, or a child. And that he did not live in Calcutta Bubble.

But he did, of course. He had been born here, schooled here, married here. At age twenty-three, he had entered service as a conductor on the King's Railroad. He could not play the piano. He had never even seen a piano, except perhaps in photographs, and on the television.

His name was, and ever had been, Terry Hawthorne.

And so it was Terry Hawthorne who watched Mr. Renault step reluctantly aside, at last. It was Terry Hawthorne who hurried past him, and began the process of removing one set of sheets and applying another. It was Terry Hawthorne who strove fruitlessly to ignore the jangling stateroom bells ringing up and down the length of the corridor outside, and it was Terry Hawthorne who reconciled himself to the stern reprimands he would now inevitably receive from the head conductor.

Virgil Smythe was present still, but only as a memory. A false memory, at that. Virgil Smythe had never existed.

3: The Pirate in Second Class

Something was happening outside. William looked up from his book and saw a crowd forming around a lady who had collapsed onto the platform. It was hard to make out her face—she was just a mound of lace and bloomers, at the moment—but she seemed young. Probably another corset incident.

A little farther away, near the platform's entrance, a small troupe of train officers were applying electrical truncheons to a flailing dromedon. William watched the poor creature convulse and shudder and flip helplessly from shape to shape.

"Good lord, what's all this about?" said his cabinmate, a young fop in a bowler hat. He peered through the window. "Ah. Some damnable dromedon mischief."

"Quite," said William. He'd reserved a private cabin, but the train was full, and they'd placed him instead in a shared berth with this creature: a spoiled wastrel heir named Percival Wiggins, who proved himself to be as loud as he was insipid, and apparently incapable of silence.

Worse: William was disguised as a spoiled wastrel heir, and was thus compelled, by the edicts of his assumed class, to carry on a conversation with this man.

"What I don't understand," said the fop, "is why we don't get rid of the lot of them. If those beastly dromedons are so unhappy living among us, why don't they just go away?"

"Indeed," said William, determined to say nothing else. And yet he said: "Of course, they didn't ask to be here."

"Oh?" Percy turned away from the window and smirked at William. "Father tells me that they sneak across the border for work. Taking jobs away from good bubble citizens, etc., etc."

"Well—I've a friend who works at the bubbleworks in Kingsbridge. Good chap, brilliant fellow. He tells me that these creatures were caught up in the causality field when the bubbles were forged. They're native betweeners, I gather, atemporal and all that. Most of them just died when we imposed time on their habitat. But a few survived. Adapted, I suppose."

"Atemporal? What on earth does that mean?"

William checked his watch. They'd be out of Hampshire Bubble in twenty minutes, and then there would be an interval of ten minutes before they could begin. So another half-hour with this ridiculous creature. "Atemporal? Oh, I think it means that they can't exist in time. There's no time in the between, you see. Just the raw substrate of events, floating free, with no particular relation to one another. Nothing really ever *happens* out there—or rather, *everything* happens, at once, and forever."

The fop laughed. "Good lord, Willy. You sound like one of those loathsome intellectuals that father dotes on. Speak English, won't you?"

William forced a chuckle. "Forgive me, old chap. Mother insisted that I attend university this term. I'm afraid some of the schooling managed to penetrate."

"Quite all right. Knowledge happens to the best of us."

"Yes. Well, as I understand it, the dromedons were a kind of lifeform that existed in the between. Not life as we'd understand it, of course, rather some sort of quasi-sentience that could withstand and even thrive in a causeless environment. Trapping them in time was like hauling a fish out of its pond, or exposing an anaerobic cell to oxygen. That's why so many of them died."

Percival was losing interest. He brushed an arrant something off his trousers, and said: "Interesting."

"Isn't it though? And think of the implications. Taking something that's completely free of the notion of time and squeezing it into a body that's utterly shackled to it. It would feel like prison, I imagine. If not torture."

"Oh dear, how melodramatic. I, for one, would welcome that kind of structure to my day."

"Quite, quite. That is their grievance, however. Or so they claim."

"Well, then, I say it again: they should just go back to their formless void, if they're so very unhappy."

"But that's the problem, you see. They can't. Once you're part of time, you simply cannot go back. The ones who made the attempt suffered the same fate as we would."

"Which is?"

"Madness."

"Oh. That." The fop shrugged. "Well, if all of that rubbish is true, I suppose they'll just have to learn to live with us. God knows they've had enough time to adjust."

"But time is exactly what they don't want, old man."

The fop threw up his hands, and laughed. "Enough! You win. The dromedons are poor downtrodden unfortunates. Humanity is a pack of beastly genocidal colonist occupiers. Satisfied?"

William thought about the machete in his valise. "Oh dear, Percy. Please don't mistake this little intellectual exercise for actual beliefs. I'm merely trying to pass the time."

"Good. I was beginning to suspect you of convictions."

"Heaven forbid," said William. They were lifting the woman on the platform onto a gurney, now, and strapping her down. She writhed and screamed, continuously. The sound filtering in through the thick glass of the window was strained, attenuated, feral. "That woman seems to be in a bad way."

"Women," said Percival. "Now *there's* a subject I can warm to."

William checked his watch again. and half-listened to Percy blather on about his latest conquest, some lady's maid in Kingsbridge Bubble. His thoughts returned to the machete secreted in his valise, and he fell happily to contemplating its many excellent uses.

4: The Dromedon in the Baggage Compartment

Jeremy Albert Benjamin tapped the lid of his small prison. He did this methodically, one action following the other: starting at the corner nearest his head, and sliding his fingers down the velvet-lined inner surface of the chest, tapping, listening for the tell-tale hollowness, tapping again.

Presently, he found what he was looking for. He curled his hand into a fist and rapped the spot with his knuckles, and then withdrew his pocketknife and cut a hole in the velvet, exposing the wood underneath. He probed the hollow area with his fingers, and then pressed. Nothing. He tried again, pressing harder, and was rewarded with a soft click. He replaced the pocketknife, and, using both hands, pushed upward on the lid, praying that nothing had been stacked on top of him. It lifted easily.

He opened it a crack, and peered out into the hulking gloom of the baggage compartment. Dark squarish shapes surrounded him, suitcases and valises, crates and chests, boxes and coffers. A cat prowled back and forth in its cage, eyes slitting the darkness like twin filaments of green flame. Moving quickly, he lifted himself out of the crate and landed crouching by its side, then paused, listening. Birdcages rattled, crates shifted, leather creaked, the cat hissed—but otherwise, silence.

He withdrew his tuxedo from the chest, and dressed quickly. He was, as ever, stymied by the bowtie, tying and retying it several times before he was satisfied. He was something of an obsessive when it came to human neckwear. A badly tied bowtie was, he maintained, a dead giveaway. He fancied himself something of an expert on the subject. This was, after all, not the first time he'd attempted to infiltrate human society.

Dressed at last, he crossed to the full-length mirror strapped to a steamer trunk near the back of the car, and studied himself. He was short and squat, though neither as short nor as squat as most dromedons. He had two hands, each with the requisite number of digits, and a head that could be compelled to stay in the same place for long stretches of time, overtopped by a thatch of something that looked very much like hair. He also had facial features that approximated the sensory organs of the sequentials: a squat nose flanked by two holes filled with gelatinous ocular balls; and an oblong hole above his chin line guarded by a pair of fleshy pink extrusions, able to both admit food and emit conversation.

Jeremy Albert Benjamin's resemblance to the men and women who had enslaved his kind was an accident of circumstance, but a fortuitous one: he was a natural spy. Today he would be Frederick Howells, a prosperous banker from Kingsbridge Bubble, bound for Piccadilly Bubble. He had a suit, a passport, a pistol, and a tiny golden device secreted in the front pocket of his waistcoat.

He adjusted his bowtie, and then closed his eyes and said a prayer. He prayed for the soul of Philip George Herbert, who had supplied the necessary distraction on the platform; for the Viceroy's daughter, sunk now in the pit of her own insanity; and for the sequentials on this train, all of whom would shortly suffer the same fate. He did not pray for himself. The things that he had done, and would do, in the service of his cause rendered him unworthy of that particular balm.

He made some final adjustments to his bowtie, took a breath, composed himself, then opened the baggage car's door, and stepped out into the train.

5: The Conductor in the Sleeping Car

Virgil reached Number 14 just as the bell sounded again, knocked, then slid the door to. A large, froggish woman, wrapped up in some monstrous pink chiffon concoction looked up at him. Her porcine face was an alarming shade of red.

"Ah, Conductor," she said. "You have come. How very good of you."

"Forgive me, Madame. I was preparing Monsieur Renault's bed for the evening."

"I rang thirteen times. Thirteen times exactly. Is that the correct number? Thirteen?"

"No, Madame. You need only ring once."

"I rang once twelve times, and you did not come. But on the thirteenth ring, you came. That is the basis for my hypothesis." She sniffed. "I suppose I should consider myself fortunate."

Virgil said: "Forgive me, Madame. It is inexcusable."

The duchess glared at him. "Fetch my spectacles."

"Of course, Madame." He paused, and said: "Would Madame be so kind as to tell me where I might find them?"

"Tonight, in my prayers," said the woman, "I will ask God to forgive me for whatever transgression has doomed me to a conductor who is not only deaf and cretinous, but *blind.*" She gestured toward a small table at the foot of her bed, which held an ashtray, a small paperback romance novel, and a pair of reading glasses. "But perhaps I should be more specific. It is that object consisting of two small circles of glass encased in a metal frame. We in the sentient classes use these devices for *reading*. You've heard of reading, Conductor? It's a kind of preserved talking."

"Indeed, Madame." He picked up the woman's spectacles, walked the two steps to the chaise on which she was splayed, and handed them to her. "Will there be anything else, Madame?"

She gave him a long, level look. Her face had dimmed from its original curried scarlet to a sort of sunset crimson, but her chins still quivered with indignation. "Not at present, thank you."

He bowed and backed out of her compartment, slid the door shut, and closed his eyes. He applied the same curative principle to anger that one did to splinters embedded in the skin—teasing it out slowly, letting it rise to the surface. *Patience,* he thought. *Patience.*

A door opened on the opposite end of the carriage and a small fat man waddled through. He was dressed in the opulent style of a bygone era, tuxedo and spats, small vermillion bowtie and matching cummerbund, black tophat.

"Good evening, sir," said Virgil.

"Good evening," said the dwarf, and smiled. He was possibly the ugliest man that Virgil had ever encountered, his features seemingly configured with the explicit purpose of triggering revulsion. And yet he had a sincere and friendly smile, and Virgil warmed to him instantly.

"I'm afraid I've quite lost track of the time," said the dwarf. "Is dinner still being served?"

"It is, sir. But you'd best hurry. The kitchen will close in twenty minutes." Virgil lifted his arm and pointed with his index and middle fingers. "Six cars down."

"Thank you, sir," said the little man, tipping his tophat, then proceeded past Virgil. He moved with a laborious rolling gait, as if crossing the pitching deck of a storm-tossed ship. Virgil smiled. The little man reminded him of

the odd academicians who'd frequented his mother's salon, back on Piccadilly Bubble.

This memory gave rise to other, less-pleasant ones, and he turned to the squat gentleman, just now reaching the end of the carriage. "Sir?"

The man turned. "Yes?"

"May I see your ticket please?"

A pause. "I believe I already showed it to my conductor."

"Yes, sir. It's merely a security precaution."

"Oh, indeed?" He began to make his way back down the carriage. "Are we in danger?"

"Oh, no sir. This is simply routine. Pirate activity has increased somewhat, of late, and there is a small fear of dromedon terrorism."

"Goodness." The little man reached into his jacket. "How distressing."

"I assure you, sir, there is no cause for concern."

"As a matter of fact, there is." The dwarf seemed a little sad. He drew out a small pistol and pointed it at Virgil.

"Terribly sorry about this," he said, and fired.

6: The Madwoman in the Infirmary

Everywhere was forever, and each atom of that endless landscape contained in turn its own eternity, complete and entire. It was a fractal explosion of time and place, simultaneously infinite and nonexistent, all of it occurring at once, and forever, and never.

Chloe's mind struggled to encompass this landscape. For all of its liquid adaptability, the human mind is founded upon a few basic prerequisites: sequentiality, finitude, smallness. It could not contain everything that she had seen on the platform. But neither could it stop trying—it bent its every effort toward taming the jumbled chaos of the disordered multiverse it had seen.

But it was all madness, madness and madness and madness. And so the lady screamed.

In some small corner of her consciousness, still tethered faintly to the objective world, she knew that she was strapped to a narrow bed in a small room; that the room contained a woman in a white nurse's uniform and a gentleman in a long frock-coat; that she was screaming, continuously. But all of that was a diaphanous filament in an ocean of churning chaos, and she could no more grasp it than she could gather sunbeams.

Suddenly, a blinding light arced across the landscape of her dementia, and her world went black, and when it swam back into view it encompassed only the small room, and the nurse, and the gentleman in the frock-coat, who was applying a pair of what appeared to be plastic earmuffs to her bare chest. Thick coiled wire emanated from each earmuff, and disappeared into a large, blinking machine beside her bed.

"Will that be enough, Doctor?" said the nurse.

"I'm afraid not. She is already regressing. Increase the voltage, if you will."

"Yes, Doctor."

They faded again, washed away on a tsunami of madness, and she screamed forever.

And then she was in the small room again. There was in the air the tangy scent of burnt flesh.

"Uncanny," said the gentleman, shaking his head. "There is no stopping this. Nurse, please…"

No more, she thought. No more. A manic strength seized her, burning down the avenues of her body like a demon conflagration. She bulged and tightened, strained and swelled, surging against her constraints until they snapped and whipped away from her like flailing adders. She surged off the table, roaring.

The nurse barely had time to scream before Chloe was on her, thrusting her back, grabbing her head with both hands, slamming it against the wall. Once, twice, three times, and with each blow Chloe felt the chaos inside of her recede a little more—her mind clearing, the terrible visions dimming, and then disappearing.

The nurse grew limp, but Chloe did not stop until she felt a hand on her shoulder. She spun, grasping a metal bedpan as she did, and dashed it against the side of the gentleman's head. He fell, and she fell with him, tearing at his eyes, sinking her teeth into the soft flesh of his throat.

When she rose, some moments later—her face wet and crimson, her shift stained with the doctor's remains, her breast rising and falling with the exertions of murder—she was calm, composed. She studied the bodies. They did nothing to dim the gentle peace that had settled over her.

But the madness was already billowing back. She could feel it, like a wolf breathing at the nape of her neck. She turned in a circle, desperate again, and then ran toward the door on bare feet, vaulting the nurse's body, her thin checkered shift billowing behind her like a bloodied sail.

She burst out of the infirmary just as a train policeman was hurrying up, and fell on him before he could draw his weapon.

His screams kept her own at bay. For this, she loved him.

7: The Pirate in the Dining Car

William sat down, and placed his valise on the floor beside him. The dining car was crowded, and alive with that uniquely aristocratic species of quiet noise—a background hum of conversation punctuated with the tinkle of silverware. He ordered lamb chops and a bottle of port, then studied the people around him, looking for the inevitable train agent. Presently he found him: a young man in sidewhiskers who seemed markedly uncomfortable in his finery, sitting by himself near the door, doing a poor job of pretending to read the newspaper. Their eyes met, briefly. William smiled and nodded, and the agent did the same.

The lamb arrived. He ate it slowly, savoring the meat's soft piquant pliancy, drank the last of his port, checked his watch, removed the napkin from his lap and placed it on the plate, then rose and drew his weapon and shot the train agent, twice. The agent's head exploded in a spray of blood and bone that spattered the wall behind him and soiled the dress of a large matronly women sitting nearby. She screamed, and then fainted. There was a general hubbub, panicked aristocrats climbing over one another in a mad aimless dash to nowhere.

William fired another round into the agent's body, and shouted: "Silence!"

The diners froze, and turned to look at him. And then settled slowly back into their seats, like a troupe of cowed schoolchildren.

"Ladies and gentlemen!" cried William. "I believe it is customary at this juncture for the assailant—that is, myself—to inform you that there is no need to be alarmed, that no harm shall come to those who cooperate. I'm afraid I can give you no such assurances." He reached into his valise and drew out the fop's head. Its face was frozen in an expression of superciliousness caught in the act of becoming terror. The stub of his neck trailed a tattered skirt of flesh, an abbreviated esophagus, a short bony tail of spine.

"It was not, strictly speaking, necessary for me to kill this man," said William. "I could have simply subdued him. It would have been the simplest thing in the world. But he displeased me exceedingly, and so I found it pleasant to separate his head from his body, using the crudest implements at my disposal." He paused. No one spoke, or made a sound. "The only reason I have not killed every one of you is because it would be inconvenient for me to do so. But I must stress that this state of affairs is balanced on a knife's edge, and could change at any moment. Is that understood?"

Silence.

"Please empty your pockets, ladies and gentlemen. Remove all of your baubles, your rings, your necklaces, your jeweled undergarments. Your money, your papers, your spectacles. In short, anything of value. Place them on the table before you. If you are unsure of an item's value, please err on the side of caution and place it on the table. If I find that anyone has withheld anything, my wrath will be biblical. Is that clear?" He put the fop's head down on the table. "Please begin."

There was a general bustle as the Vickies went about the business of disgorging their valuables. William watched, amused, as women stripped rings from their fingers and tore pendants from their necks, men fumbled watches out of their waistcoats, cufflinks from their sleeves, tiepins from their cravats. The better-dressed passengers went so far as to remove their outer garments entirely. Soon the small dining tables were piled with a dragon's-horde of treasure.

William checked his watch. If all was proceeding according to plan, his confederates would soon begin ransacking the first-class cars. He pulled two large plastic bags from his valise and held them out to two men sitting at a nearby table. "Gentlemen," he said. "If you would be so kind as to collect my possessions." The men did not move. He sighed. "Please rest assured that you will not be harmed for doing my bidding. In fact, quite the opposite."

The first man rose, took a halting step, then stopped. His eyes went to a point just above William's shoulder, and widened.

William reacted instantly. He thrust himself backward, pressing himself against the wall of the dining car, and—keeping his firearm pointed at his trembling prisoners—drew a second weapon and trained it on the carriage door.

A fantastically unattractive dwarf stood in the open doorway, an expression of deepest surprise on his face.

"Good evening, sir," said William. "Please join us."

But the dwarf simply stood, regarding William now with an air of bemusement.

"I do not like to repeat myself, sir," said William.

The dwarf laughed. It was a strange sound, a sort of lilting, giggling cough, as infectious as it was odd. William found himself smiling. "You find this amusing?"

"Oh, infinitely," said the dwarf. "Have you read Sartristosophocles, sir?"

There was a restless shifting in the car. William cast a quick glance down the length of his right arm, then returned his attention to the funny little man. "The halfbreed dromedon? I'm afraid I have not had the pleasure. But I'm afraid that I do not have time to discuss philosophy."

"In his Atemporal Atales," said the dwarf, "Sartristosophocles wrote: 'I find myself on far more slippery footing in the sequential world. For the atemporal universe is reliably astonishing, while the sequential is only sporadically so.' I have never fully apprehended his meaning, until this moment." The dwarf reached into a pocket and removed a small golden sphere.

William recognized it instantly. Unless he missed his guess, it could fell cities.

"I believe that we are confederates, sir," said William.

The small man shook his head. "No. Confederates in sin, perhaps, but that is all. The paths we travelled to this moment were quite different."

"Nevertheless," said William. "There is no need for you to trouble yourself. My men will soon do your work for you."

"It is my policy not to trust pirates. Even when their goals appear to align with mine."

"But I cannot allow you to detonate that, sir."

The man smiled. "Allow?"

"Indeed."

"There is no allowing, sir. There is only the act, and its consequences." The little man cradled the golden ball in his palm, and turned his attention to the dining car's occupants. "I had hoped to explain my cause to you," he said, raising his voice. "But circumstances have intervened. All I can do is assure you that what I do now, I do for the best of all reasons. Forgive me." He tilted his hand, and let the orb drop.

William watched it fall. It touched the floor, and then sank through. The tiny hole it left in its wake quickly grew from a circle the size of a shilling to one the size of a fist, a pomegranate, a cannonball. Cracks issued from its circumference, ramifying down the surface of the dining car like black lines of lightning.

One of the lines touched a gentleman in a dark frock-coat. He became every moment of himself, from the instant he was born, to the instant he died. The space that he occupied, in his multitudes, imploded.

William turned away. The carriage door was open, the dromedon gone. He holstered his weapons, and ran.

8: The Conductor in the Linens Closet

Virgil awoke to darkness and pain.

He touched his side, and felt dampness, warmth. He touched his head, and flinched away from an electric stab of pain. And then he turned his hand outward, grasping blindly at the dark. His fingers brushed a soft mound of silk, a pile of terrycloth, a stack of pillows. He was in the linens closet.

This seemed to him a very strange place to be. He felt certain that, all things being equal, and given his many duties, it was not a place he should have been at the moment.

He waited for his mind to supply him with answers, which it did, presently: the ugly little man, the gun, the shot. Pain blossoming in his side, his legs growing weak. Crumpling to the ground, hugging his belly. Looking up to see the dwarf standing over him, revolver pointed at his head.

He remembered opening his mouth to plead for his life, but instead saying this: "I am not a conductor, sir. I am not Terry Hawthorne. I trafficked in the forbidden mysteries of the between, and have suffered the consequences. I am Virgil Smythe, and it is my ambition to become a concert pianist." Because now, at the end of his life, all he wanted was to be known.

The dwarf studied him. Turned his head and studied him again, out of the corner of his eye. "Oh dear," he said. "You poor man."

And then the most extraordinary thing: the dwarf lowered his arm, letting his jumbleshop tumble of features settle into something like sadness. "I cannot," he said. "You will die with the rest of them, but I cannot." He sighed, and turned his weapon about, grasping it by the barrel—and then paused again, and seemed to consider. "I will come back for you," he said, and brought the butt down sharply on Virgil's head.

You will die with the rest of them. Virgil struggled to his feet, and stood leaning against the wall, waiting for the waves of nausea and pain to subside. He must alert train security. He fumbled about until he found the door handle, and opened it, and stepped out.

For a moment, before he was able to collect himself, he simply stared. The walls of the carriage had become a mass of insects, and their rapid, restless scurrying filled the hall with a chitinous, sibilant hissing. Portions of the skittering horde occasionally arranged themselves into recognizable configurations. There was a flickering rendition of his mother—Virgil's mother—her face a mask of tragedy, streams of cockroach tears falling from her cockroach eyes. There was a bas-relief of his wife—Terrence's wife—ants and beetles, cradling a squirming spider-sculpture of his daughter—she looked up and opened her mouth, and a passing phalanx of centipedes paused in their travels to arrange themselves into a cartoon speech bubble above her head. *Don't forget to pick up the baklava in Kingsbridge,* she said. *Be careful. I love you.* And then she disappeared, and the insects erupted into a mad frenzy, like a snowstorm in a hurricane.

Virgil had read about this, of course. When a causality field is in the first stages of collapse, and the mind is presented with a glimpse of the between, it attempts to interpret it in terms of the familiar, grasping desperately for metaphors. The chaos usually manifests as insects, or rain, or sandstorms: anything multitudinous, small, and chaotic.

Quite suddenly, the carriage returned to its former aspect: thick carpeting, dark wood-paneled walls, bronze gaslight fixtures. The field seemed to have reasserted itself—but only weakly, as artifacts were already appearing: doors shifted from one end of the hall to the other, side tables wrenching themselves free of their moorings and stumbling away, untethered lamps and papers and pens falling upwards in small pockets of inverse gravity. The door to Number 8 flew open and Mr. and Mrs. Treppany and their two children squeezed out, combined now into a single mass, a tumbleweed of arms and legs, faces scattered randomly across the surface of their shared body. Virgil stepped aside as they rolled past, reaching out to him with all of their arms, mouthes open on a silent plea.

And so the train was already compromised. The only thing left was to gather up as many passengers as possible, and get them to a lifeboat.

Virgil ran down the hall, hunched over his injury, opening doors, finding fresh scenes of horror behind each. Mr. Braithwait had become his room: the walls, a stretched drumhead of tearing skin, pulsed with the warmth of a waning life, and the floor surged hungrily toward him, in a rippling tidewall of Braithwait; Ms. Cragstone was bifurcating steadily, splitting off into new Cragstones with every passing second, slowly becoming a crowd of herself; Mr. and Mrs. Clarendon were devolving into their predecessor species, heads expanding, brows sloping, backs bowing, arms becoming legs, hands becoming feet, feet becoming paws. The crackle of reconfiguring bones filled the room, along with the increasingly animalian cries of its occupants.

Virgil shut the last door and stepped back. The floor surged under his feet, undulating like waves on a choppy sea. He began to despair of finding anyone to save.

Just then the carriage door opened and a woman stepped through. She wore a white checkered shift as bloodstained as a birthing sheet. Her eyes were large and open so wide as to appear lidless, her hair wild and disordered, thrusting out at tentacular and improbable angles. Her face was filthy, covered in a viscous film. She stopped, and studied him.

Virgil moved quickly to her side. "We must hurry, Madame," he said. "If you would come with me…"

The woman did not move. There was about her a sense of unearthly calm, a preternatural stillness. Presently, she opened her mouth, exposing a hedge of ochre-stained teeth. And then continued to open it, until the hedge became a hole, the hole a cavern, the cavern an abyss—until her mouth was open wider than any mouth had any right to be.

Virgil had all but convinced himself that the woman was simply another chaos hallucination when she dipped her head and sunk her teeth into his shoulder. The pain was quite real, and he cried out. She lifted her head and stared at him with wide and curious eyes. Her blonde and matted hair shimmered above her like an aureole of serpents. And then she began in earnest the process of destroying him.

9: The Pirate in Flight

William ran, the train's dissolution close on his heels, transforming, consuming, unbecoming the carefully ordered realities around him. He went from carriage to carriage, shouldering aside the panicked throngs spilling out of their rooms, moving as quickly as he could. But the waddling little man was nowhere to be seen. William had begun to despair of catching up to him when he burst through the door of the first-class sleeping carriage, and came to a skidding halt.

A train conductor lay writhing on the floor, torn open and spilling himself onto the thick carpet, breathing in sporadic, dying heaves.

A woman in a bloodied shift knelt with her back to him, quietly mauling the little man.

And the little man lay squirming on his back, like an overturned beetle, fending away the woman's attacks, and doing a generally poor job of it.

William drew his weapon and shot the woman. She shuddered, drooped, then rose and staggered toward him. He shot her again, and then again, and then a third time. She fell, at last, but continued to move toward him, hand over hand, dragging herself across the buckling landscape of the dissolving carriage.

The little man stood, and brushed himself off. "Thank you, sir."

"My motives are entirely selfish, I'm afraid," said William. "You've rather ruined my plans for escape, so I would very much like to share in yours."

"Of course. If you'll grant me a moment." The little man began to disrobe, methodically: first his bowtie, then his waistcoat, his trousers, chemise, boots, stockings, smallclothes. When he was done, a dromedon stood in his place, grey skin glistening in the flickering light of the gaslamps.

William blinked, blinked again, and then smiled. "Oh, well done, sir."

The dromedon bowed, then drew a taper from his discarded waistcoat, stood on his toes, and thrust it into the nearest gaslamp. When it ignited, he lowered it into the pile of clothing. After a moment, tendrils of smoke began to rise from the pile. But the smoke did not behave as smoke should. For one thing, it was lavender. For another, it seemed quite solid. For a third, it appeared to be arranging itself into some sort of opaque archway. A portal.

"Where does it lead?" asked William.

"The question isn't where, really," said the dromedon. "It reconfigures the reality of those who pass through it. It's more of a what, I suppose."

"That will do," said William, and raised his weapon. "Please step aside."

"I would advise against killing me just yet, sir. It is not as simple as passing through. You will need me to mediate the means and circumstances of the journey."

"Ah." William thought about this. "You are lying to me, perhaps?"

"Perhaps. Please help me with the conductor." The dromedon crossed to where the twitching and bloodied man lay dying. After a moment, William joined him. Together, they dragged him to the portal. The dromedon placed his hand on its shimmering surface, and closed his eyes. "Good," he said, and, with William's help fed the man into the aperture. He disappeared, inch by inch, until he was gone.

"One of your accomplices?" said William.

"No. I only just met him today."

"I see." William paused. "Although I don't, actually."

"I made him a promise." The dromedon looked at the woman. "Now her."

"Did you make her a promise as well? While she was attempting to extract your viscera, perhaps?"

The madwoman had by now stopped struggling. She lay in a ball, shuddering, emitting small keening noises. They grasped her by her feet and slid her to the portal. The dromedon repeated his incantation, and they pushed her through.

William straightened. "Now for myself, if you please, I would like—" He stopped, and looked at the portal. It was thinning, now, shimmering, losing its consistency. It flickered, dimmed, returned. And then it was gone.

There was a silence. William said: "Ah."

"I'm afraid I have been less than candid with you," said the dromedon. "The device was only designed to accommodate two souls."

William sighed. "We are two souls, you and I."

"But those two deserved salvation more than we, don't you think?"

William shook his head. "As a matter of fact, I don't." He looked around at the carriage. The walls were fading away now, turning slowly to shadow. Troubling shapes lurked in the darkness beyond. "How long?"

"Not long," said the dromedon. He extended a hand. "We have not been formally introduced. I am Jeremy Albert Benjamin."

William looked at him for a long moment, and then took his hand. "William Thackery. Pleased to meet you, sir."

"The pleasure is all mine," said Jeremy Albert Benjamin. And they stood together, smiling vaguely, as the world dissolved quietly around them.

10: The Conductor in His Parlor

Virgil bent over the piano, eyes closed, and let his fingers fly over the last bars of the movement—felt the music course through him and play along his body. It wasn't perfect, not yet, but it was quite good. He'd have it in time for his performance at Marshracht Hall, he thought. After that, he was scheduled for the Vozenkult, and then a private recitation for Prince Reagar himself.

He straightened and looked to his wife, knitting beside him on the settee. "How was that, my love?"

Chloe looked up. "Fair," she said.

"Ah. Do you mean sublime?"

"Is that what you want me to mean, my dear?"

"It is."

"Then that is what I mean."

Virgil smiled. "You are an excellent wife."

"So you've said. Although it strikes me that you only say it after I compliment you on the sublimity of your performances."

"Nonsense. I seem to recall granting you your excellence, just last week, when you thought one of my recitations merely inspired."

She smiled, and put her work aside. "I must see to dinner."

Virgil rose from his bench, took her hands and kissed them lightly. "I do love you, Katerina."

She lifted an eyebrow. "And I you," she said. She glanced over her shoulder, making sure that none of the servants were about, then stood on her toes and kissed him on the cheek. "Now you must excuse me, Jan."

Virgil watched her leave the parlor. She was quite as beautiful as she'd been when they met at the Prince's Ball, so long ago. Could it have been ten years already? Could it be that their children were entering preparatory school? Truly, could the store of memories they'd built together be so very large?

But there were other memories, of course, lurking behind the real ones: a terrible sundering in a filthy Yorkshire apartment; a wife and a child abandoned in Calcutta Bubble; a raving, bloodstained woman who resembled his wife in every particular, clawing at his eyes, tearing at his face, steadily destroying him. And others, more distant still: the memories of a young Englishman, yearning for a talent he could not have.

He did not know if Katerina had her own store of false memories. If so, she never spoke of them. And this was right and proper. She was Katerina Lichtman, formerly Katerina Vogel. He was Jan Niklas Lichtman, son of Albrecht and Hedda Lichtman, and the most sought-after concert pianist in Leipzig Bubble. This was the reality. The rest were dreams.

He sat down at the piano, rested his fingers lightly on the keys, and paused to whisper a few words of thanks—the same words he repeated before each of his performances.

His friends generally assumed that he was thanking God.

He was not.

He began to play.

The Mechanical Aviary of Emperor Jalal-ud-din Muhammad Akbar

Shweta Narayan

SHWETA NARAYAN was smelted in India's summer, quenched in the monsoon, wound up on words in Malaysia, and pointed westward. She surfaced in Saudi Arabia, The Netherlands, and Scotland before settling in California, where she lives on language, veggie tacos, and the Internet. Other Artificer bird stories can be found in *Realms of Fantasy* and *Clockwork Phoenix 3*; Shweta also has fiction in *Strange Horizons* and *Beastly Brides*. She was the Octavia E. Butler Memorial Scholarship recipient at the 2007 Clarion workshop and can be found online at WWW.SHWETANARAYAN.ORG. Of her story, she writes that it is "based on a South Indian epic, the Cilappatikaram (The Tale of an Anklet, 5th CE); the original is quite a bit stranger. The mechanical cities were inspired by the work of Alberuni, an 11th-century Persian scholar. In his great tome on India, in a listing of the peoples of India, he mentions a race of golden and silver people in the south who live on sunlight. Akbar the Great is of course historical, but his aviary is not."

BULBUL AND PEACOCK

Now AKBAR-E-AZAM, THE Shah-en-Shah, Emperor of the World, who is called the Light of Heaven, has built markets and mosques and schools for his people of flesh and of metal and for the eternal glory of God. But he commissioned the mechanical aviary for himself and only himself. Not even his favorite wives could enter—only the Emperor, his slaves, and the Artificer, who is herself a bird of metal.

It was a small aviary, notable only for its roof: panes of thin clear glass which cast no latticed shadows but let the Sun light up the birds unhindered. Birds of cog and gear and lever, their mechanical lives powered by springs, they were made from shining copper and silver and bronze. Enamel coated their heads, their tails, their wing-tips, in gleaming colors for the Shah-en-Shah's delight. From Falcon, whose beak and claws were edged with diamond, who had once brought down a tiger, to Phoenix, whose mechanism built a child within her and sealed its final seams in the fire that melted her away—every bird was a wonder. Not a feather rusted, not a joint squealed, not a single spring wound down, for the merely human aviary slaves were careful and skilled.

The Shah-en-Shah (blessed with long life, Allah be praised) was at that time barely more than a boy. He loved his birds and denied them nothing. Most especially he could not deny his favorites, Peacock and Bulbul.

For though he was proud of Falcon and Phoenix, he came most often to hear Bulbul's sweet song and see the flashing colors of Peacock's dance; or to have Bulbul sit on his shoulder while he rubbed jasmine oil onto Peacock's feathers. This brought him peace; and to Akbar, who inherited a crown and a war when he was thirteen years old, who had to execute his own foster brother for treachery, peace has always been harder won than pride. For the joy of their music and dance he loved Bulbul and Peacock above all others—and for the joy of their music and dance they grew to love each other.

And so they approached the Artificer.

"O Lady with human hands," sang Bulbul, "will you build us a child who can both dance and sing?"

But the Artificer bird would not.

"O brightest of eye and feather," said Peacock, "does our wish displease you? Do you find these slaves presumptuous?"

"Not presumptuous," said the Artificer, "but certainly unwise."

They were so distraught that Peacock tripped over his own tailfeathers when he next tried to dance, while Bulbul piped one thin, flat, endless note.

"Are you ill?" asked the Emperor. "Are your cogs slipping, one from the other?"

"Son of Heaven," Peacock said, "the illness is in our heartsprings. We wish to make a child together, but the Lady will not help."

At this the Emperor frowned. "Is such a task below you?" he asked her. For the Artificer was no slave; she had once been his teacher, and was now an honored guest.

She rustled her copper tailfeathers. "Far below me," she said, "to betray you so. Every bird here has one purpose, and one bird fulfills each purpose, and thus is peace maintained. Will you breed strife in your sanctuary?"

"Children strive against us," said the Shah-en-Shah (who had yet no children). "We raise them in love nonetheless. If you are truly my friend, give my birds their wish."

The Artificer was silent for a long time. Finally she said, "As I am your friend, I shall. But hear me first."

The Dancing Girl

In the Golden City of legend, Mechanical Pukar (which Westerners called Khaberis), there were wonders lost now to the ages. Rooftops and roads inlaid with yellow sapphire, emerald, cinnamon stone, and the other astrological gems; mechanical people wearing spun and filigreed gold; markets piled with ingots and fine tools. There were slaves of flesh to tend to people and wind them up. There were pools of fragrant oil to bathe in, tiled with obsidian and warmed by the Sun. And there were temple dancers, who also sang.

Nothing compared to the dancers' beauty; but having both abilities wound their heartsprings so tightly that they could think only of themselves and their art. So too could any who grew close to them think only of them.

There was an artificer once, a young man of gleaming bronze, with sharp eyes and skillful fingers. He and his wife worked hard and well together. They made a fortune. Then he made a dancing girl and fell in love.

He squandered everything he owned, everything his wife owned, save only her anklets. Instead of his commissions he built treasures for his dancer, treasures which the Shah-en-Shah himself would gladly accept if they existed today. But the girl thought only of her dance and her song.

She danced away, in time. His heartspring nearly snapped, but he woke from that dream and found that, despite everything, he still had a wife. They left Pukar together that day, in shame, walking barefoot through the dust.

Devadasi

"So I shall make them a child," said the Artificer, "but it shall either sing or it shall dance. Not both."

"We could not love such a child equally," said Peacock.

Bulbul said, "It must do both."

"Pukar is but an old legend," said the Shah-en-Shah. "Will you deny them for a story?"

"A story?" The Artificer clicked her beak. "I wear one of those anklets around my neck."

Akbar smiled, but as he smiled in court, with grace rather than belief.

"What you ask worries me," said the Artificer. "But it worries me more that I seem to have taught you nothing. So be it, King of Kings; bring me beaten silver to replace the worn copper in my tail, and precious metal and enamel enough for this task, and they shall have what they want."

And so it was; she made a little golden child with wings and tail enamelled green, and named her Devadasi. Bulbul and Peacock raised her and taught her with love and patience. Being made by the Artificer, whose skill exceeds all others', she soon sang with greater range and sweetness than her father and danced with more grace and expression than her other father. All the birds were entranced—except the Artificer, who stayed away.

One day, when Akbar came to the aviary with trouble on his shoulders, Devadasi fluttered down to him. "May this slave sing to ease your soul?" she asked. "May I dance to give joy to the brightest star in the Heavens?" For her fathers had also taught her manners.

Now, the Shah-en-Shah had just abolished the pilgrim tax, and he was anxious to forget his mother's anger (remember that he was very young in those days). So he smiled, and accepted, and Devadasi sang for him and danced. And like all others, the Emperor of the World was entranced.

"What a clever bird you are," he said afterwards.

Devadasi preened and asked, "Do you not think my singing sweeter than Bulbul's, O my lord?"

The Emperor said, "Yes, little bird, it is sweeter than any other music in the world." This was thoughtless of him; but indeed he was not thinking.

"And do you not think my dancing prettier than Peacock's?"

"I do, little one," he said.

Bulbul and Peacock had approached to see how their daughter fared; but their heartsprings broke at Akbar's words, and they sang and danced no more. Struck by grief and guilt, the Shah-en-Shah bent his head and wept.

"Do not mourn, Great One," said Devadasi. "They are merely metal now, it is true, but surely it would please their springs and screws to be made beautiful. Have the Artificer bird use them to build more birds like myself, and my fathers' very cogs will rejoice."

And so the Light of Heaven commanded.

The Lady obeyed (for even an honored guest obeys the Ruler of All). She sawed Bulbul and Peacock apart, melted them down, reformed them. But their balance wheels and their broken heartsprings she quietly set aside.

The Devadasi birds exulted. They sang in complex harmony and choreographed elaborate dances, their different colors flashing in varied patterns. And they wanted, always, to make more complex music, more complex patterns. They wanted more of themselves.

So too did the Light of Heaven want more of them, for the memory of Bulbul and Peacock made him doubt his every thought and judgment. In the Devadasi birds' presence he could forget the new torture of shame and indecision; he came more and more often to the aviary, sometimes even cancelling his open court. And each time he came, the birds asked for something more.

They asked for bronze from the aviary's central fountain, and copper from the pipes that pumped in warm oil. He granted their wish, though it meant the other birds grew creaky and stiff. They wanted the solder that held together the aviary's panes of glass; and they had it, though the roof shattered and the rain came in.

They asked him, then, for stories of warfare. He spoke of swords and guns and killing machines, of strategy and of treachery on the field. And Falcon heard, and knew that her hunting was only a game for princes, and her heartspring broke. Then they asked whether owls of flesh could spin their heads all the way around; and Owl tried it, and unscrewed his head until it fell right off and smashed. They asked about wild swans, how gracefully they could glide through still water; and Swan tried to swim, and sank.

As each bird died there was more metal, and more still, and Devadasis' wishes kept the Artificer busy. But she saved every heartspring, and every special movement plate and wheel, and she hid them away. And late at night when she would not be disturbed, she spent long fraught hours patching broken heartsprings with copper from her old tailfeathers.

The day came when there were no birds left to murder for salvage, nothing more to harvest from the aviary itself. On that day the flock asked the Shahen-Shah if they might go with him to the Artificer's workshop, and on that day he did once again as they asked.

"See what you have wrought?" sang the Devadasi birds, their pure voices interweaving. "If not for you, the aviary would still be whole. You are flawed, Artificer; we are perfect. It is fit that you scrap your wings and make more of us."

But the Artificer said, "You will not find it so easy to break my heartspring."

"Then at least take that ugly anklet from around your neck," they chorused. "It is not fitting for a bird to wear jewellery, and it will help make one of us."

"Do you know the cost of an anklet?" said the Lady. "I shall tell you."

"We care nothing for your stories," they called.

"You will listen anyway," she said; and they did.

The Anklet

Once a young couple from Pukar came to Maturai, ruin of the south, in search of work and a new life. In that time, the city that is no more was thriving, rich in the manner of the flesh people, with fruit and meat and wandering cows and children and elaborate, painted woodwork.

The couple were barefoot, their skin scratched and muddy from travel. They owned nothing of value but her gleaming golden anklets. Ragged lengths of dyed silk fell from their shoulders, a mockery of the spun-gold robes they once had worn. But these were no paupers; they were master artificers both, and hoped to rebuild their fortune in Maturai.

Settling beneath a banyan tree on the edge of the city, they waited for sunrise. She beat a rhythm on her right anklet, her copper fingers dark against the gold. It sprung open with an oiled click-whirr. Moonlight caught on its tiny hinges and on the nine precious stones on their internal belt.

"Will you calculate our future?" asked her husband. For her right anklet was an astrological device; each stone represented a star.

"No," she said. "How would knowing help? We must speak to this raja's artificer; we have no choice."

Her husband bent his head. "Forgive me." His voice was dull as his once-gleaming skin.

She said only, "You were not yourself."

He slumped, silent, until she closed the anklet up and handed it to him; then he raised one brushed-bronze eyebrow in a question.

"You will need proof of our skill," she said.

"Should I not take my masterwork, rather than yours?"

"Yours is too useful," she said. "He might take it away." Her left anklet was a measuring device, its belt set with magnifying lenses. She did not mention that she preferred losing her own masterwork to his.

So when the stars to the east started to fade, he rose with her anklet in his hand and trudged into Maturai. He did not return.

Three days and three nights passed before she ventured into the city. She waited because flesh women did not conduct business, and because she was ashamed to enter the city with an ankle bare. But she also waited because she wished to trust her husband.

So it is that we can make terrible mistakes with the best of intentions. For by the time she entered the city, her husband was three days dead.

She learned from the flesh people that a metal man had stolen the queen's anklet and tried to sell it to the raja's own artificer. She asked where he was. "With the artificer," they said. "In pieces, by the raja's command. As the thieving device deserves."

She said, "The one you speak of was neither thief nor mere machine, but my husband."

As one, they turned away from her.

So she went to the palace. The raja's guards tried to stop her, of course; her hair filaments were unbraided, her copper skin dented and green in places. But they knew nothing of Pukar's people, of their strength and their speed. The woman of metal brushed them aside and clanged into court, where she cried, "Is this the justice of Maturai? Her raja is a murderer; her queen wears stolen goods."

"The device is raving," said the courtiers. But the queen looked at her and paled. For the copper woman's single anklet was a perfect golden band, just like the queen's two.

The raja said, "What nonsense. My artificer made the queen's anklets himself."

"Perhaps." The woman flexed her finger hinges. "But I made one that she wears."

"Do you claim my artificer lied?"

"Claim?" she said. "Call your artificer, O murderer, and I will prove it."

The raja took an angry breath, then stopped and smiled. "If I shame him so, he will leave," he said, as oiled as the copper woman's hinges. "I must have an artificer."

"Give me his workshop and his goods," she said, "and I will take his place."

The raja called gleefully for his artificer then, and bade the queen slip off her anklet.

The metal woman watched quietly. When the queen had eased an anklet off, she said, "But surely you knew which one you lost? Mine is the other."

The queen flushed and bowed her head, then fumbled her other anklet off. She held it out to the metal woman without looking up.

The artificer came in then, flanked by guards and protesting with every step. "What travesty is this?" he cried. "I have never been so insulted! Majesty, have I given you cause to doubt me? Surely I must know my own work!"

The copper woman said, "Then trigger its mechanism."

"What mechanism?" he sneered. "Do you see seams in my craftwork?" He held the anklet up to the window and turned it in the fractured light. "Do edges glint? Do hinges mar the surface? Show me one single imperfection—Thing."

She took the anklet from him, tapped it, and held it up as it click-whirred open. "In Pukar," she said, "jewellery is more than merely art."

The raja had his artificer put to death. The copper woman watched and smiled. She smiled more when the raja cast suspicious glances towards his queen.

And so the woman of Pukar became a raja's artificer. But she did not promise him loyalty, for she was too honorable to lie.

In the workshop she found her husband's armpieces, legpieces, breastplate, and skull. She found his gears arranged by size. She found a dozen plates, a thousand screws, a counterspring, a ratchet spring, a regulating spring. If she had found his heartspring intact, she might not have destroyed Maturai.

But she had given the old artificer three days and three nights with the body, and the flesh people have always wanted to know how heartsprings work. She could not repair it. Her husband was truly dead. And she had never told him that she treasured his anklet over her own. Her own heartspring might have broken then. It tightened, instead, in anger.

So she promised the raja a present in thanks for his justice, and she locked herself away. She kept her heartspring tight, and thought only of her art. For nine months she made children, scavenged from her husband's parts and her own. Nine monstrous children, each with one leg, one arm, and one eye. Each eye was a stone from her astrological anklet.

From the remaining parts she made a bird, copper from its tailfeathers to its wingtips. But its beak was the bronze of her husband's skin, and its articulated hands were human.

She was barely a framework by then. She unscrewed her breasts, filled their cups with gems from workshop stores, and with poison; then she soldered them together. She told her children their task: hop to the funerary grounds, steal burning branches from the pyres, and set Maturai aflame. She wound their heartsprings so tightly that they could think of nothing else. Then she set them loose.

Finally she clasped her measuring anklet around the bird's neck, pulled out her heartspring, and in one automated movement transferred it into the copper bird.

Then she stretched out her wings and flew.

She flew first into the raja's court, holding the sphere made from her breasts; and there she dropped it. It hit the marble tiles and burst open (for solder is not strong). Shining gems bounced everywhere. Some cut gashes in the courtiers and guards. They did not care. The copper bird's last view of the court of Maturai was a frenzy of men and women grabbing for rubies, emeralds, pearls; and every stone was coated in poison.

Heartsprings

"Poison kills flesh very quickly," said the Artificer thoughtfully. "And carved-wood buildings burn fast. So ended Maturai and so, as I flew high above and far away, was justice finally done."

There was a silence in the workshop when she finished. Even the flock was a little bit impressed, and the Emperor looked at his friend with a first hint of fear. She was both teacher and maker; just how tightly was *her* heartspring wound?

The flock recovered first. "Your price has been met," they warbled, "and we outnumber you still. If you will not give us your anklet, we will rip it from your neck."

"But the story is not done," said the Artificer. "For I made you, and I must tell you one thing more. I made you in the image of the temple dancers of golden Pukar, those who stole away my husband for one long and heartsore year. I even named the first of you after them: Devadasi. They were beautiful and skilled, and their grace was unmatched in this world."

As one, the flock preened.

"Yes, you were made in their image," said the Artificer. "But what I must tell you is that I failed. My skill was not sufficient. They are still unmatched, for they were better than you."

And hearing this, the entire flock's heartsprings broke in one discordant twang, and they fell, littering the floor, the table, the cabinets.

The Shah-en-Shah flinched. He looked around, a dreamer slowly waking into nightmare. Tears formed in his eyes. "What have I done?" he said.

The Artificer collected Devadasi bodies. She cut feathers and plates and counter-nuts apart. "You have learned something, my friend," she said, pulling heartsprings out of their hidden drawers. "The hard way, of course, like all the young."

And she set to remaking the birds of the aviary.

Akbar

He did learn, that young ruler. He learned whom to trust, and whom to heed, and that the two are not always the same. And that is surely why he lives to tell you this story today.

☉ One

Chris Roberson

CHRIS ROBERSON has published some three dozen short stories and more than a dozen novels, including the Celestial Empire series (*The Dragon's Nine Sons, Three Unbroken*, and *Iron Jaw and Hummingbird*) and the Bonaventure-Carmody sequence (*Here, There & Everywhere, Paragea: A Planetary Romance, Set the Seas on Fire, End of the Century*, and *Book of Secrets*), and his comic book work includes the miniseries *Cinderella: From Fabletown with Love,* and the ongoing series *I, Zombie*, both from Vertigo. Along with his business partner and spouse Allison Baker, he is the publisher of MonkeyBrain Books, an independent publishing house specializing in genre fiction and nonfiction genre studies. Visit him online at WWW.CHRISROBERSON.NET. "At the 2001 World Fantasy Convention in Montreal, anthologist and editor Lou Anders invited me to submit a story to his *Live Without a Net*. On the flight home, I outlined a story entitled 'O One,' which featured a conflation of an incident from Richard Feynman's autobiography *Surely You're Joking, Mr. Feynman!* with the story of John Henry and the steam engine, set in an alternate history heavily inspired by Bernardo Bertolucci's *The Last Emperor*. The resulting story ultimately appeared in the anthology, and went on to be nominated for a World Fantasy Award and to win a Sidewise Award for Short Form Alternate History."

T SUI STOOD IN the golden morning light of the Ornamental Garden, looking over the still waters of the abacus fish ponds and thinking about infinity. Beyond the walls, the Forbidden City already hummed with the activity of innumerable servants, eunuchs, and ministers bustling along in the Emperor's service, but in the garden itself was only silence and serenity.

Apart from the Imperial House of Calculation, which Tsui had served as Chief Computator since the death of his predecessor and father years before, the Ornamental Garden was the only place he lingered. The constant susurration of beads shuttling and clacking over oiled rods was the only music he could abide, and as dear to him as the beating of his own heart, but there were times still when the rhythms of that symphony began to wear on him. On these rare occasions the silence of the fish ponds and the sculpted grounds surrounding them was the only solace he had found.

His father, when he had been Chief Computator and Tsui not yet an apprentice, had explained that time and resources were the principal enemies of calculation. One man, with one abacus and an unlimited amount of time, could solve every mathematical operation imaginable, just as an unlimited number of men working with an infinite number of abacuses could solve every operation imaginable in an instant; but no man had an infinity in which to work, and no emperor could marshal to his service an infinite number of men. It was the task of the Chief Computator to strike the appropriate balance. The men of the Imperial House of Calculation worked in their hundreds, delicately manipulating the beads of their abacuses to provide the answers the Emperor required. That every click of bead on bead was followed a moment of silence, however brief, served only to remind Tsui of the limits this balance demanded. In that brief instant the enemies of calculation were the victors.

As a child Tsui had dreamt of an endless plain, filled with men as far as the eye could see. Every man in his dream was hunched over a small wooden frame, his fingers dancing over cherry-wood beads, and together they simultaneously solved every possible operation, a man for each calculation. In his dream, though, Tsui had not heard the same clatter and click he'd found so often at his father's side; with an endless number of permutations, every potential silence was filled with the noise of another bead striking bead somewhere else. The resulting sound was steady and even, a constant hum, no instant distinguishable from any other.

Only in pure silence had Tsui ever found another sensation quite like that, and the only silence he had found pure enough was that of the Ornamental Garden. Without speaking or moving, he could stand with eyes closed at the water's edge and imagine himself on that infinite plain, the answer to every problem close at hand.

The sound of feet scuffing on flagstone broke Tsui from his reverie, and he looked up to see Royal Inspector Bai walking leisurely through the garden's gate. Like Tsui, the Royal Inspector seemed to find comfort within the walls of silence, and the two men frequently exchanged a word of pleasantry on their chance encounters.

"A good morning, Chief Computator?" Bai asked. He approached the fish ponds, a package of waxed paper in his hands. He stopped opposite Tsui at the water's edge of the southernmost of the two ponds and, unwrapping his package with deft maneuvers, revealed a slab of cold pork between two slices of bread. A concept imported from the cold and distant England on the far side of the world, it was a dish that had never appealed to Tsui, more traditional in his tastes than the adventurous Inspector.

"As good as I might deserve, Inspector," Tsui answered, inclining his head a fraction. As he was responsible for the work of hundreds, Tsui technically ranked above the Inspector in the hierarchy of palace life, but considering the extensive influence and latitude granted the latter by imperial decree, the Chief Computator always displayed respect shading into submissiveness as a matter of course.

Bai nodded in reply and, tearing pieces of bread from either slice, dropped them onto the water before him. The abacus fish in the southern pond, of a precise but slow strain, moved in a languid dance to nibble the crumbs floating on the water's surface. The brilliant gold hue of their scales, iridescent in the shifting light, prismed through the slowly shifting water's surface, sparkled from below like prized gems. The fish, the result of a failed experiment years before to remove man from the process of calculation, had been bred from ornamentals chosen for their instinct of swimming in schools of close formation. In tests of the system, though, with a single agent flashing a series of lights at the water's edge representing a string of digits and the appropriate operation, it was found that while accurate to a high degree, the slowness of their movements made them no more effective than any apprentice of the House of Calculation. The biological and chemical agents used in breeding them from true, however, had left the scales of the languid abacus fish and their descendants much more striking that those of the base stock, and so a place was found for the failed experiment in the gardens.

"Your pardon, O Chief Computator," Bai remarked, shaking the last dusty crumbs from the pork and moving to the northern pond. "But it seems to me, at such times, that the movements of these poor doomed creatures still suggests the motions of your beads over rods, even in their feeding the fish arranging themselves in columns and rows of varying number."

Tearing off strips of pork, the Inspector tossed them onto the water, which frothed and bubbled the instant the meat hit the surface. Silt, kicked up by the force of the sudden circulation, colored the water a dusty gray.

"I can only agree, of course," Tsui answered, drawing alongside the Inspector and looking down on the erratic dance beneath the surface of the pond. This strain of abacus fish was, in contrast to its languid neighbor, much swifter but likewise far less consistent. They had been mutated from a breed of carnivorous fish from the Western Hemisphere's southern continent, the instinct of hunger incarnate. The operations they performed, cued by motions in the air above and enticed by offerings of raw flesh, were done faster than any but the most accomplished human operator could match, but with an unacceptably high degree of error. Like their languid cousins before them these fierce creatures were highly prized for their appearance, strangely viridescent scales offset by razor teeth and jagged fins, and so they were relocated from the Imperial Ministry of Experimentation into the garden when Tsui was only a child. "They mimic the process of calculation as a mina bird does that of human speech. Ignorant, and without any comprehension. Man does not, as yet, have any replacement."

"Hmm," the Inspector hummed, tossing the last of the pork into the water. "But what does the abacus bead know of its use? Is it not the computator only who must understand the greater meaning?"

"Perhaps, O Inspector, this may be how the Emperor himself, the-equal-of-heaven and may-he-reign-ten-thousand-years, rules over the lives and destinies of men. Each of us need not know how we work into the grander scheme, so long as the Emperor's hand guides us." It was not a precise representation of Tsui's thoughts on the matter, but a more politic answer than that which immediately suggested itself, and one better fit for the ears of the Emperor's justice.

The Inspector hummed again, and wiped his fingers clean on the hems of his sleeves. Looking past Tsui's shoulder at the garden's entrance, Bai raised his eyebrows a fraction and nodded.

"You may be right, Chief Computator," the Inspector answered, grinning slightly. "I believe either of two beads, you or I, will in short order be guided from here. Can you guess which?"

Tsui turned his chin over his shoulder, and saw the approach of the Imperial page.

"Neither can I," the Inspector said before Tsui could answer. When the page presented the parchment summons to the Chief Computator with an abbreviated bow, Bai smiled and nodded again, and turned his attention back to the abacus fish. The last of the pork was gone, but white foam still frothed over the silty gray waters.

Within the hall they waited, ministers and courtiers, eunuchs and servants, the Empress Dowager behind her screens, her ladies with faces made painted masks, and the Emperor himself upon the Golden Dragon Throne. All watching the still form of the infernal machine, squatting oily and threatening like a venomous toad on the lacquered wooden floor, its foreign devil master standing nervously to one side.

Tsui was met in the antechamber by the Lord Chamberlain. With a look of stern reproach for the Chief Computator's late arrival, the Chamberlain led Tsui into the hall, where they both knelt and kowtowed to the Emperor, touching foreheads to cold floor twice before waiting to be received.

"The Emperor does not like to be kept waiting," said the Emperor, lazily running his fingers along the surface of the scarlet and gold object in his hands. "Begin."

As the Emperor leaned forward, elbows resting on the carved arms of the ancient Manchurian throne, Tsui could see that the object in his hand was a representation in miniature of the proposed Imperial Space Craft. A much larger version, at fifty-percent scale, hung from the rafters of the hall overhead. It presented an imposing image of lacquered red cherry-wood and finely wrought gold, delicately sweeping fins and the imperial seal worked into the bulkheads above the forward viewing ports. That the Emperor did not like to be kept waiting was no secret. Since he'd first ascended to the Dragon Throne a decade before, he'd wanted nothing more than to travel to the heavens and had dedicated the resources of the world's most powerful nation to that end. His ancestors had conquered three-quarters of the world centuries before, his grandfather and then his father had gone on to bring the remaining rogue states under the red banner of China, and now the Emperor of the Earth would conquer the stars.

In the years of the Emperor's reign, four out of every five mathematical operations sent to the Imperial House of Calculation had been generated by the Ministry of Celestial Excursion, the bureau established to develop and perfect the art of flying into the heavens. Tsui had never given it a great deal of thought. When reviewing the produced solutions, approving the quality of each before affixing his chop and the ideogram, which represented both "Completion" and "Satisfaction," he had never paused to wonder why the scientists, sages, and alchemists might need these answers. The work of the Chief Computator was the calculation, and the use to which the results were put the concern of someone else.

Now, called for the first time to appear before his Emperor, it occurred to Tsui that he might, at last, be that someone else.

The Lord Chamberlain, at Tsui's side, motioned for the foreign devil to step forward. A tall, thin white man, he had a pile of pale brown hair on his head, and wispy mustaches which crept around the corners of his mouth towards his chin. A pair of round-framed glasses pinched the bridge of his nose, and his black wool suit was worn at the edges, the knees worn thin and shiny.

"Ten thousand pardons, Your Majesty," the Lord Chamberlain began, bowing from the waist, "but may I introduce to you the Proctor Napier, scientific attaché to the Imperial Capital from the subjugated land of Britain, conquered in centuries past by your glorious ancestors."

The Emperor inclined his head slightly, indicating that the foreign devil could continue.

"Many thanks for this indulgence, O Emperor," Proctor Napier began. "I come seeking your patronage."

The Emperor twitched the fingers of one hand, a precise motion.

"I was sent to these shores by your servant government in my home island," Napier continued, "to assist in Imperial research. My specialty is logic, and the ordering of information, and over the course of the past years I have become increasingly involved with the questions of computation. The grand designs of Your Majesty's long-range plans, whether to explore the moon and far planets, or to chart the course of the stars across the heavens, demands that complex calculations be performed at every step, and each of these calculations requires both men, materials, and time. It is my hope that each of these three prerequisites might be eliminated to a degree, so as to speed the progress towards your goals."

Tsui, not certain before this moment why he had been called before the Emperor, now harbored a suspicion, and stifled the desire to shout down the foreign devil. At the Chamberlain's side, he listened on, his hands curled into tense fists in his long sleeves.

"With Your Majesty's kind indulgence," Napier said, "I would take a moment to explain the fundaments of my invention." With a timid hand, he gestured towards the oily contraption on the floor behind him. "The basic principle of its operation is a number system of only two values. I call this system 'binary.' Though an innovation of Europe, this system has its basis in the ancient wisdom of China, and as such it seems appropriate that Your Divine Majesty is the one to whom it is presented.

"The trigrams of the I Ching are based on the structure of Yin and Yang, the complementary forces of nature. These trigrams, the building blocks of the I Ching, are composed either of broken or of unbroken lines. Starting from this pair of values, any number of combinations can be generated. Gottfried Leibniz, a German sage, adapted this basic structure some two hundred years ago into a full number system, capable of encoding any value using only two symbols.

He chose the Arabic numerals '1' and '0,' but the ideograms for Yin and Yang can be substituted and the system still functions the same. The decoding is key. Using the Arabic notation, the number 1 is represented as '1,' the number two as '10,' the number three as '11,' the number four as '100,' and so on."

The Emperor sighed, pointedly, and glanced to the space craft model in his lap, signifying that he was growing weary of the presentation.

"Oh, dear," Napier whispered under his breath, and then hastened to add, "Which brings me to my invention." He turned, and stepped to the side of the construct of oily metal and wood on the floor. It was about the height of a man's knee, almost as wide, a roughly cubical shape of copper and iron, plain and unadorned. The top face was surmounted by a brass frame, into which was set a series of wooden blocks, each face of which was carved with a number or symbol. On the cube face presented towards the Emperor was centered an array of articulated brass buttons, three rows of fifteen, the brassy sheen dulled by smudges of oil and grime.

"I call it the Analytical Engine. Powered by a simple motor, the engine comprises a series of switches, each of which can be set either to an 'on' or 'off' state by the manipulation of gears and cogs. By assigning a binary value to each of the two states, we are then able to represent with the engine any numerical value conceivable, so long as there are a sufficient number of switches available. With the inclusion of five operational variables, and the ability to display results immediately," he indicated the series of blocks crowning the device, "a fully functional Analytical Engine would theoretically be capable of solving quickly any equation put to it. Anyone with a rudimentary ability to read and input values can produce results more quickly and efficiently than a team of trained abacists. This is only a prototype model, of course, capable of working only up to a limited number of digits, but with the proper funding I'm confident we could construct an engine free of this limitation."

Tsui's pulse raged in his ears, though he kept silent and calm in the view of the Emperor.

"If I may?" Napier said, glancing from the Emperor to his invention with an eyebrow raised.

The Emperor twitched, almost imperceptibly, and in response the Chamberlain stepped forward.

"You may exhibit your device," the Chamberlain announced, bowing his head fractionally but never letting his eyes leave Napier's.

Wiping his hands nervously on the thin fabric of his pants, Napier crouched down and gripped the wood-handled crank at the rear of the engine. Leaning in, the strain showing on his pale face, he cranked through a dozen revolutions that produced a grinding clatter that set Tsui's teeth on edge. Finally, when the Chief Computator was sure he could stand the torture no longer, the engine sputtered, coughed, and vibrated to clanking life. Little plumes of acrid smoke bellowed up from the corners of the metal cube, and a slow drip of oil from one side puddled in a growing pool on the lacquered floor.

Licking his lips, Napier worked his way around to the front of the device, and rested his fingers on the rows of brass buttons.

"I'll start with a simple operation," he announced. "Can anyone provide two numbers?"

No one ventured an answer, all too occupied with the clattering machine on the floor, afraid that it might do them some harm.

"You, sir?" Napier said, pointing at Tsui. "Can you provide me with two numbers for my experiment?"

All eyes on him, not least of which the Emperor's, Tsui could only nod, biting back the answer that crouched behind his teeth, hoping to pounce.

"One and two," Tsui answered simply, eyes on the floor.

With a last look around the assembled for any other response, Napier hit four buttons in sequence.

"I've just instructed the engine to compute the sum of the two provided values," he explained, pausing for a brief resigned sigh, "and when I press this final button the calculation will occur immediately and the result will be displayed above."

Demonstrating a flair for the dramatic, Napier reached back his hand, and stabbed a finger at the final button with a flourish. The engine smoked and wheezed even more than before, and with a final clatter the rightmost of the blocks crowning the device spun on its brass axis and displayed the symbol for "3" face up.

"There, you see?" Napier said. "The answer produced, without any human intervention beyond the initial input."

"I have seen horses," the Emperor replied in a quiet voice, "clopping their hoofs on cobblestones, do more complicated sums than this."

"Perhaps, Your Majesty," the Chamberlain said, stepping forward, "a more evaluative demonstration is in order. Chief Computator Tsui?" The Chamberlain motioned to him with a brief wave of his hand, and Tsui inched forward, his fingers laced fiercely together in front of him.

The Chamberlain then snapped his fingers, and a page glided out of the shadows into the center of the hall, a small stool in one hand, an abacus in the other. Setting the stool down a few paces from the foreign devil's instrument, the page presented the abacus to Tsui and, bowing low, glided back into the shadows.

"I would suggest, with Your Majesty's permission," the Chamberlain said, "that a series of calculations be performed, both by the Proctor Napier and his machine, and by our own Chief Computator and his abacus. Which of the two performs more reliably and efficiently will no doubt tell us more than any other demonstration could."

The Emperor twitched his eyebrows, slightly, suggesting a nod.

"Let us begin," said the Chamberlain.

Tsui seated himself on the stool. The abacus on his lap was cool and smooth at his touch, the beads when tested sliding frictionless over the frame of rods. Tilting the frame of the abacus up, he set the beads at their starting position, and then left his fingers hovering over the rightmost row, ready to begin.

The Chamberlain officiated, providing values and operations from a slip of paper he produced from his sleeve. That he'd anticipated this test of man and machine was obvious, though it was inappropriate for any involved to suggest the Chamberlain had orchestrated the events to his ends.

The first calculation was a simple addition, producing the sum of two six-digit numbers. Tsui had his answer while Napier's engine was still sputtering and wheezing, taking less than a third of the time needed for the machine to calculate and display the correct answer on blocks.

The second calculation was multiplication, and here again Tsui finished first. The lapse of time between Tsui calling out his answer and Napier calling out his, though, dwindled in this second round, the engine taking perhaps only twice as long.

The third calculation was division, a four-digit number divided into a six-digit one. Tsui, pulse racing, called out his answer only an instant before Napier. The ruling of the Chamberlain named the Chief Computator the victor, even after Napier protested that he had inadvertently set his engine to calculate to two decimal places, and that as a result his answer was in fact more accurate.

The fourth and final calculation was to find the cube root of a six-digit number. This time, with his previous failure in mind, Napier shouted out after the numbers had been read that the answer should be calculated to two decimal points. The Chamberlain, eyes on the two men, nodded gravely and agreed to this condition. Tsui, who was already fiercely at work on the solution, felt the icy grip of dread. Each additional decimal place in a cube root operation increased the time necessary for the computation exponentially, and even without them he wasn't sure if he would finish first.

Fingers racing over the beads, too tense even to breathe, Tsui labored. The answer was within reach, he knew, with only seconds until he would be named the victor. The abhorrent clattering machine of the foreign interloper would be exposed for a fraud, and the place of the Chief Computator, and of the Imperial House of Computation, would be secure.

"I have it!" Napier shouted, and stepped back from the Analytical Engine to let the assembled see the displayed solution. There was a manic gleam in his eyes, and he looked directly at the Emperor without reservation or shame, as though expecting something like applause.

Tsui was frozen, struck dumb. Reviewing his mental calculations, he realized he'd been nowhere near an answer, would have required minutes more even to come close. He looked up, saw the symbols displayed on the first blocks of the device, and knew that Napier's answer was the correct one.

"It is decided, then," the Chamberlain announced, striding to Tsui's side. "Of the four tests, the methods of our tradition won out more often than they did not, and only by changing the parameters of the examination after calculations had begun was the Proctor Napier able to prevail. Napier's device is a failure."

"But..." Napier began, on the edge of objection. Seeing the stern expression on the Chamberlain's face, and looking to the palace guards that ringed the room, the foreigner relented. He'd agreed that his machine should be judged by a majority of tests, and had to abide by the results. To object now would risk a loss of face, at best, and a loss of something much more dire at worst.

Tsui, too numb still to speak, rose shakily to his feet and handed the abacus back to the page who appeared again from the shadows. Bowing to the Emperor, he backed towards the exit, face burning with self-recrimination.

"The Emperor demands a brief moment," the Emperor announced, sitting forward with something resembling interest. "British, how much time and work would be needed for you to complete the improvements you mentioned earlier? How many of your countrymen are trained in the arts of this device, who could assist you in the process?"

Napier, already in the process of packing up his engine dejectedly, rose to his feet. Rubbing his lower lip with an oil-stained finger, he answered.

"A matter of months to eradicate the current limitations, Your Majesty," he said. "Perhaps a year. But I would need easily as much time to instruct a staff of men, as at present I am the only one who understands all the aspects of the engine's manufacture."

The Emperor, uncharacteristically demonstrative, nodded twice.

"Leave now," the Emperor commanded, and they did.

In the antechamber, while Napier led a collection of pages and eunuchs in dismantling and boxing up his device, the Chamberlain caught Tsui's elbow.

"A moment, Chief Computator," the Chamberlain said in a low voice, drawing him into an alcove and well out of earshot.

"My thanks, O Lord Chamberlain," Tsui said, his tones hushed, "for allowing me to perform this small service for our master the Emperor."

"We all serve our part," the Chamberlain answered. "Remember, though, that the Emperor's remembrance of this good office will serve only to balance his displeasure that you kept him waiting."

"And for that, you have my apologies," Tsui answered. "But it is strange, I should think, that you would send for me at the House of Computation, in an hour during which it is well known to you that I am elsewhere at my leave. Would not one of my journeymen have been a suitable representative to hear the foreigner's presentation, and to offer any service you might require?"

"Perhaps," the Chamberlain replied, eyes narrowed. "Perhaps it slipped my memory that you would not be found in the House of Computation at this hour, and perhaps it did not occur to me that one of your able journeymen might be as suited for our purposes. But perhaps," the Chamberlain raised a long finger, "it was best that a member of the House of Computation in your position of leadership was present to see and hear what you have. I have always counted on you, O Chief Computator, to find solutions to problems others thought without resolution. Even, I add, solutions to things others did not even see as problems."

Tsui nodded.

"Yes," he said, "but of the many hundreds who labor under me in the art of calculation there are others very nearly as adept." He paused, and then added, "Many hundreds."

"Mmm," the Chamberlain hummed. "It is best, then, do you not think, that this device of the British does not meet the Emperor's standards, that so many hundreds of adepts are not removed from their productive positions?"

That the standards proposed had not been the Emperor's, but had instead been proposed by the Lord Chamberlain himself, was a point Tsui did not have to raise. The Emperor, in fact, as evidenced by his uncharacteristic inquiry into the production cycle of Napier's invention, seemed not entirely swayed by the Lord Chamberlain's stage-craft, the question of the utility of the Analytical Engine not nearly so closed as Tsui might have hoped.

"I could not agree more," Tsui answered, thin-lipped and grave. "I thank you for this consideration, and value our exchange."

The Chamberlain nodded, and drawing his robes around him, slid away into the antechamber and beyond, leaving Tsui alone.

The next morning found Tsui in the Ornamental Garden, eyes closed by the northernmost abacus fish pond.

The noise of shoes scuffing on gravel at his side startled him, and he opened his eyes to see Royal Inspector Bai standing at his side. He'd made no other sound in his approach.

"Good morning, Chief Computator," Bai said, a statement more than a question.

"Yes, Inspector," answered Tsui, looking down into the waters of the pond. They were silty and gray, the carnivorous fish almost hidden below the surface. "I would say that it is."

"Surprising, one might argue," Bai went on, "after the excitement of the evening." The Inspector pulled a wax-paper-wrapped lump of meat and bread from within his sleeve and, unwrapping it, began to drop hunks of dried pork into the waters.

"Excitement?" Tsui asked, innocently.

"Hmm," the Inspector hummed, peering down into the water, quiet and still but for the ripples spreading out from the points where the meat had passed. "The fish seem not very hungry today," he said softly, distracted, before looking up and meeting Tsui's gaze. "Yes," he answered, "excitement. It seems that a visitor to the Forbidden City, a foreign inventor, went missing somewhere between the great hall and the main gate after enjoying an audience with the Emperor. The invention which he'd brought with him was found scattered in pieces in the Grand Courtyard, the box which held it appearing to have been dropped from a high story balcony, though whether by accident or design we've been unable to determine. The Emperor has demanded the full attentions of my bureau be trained on this matter, as it seems that he had some service with which to charge this visitor. That the visitor is not in evidence, and this service might go unfilled, has done little to improve the temper of our master, equal-of-heaven and may-he-reign-ten-thousand-years."

Tsui nodded, displaying an appropriate mixture of curiosity and concern.

"As for the man himself," Bai said, shrugging, "as I've said, he seems just to have vanished." The Inspector paused again, and in a practiced casual tone added, "I believe you were present at the foreign inventor's audience yesterday, yes? You didn't happen to see him at any point following his departure from the hall, did you?"

Tsui shook his head, and in all sincerity answered, "No."

The Chief Computator had no fear. He'd done nothing wrong, after all, his involvement in the business beginning with a few choice words to his more perceptive journeymen and foremen on his hurried return to the Imperial House of Computation, and ending in the early morning hours when a slip of paper was delivered to him by one of his young apprentices. On the slip of paper, unsigned or marked by any man's chop, was a single ideogram, indicating "Completion" but suggesting "Satisfaction."

Tsui's business, since childhood, had been identifying problems and presenting solutions. To what uses those solutions might be put by other hands was simply not his concern.

"Hmm," the Inspector hummed again and, looking at the still waters of the pond, shook his head. "The abacus fish just don't seem interested today in my leavings. Perhaps they've already been fed, yes?"

"Perhaps," Tsui agreed.

The Inspector, with a resigned sigh, dropped the remainder of the meat into the northernmost pond, and then tossed the remaining bread into the south-ernmost, where the languid fish began their slow ballet to feed themselves.

"Well, the Emperor's service demands my attention," Inspector Bai said, brushing off his hands, "so I'll be on my way. I'll see you tomorrow, I trust?"

Tsui nodded.

"Yes," he answered, "I don't expect that I'll be going anywhere."

The Inspector gave a nod, which Tsui answered with a slight bow, and then left the Chief Computator alone in the garden.

Tsui looked down into the pond, and saw that the silt was beginning to settle on the murky bottoms, revealing the abacus fish arranged in serried ranks, marking out the answer to some indefinable question. The Chief Computator closed his eyes, and in the silence imagined countless men working countless abacuses, tirelessly. His thoughts on infinity, Tsui smiled.

Wild Copper

Samantha Henderson

SAMANTHA HENDERSON lives on the outskirts of Los Angeles, with an excellent view of the burning hills every summer. Her short fiction and poetry have been published in *Realms of Fantasy, Strange Horizons, ChiZine, Fantasy, Abyss & Apex, Weird Tales*, and *Ideomancer* and have been podcast on *Escape Pod, Podcastle, Drabblecast*, and *StarShipSofa*. Her first novel, *Heaven's Bones*, was released in 2008 and was a nominee for the Scribe Award. You can stalk her at her LiveJournal (SAMHENDERSON.LIVEJOURNAL.COM) or website (WWW.SAMANTHAHENDERSON. COM). Of "Wild Copper," she writes that "it had its genesis both in my childhood reading of a collection of tales of the Pacific Northwest Native Americans and a visit to Puget Sound a few years ago to visit my in-laws. The beauty of the area is almost unbearable; I sat on a log cast up on a beach of pebbles and watched the dark, choppy waters where orcas sometimes venture, imagining what lay beneath the surface."

I

THIS TIME OBERON turned Megan into a deer from the waist down, and nothing remained of yesterday's snake-tail but the memory of leaves against her belly-plates. She tapped cautiously on the trail with four small hooves.

Oberon did it to amuse himself, and to annoy the Queen. Titania wouldn't hesitate to transmogrify Megan herself, but the Queen did not appreciate Oberon's play in metamorphosing her handmaid. What chimera would present herself, dusk by dawn, to do the Fae Queen's bidding?

Megan knew he was angry. So angry.

Tap, tap on the mossy path. A day to grow into a deer's grace, then perhaps he would leave her alone for a while.

He would look at her with thousand-year-old eyes, and she'd feel his anger take hold like a tremendous hand, and he'd twist and shape her body until the craving was appeased.

Once he changed her head into a donkey's, and laughed his black-moss laugh every time he saw her. Titania bit her lip at that, casting her eyes down, and made her bower so cold that Oberon finally went off in a huff. Megan knelt out of sight in the ferns, since the Queen would not look at her. Her shoulders ached, and hot tears crept down her cheeks, under the coarse, itchy hair.

She'd thought she was so lucky. Lucky her uncle was a Ranger, lucky she and Casey and Mom and Dad could see, close as any mortal could, the borders of the Fae Reserve.

Usually Titania's attendants laughed at Megan's human clumsiness and the shapes Oberon forced her into—but they didn't laugh at the donkey's head. They crept about her, silently, until she slept. Later she woke with a crick in her neck and her own face and a crust of dried tears.

She scrubbed them away and stretched, feeling the rustle of the fairies around her in the weak green light before dawn. The Fae slept through the darkest part of the night and the middle of the day. Dawn and morning, dusk and twilight they woke. She must too, since she had given herself to them of her own free will.

Most nights and afternoons now she nested at the foot of a huge, lightning-twisted cedar. The Fae didn't like the shattered tree, and left her alone while she slept. Before she found this small sanctuary she'd wake to find her hair tied in elaborate knots, and the laces of her worn sneakers twisted in a way that took her hours to undo.

Megan scrabbled at the roots for the little hollow where she kept her comb—a gift from Titania in a generous mood—and dragged it through her hair. She gritted her teeth as she worked at the knots. This last summer she had let them stay, let Peaseblossom and Moth weave her hair high and wild, let them dress her in acorns and fern, shed her sneakers and had danced like a dervish on the moonlit paths that wound through green pillars and velvet moss and the jet-black, diamond-sprinkled waters of Puget Sound. She knew it pleased the Queen, and Oberon too as he watched from under a canopy of boughs under the starpricked sky.

And in summer's magic, it pleased her.

But now fall was in the air, and she was recalled to herself, and shed her frond-skirt and put on her shoes. She wanted to be human again.

Maybe that was why Oberon was angry.

So lucky, she thought bitterly.

"It's no use. They'll do it again tonight."

A man leaned against the tree, dressed in worn jeans and a plaid shirt. His hair was dull auburn, but gold sparked from it when he moved in the shaft that struck from a break in the canopy.

He wasn't quite human. Years of living with the Fae had sharpened her senses. Yet he was nothing like a fairy. The air around him tasted of earth and musk, and a little of the sweat of a working man or hunter.

He knelt, watching her.

"A human come to live with the Fae, to be Titania's handmaiden. I heard of it, but didn't believe. I haven't been surprised in a hundred years. Tell me how this happens."

He narrowed his eyes, and memories, unbidden, bubbled up like blisters. She tried to fight it but it was like fighting Oberon when he changed her, like trying to swim in mud.

So lucky and it was cool at first but what was the use when you couldn't go exploring the Reserve anyway just peer in from the edge with Uncle Leroy and the other Rangers hovering over you and she was in charge because she was the oldest and Dad was always fishing and Mom was always shopping in those frou-frou shops like they did on every vacation and when Casey said he wanted to see more she might as well go with him because he'd sneak off anyway it wasn't like she could tie him up and...

2

...Casey found a place where the thin, taut wires of the electric fence sagged apart, their metal supports rusting away, the recurrent "NO TRESPASSING—U.S. GOVERNMENT PROPERTY" sign rotting in the damp air. They'd go inside, just for a moment, just to say they'd done it, and be back before Uncle Leroy was done with his pile of paperwork back at the station. What could a couple sad fairies do to them, anyway, even if they were Oberon and Titania? England chased them away at the time of Cromwell, and they'd been pushed from refuge to refuge across the United States, shelter given and taken away as the lands they inhabited became valuable, moving west until they came to rest here, at the edge of the continent. How dangerous could they be in their defeat?

Past the thin line of trees at the fence there was a strip of meadow before the imposing, ancient trees of the forest proper began. Casey walked ahead, eager, while Megan trailed behind, so she was a good hundred feet away from him when she realized what he was doing.

Casey had scooped up a handful of wet rocks and started to hurl them at the solid wall of trees. The bark of the nearest cedars bruised with a wet spatter.

"Casey! Casey, stop!" Her voice still echoed in her head. "What do you think you're doing?" She ran at him, but he didn't stop. The meadow grass tangled her ankles. Casey threw faster and faster and harder, and just as she reached him she saw two eyes blink open on the bark of a cedar, and then the faint outline of a shoulder, and she tried to grab his arm, but he hurled the last stone as hard as he could and it struck beside the eyes and the sound was different, still wet but with a crunch like clay breaking instead of bark, and the eyes closed, and all she could see was a dark viscous splatter.

Casey froze, his mouth in a horrified "o."

Splayed against the tree, like a dark-speckled moth on a light-speckled tree, was a hunched outline, slender and bark-clad. It slumped down the trunk, and a wide, dark streak followed it down.

"It's a dryad," Megan whispered. All the dark spaces between the trees seemed to lean forward and listen. "Casey, I think you killed her."

"No," he said. "You can't kill a fairy. They're immortal. You can't kill them."

She walked forward in the squelchy undergrowth. The dryad was hunched at the foot of her tree. Even from this distance Megan could see that the side of her head was caved in.

The bile rose in her throat and she turned aside to vomit.

"I didn't mean to," said Casey, his voice hoarse. "I didn't mean to. I didn't *know…*"

"Shut up," she snapped, kneeling over her mess. She wiped her mouth with her sleeve. "Shut *up.*"

The dark places between the cedars did lean forward then, and things moved in the shadows, and *they* came: Oberon, tall and clad in black and spangled with rain, crowned with broken sticks and spiderwebs; Titania, all russet and ochre, with hair that rippled to her waist and eyes that robbed every living leaf of its green. With them, a multitude of fairies, nymphs, fauns, and tiny, nameless things that crawled between the cracks in the bark and through the litter of leaves.

Big, they were so big, and it wasn't so much their size as the fact that when you looked at them, you couldn't think of anything else. They possessed the senses.

* * *

She stayed on her knees in front of them and something twisted in her heart. You could die from seeing something so beautiful.

A faun crouched by the dryad and touched her head. Somewhere someone started to weep, a dry, scratchy sound, grating in the wet silence.

"She is dead," said Oberon. His voice was deep and rough.

"Dead," he said again, and his gaze caught the rock by the dryad's head and went to the gash and the smear on the bark.

"Dead." He looked straight at Casey. Casey shuddered.

Human footsteps behind them, crunching through the leaves. For a second Megan was angered at their intrusion, their *bulk,* the way they pushed through air instead of incorporating air.

Rangers, three of them. Uncle Leroy on the right; she didn't know the others. They stared at the Fae, astonished.

Even Rangers, keeping the boundary of the Fae Reserve, only caught occasional glimpses of sprites and pixies, and the dryads of the border. Uncle Leroy had told them that fifty, seventy-five years ago, one might catch a glimpse of a procession through the trees. But then the Court withdrew into the heart of the forest, and no one ever saw them these days. Megan saw in the three human faces the glad heartbreak she had felt.

Then Uncle Leroy saw Casey stricken and Megan kneeling.

"Megan?" He spoke to her because she was *in charge.* "Megan, honey, what's going on?"

"This boy," said Oberon in his deep woodsmoke voice, mouthing the "b" as if it tasted bad, "this *boy* killed a dryad. Not since Cromwell's Bane drove us from Albion has a human killed a fairy."

You lie, thought Megan, startled that she knew. Oberon glanced at her, sharp as obsidian, and at first she thought she'd spoken out loud.

Oberon pointed at the dark streak on the bark. "Blood calls for blood," he said. "Within the fairy's domain is fairy's law. He has trespassed and killed one of our own. He will die."

Uncle Leroy opened his mouth, but nothing came out. Who was the last human to speak to Oberon? Washington? Lincoln?

Megan's heart beat hard in her chest, and her throat hurt. "You can't do that," she whispered.

His look was like a blow.

"Can't I?" Oberon raised his hand and spread the fingers wide. Suddenly he clenched them and spread them again. One beat of a heart.

Casey cried out and fell to one knee. His hand flew to his chest, leaving a smear on his t-shirt.

"No!" cried Megan, starting to her feet, and the Rangers advanced.

Oberon clenched again, and Casey fell into the ferns. His lips were blue.

"Stop it!" shouted Megan.

Oberon stared at her, but kept his hand open.

"That's not necessary," Uncle Leroy said finally, his voice tight with the strain. "We have laws to deal with this kind of situation."

Uncle Leroy knelt beside Casey. "Breathe. You'll be okay, son. Just breathe."

Oberon threw the Ranger a withering glance. "Human laws," he said. "Cromwell's laws, Natural Law, law of supply and demand. I've had enough of your laws. The boy will die." His hand tensed.

He wants something, thought Megan. Or else he would have killed Casey by now. He wants something from me. And I was in charge.

"A trade," she said, fighting to keep her voice steady, as if she was not terrified. *Was that what Oberon wanted?*

Oberon smiled, frosty. He said, "A trade, then, your life for his?" Uncle Leroy was protesting, and the other Rangers too, but their words were unimportant, an officious human babble.

"Is there a law?" Megan looked past Oberon. Titania stood there, in her rustling garments with her eyes like leaves. "One of your laws? Is there?"

Uncle Leroy's voice penetrated, finally. "Megan. Let us handle this. You don't know what you're getting yourself into."

Titania tilted her head, ignoring Uncle Leroy. "There is a law." Her voice was a tinkling bell to the King's basso. "The law of *geis,* if my lord agrees."

Oberon lowered his hand. "If it pleases my lady," he said, and grinned.

His teeth were pointed. Megan felt sick.

"Oh God," said Uncle Leroy. Megan couldn't look at him, looked instead at Casey, white and shaking, still holding a stone in his left hand.

"Geis!" said the fox-faced man, licking his lips as if tasting something new. "Your service for your brother's life. For how long?"

Megan shook away the fragmented images in her head—Uncle Leroy, red-faced, arguing with the other Rangers; Casey, his eyes huge, watching as Titania's fairies drew her away between the trees. "Until My Lady pleases," said Megan.

The man jumped back and cocked his head to one side. Megan was startled. He looked human until then.

"I wonder," he said, "if Oberon planned it that way, as soon as he saw the dead dryad. He is almost as clever as me."

"Why would he do that?"

"To have a human bondservant, not a child stolen from the cradle, but a girl-woman, of her own free will? Such a thing has not been done since before the Ban. Tell me, are you bleeding yet?" His head wagged and he looked more and more like some long-snouted animal.

She gasped and laughed at the same time. "That's none of your business! And why would…"

"Because your kind is made of dirt and blood-and-snot and spit, and there's power in that," he said. She saw he'd grown a tail.

"He promised no harm would come to me. That was part of it." She looked at her hands, feeling again Oberon's, Titania's clasped about them, in front of Casey, the Rangers, a stone digging into her knee. Pledging her service. *Geis.*

"Harm?" He barked the word. "The Fae aren't human. You don't know what they mean when they say 'no harm.' What does a war chief mean when he says 'no harm'? A midwife? A slaver? A man of God? He wants you like a pregnant woman wants to eat clay." He was yipping, and his ears were growing long and pointed.

"Who are you?" she said, sharply. He was more than half a dog already.

Suddenly he was again a man. "I am Coyote," he said. "And I was here long before the exile Fae. And I have come back. And tonight, in the dark of the moon, I will come and tell you a story, since you told me yours so prettily."

"Wait!" she said, although he hadn't moved. "Tell me…why is he so angry?"

"Angry?" he said, surprised and amused, as if she had guessed the answer to a riddle.

"Yes. Every time he looks at me, even when he doesn't hate me, I feel it."

"Exiles are angry," he said. "I should know. When the Fae came from Albion, hunted from their domains, how welcome they were in this grand new land. And then they were pushed west, west, west again, as people, humans, strong in their earth-bound, flat-footed, blood and snot way, planted and ate and planted more to eat. Pushed the Fae, and the Fae pushed the Indian: Oberon and Custer together. And when they were, oh so kindly, deeded these lands, they pushed out my people, and with them Raven, and Eagle, and Bear, and the Thunderbird, and the demons of the lakes. I know how Oberon feels."

Megan saw a cliff, scattered with small white flowers, and at its lip tiny figures falling, over and over, into the sea. She blinked the image away.

Coyote stepped behind the tree and Megan knew if she looked, she would not find him on the other side. The fairies played that trick often enough.

3

The next day, Titania wanted sand dollars, and that chore drove the Coyote from her thoughts. Megan went to the shore alone: the fairies didn't like the water. Megan wondered why, because it was beautiful here, with dawn streaking the low waters blue and pink, and blackberry brambles growing to the water's edge. Sea-polished logs nestled in the flat pebbles of the shore. Sometimes she liked to sit and watch the faint blur across the sound—a harbor town outside of the Reserve. For some time she had not been able to remember its name, although she thought perhaps that was where she and Casey and her parents has been staying. She had a memory, sometimes, of discarded clothes wadded up on a motel floor, and Mom's voice telling them to pick up their mess. Or the taste of soda, forbidden at home, in a touristy burger stand.

But perhaps it was somewhere else. She couldn't recall. How long did they stay, trying to force human law on the Fae, trying to free her? When had they given up? A driftwood log moved, the pebbles underneath clanking. A seal? She saw them, sometimes, their heads bobbing up and down in the waters of the Sound. They didn't ever seem to come up on the beach at the Fae Reserve, however.

It was bigger than a seal: walrus-sized, smooth and shiny. It shifted again and she heard a faint moan. She went closer, and the breeze brought her a distinctly fishy odor.

The stranded creature was glossy, with black-and-white markings like a killer whale. But it wasn't a whale—Megan had never seen anything like it.

It did have a large, whalelike paddle of a tail, and a set of flippers. But the head was blunt and round, and it had two enormous eyes, disproportionately large for the head. They were the size of coconuts and had hardly any white at all—all brown iris and dull black pupil. The mouth was huge, a long slit that bisected the head halfway round, with bulbous, rubbery lips. When the creature gasped for air, she glimpsed rows of pointed teeth.

Over the eyes sprouted feelers, like a catfish's: three above each eye, thin

and supple—about two feet long and tipped on the ends with small round knobs. There was a whistling sound as it tried to breathe and the fishy smell was very strong.

The huge brown eyes rolled up at her, and the creature stirred again. It seemed to be trying to roll towards the water, fifty feet away, but could not gain purchase on the smooth rocks. Megan studied its smooth black-and-white flank and saw a gash, about two inches wide. Something protruded from the wound, and small bubbles of the creature's reddish-ochre blood oozed around it.

She knelt beside it, hoping it wouldn't whip around with those wicked teeth. She touched its side with the flat of her hand. It jerked once.

The object inside the gash looked like a thick stone sliver. She touched it, and the creature flinched, then held still. She grasped the splinter and pulled it hard—it was slippery and she had to wiggle it free. Dark thick fluid flowed from the wound. Then, like a seamless zipper, the slit closed up on its own. Except for the blood, there was no mark on the glossy hide.

She looked at the object in her palm. It *was* stone, a flint, chipped and crafted into a sharp blade. It looked like an Indian arrowhead, but she knew it wasn't. She'd seen these before, on the forest paths. It was a fairy point.

The creature shifted again. Dropping the Fae weapon, Megan braced herself against the smooth side and pushed as hard as she could. The thing was solid, and heavy, and it took all her strength to roll it halfway over.

Her efforts seemed to hearten the creature, and it pushed with its flippers and tail. Again she rolled it, and again. The muscles in her back protested, but she kept on, grimly.

She was strong. She was dirt and blood and sweat and snot.

Her shoulders were cramping by the time they reached the water's edge.

As the Sound washed against the creature's side it found new vigor and with a last mighty push it rolled into the water. Salt sprayed her face as it cracked its tail on the surface, propelling itself into the depths. She watched its wake arrow away from the shore of the Reserve.

Quickly she gathered as many sand dollars as she could for the Queen. When she went to look for the fairy point she found nothing but a smear of black ash.

"You stink of fish," said Titania, when Megan brought her the shells. "Don't come back in to my presence until you're clean again."

Dirt and sweat. Snot and blood.

4

The night was chilly and the smaller fairies liked to sleep on top of Megan, for she was warmer than they were. Their cold bodies made her shiver. Still, she managed to push free and sought the roots of her cedar.

She dozed off and woke with a start, not to a stray Fae weaving sticks in her hair, but the silhouette of a man against the stars.

"You owe me a story," she said.

"What did you do today? You smell."

"Titania wanted shells, so I went to the water. They don't like to look at the sea."

"They used to, when it was new to them. I remember."

Megan hesitated, then asked: "What has markings like a killer whale and huge brown eyes and feelers on the top of its head?"

He quirked an eyebrow. "*Kooshinga,*" he said. "A water-demon. Could it be you saw one?"

She didn't like his mocking tone, and besides, the incident with the *Kooshinga* was one of the only things that belonged to her alone. "You owe me a story," she said again.

Coyote bent close and his eyes were enormous.

"There was a girl," he said, "a slave of a great chief. One day, she found a lump of copper in the stream. She found another, and another, and knew they must have their source upstream.

"She tracked the copper, until she found a tremendous lump, an entire boulder. Enough to buy her freedom, the freedom of a hundred slaves.

"She took the lumps she'd found, hid them in her skirt, and polished them until they glowed. Then she waited until the great chief held a potlatch, a feast for all his tribe and their allies. She waited with the other women by the cooking fires, until she knew it was time for the hosts and their guests to outdo each other by offering rich gifts.

"She walked into the lodge, straight and proud, walked to the bench where her master sat, and everyone fell silent and stared as she passed by. She looked neither to the left nor the right. She walked straight to the chief and stood before him.

"He had feasted well, so he was in a good mood.

"'What do you want, Little Maid?' he said. 'A blanket, or a bowl, or a necklace?'"

"'None of these,' she replied. 'I want my freedom.'

"'And what do you have that would buy the freedom of a pretty slave?' he said, admiring her courage.

"For answer, she reached out her hand and dropped three pieces of copper on the hem of his robe. In the firelight they shone like fragments of the setting sun.

"'A fair gift, but not enough to purchase a slave,' he said. 'You price yourself too cheaply.'

"'This is nothing,' she said. 'In the woods is a great boulder of copper that I will show you and make no claim to, if I may be free. More copper than anyone has ever had before.'

"'Tomorrow,' he said. 'Tomorrow you will show me. If you speak the truth, you shall go free. But if you are lying, little slave, you will die.'

"The next day she led the chief to the boulder, and gained her freedom, and found her own man and lodge in the lands of the Kwakiutl. And so my story ends happily."

"What happened to the chief?" asked Megan.

Coyote grinned. "Given so much copper, he was overcome with greed and kept it all himself, refusing to give rich gifts to his friends and rivals and allies. And so he diminished in honor and stature, growing old before his time, and died clutching his boulder of copper, wizened like a spider.

"But we are not concerned with him. We speak of the girl, who bargained with copper for her freedom."

She stared at him. "The Fae want copper?"

"Ah," he replied. "Not anything so simple. I'm going to have to tell you another story."

Coyote slid to the ground, crossing his legs and resting his hands on his knees. "There was a time when all the animals walked the earth on two feet and spoke together, and Man was just another animal. Then everything changed. Something made it change.

"Sometimes it was one thing and sometimes it was another. Sometimes it was the Bears and sometimes it was Thunderbird. But this is what I remember best. I remember a shadow blotting out the sun. I remember something like a great warship sailing the sky. Immense and streamlined, like a dolphin, and the red-gold color of copper. And how it sang…"

He closed his eyes. "Such a strange song, so alien, maybe even not music at all, it shouldn't have been so beautiful. But it was sad, and lovely, and all the animals stopped, staring up at the sky. Some wept, some covered their ears and turned away, and some laughed. That's when everyone started to change, to become the way they are now. The Beaver and the Wolf and the Frog and the Man.

"I was one of those who laughed. And then…"

He opened his eyes. "It fell.

"There are many stories about Copper Woman. How she was made by the One Who Made The World and made mankind from the stuff that came from her body. How she married the Wealthy Chief who lives under the sea. How she controls the volcanoes.

"But this is what I remember: Copper Woman came from the sky and fell, hard and enormous, into the soft earth beneath the shallow sea. She sank deep, and the islands grew above her. She made things change. So long ago, I can hardly remember. Sleeping, she changed the world. I wonder, what might she do if she was awake?

"Pieces of her still work their way up through the dirt. Copper, but different from the native copper of the place—crafted, twisted, Wild Copper. Every piece plays a part. Every fragment tells a story. This is what the Sidhe Queen craves. Wild Copper.

"Since I came back I've whispered stories about Copper Woman, Wild Copper, every night, every noon to Titania as she sleeps. I've made her dream of it, and crave it. She thinks it will give her the power to break free of these inlet woods, this tiny finger of land your people have driven them to. She thinks the Wild Copper is tiny parts of a great magic.

"The Fae don't know anything about machines. Sitting cheek by jowl with humans a thousand years, they think they do. But they were never at Trinity, never at Hiroshima, like I was. They don't know a damn thing.

"But you're still human. You don't get distracted by the pattern of the bark or a moonbeam. You're still dirt: you understand machines. I'll help you find it. You can buy your freedom from Titania."

Freedom. From Oberon. From the fairies' teasing. From the fear that soon she would not want to be free at all.

"What will happen, when Titania has her machine?"

His face flickered, becoming birdlike, bearlike, again vulpine.

"This is what I think will happen. Copper Woman will hatch out of the deep mud. She will awaken and break free."

"Out of the Sound?"

"Out of the Sound."

"Under the hills?"

He thumbed an itch away from his forehead and sighed.

"Under the hills. She'll tear them away from the wet bosom of the world like a scab."

"But—everything will be destroyed!"

He shrugged. "I am Coyote. I ate my sisters to keep them in my belly and give me advice. I slept with my daughters because I felt like it. I changed a girl to stone because she wouldn't marry me. What wouldn't I do? I would destroy the world as a joke. I have, many times. At least, I think so. My memory's not what it was.

"The question is: what would you do?"

She looked at the ground before answering, and when she looked up again, he was gone, as she knew he would be.

5

Coyote showed her where to look: at the rim of the water, where the fairies wouldn't go. At the base of a sea-twisted pine she shoved pebbles aside until her fingers were sore, until she reached soggy sand. She was about to give it up as one of Coyote's jokes until she felt a force pushing back at her hands. Fuzzy, like a mild electrical shock, it was almost-pleasant-unpleasant, like an itch begging to be scratched. She dug a few inches deeper and found, sand-crusted, a delicate reddish coil that looked like the broken links of an old necklace she'd found in the bottom of her mom's jewelry case...

She sat there looking at it until the sun began to set, and she knew Titania was awakening.

6

"I want my freedom. I want to go home."

She knelt with her knees deep in the moss at the edge of Titania's bower.

The Fae Queen flashed her a look, not unkindly.

"So do I child," she said. "But neither of us is going to get what we want this day."

In answer, Megan held out the copper coil. She heard the hiss of Titania's indrawn breath.

"You know what it is, don't you? I'll find you all the pieces I can," she said. "I'll bring you every one of them. But then I want to go home."

Cautiously, almost flinching, the Queen spread her long pale fingers towards her and Megan fought the urge to scramble backwards, because suddenly the fingers looked like tentacles, the beautiful hand like an abbreviated octopus. But she made herself hold still as Titania gathered the fragment between her fingertips. Her face twitched as if it stung her, but she did not let go.

"Yes," she said. "Bring me the pieces and I'll let you go. I'll break the *geis*."

She drew in her breath as if to say more, and her expression was sad, but she looked again at the object in her hand and something else smoothed the sadness away.

There was a stir in the undergrowth, a scattering of fairies, and Megan looked up, expecting to see Coyote. But it was Oberon, in his silvery blackness.

He was in a foul mood: she could smell it, burnt fern and feathers in the dusk breeze. Automatically she drew inwards, bracing herself against him and against the pleasure she was beginning to feel when he changed her.

Oberon looked at her with hooded eyes. But Titania put out her hand, her attention still on the copper spiral. "No."

Oberon's face became sharp and glassy. "What did you say?"

"Leave the girl alone. Your games tire me."

He shot Megan a look that prickled across her skin, and she felt like a ball of clay in the grubby hand of a toddler. But then something stole through her, penetrating as Titania's octopus fingers, but cool, green, comforting. Her center, which was beginning to quiver and melt, stilled and became solid. Titania's green power met Oberon's force, and this time, like paper embracing rock in a child's game, prevailed.

She had not once looked at him. "Go," she said. "Until you can come here in peace, go."

The Fae King stood, a cold black flame of rage. For a second Megan feared he would rise and consume the bower, herself, Titania, the Sound, perhaps the world. But as a flame flickers he vanished, leaving the smell of soot behind.

Titania stayed, staring at her hand.

7

"Why does she want it, Coyote? Why does a Fae want a machine?"

She was digging in the soft earth beneath a bank of ferns. Coyote had told her to look there yesterday. She didn't see him but spoke out loud, on the chance that he was spying.

He didn't respond at first. But presently his voice came from behind her.

"Do you think Titania likes having you for a handmaid? Dirt-girl? Mucus-woman?"

She didn't answer, still digging in the soft decomposed mulch.

"Do you think she enjoys Oberon's games?"

Megan took a moment to answer. "I don't think she cares."

"She has learned not to care."

He appeared at the periphery of her vision and sat, well clear of the ferns.

"Once they were Lord and Lady of the Wood. Once all was in harmony between them.

"But things change. Love intensifies and fades and grows again. One seeks power. One plays politics. One is jealous and seeks revenge for wrongs real and imagined. One wants a changeling boy for himself. One falls in love with a mortal, and out again. Cromwell's Bane would have had no power against what they once were."

Two feet down, and something tingled in her fingers. The force that surrounded the Wild Copper.

"How do you know?" She dug faster. "How do you know what happened in Albion?"

He had gone, and his voice came from behind again, distantly.

"Of course I don't know. I'm making it up, like I made up the world."

Her roughened fingertips touched smooth metal.

"Silly Coyote," she said, smiling. "Raven made the world."

"Ah. You are learning."

He was gone, leaving behind a coil of laughter.

8

"It's the last piece," Megan told Titania.

"How do you know?"

"I'm dirt. I know." Nothing else had worked itself free. The rest lay buried underneath the peninsula.

She held it out on her palm, and it gleamed like burnished gold.

Titania reached for it but Megan drew it back, fisting her hand by her shoulder, and for the first time her eyes met the Fairy Queen's.

Leaf green and leaf brown and stormy, like the tops of trees tossing in high wind. She smelled ozone and lightening, and felt the pull to run wild in that wind. If Oberon's power was that of spider-webs and the dark places between the trees, Titania's was of storms slashing though the forest.

Megan didn't look away, but she squinted until her eyes couldn't hold any more storm.

"Your promise, Majesty," she said. "You promised my freedom with this last piece."

"I did," said Titania, in a gentle voice that was a soft breeze counterpoint to her wind-tossed eyes. "I will. Give it to me."

"Break the *geis.*" Megan kept her hand clenched. She heard a Coyote-size rustle in the dry leaves.

Titania's eyes narrowed and Megan learned a new thing: the wind has the power to tear you apart. She felt dog's-warmth behind her and pulled the fibers of her being back around her, like a cloak.

The Fairy Queen's beautiful eyes widened and the tempest became a gentle breeze, winding around her, caressing and seductive.

"Stay with me, girl," said Titania. "Come with me across the sea, when I break Cromwell's Bane. I will be Queen of Albion then, and you will stay at my side.

"No, Majesty," said Megan, her heart breaking. "Our bargain. Break the *geis.*"

"Don't you understand?" said the Fae, with a contemptuous sympathy. "Don't you know that your people, your family, died years ago? Have you no concept of how long you have been here?"

Megan couldn't answer. Her mouth was dry, and a small brittle hope she'd hardly been aware of crumpled away.

"A hundred years, two hundred. You have lived with the Fae. In a season with us, your mother grows grey and brittle, and fades away. In a year, your brother ages and dies. For all you know, the world of men is gone. Stay with us. Live in beauty."

Megan cried, although no tears came. She shook her head.

Titania's eyes narrowed, but there were no storms left for Megan. "Very well then," she said. "I would have crowned you with English daisies, and shown you secrets no mortal has dreamed of, but you are a silly girl after all, in love with your human flesh and mortality. Give me your hand."

Megan stretched out her left hand, a grubby paw, and the Queen's fine ivory fingers closed around it briefly and there was a prickle like nettles and that was all.

She was free.

Titania held out her hands: on her palm were six twisted fragments of copper. Her beauty was terrible and cold and immense.

Megan unfisted her hand and dropped the last piece into the Queen's hands.

For a second they lay on her white skin like dull garnets. Then they began to move.

She watched, and the Queen in her beauty watched, as the Wild Copper twisted and turned and crawled together, piece to piece, crawled together and joined together, one by one.

Megan stepped back, stepped back again. Titania was immobile, a smile playing on her lips, and something glowed in the cup of her hands.

Megan forced herself to turn away and stumbled through the trees. A rustle told her Coyote followed; he emerged from behind a cedar and waited for her.

9

Despite herself and needing comfort, she drew close to Coyote's side. He was warm, and smelled rank and foxy. She knew he was afraid, too.

"What is going to happen?" she whispered.

He whispered back. "I don't know. There is much I don't remember." He rubbed at his forehead with the heel of his hand. "Sometimes I think I dreamed it all. Copper Woman with her balls of dirt and snot and sweat, the Bears standing upright with their bows and arrows, marrying chieftain's daughters.

"Did you know people cooked their food by the heat of the sun, until I gave them fire? Did you know they went hungry until I made the Beaver sisters give the Salmon back?"

"No. I didn't know that."

"I taught them how to live as men, and I bargained with River and Wind and Bear and Eagle to ease their lives, to give them time to weave and make pots and store food and create a people out of an animal.

"But sometimes it wasn't me, but Raven."

His features flickered and looked, momentarily, birdlike.

Back in the grove, out of sight in her bower, Titania screamed.

"Run." Coyote's breath was hot on her ear. "Run as if *Tsonoqua* was coming after you."

She didn't think, but turned and ran, and sprawled as the earth shook beneath the trees.

Oh for four legs and a tail, she thought, and something inside her, the same something that knew to ask Oberon for her brother's life, that knew about the laws of *geis,* something reached deep inside her and made her blood and bones remember what it was like to be a deer.

She sprang to all four feet and saw Coyote waiting for her, and ran until the woods closed in and became brambles.

Snake, said something. She saw the ferns grow over her head and she slithered through the undergrowth, rocks round and cool and bark scraping against her belly, and her way was barred by thick spiny stalks of blackberries and something said…

…mouse…

…skitter scatter between the thorns like she was born to them and clitter clatter of tiny claws on the beach pebbles that were starting to shake and could crush a little mouse, break her skull like a dryad, and something said…

…*girl.*

Megan crouched at the rim of the water. In the middle of the Sound the water was shaking like jelly, and wavelets crashed on the shore frantically, out of their natural rhythm. Coyote was beside her, with his man-body and his dog-face. Behind them the slope of cedars and close-knit ferns was shaking apart.

She turned to the water. She could swim, but not fast enough, and Oberon had never changed her into a water-creature. She didn't have that pattern knit inside her. Coyote watched her, eyes wide, and understood.

"Leave me," she said.

"Never," said Coyote.

Something tore free deep underneath. From the woods came a high-pitched keening.

She stepped into the water and the cold of it struck to the bone. Pebbles and shells scraped against her bare feet and she made herself push on. She was up to her waist, up to her neck, and now she had to kick off by herself. The cold water made her limbs leaden and ripples were turning into waves, knocking into her and filling her mouth with salt.

Just behind her and to the side was a flash of silver as a salmon leapt out of the Sound: grey and pink with Coyote's lazy eyes. It darted around her and underneath, brushing against her flank, her toes, but he couldn't help her, and the waters were getting rougher.

The rumble of the land stirring sounded like a freight train, like an earthquake. She managed to float on her side and looked over her shoulder.

The peninsula was lifting as something huge ripped from underneath it. Birds flew, and other animals, squirrels and snakes and deer, darted from the undergrowth by the shore and plunged into the water.

A hundred feet up the shore the earth gaped. As it lifted and lengthened, Megan saw what was inside, what had been buried under the peninsula for millennia, what made it, and what would destroy it now: the flank of an enormous, copper-colored vessel, the same color as the coils and knobs of Wild Copper she had given Titania, some kind of trigger that rebirthed the ship when allowed to reassemble.

The submerged land beneath her was shaking and clots of dirt from the land were flying by her head. She couldn't swim away fast enough. The little snakes that arrowed past her on the surface of the water had a chance: she didn't. She would die along with the Fae. The silver salmon darted about her like a reflection itself.

She looked down at him, willing him to swim for the other side, and saw two bulbous, brown eyes beneath her, behind them, a smooth black-and-white body. She was paralyzed with the cold and hardly moved as the long feelers tickled her feet.

It surfaced beside her and it wasn't until it nudged her that she understood. She grasped one of the flippers and wrapped her legs around what she could of the slippery body.

It took all her strength to cling to the water-demon as it drove towards the far shore, the harbor town, with powerful strokes of its tail. She willed her muscles to lock into place, shutting her eyes against the stinging salt spray. She could not block out the sound of the land behind her and all its creatures being torn asunder.

Rocks beneath her bare leg: the *Kooshinga* had brought them to the opposite shore. Numb, she released her grip on its flippers and stumbled onto land. Something silver flipped beside her and Coyote stood on the shore.

The *Kooshinga* rolled into the deep choppy water and vanished.

The sky was darkening, the sun turning sunset-copper although it was still over the horizon. She spared a glance for the town splayed across the shore.

Stores and restaurants and little cottages were crumbling away, their paint long gone. There was no sign of any people. A rusty car squatted on a ragged shelf of asphalt that jutted where a pier had fallen apart, driver and passenger doors spread open as if the occupants had fled a hundred years ago.

Across the Sound the peninsula was ripping itself apart. As they watched, the land split open.

The craft that rose from its deep womb was larger than any ship or building Megan had ever seen. Clumps of dirt, not clumps really but clots of land with boulders and trees, dropped from its terraces.

It was a dull red-gold that blanched the bloody sun, it had wings and sails and delicate towers laced along its sides, it moved through the air with the controlled strength and grace of a seal in water, and as it moved it sang. It sang a song to make you cry and laugh and cover your ears.

Copper Woman.

Megan felt Coyote's hand warm on her shoulder. She closed her eyes and let the song inside, free within her.

The song coiled and lapped at her very core, coiling like copper wire through her flesh. It pulled and tugged and caressed. It found the places soft and bruised from Oberon's tinkering, and healed them. It found the defenses she had built against him, and broke them apart. It found the years she had spent with the Fae and braided them together. It found the wet sound of a dryad's skull breaking and pondered that.

She opened her eyes. The ship was gone.

She stood on the pebbles of the Sound. She had the legs of a deer, the tail of a snake, and the ears of the mouse. And then, with a thought, she didn't.

Megan laughed.

The waters of the Sound poured into the great wound Copper Woman made. Soon, except for an occasional tree that bobbed to the surface, no sign remained of that tongue of land.

"What do we do now?" said Megan, when she had stopped laughing.

"Now we make the world," said Coyote.

The Bold Explorer in the Place Beyond

David Erik Nelson

DAVID ERIK NELSON is a freelance writer living in Ann Arbor, Michigan. His stories have appeared in *Shimmer, Asimov's Science Fiction*, and *The Best of Lady Churchill's Rosebud Wristlet*. You can find him online at WWW.DAVIDERIKNELSON.COM. "The Bold Explorer in the Place Beyond" is "one of several interlocking stories set in an America where the Union won the Civil War by [using] a large body of Chinese clockwork soldiers. After the war many discharged clockies, feared and reviled for their efficiency on the battlefield, went west to live peacefully apart from a citizenry that neither appreciated their contribution to the war effort nor their company. The most noted of my clockie stories (and also the sequel to the following story) is the novelette 'Tucker Teaches the Clockies to Copulate' (Spring 2008 *Paradox*). That novelette, and thus the whole of the 'Clockie' universe, grew out of a riff on a Zuni Trickster story, 'Teaching the Mudheads How to Copulate.' While the story you are about to read is framed by the Clockie universe, its heart—the misadventure of the Bold Explorer—is a bedtime story I told to my son when he was about a year old. In other words, 'The Bold Explorer in the Place Beyond' is a kid's story wrapped in a dirty joke."

"S O, THAT LIL squid, the bold explorer, had just knocked his whole damn operation into a cocked hat, is what he'd done." That voice came chopping out of the crisp spring dark and scared the tar out of me. I'd been creeping down to peep into the windows of Two-Ton Sadie's Dancehall—catch me a look at them dancing girls she's got—when that crippled ole Johnny Reb, Dickie Tucker, came bellowing out of the dark alley alongside the General Mercantile Emporium, bottle in hand. He stomped up to Rev. Habit's First Church of the Latter-Day Saints, and I went hopping into Sheriff Plume's high hedge like a jackrabbit.

The fat, spring moon gleamed on Dickie's single good eye and made plain the hard fist of scars clenching the right side of his head as he hectored the big double doors of Rev. Habit's church. He looked like the Devil's own fist hammering down the Lord's door.

"That lil squid had kitted himself together a clever ole clockwork diving engine—an *undiving* engine. Looked like a lil crab stitched outta scraps of copper, rubber, and greased leather." Dickie made obscure gestures in the air, like he was telling a Chinaman how to put together a pump head, but I already had a notion of what his *bold explorer* looked like: like them Union automatic clockwork soldiers that keep their camp up on Windmill Mesa, now that they's retired from Sherman's dreaded First Mechanical Battalion. Word was that Dickie'd lost his face to a clockie platoon at the Battle of Atlanta. No one knew if that was true—you couldn't hardly talk to Dickie Tucker, no more than you could talk to a rabid dog, but the way he lashed into the clockies when he'd see them in the street…it seemed credible.

"Started okay: The bold explorer, he'd crept up out of the water, peering from behind a curved shard of a Chinese blowed-glass fishing float, not knowin' what to expect of the Place Beyond. He'd clicked and clacked up out of the surge and scuttled into the sedges, not just blinded by the clean, pure light of that slitted sliver of moon, but by his sense of wonder and terror. He'd skidded right through the scintillant edge of everything, and was still live and sane." Dickie wavered in the street and held his bottle up to see its level in the moonlight. I couldn't see how much he had, or had had, or would have. Probably God couldn't, neither. Behind him, the dancehall thumped and jangled. With its swaybacked roof and lit-up windows, it looked like a November jack-o'-lantern gone soft, waiting to fall in on itself.

"Before he'd even gotten over congratulating hisself on bein' so damn brave and clever," he told the bottle, "the bold explorer had already bumbled his way through the thickets of sharp bentgrass, tumbled down the backs of the dunes, and stumbled into the forest." Dickie took another slug.

"The forest was thick," he said, taking the church steps like he was charging a trench through a mucky field, "and the leafy branches of the old beeches and buckeyes cut the glare off the moonlight. His lil optically perfect eyes could focus again, and he saw a sick world of wonders. It was crowded with what he took for corals and anemones, but these reefs was fishless and vacant, the piebald corals bleached of their living color, the anemones listless. No wonder, he thought, that the few that got pulled up through the Silver Edge came back broken and dead, and the survivors mad; the Place Beyond was a dead world." Dickie knelt shakily, set down his bottle on the top step, and peered through the door crack like he was peeping on Jesus in the bath. Then he started to whisper into the doorknob.

"The bold explorer's lil legs whirred and clicked as he scuttled through the dry leaves," Dickie crawled the fingers of his left hand over the wooden door, like a giant spider tickling a lady's bottom over her silk knickers, "whirred and ticked as he scrambled over logs, whirred and tocked as he skittered over knobby old roots. Even if it was a dead world, there was still much to see, and he aimed to look his fill while he had the chance. He was slipping into a dip under a big ole uprooted paper birch when his suit whirred and sproinged, and one of his front legs gave out limp." Dickie made his index finger flop lamely. "He stopped in his tracks, and gave the leg a test jiggle. It did nuthin'. He gently tested the other seven; two more sproinged. He backtracked up out of the dip, but was hardly clear of the tree's lee when the suit *crack!*ed" he clapped his hands, "sproinged, whirred, whistled, and keeled over." Dickie's left hand dropped dead on the church's wide top step. "He rolled a half turn, and looked up through a break in the canopy at the drowsy, half-lidded moon." Dickie himself rocked back on his heels, almost tumbling down the steps, then spun and planted his skinny hams on the narrow threshold. He leaned back into the door's embrace, closed his eye, and basked in the spring moonlight.

"Soon enough," Dickie grunted, "bold explorer discovered that the forest wasn't so empty like he thought. But till then, he had hisself a time to lay out orderly how he'd got where he was. If there's such as sin, then the bold explorer, his sin was *pride*. All his days, as a young squidlet at the bottom of the goddamn sea, he'd been too *fancy* to socialize proper with all them other lil squiddies. When they'd spurt up to ask him to play at races and crack-the-whip, or to twirl it up at the annual squid cotillion, he was always too busy studyin' up and schemin' on his glorious *future*. He's too busy to even be proper and polite and express his *regrets,* and so it wasn't too soon before every other lil squid stopped tryin' to pal up to him. Not that the damn thick bastard even might notice." Dickie opened his eye and there was fire in it. He shot to his feet, and shouted in the moon's face.

"'Cause ole Mr. *Fancy Pants* had him a notion that there was somethin' worth knowing up beyond the undulant, silver top edge of the waters, somethin' more than plain, ole Death. The squids, they all *knew* there was somethin' out Beyond, but didn't reckon it was somethin' worth knowin'. Why? 'Cause on account now and again some poor damn bastard would get caught in a net, or lay into a baited hook, and get whisked up clean out of their world. Mostly, that was the end of the story. Occasionally, his corpse might get coughed back out, limp and torn. And very, very, very…" his steam had run down. Dickie seemed like a locomotive that might start rolling back down hill, devil may care and no survivors when it jumps track. He took the steps back down in a loose-limbed trot, then looked at his hands quizzically.

"Very, very rare," he mumbled absently, looking about him on the ground, "that unlucky squid would come back live. But what he could say of what he'd seen…" Dickie finally caught a glimpse of his bottle, left neglected on the church steps, and his single eye sparkled, "There weren't much to it. It was crazy babble," Dickie leaned over the steps, laying out across them, snatched up his hooch, and took a long, reflective gulp before standing. "He'd tell 'em, of a *thin* place up above and beyond the world, a searing place of blinding light, of roars and shudders, of helpless flopping and hopeless incomprehensibility. All them other squids pitied these madmen that had seen the Place Beyond. And, jus' like us, sayin' they *pitied* these luckless travelers is to say they *ignored* them."

Dickie rubbed his face then knuckled his good eye. "But the bold explorer," he sighed, "he lacked the good goddamn sense to ignore crippled lunatics."

Dickie rocked on his heels, starring into the moon, and then muttered, "He was a brave, dumb sonofabitch. I'd pity the bastards too. Pity 'em all."

Dickie strutted up the street, like an actor across the boards. He took a deep breath and blew out his contemplative mood. "And then," he kicked a horse apple, aiming for Sheriff's door. It pounded into the bushes where I crouched, off to my left. "As the bold explorer laid there, thinkin' on his progress, cats oiled in on the darkness, like eels 'cross ice. Feral old toms, refugees from a torched plantation. One still wore his leather collar, which was cracked and dry, but had its silver bell. Though tarnished black, that bell tinkled high and pretty in the moon-bright night." He kicked another turd. "Not that the bold explorer could hear." And it went extremely wide, skittering up the street. "They was cats and didn't know much, but they remembered the sorts of fancy food what came out of cans and jars, once upon a time, afore them clockie sonsabitches brought their fire down through Atlanta and clear to the sea." He kicked another turd, hard. It disintegrated to a mist of manure on impact with his boot toe, but he still squinted into the distance to see where it had landed.

"Them cats flowed out of the dark and knotted around the bold explorer who, bless his stupid heart, was glad to see 'em. He watched the cats glide through the air, slick as fish, and blushed a warm *hello* and gracious salutation, such as you might to diplomats and ambassadors. 'Course," he kicked, and a horse apple shot into the bush directly above me, raining down leaves and filth, "they didn't give a good God damn for greetings. Them toms couldn't even imagine the full-color skin semaphore that's squid talk. All they saw was pretty fish in a Mason jar." Two more horse apples came in quick succession, cutting right into the trail of the last, and dusting me with stink to match my regret.

"But the bold explorer, he just kept grinnin' like a blue-ribbon asshole, and flashin' his *howdy-do?* and swirlin' his embarrassed relief, and jiggin' an excruciatingly boring explanation of his predicament. He was explicating his situation when the first swat knocked him and his little bubble of sea into the brush." Dickie cracked his hard palm smartly across his thigh, "And they was off to the races. The trio of toms swirled off into the forest, drivin' that squid in his clockwork divin' bell before 'em like injuns runnin' buffalo off a cliff. They went ricochetin' off trees, tumblin' down banks, and sprintin' up hills. Soon as they started they'd lost the sense of the goal of the task, and was just runnin' after the savage joy of it. Once that dome cracked the party'd be done, and maybe they'd mourn the loss of the game, but a full belly goes a long way to soothe a sad heart. Least when you's livin' rough." Dickie made to drink, but lost his grip. The bottle tumbled to the dirt. He shook his head, watching his tonic glug away into the rutted lane. Sadie's thumped and rocked, like a distant train passing on a track that don't go nowhere near your town. The girls all whooped together, high and pretty, and the sound of it in the spring night made my heart crinkle till I was near to crying.

"But the cats," Dickie said, "they didn't get their supper. They was all legs and cartwheels, time a-their life, when somethin' big and angry, somethin' that wanted what they had, pounded up the brush and loosed a single screechin' roar. Stopped them three toms dead in their tracks, and sent 'em yowlin' to the four points of the compass, leaving the bold explorer to rock and froth and shudder to rest among the roots and bracken."

Dickie squatted shakily and dabbled his fingers in the puddle of booze that was mingling with everything else in the street—hog slop and horse piss and cowflops and God even don't imagine what. "The cat's yowls and ruckus drifted off into the night, with the tinkle of that age-black silver bell followin' after." He brought his fingers to his mouth and my guts clenched up tight and greasy. He scowled, then nodded.

"Soon, out from the brush, crept the 'possum, gopher, and two squirrels who'd made that racket." Dickie got shakily to all fours. "They circled up 'round the bold explorer. His little undiving engine was worse for wear: Three of the legs was gone altogether, with toothy gears and useless snarls of spring-steel protruding from their empty sockets. The other five were twisted beyond all hope of repair, bent back and around the dome of his lil anti-bathysphere like the green sepals pulled up around a dandelion's fluff." He carefully lowered his face to the puddle. "The glass was still whole—maybe for the luck of being shielded by them bust-up legs—but there was a trickle of water running out from between the tarred plates on his undercarriage." Dickie was bringing his lips to the dirt-flecked surface of that grotesquely filthy whiskey puddle when the better angels of his nature reared their heads. My guts hitched into my throat and stuck there, even when Dickie flopped onto his backside instead of slurping up that mess. He sighed like an abandoned dog.

I was scared of getting skinned by my pa', and scared of Dickie Tucker, and sick sad that I was missing on seeing those dancing girls that Pa' calls "prairie nymphs," like the words are a mouthful of spoilt milk. Maybe they're cheap trash, but to see them twirling in the light of a hundred candles, their curls shining, to see them lounge against the bar like cats, to see their legs and arms and necks, to see their coyness that ain't coy when they set hand to a man's arm or chest—it's warm and dizzy and worth any kind of scared. It settled my gut, thinking about them.

"The bold explorer himself was bruised all to hell," Dickie said, "with one eye swelled shut like a county fair pugilist, but he's just as optimistic as ever. He smiled tentative, then blushed and wigwagged his color-talk, 'splaining how he'd got there—which they knew plain enough, from seein'—and askin' their help in diagnosing the ailments of his suit—which was beyond their capacities." Dickie stood and turned back toward the church doors, serendipitously catching sight of his dropped bottle. A bare inch of liquor lay in the curve of the bottle's belly, and Dickie perked up seeing it. "All's to say that it was probably just fine that they couldn't understand a damn thing he said." Dickie scooped up the bottle and drained her.

Though it seems unlikely, Dickie was even less steady on his feet than before, pacing careful, his eyes glued to the dirt. He brought each step to bear with ferocious concentration, as though he expected the ground to squirt out from under foot.

"The squirrels, 'possum, and whistlepig held a lil powwow, and agreed that they didn't know what in the hell they'd stumbled into, or where it belonged. They figured it was some manner-ah tadpole 'r salamander, and needed water, which it was quickly runnin' shy on in its leaky fishbowl." Dickie stood at the base of the steps, staring down the doors.

"The bold explorer smiled hopefully up at his saviors, even as the water level inched down his dainty, color-swirled mantle."

Dickie undid the buttons on his pants, and proceeded to loose a powerful stream on the church steps, his hands, and his trousers, sighing his satisfaction.

"These four crusaders had never seen the sea, nor had any notion of it, so they did best they could," Dickie buttoned up crooked, then rubbed his face, like a night watchmen warding off sleep. "They hauled him up, set him on their shoulders, and carried him, like a fallen hero, to the charred ruins of the plantation house. Round back, down to the old slave shacks, the 'possum and whistlepig cradled the bold explorer. He's beamin' at all he'd saw, and what he'd see yet, imaginin' his hero's welcome back to the sea, his lecture circuit on the Place Beyond. The squirrels scrabbled up to the crumblin' lip of the old well. The 'possum and groundhog heaved the lil suit up—weighed almost nuthin', what with most of the water drained away—and the squirrels hauled it over, and dropped it down. The bold explorer tumbled into the dark with the moon's silver light frostin' the copper and glass, shinin' in his perfect, expectant eyes. It was a thin slice of moon, a droopin' eye, like a lazy God almost sorta watchin' over his passage. Then he was gone."

Dickie stood, swaying like he was on a foundering frigate.

"He didn't make no sound on the way down, but he splashed when he hit bottom."

Dickie fixed the big double doors in a baleful stare.

"The four a-them standin' in the moonlight looked down inna that well. They knew they hadn't done right, 'xactly, but they'd done best they could." His breath hitched, like he might sick up. "Didn't feel much good 'bout it, tho'."

Dickie took a breath, looked as to continue, but instead passed out. His right knee buckled while the left held, and he twirled like a ballerina before flopping on his back into the lane's filth.

We sat together, alone in the dark. Dickie snorted. Down the lane, lady laughter bubbled out of Sadie's. I shivered, even though the night was warm.

I wanted to help Dickie home, but his place is so far west of town that doing so would have meant getting caught out for sure. And the fact is, I wanted—I needed—to have my look at Sadie's gals, I needed to go get my fill, even though I knew: Needing to see is where the trouble starts; ain't no amount of looking that fills you.

Besides, sleeping out couldn't possibly bother Dickie Tucker; sleeping in his crumbling shack wasn't much better than sleeping out. At least on the church steps he had fresh air and the Lord watching.

But it didn't matter. I was still tangled in Sheriff's hedge when I heard clicking and clanking come from the darkness out west of the church. I looked up and seen that it was four clockies from the bunch that make their camp up on Windmill Mesa, refugees and veterans of that same Long War that had taken Dickie's good right eye. They looked down at Dickie, their eyes glowing like pairs of coals peeking out from a stove grate. One hunkered and nudged Dickie, who snored deep and didn't stir. The croucher clicked at his mates, and one tick-tocked off, returning with a wheelbarrow snitched from the side of Emet Kohen's Mercantile Emporium. They hauled Dickie up, then wheeled him down the lane, right past my nose. Dickie smelt terrible of manure and I can't even guess what, but the clockies were clean. They smelled like copper and gun oil, and water from the springs way back in the box canyons.

As he was wheeled past, Dickie's one good eye rolled open. It fixed on me blearily, and he mumbled, "Go have yer look, Seth Everett. Couldn't *possibly* do no harm."

At the next alley the party cut west, into the darkness, and if they dumped Dickie back into his own pitiful sod hut, or rolled him right past, all the way to their neat homestead on top of Windmill Mesa, I really can't say.

Lost Pages from
"The Encyclopedia of
Fantastic Victoriana"

Jess Nevins

JESS NEVINS is a college librarian by trade and manic geek researcher by preference. He is the author of *The Encyclopedia of Fantastic Victoriana* (2004) and the forthcoming *Heroes of the World: An Encyclopedia of Global Pulp Heroes.* As for this excised section of his Victoriana encyclopedia, he writes, "The idea of steampunk existing in the nineteenth century is certainly an attractive one, but, sadly, the reality of such a thing would result in its use at war and its catastrophic failure. War so often drives technological innovation, and there's no reason steampunk would be immune to that, especially in the bloody and war-torn nineteenth century. And so much of nineteenth-century war was futile, appallingly fatal, and generally abortive, so it seemed fitting to me that steampunk vehicles would prove likewise." Visit him at RATMMJESS.LIVEJOURNAL.COM.

S TEAM DEVICES. The symbiotic relationship between real events and nineteenth-century popular literature is underappreciated by critics and academics where it is not entirely ignored. The reality of female private investigators, and their influence on fictional female detectives (see: LADY DETECTIVES), has gone unnoticed by modern writers. Of course, much of what appears in fiction is romanticized, sentimentalized, and made more neat and suitable for fiction—reality is often disappointing in that regard. One prominent example of this is the numerous experiments with steam weapons and steam vehicles—"steam devices," in the phraseology common to the era—during the nineteenth-century.

Steam power was a constant throughout the nineteenth century; the first real steamboat, the *Charlotte Dundas,* debuted in 1803. But it was the addition of the screw propeller to a steam-powered ship, first with the S.S. *Archimedes* in 1839 and then, via noted English engineer Isambard Kingdom Brunel, the S.S. *Great Britain* in 1843, that caused a revolution in both real-life transportation and in the thinking of authors. Before the *Archimedes* and the *Great Britain,* science fictional voyages used existing forms of transportation, usually balloons and wind-powered ships. But the introduction of successful steam-powered ships spurred authors to create new vehicles and new energies to power them, and spurred real-life engineers and inventors to create them.

The first known example of this took place in April 1855 during the Crimean War. The siege of Sevastopol had so far been a bloody and futile effort, and Thomas Cochrane, the tenth Earl of Dundonald (and model for both C. S. Forester's Horatio Hornblower and Patrick O'Brian's Jack Aubrey) had what he thought was a solution. Cochrane was a foresighted thinker where nautical technology was concerned: he had proposed a saturation bombing ship and a gas warfare ship in 1812 for use against the French, he patented a tunneling shield with Marc Isambard Brunel (father to Isambard Kingdom Brunel), and Cochrane was an early proponent of steamships. In 1854, in response to the negative news from Crimea, he had collaborated with Isambard Kingdom Brunel on the creation of an "armoured land vehicle" for use in the siege of Sevastopol. Together with engineer Henry Bessemer, who had developed a method for spin-stabilized artillery shells, Cochrane and Brunel created a "landrover"—in other words, a working, steam-powered prototypical tank. On 31 April 1855 the landrover was at the forefront of an attack on the city. Unfortunately, as one survivor of the attack wrote in a letter to the *Times of London*, the results were not positive:

But, alas! what misery awaited us. The landrover was emitting a perfect hailstorm of grape, canister, round shot, shell, and bullets, the Bessemer rockets in particular mangling the Russians in a most frightful manner, and our brave boys were engaged at bayonet range with the Cossacks, who were beginning to melt away in the face of the landrover's fire, when a harsh screaming sound, increasing in vehemence, came from the landrover and struck us numb with horror. Then, with "a mighty and a strong wind," the landrover exploded. Even at head-quarters, two and a-half miles, perhaps, distant, the explosion burst open and broke windows. I, tripped up by one of the thick low scrubby bushes which break our every march, was thrown into the air, but by providence was spared the worst. Men lay on every side of me gashed and torn, cut in two as if by a knife or their bodies doubled up like so many strips of brown paper. Those few survivors fled in a disorderly chaos back up the ravine, our losses distressingly heavy and our spirits low....

Forgotten today, not least because the explosion of the landrover killed so many British soldiers, the landrover gained no small amount of attention at the time. Rani Lakshmi Bai (1835–1858), queen of the Indian state of Jhansi, reportedly began work on a mobile steam-powered version of Tipu's Tiger, a clockwork device showing a tiger devouring a European soldier. But the steam Tiger, if it existed, disappeared when the British sacked Jhansi in 1858. And iterations of the landrover, or at least references to it, regularly appeared for many years in both casebook fiction (see: THE CASEBOOK), such as R. Reid's *Revelations of an Indian Detective* (1885), which claimed that a new version of the landrover was in use against the Thugs, and in penny bloods, either as *deus ex machina* saviors (as in the Kabul climax of the first half of *English Jack Amongst the Afghans; or, The British Flag—Touch It Who Dare!* (see: ENGLISH JACK) or as machines of horror in the Depraved Dreadfuls of the 1860s and 1870s (as, for example, the "unspeakable vehicle" in Lord Manningtree's "special yard" in *Fanny White and Her Friend Jack Rawlings. A Romance of a Young Lady Thief and a Boy Burglar* (circa 1865) (see: FANNY WHITE)).

Regrettably, the next appearance on record of a steam device is even less salutary, or successful, than the Earl of Dundonald's landrover. The Russia of Tsar Alexander II (1818–1881, Tsar from 1855 to 1881) was notoriously cruel, treating Poles (in the 1863 January Uprising), Kazakhs (the 1871 invasion of the country of Ili), and separatist and rebellious Russians (throughout Alexander's reign) with equal brutality. But Alexander, though autocratic, wanted to reform Russia and make it a modern country worthy of comparison with the European powers. Alexander saw the value of modern technology—he modernized and expanded Russia's railway system, among other things—and was struck by the potential of the Earl of Dundonald's landrover. Since the 1850s Russia had been attempting to match European colonial expansion in Asia by annexing parts of China, forcing three treaties on the Chinese government between 1858 and 1860, and in 1871, when the Kazakh country of Ili (northeast of modern Sinkiang) revolted against Chinese rule and declared itself independent, Alexander saw yet another territory which Russia could acquire, as well as an opportunity to create a steam device. He ordered the creation of a steam-powered weapon-carrying vehicle for use in Ili—and with an eye to the constant peasant rebellions he ordered it made into the shape of something which Russian peasants would reflexively fear: the hut of Baba Yaga, the cannibalistic witch of Russian folklore.

The Russian conquest of Ili was quick and thorough, but the steam device was a failure: with all the will in the world, Russian engineers could not make a steam-powered vehicle which would both walk and carry artillery. Reportedly Alexander was furious at the device's failure. However, Russian revolutionary activists believed that the problem was not with the concept but with the shape of the vehicle, and like Alexander saw the potential battlefield utility of a steam vehicle.

In the early 1870s the peasants of Chyhyryn, in the central Ukraine, revolted against a proposed land reallocation program. The revolt was more passive than active and was rarely violent, but revolutionary activists saw the potential in it—the peasants of Chyhyryn were the descendants of Cossacks and could be relied upon to revert to their Cossack roots, given the right impetus. Iakov Stevanovich, organizer of the "Secret Druzhina" uprising in Chyhyryn, later wrote in his *The Chyhyryn Affair* (1881):

The primary task I set myself was injecting a revolutionary element into this dumb protest. It was in the guise of a peasant from Kherson Province that I first became acquainted with Lazar Tenenik. After several meetings with him, I let him know that I had something important to impart. His interest caught, he asked, "Tell me, good fellow, is it good or evil you bring for us?" I explained that I brought special plans which would allow the muzhiks to build a weapon which would allow them to defy the authorities....

Stevanovich does not go into detail about the weapon, and contemporary accounts of what happened in Chyhyryn are vague. A *Times of London* article from 14 May 1877 says only:

A telegram from Odessa states that the Cossacks of Chyhyryn, north of Odessa, attacked a posse of rural police. The body of Cossack peasants offered resistance to a squadron of dragoons, who thereupon charged them. An explosion of unknown origin killed several dozen on both sides.

But tradition has it that Stevanovich's "weapon" was steam vehicles in the shape of horses, designed to ignite the imagination of the Cossacks of Chyhyryn and give them an advantage against the government troops.

Failures like Stevanovich's steam horses, the mechanical ostrich of the 1880s, and Archibald Campion's abortive robot soldier in 1893 did not stop the major powers of the world from trying to make the Earl of Dundonald's concept a working reality. These attempts were also failures, but far more damaging ones. Japan, Russia, France, and Great Britain all saw the Boxer Rebellion as an ideal situation for testing new steam devices. As French novelist and journalist Pierre Loti described in *Les Derniers Jours de Pékin* (1902), these devices failed catastrophically:

> The wall of Pekin dwarfs us. It is Ozymandian in scale, a dead black in the bleak light of a snowy autumn morning. No witnesses as we approach the city, not one, our only escort the rows of the Chinese dead, left where they fell. Ravaged, lifeless earth along the walls; the ground churned, sinister with ashes, with still-smouldering machines, what is left of human bodies. Only crows, attending to the bodies, salute us with their deathly cawing. The dogs had already eaten their fill.
>
> The triple gates, once five storeys high, impregnable, now shapeless broken stumps torn by Allied machinery, now house-high piles of brick being slowly buried beneath the ash and snow. Our horses' hooves disappear into the coal-black dust, which blinds and coats all in spite of the rain and the snowflakes which sting our faces.
>
> Silently, as though we were riding upon felt, we pass under the broken arches and enter a land of ruin and ashes. Allied sentries, and a few squalid beggars shivering in corners. That is all. Hushed solitude inside the walls. Nothing but rubbish and smoke. Little gray bricks, the sole material of which Pekin was built, scattered in myriads. A city of small low houses adorned with gilded wooded lacework, a city of which only a mass of queer debris is left. Fire and shell and Allied machinery have reduced the tidy order of Pekin to chaos and abomination.
>
> We enter the city at the Tartar quarter, where there was the fiercest fighting—it contained the European legations. Legation Street and Ha Ta Men Avenue may still be discerned from this endless labyrinth of smoking ruin, but Pekin's former decorous order is now a chaos of shattered brick, human remains, and what is left of the Allied machinery.

All is gray or black. The gloomy, silent monotony which follows every apocalyptic fire is broken only by the rare glimpse of porcelain or cloisonné peeking through the eternal ash.

After a few hundred meters we enter Legation Street, the focus of the whole world's anxious attention for so many months. Everything is in ruins, much still smoking, the Russian "Yaga hut" device leaning against one wall, its iron chicken legs all that remains of the mobile gun platform. In an inner square near a chapel is what is left of the Japanese "Archer Boy." Only the end of its bow is visible, all else destroyed or submerged beneath the universal little gray bricks

We finally dismount at the entrance of the French Legation. All around us are piles of rubbish and Chinese corpses not yet carried away. The Legation walls are so pierced with balls that one wonders they still stand. The rubble to our right is the Legation proper, destroyed by the crash of our *Fusil Aerienne*. At our left is the Chancellor's home, where the defenders took refuge during the siege, because it was in a less-exposed situation. Few survived the explosion of the British "Nelson" vehicle.

Tanglefoot
(A Clockwork Century Story)

Cherie Priest

CHERIE PRIEST is the author of seven novels from Tor and Subterranean Press, including the Nebula award nominee *Boneshaker*, *Dreadful Skin*, and the Eden Moore trilogy. Her short stories and nonfiction articles have appeared in such publications as *Weird Tales*, *Subterranean Magazine*, *Publishers Weekly*, and the Stoker-nominated anthology *Aegri Somnia* from Apex. Though she spent most of her life in the southeast, she presently lives in Seattle, Washington, with her husband and a fat black cat. You can find her online at WWW.CHERIEPRIEST.COM. "Tanglefoot" was sparked by an incident in which she and a friend "were chased away from the Waverly Hills Sanitarium by the cops. We knew it wasn't 'open,' which is to say, we'd arrived well after tours of the old hospital had come to a close; but we wanted to take pictures of the building, the grounds outside, and the 'guardians'—an assortment of enormous gargoyles hunkering on the roof, overlooking the front entryway. In our defense, we were only trespassing. It's not like we were breaking and entering."

HUNKERED SHOULDERS AND skinny, bent knees cast a crooked shadow from the back corner of the laboratory, where the old man tried to remember the next step in his formula, or possibly—as Edwin was forced to consider—the scientist simply struggled to recall his own name. On the table against the wall, the once estimable Dr. Archibald Smeeks muttered, spackling his test tubes with spittle and becoming increasingly agitated until Edwin called out, "Doctor?"

And the doctor settled himself, steadying his hands and closing his mouth. He crouched on his stool, cringing away from the boy's voice, and crumpling his over-long work apron with his feet. "Who's there?" he asked.

"Only me, sir."

"Who?"

"Me. It's only...me."

With a startled shudder of recognition he asked, "The orphan?"

"Yes sir. Just the orphan."

Dr. Smeeks turned around, the bottom of his pants twisting in a circle on the smooth wooden seat. He reached to his forehead, where a prodigious set of multi-lensed goggles was perched. From the left side, he tugged a monocle to extend it on a hinged metal arm, and he used it to peer across the room, down onto the floor, where Edwin was sitting cross-legged in a pile of discarded machinery parts.

"Ah," the old doctor said. "There you are, yes. I didn't hear you tinkering, and I only wondered where you might be hiding. Of course, I remember you."

"I believe you do, sir," Edwin said politely. In fact, he very strongly doubted it today, but Dr. Smeeks was trying to appear quite fully aware of his surroundings and it would've been rude to contradict him. "I didn't mean to interrupt your work. You sounded upset. I wanted to ask if everything was all right."

"All right?" Dr. Smeeks returned his monocle to its original position, so that it no longer shrank his fluffy white eyebrow down to a tame and reasonable arch. His wiry goatee quivered as he wondered about his own state. "Oh yes. Everything's quite all right. I think for a moment that I was distracted."

He scooted around on the stool so that he once again faced the cluttered table with its vials, coils, and tiny gray crucibles. His right hand selected a test tube with a hand-lettered label and runny green contents. His left hand reached for a set of tongs, though he set them aside almost immediately in favor of a half-rolled piece of paper that bore the stains and streaks of a hundred unidentifiable splatters.

"Edwin," he said, and Edwin was just short of stunned to hear his name. "Boy, could you join me a moment? I'm afraid I've gone and confused myself."

"Yes sir."

Edwin lived in the basement by the grace of Dr. Smeeks, who had asked the sanitarium for an assistant. These days, the old fellow could not remember requesting such an arrangement and could scarcely confirm or deny it anymore, no matter how often Edwin reminded him.

Therefore Edwin made a point to keep himself useful.

The basement laboratory was a quieter home than the crowded group ward on the top floor, where the children of the patients were kept and raised; and the boy didn't mind the doctor's failing mental state, since what was left of him was kind and often friendly. And sometimes, in a glimmering flash between moments of pitiful bewilderment, Edwin saw the doctor for who he once had been—a brilliant man with a mind that was honored and admired for its flexibility and prowess.

In its way, the Waverly Hills Sanitarium was a testament to his outstanding imagination.

The hospital had incorporated many of the physicians' favorites into the daily routine of the patients, including a kerosene-powered bladed machine that whipped fresh air down the halls to offset the oppressive summer heat. The physicians had also integrated his Moving Mechanical Doors that opened with the push of a switch; and Dr. Smeeks's wonderful Steam-Powered Dish-Cleaning Device was a huge hit in the kitchen. His Sheet-Sorting Slings made him a celebrity in the laundry rooms, and the Sanitary Rotating Manure Chutes had made him a demi-god to the stable-hands.

But half-finished and barely finished inventions littered every corner and covered every table in the basement, where the famed and elderly genius lived out the last of his years.

So long as he did not remember how much he'd forgotten, he appeared content.

Edwin approached the doctor's side and peered dutifully at the stained schematics on the discolored piece of linen paper. "It's coming along nicely, sir," he said.

For a moment Dr. Smeeks did not reply. He was staring down hard at the sheet, trying to make it tell him something, and accusing it of secrets. Then he said, "I'm forced to agree with you, lad. Could you tell me, what is it I was working on? Suddenly…suddenly the numbers aren't speaking to me. Which project was I addressing, do you know?"

"These are the notes for your Therapeutic Bath Appliance. Those numbers to the right are your guesses for the most healthful solution of water, salt, and lavender. You were collecting lemongrass."

"Lemongrass? I was going to put that in the water? Whatever would've possessed me to do such a thing?" he asked, baffled by his own processes. He'd only drawn the notes a day or two before.

Edwin was a good student, even when Dr. Smeeks was a feeble teacher. He prompted the old fellow as gently as he could. "You'd been reading about Dr. Kellogg's hydrotherapy treatments in Battle Creek, and you felt you could improve on them."

"Battle Creek, yes. The sanitarium there. Good Christian folks. They keep a strict diet; it seems to work well for the patients, or so the literature on the subject tells me. But yes," he said more strongly. "Yes, I remember. There must be a more efficient way to warm the water, and make it more pleasing to the senses. The soothing qualities of lavender have been documented for thousands of years, and its antiseptic properties should help keep the water fresh." He turned to Edwin and asked, with the lamplight flickering in his lenses, "Doesn't it sound nice?"

"I don't really like to take baths," the boy confessed. "But if the water was warm and it smelled real nice, I think I'd like it better."

Dr. Smeeks made a little shrug and said, "It'd be less for the purposes of cleanliness and more for the therapy of the inmates here. Some of the more restless or violent ones, you understand."

"Yes sir."

"And how's your mother?" the doctor asked. "Has she responded well to treatment? I heard her coughing last night, and I was wondering if I couldn't concoct a syrup that might give her comfort."

Edwin said, "She wasn't coughing last night. You must've heard someone else."

"Perhaps you're right. Perhaps it was Mrs.... What's her name? The heavy nurse with the northern accent?"

"Mrs. Criddle."

"That's her, yes. That's the one. I hope she isn't contracting the consumption she works so very hard to treat." He returned his attention to the notes and lines on the brittle sheet before him.

Edwin did not tell Dr. Smeeks, for the fifth or sixth time, that his mother had been dead for months; and he did not mention that Mrs. Criddle's accent had come with her from New Orleans. He'd learned that it was easier to agree, and probably kinder to agree.

It became apparent that the old man's attention had been reabsorbed by his paperwork and test tubes, so Edwin returned to his stack of mechanical refuse. He was almost eleven years old, and he'd lived in the basement with the doctor for nearly two years. In that time, he'd learned quite a lot about how a carefully fitted gear can turn, and how a pinpoint-sharp mind can rust; and he took what scraps he wanted to build his own toys, trinkets, and machines. After all, it was half the pleasure and privilege of living away from the other children—he could help himself to anything the doctor did not immediately require.

He didn't like the other children much, and the feeling was mutual.

The other offspring of the unfortunate residents were loud and frantic. They believed Edwin was aloof when he was only thoughtful, and they treated him badly when he wished to be left alone.

All things considered, a cot beside a boiler in a room full of metal and chemicals was a significant step up in the world. And the fractured mind of the gentle old man was more companionable by far than the boys and girls who baked themselves daily on the roof, playing ball and beating one another while the orderlies weren't looking.

Even so, Edwin had long suspected he could do better. Maybe he couldn't *find* better, but he was increasingly confident that he could *make* better.

He turned a pair of old bolts over in his palm and concluded that they were solid enough beneath their grime that a bit of sandpaper would restore their luster and usefulness. All the gears and coils he needed were already stashed and assembled, but some details yet eluded him and his new friend was not quite finished.

Not until it boasted the finer angles of a human face.

Already Edwin had bartered a bit of the doctor's throat remedy to a taxidermist, an act which gained him two brown eyes meant for a badger. Instead, these eyes were fitted in a pounded brass mask with a cut strip of tin that made a sloping nose.

The face was coming together. But the bottom jaw was not connected, so the facsimile was not yet whole.

Edwin held the bolts up to his eye to inspect their threadings, and he decided that they would suffice. "These will work," he said to himself.

Back at the table the doctor asked, "Hmm?"

"Nothing, sir. I'm going to go back to my cot and tinker."

"Very good then. Enjoy yourself, Parker. Summon me if you need an extra hand," he said, because that's what he always said when Edwin announced that he intended to try his own small hands at inventing.

Parker was the youngest son of Dr. and Mrs. Smeeks. Edwin had seen him once, when he'd come to visit a year before at Christmas. The thin man with a fretful face had brought a box of clean, new vials and a large pad of lined paper, plus a gas-powered burner that had been made in Germany. But his father's confusion was too much for him. He'd left, and he hadn't returned.

So if Dr. Smeeks wanted to call Edwin "Parker" once in a while, that was fine. Like Parker himself, Edwin was also thin, with a face marked by worry beyond his years; and Edwin was also handy with pencils, screwdrivers, and wrenches. The boy figured that the misunderstanding was understandable, if unfortunate, and he learned to answer to the other name when it was used to call him.

He took his old bolts back to his cot and picked up a tiny triangle of sandpaper.

Beside him, at the foot of his cot underneath the wool blanket, lay a lump in the shape of a boy perhaps half Edwin's size. The lump was not a doll but an automaton, ready to wind, but not wound yet—not until it had a proper face, with a proper jaw.

When the bolts were as clean as the day they were cast, Edwin placed them gently on his pillow and reached inside the hatbox Mrs. Williams had given him. He withdrew the steel jawbone and examined it, comparing it against the bolts and deciding that the fit was satisfactory; and then he uncovered the boy-shaped lump.

"Good heavens, Edwin. What have you got there?"

Edwin jumped. The old scientist could be uncannily quiet, and he could not always be trusted to stick to his own business. Nervously, as if the automaton were something to be ashamed of, the boy said, "Sir, it's…a machine. I made a machine, I think. It's not a doll," he clarified.

And Dr. Smeeks said, "I can see that it's not a doll. You made this?"

"Yes sir. Just with odds and ends—things you weren't using. I hope you don't mind."

"Mind? No. I don't mind. Dear boy, it's exceptional!" he said with what sounded like honest wonder and appreciation. It also sounded lucid, and focused, and Edwin was charmed to hear it.

The boy asked, "You think it's good?"

"I think it must be. How does it work? Do you crank it, or—"

"It winds up." He rolled the automaton over onto its back and pointed at a hole that was barely large enough to hold a pencil. "One of your old hex wrenches will do it."

Dr. Smeeks turned the small machine over again, looking into the tangle of gears and loosely fixed coils where the brains would be. He touched its oiled joints and the clever little pistons that must surely work for muscles. He asked, "When you wind it, what does it do?"

Edwin faltered. "Sir, I…I don't know. I haven't wound him yet."

"Haven't wound him—well, I suppose that's excuse enough. I see that you've taken my jar-lids for kneecaps, and that's well and good. It's a good fit. He's made to walk a bit, isn't he?"

"He ought to be able to walk, but I don't think he can climb stairs. I haven't tested him. I was waiting until I finished his face." He held up the metal jawbone in one hand and the two shiny bolts in the other. "I'm almost done."

"Do it then!" Dr. Smeeks exclaimed. He clapped his hands together and said, "How exciting! It's your first invention, isn't it?"

"Yes sir," Edwin fibbed. He neglected to remind the doctor of his work on the Picky Boy Plate with a secret chamber to hide unwanted and uneaten food until it was safe to discreetly dispose of it. He did not mention his tireless pursuit and eventual production of the Automatic Expanding Shoe, for use by quickly growing children whose parents were too poor to routinely purchase more footwear.

"Go on," the doctor urged. "Do you mind if I observe? I'm always happy to watch the success of a fellow colleague."

Edwin blushed warmly across the back of his neck. He said, "No sir, and thank you. Here, if you could hold him for me—like that, on your legs, yes. I'll take the bolts and…" with trembling fingers he fastened the final hardware and dabbed the creases with oil from a half-empty can.

And he was finished.

Edwin took the automaton from Dr. Smeeks and stood it upright on the floor, where the machine did not wobble or topple, but stood fast and gazed blankly wherever its face was pointed.

The doctor said, "It's a handsome machine you've made. What does it do again? I think you said, but I don't recall."

"I still need to wind it," Edwin told him. "I need an L-shaped key. Do you have one?"

Dr. Smeeks jammed his hands into the baggy depths of his pockets and a great jangling noise declared the assorted contents. After a few seconds of fishing he withdrew a hex, but seeing that it was too large, he tossed it aside and dug for another one. "Will this work?"

"It ought to. Let me see."

Edwin inserted the newer, smaller stick into the hole and gave it a twist. Within the automaton springs tightened, coils contracted, and gears clicked together. Encouraged, the boy gave the wrench another turn, and then another.

It felt as if he'd spent forever winding, when finally he could twist no further. The automaton's internal workings resisted, and could not be persuaded to wind another inch.

The boy removed the hex key and stood up straight. On the automaton's back, behind the place where its left shoulder blade ought to be, there was a sliding switch. Edwin put his finger to it and gave the switch a tiny shove.

Down in the machine's belly, something small began to whir.

Edwin and the doctor watched with delight as the clockwork boy's arms lifted and went back down to its sides. One leg rose at a time, and each was returned to the floor in a charming parody of marching-in-place. Its bolt-work neck turned from left to right, causing its tinted glass eyes to sweep the room.

"It works!" The doctor slapped Edwin on the back. "Parker, I swear—you've done a good thing. It's a most excellent job, and with what? My leftovers, is that what you said?"

"Yes sir, that's what I said. You remembered!"

"Of course I remembered. I remember you," Dr. Smeeks said. "What will you call your new toy?"

"He's my new friend. And I'm going to call him…Ted."

"Ted?"

"Ted." He did not explain that he'd once had a baby brother named Theodore, or that Theodore had died before his first birthday. This was something different, and anyway it didn't matter what he told Dr. Smeeks, who wouldn't long recall it.

"Well he's very fine. Very fine indeed," said the doctor. "You should take him upstairs and show him to Mrs. Criddle and Mrs. Williams. Oh—you should absolutely show him to your mother. I think she'll be pleased."

"Yes sir. I will, sir."

"Your mother will be proud, and I will be proud. You're learning so much, so fast. One day, I think, you should go to school. A bright boy like you shouldn't hide in basements with old men like me. A head like yours is a commodity, son. It's not a thing to be lightly wasted."

To emphasize his point, he ruffled Edwin's hair as he walked away.

Edwin sat on the edge of his cot, which brought him to eye-level with his creation. He said, "Ted?"

Ted's jaw opened and closed with a metallic clack, but the mechanical child had no lungs, nor lips, and it did not speak.

The flesh-and-blood boy picked up Ted and carried him carefully under his arm, up the stairs and into the main body of the Waverly Hills Sanitarium. The first-floor offices and corridors were mostly safe, and mostly empty—or populated by the bustling, concentrating men with clipboards and glasses, and very bland smiles that recognized Edwin without caring that he was present.

The sanitarium was very new. Some of its halls were freshly built and still stinking of mortar and the dust of construction. Its top-floor rooms reeked faintly of paint and lead, as well as the medicines and bandages of the ill and the mad.

Edwin avoided the top floors where the other children lived, and he avoided the wards of the men who were kept in jackets and chains. He also avoided the sick wards, where the mad men and women were tended to.

Mrs. Criddle and Mrs. Williams worked in the kitchen and laundry, respectively; and they looked like sisters though they were not, in fact, related. Both were women of a stout and purposeful build, with great tangles of graying hair tied up in buns and covered in sanitary hair caps; and both women were the mothering sort who were stern with patients, but kind to the hapless orphans who milled from floor to floor when they weren't organized and contained on the roof.

Edwin found Mrs. Criddle first, working a paddle through a metal vat of mashed potatoes that was large enough to hold the boy, Ted, and a third friend of comparable size. Her wide bottom rocked from side to side in time with the sweep of her elbows as she stirred the vat, humming to herself.

"Mrs. Criddle?"

She ceased her stirring. "Mm. Yes dear?"

"It's Edwin, ma'am."

"Of course it is!" She leaned the paddle against the side of the vat and flipped a lever to lower the fire. "Hello there, boy. It's not time for supper, but what have you got there?"

He held Ted forward so she could inspect his new invention. "His name is Ted. I made him."

"Ted, ah yes. Ted. That's a good name for…for…a new friend."

"That's right!" Edwin brightened. "He's my new friend. Watch, he can walk. Look at what he can do."

He pressed the switch and the clockwork boy marched in place, and then staggered forward, catching itself with every step and clattering with every bend of its knees. Ted moved forward until it knocked its forehead on the leg of a counter, then stopped, and turned to the left to continue soldiering onward.

"Would you look at that?" Mrs. Criddle said with the awe of a woman who had no notion of how her own stove worked, much less anything else. "That's amazing, is what it is. He just turned around like that, just like he knew!"

"He's automatic," Edwin said, as if this explained everything.

"Automatic indeed. Very nice, love. But Mr. Bird and Miss Emmie will be here in a few minutes, and the kitchen will be a busy place for a boy and his new friend. You'd best take him back downstairs."

"First I want to go show Mrs. Williams."

Mrs. Criddle shook her head. "Oh no, dear. I think you'd better not. She's upstairs, with the other boys and girls, and well, I suppose you know. I think you're better off down with Dr. Smeeks."

Edwin sighed. "If I take him upstairs, they'll only break him, won't they?"

"I think they're likely to try."

"All right," he agreed, and gathered Ted up under his arm.

"Come back in another hour, will you? You can get your own supper and carry the doctor's while you're at it."

"Yes ma'am. I will."

He retreated back down the pristine corridors and dodged between two empty gurneys, back down the stairs that would return him to the safety of the doctor, the laboratory, and his own cot. He made his descent quietly, so as not to disturb the doctor in case he was still working.

When Edwin peeked around the bottom corner, he saw the old scientist sitting on his stool once more, a wadded piece of linen paper crushed in his fist. A spilled test tube leaked runny gray liquid across the counter's top, and made a dark stain across the doctor's pants.

Over and over to himself he mumbled, "Wasn't the lavender. Wasn't the…it was only the…I saw the…I don't…I can't…where was the paper? Where were the plans? What was the plan? What?"

The shadow of Edwin's head crept across the wall and when the doctor spotted it, he stopped himself and sat up straighter. "Parker, I've had a little bit of an accident. I've made a little bit of a mess."

"Do you need any help, sir?"

"Help? I suppose I don't. If I only knew…if I could only remember." The doctor slid down off the stool, stumbling as his foot clipped the seat's bottom rung. "Parker? Where's the window? Didn't we have a window?"

"Sir," Edwin said, taking the old man's arm and guiding him over to his bed, in a nook at the far end of the laboratory. "Sir, I think you should lie down. Mrs. Criddle says supper comes in an hour. You just lie down, and I'll bring it to you when it's ready."

"Supper?" The many-lensed goggles he wore atop his head slid, and their strap came down over his left eye.

He sat Dr. Smeeks on the edge of his bed and removed the man's shoes, then his eyewear. He placed everything neatly beside the feather mattress and pulled the doctor's pillow to meet his downward-drooping head.

Edwin repeated, "I'll bring you supper when it's ready," but Dr. Smeeks was already asleep.

And in the laboratory, over by the stairs, the whirring and clicking of a clockwork boy was clattering itself in circles, or so Edwin assumed. He couldn't remember, had he left Ted on the stairs? He could've sworn he'd pressed the switch to deactivate his friend. But perhaps he hadn't.

Regardless, he didn't want the machine bounding clumsily around in the laboratory—not in that cluttered place piled with glass and gadgets.

Over his shoulder Edwin glanced, and saw the doctor snoozing lightly in his nook; and out in the laboratory, knocking its jar-lid knees against the bottom step, Ted had gone nowhere, and harmed nothing. Edwin picked Ted up and held the creation to his face, gazing into the glass badger-eyes as if they might blink back at him.

He said, "You're my friend, aren't you? Everybody makes friends. I just made you for *real.*"

Ted's jaw creaked down, opening its mouth so that Edwin could stare straight inside, at the springs and levers that made the toy boy move. Then its jaw retracted, and without a word, Ted had said its piece.

After supper, which Dr. Smeeks scarcely touched, and after an hour spent in the laundry room sharing Ted with Mrs. Williams, Edwin retreated to his cot and blew out the candle beside it. The cot wasn't wide enough for Edwin and Ted to rest side-by-side, but Ted fit snugly between the wall and the bedding and Edwin left the machine there, to pass the night.

But the night did not pass fitfully.

First Edwin awakened to hear the doctor snuffling in his sleep, muttering about the peril of inadequate testing; and when the old man finally sank back into a fuller sleep, Edwin nearly followed him. Down in the basement there were no lights except for the dim, bioluminescent glow of living solutions in blown-glass beakers—and the simmering wick of a hurricane lamp turned down low, but left alight enough for the boy to see his way to the privy if the urge struck him before dawn.

Here and there the bubble of an abandoned mixture seeped fizzily through a tube, and when Dr. Smeeks slept deeply enough to cease his ramblings, there was little noise to disturb anyone.

Even upstairs, when the wee hours came, most of the inmates and patients of the sanitarium were quiet—if not by their own cycles, then by the laudanum spooned down their throats before the shades were drawn.

Edwin lay on his back, his eyes closed against the faint, blue and green glows from the laboratory, and he waited for slumber to call him again. He reached to his left, to the spot between his cot and the wall. He patted the small slip of space there, feeling for a manufactured arm or leg, and finding Ted's cool, unmoving form. And although there was scarcely any room, he pulled Ted out of the slot and tugged the clockwork boy into the cot after all, because doll or no, Ted was a comforting thing to hold.

Morning came, and the doctor was already awake when Edwin rose.

"Good morning, sir."

"Good morning, Edwin," the doctor replied without looking over his shoulder. On their first exchange of the day, he'd remembered the right name. Edwin tried to take it as a sign that today would be a good day, and Dr. Smeeks would mostly remain Dr. Smeeks—without toppling into the befuddled tangle of fractured thoughts and faulty recollections.

He was standing by the hurricane lamp, with its wick trimmed higher so that he could read. An envelope was opened and discarded beside him.

"Is it a letter?" Edwin asked.

The doctor didn't sound happy when he replied, "It's a letter indeed."

"Is something wrong?"

"It depends." Dr. Smeeks folded the letter. "It's a man who wants me to work for him."

"That might be good," Edwin said.

"No. Not from this man."

The boy asked, "You know him?"

"I do. And I do not care for his aims. I will not help him," he said firmly. "Not with his terrible quests for terrible weapons. I don't do those things anymore. I haven't done them for years."

"You used to make weapons? Like guns, and cannons?"

Dr. Smeeks said, "Once upon a time." And he said it sadly. "But no more. And if Ossian thinks he can bribe or bully me, he has another thing coming. Worst comes to worst, I suppose, I can plead a failing mind."

Edwin felt like he ought to object as a matter of politeness, but when he said, "Sir," the doctor waved his hand to stop whatever else the boy might add.

"Don't, Parker. I know why I'm here. I know things, even when I can't always quite remember them. But my old colleague says he intends to pay me a visit, and he can pay me all the visits he likes. He can offer to pay me all the Union money he likes, too—or Confederate money, or any other kind. I won't make such terrible things, not anymore."

He folded the letter in half and struck a match to light a candle. He held one corner of the letter over the candle and let it burn, until there was nothing left but the scrap between his fingertips—and then he released it, letting the smoldering flame turn even the last of the paper to ash.

"Perhaps he'll catch me on a bad day, do you think? As likely as not, there will be no need for subterfuge."

Edwin wanted to contribute, and he felt the drive to communicate with the doctor while communicating seemed possible. He said, "You should tell him to come in the afternoon. I hope you don't mind me saying so, sir, but you seem much clearer in the mornings."

"Is that a fact?" he asked, an eyebrow lifted aloft by genuine interest. "I'll take your word for it, I suppose. Lord knows I'm in no position to argue. Is that…that noise…what's that noise? It's coming from your cot. Oh dear, I hope we haven't got a rat."

Edwin declared, "Oh no!" as a protest, not as an exclamation of worry. "No, sir. That's just Ted. I must've switched him on when I got up."

"Ted? What's a Ted?"

"It's my…" Edwin almost regretted what he'd said before, about mornings and clarity. "It's my new friend. I made him."

"There's a friend in your bunk? That doesn't seem too proper."

"No, he's…I'll show you."

And once again they played the scene of discovery together—the doctor clapping Edwin on the back and ruffling his hair, and announcing that the automaton was a fine invention indeed. Edwin worked very hard to disguise his disappointment.

Finally Dr. Smeeks suggested that Edwin run to the washrooms upstairs and freshen himself to begin the day, and Edwin agreed.

The boy took his spring-and-gear companion along as he navigated the corridors while the doctors and nurses made their morning rounds. Dr. Havisham paused to examine Ted and declare the creation "outstanding." Dr. Martin did likewise, and Nurse Evelyn offered him a peppermint sweet for being such an innovative youngster who never made any trouble.

Edwin cleaned his hands and face in one of the cold white basins in the washroom, where staff members and some of the more stable patients were allowed to refresh themselves. He set Ted on the countertop and pressed the automaton's switch. While Edwin cleaned the night off his skin, Ted's legs kicked a friendly time against the counter and its jaw bobbed like it was singing or chatting, or imagining splashing its feet in the basin.

When he was clean, Edwin set Ted on the floor and decided that—rather than carrying the automaton—he would simply let it walk the corridor until they reached the stairs to the basement.

The peculiar pair drew more than a few exclamations and stares, but Edwin was proud of Ted and he enjoyed the extended opportunity to show off.

Before the stairs and at the edge of the corridor where Edwin wasn't supposed to go, for fear of the violent inmates, a red-haired woman blocked his way. If her plain cotton gown hadn't marked her as a resident, the wildness around the corners of her eyes would've declared it well enough. There were red stripes on her skin where restraints were sometimes placed, and her feet were bare, leaving moist, sweaty prints on the black and white tiles.

"Madeline," Dr. Simmons warned. "Madeline, it's time to return to your room."

But Madeline's eyes were locked on the humming, marching automaton. She asked with a voice too girlish for her height, "What's that?" and she did not budge, even when the doctor took her arm and signaled quietly for an orderly.

Edwin didn't mind answering. He said, "His name is Ted. I made him."

"Ted." She chewed on the name and said, "Ted for *now*."

Edwin frowned and asked, "What?"

He did not notice that Ted had stopped marching, or that Ted's metal face was gazing up at Madeline. The clockwork boy had wound itself down, or maybe it was only listening.

Madeline did not blink at all, and perhaps she never did. She said, "He's your Ted for now, but you must watch him." She held out a pointing, directing, accusing finger and aimed it at Edwin, then at Ted. "Such empty children are vulnerable."

Edwin was forced to confess, or simply make a point of saying, "Miss, he's only a machine."

She nodded. "Yes, but he's your boy, and he has no soul. There are things who would change that, and change it badly."

"I know I shouldn't take him upstairs," Edwin said carefully. "I know I ought to keep him away from the other boys."

Madeline shook her head, and the matted crimson curls swayed around her face. "Not what I mean, boy. *Invisible* things. Bad little souls that need bodies."

An orderly arrived. He was a big, square man with shoulders like an ox's yoke. His uniform was white, except for a streak of blood that was drying to brown. He took Madeline by one arm, more roughly than he needed to.

As Madeline was pulled away, back to her room or back to her restraints, she kept her eyes on Edwin and Ted, and she warned him still, waving her finger like a wand, "Keep him close, unless you want him stolen from you—unless you want his clockwork heart replaced with something stranger."

And before she was removed from the corridor altogether, she lashed out one last time with her one free hand to seize the wall's corner. It bought her another few seconds of eye contact—just enough to add, "Watch him close!"

Then she was gone.

Edwin reached for Ted and pulled the automaton to his chest, where its gear-driven heart clicked quietly against the real boy's shirt. Ted's mechanical jaw opened and closed, not biting but mumbling in the crook of Edwin's neck.

"I will," he promised. "I'll watch him close."

Several days passed quietly, except for the occasional frustrated rages of the senile doctor, and Ted's company was a welcome diversion—if a somewhat unusual one. Though Edwin had designed Ted's insides and stuffed the gears and coils himself, the automaton's behavior was not altogether predictable.

Mostly, Ted remained a quiet little toy with the marching feet that tripped at stairs, at shoes, or at any other obstacle left on the floor.

And if the clockwork character fell, it fell like a turtle and laid where it collapsed, arms and legs twitching impotently at the air until Edwin would come and set his friend upright. Several times Edwin unhooked Ted's back panel, wondering precisely why the shut-off switch failed so often. But he never found any stretched spring or faulty coil to account for it. If he asked Ted, purely to speculate aloud, Ted's shiny jaw would lower and lift, answering with the routine and rhythmic clicks of its agreeable guts.

But sometimes, if Edwin listened very hard, he could almost convince himself he heard words rattling around inside Ted's chest. Even if it was only the echoing pings and chimes of metal moving metal, the boy's eager ears would concentrate, and listen for whispers.

Once, he was nearly certain—practically *positive*—that Ted had said its own name. And that was silly, wasn't it? No matter how much Edwin wanted to believe, he knew better…which did not stop him from wondering.

It was always Edwin's job to bring meals down from the kitchen, and every time he climbed the stairs he made a point to secure Ted by turning it off and leaving it lying on its back, on Edwin's cot. The doctor was doddering, and even unobstructed he sometimes stumbled on his own two feet, or the laces of his shoes.

So when the boy went for breakfast and returned to the laboratory with a pair of steaming meals on a covered tray, he was surprised to hear the whirring of gears and springs.

"Ted?" he called out, and then felt strange for it. "Doctor?" he tried instead, and he heard the old man muttering.

"Doctor, are you looking at Ted? You remember him, don't you? Please don't break him."

At the bottom of the stairs, Dr. Smeeks was crouched over the prone and kicking Ted. The doctor said, "Underfoot, this thing is. Did it on purpose. I saw it. Turned itself on, sat itself up, and here it comes."

But Edwin didn't think the doctor was speaking to him. He was only speaking, and poking at Ted with a pencil like a boy prods an anthill.

"Sir? I turned him off, and I'm sorry if he turned himself on again. I'm not sure why it happens."

"Because it wants to be *on*," the doctor said firmly, and finally made eye contact. "It wants to make me fall, it practically told me so."

"Ted never says anything," Edwin said weakly. "He can't talk."

"He can talk. You can't hear him. But *I* can hear him. I've heard him before, and he used to say pleasant things. He used to hum his name. Now he fusses and mutters like a demented old man. Yes," he insisted, his eyes bugged and his eyebrows bushily hiked up his forehead. "Yes, this thing, when it mutters, it sounds like *me.*"

Edwin had another theory about the voices Dr. Smeeks occasionally heard, but he kept it to himself. "Sir, he cannot talk. He hasn't got any lungs, or a tongue. Sir, I promise, he cannot speak."

The doctor stood, and gazed down warily as Ted floundered. "He cannot flip his own switches either, yet he *does.*"

Edwin retrieved his friend and set it back on its little marching feet. "I must've done something wrong when I built him. I'll try and fix it, sir. I'll make him stop it."

"Dear boy, I don't believe you *can.*"

The doctor straightened himself and adjusted his lenses—a different pair, a set that Edwin had never seen before. He turned away from the boy and the automaton and reached for his paperwork again, saying, "Something smells good. Did you get breakfast?"

"Yes sir. Eggs and grits, with sausage."

He was suddenly cheerful. "Wonderful! Won't you join me here? I'll clear you a spot."

As he did so, Edwin moved the tray to the open space on the main laboratory table and removed the tray's lid, revealing two sets of silverware and two plates loaded with food. He set one in front of the doctor, and took one for himself, and they ate with the kind of chatter that told Edwin Dr. Smeeks had already forgotten about his complaint with Ted.

As for Ted, the automaton stood still at the foot of the stairs—its face cocked at an angle that suggested it might be listening, or watching, or paying attention to something that no one else could see.

Edwin wouldn't have liked to admit it, but when he glanced back at his friend, he felt a pang of unease. Nothing had changed and everything was fine; he was letting the doctor's rattled mood unsettle him, that was all. Nothing had changed and everything was fine; but Ted was not marching and its arms were not swaying, and the switch behind the machine's small shoulder was still set in the "on" position.

When the meal was finished and Edwin had gathered the empty plates to return them upstairs, he stopped by Ted and flipped the switch to the state of "off." "You must've run down your winding," he said. "That must be why you stopped moving."

Then he called, "Doctor? I'm running upstairs to give these to Mrs. Criddle. I've turned Ted off, so he shouldn't bother you, but keep an eye out, just in case. Maybe," he said, balancing the tray on his crooked arm, "if you wanted to, you could open him up yourself and see if you can't fix him."

Dr. Smeeks didn't answer, and Edwin left him alone—only for a few minutes, only long enough to return the tray with its plates and cutlery.

It was long enough to return to strangeness.

Back in the laboratory Edwin found the doctor backed into a corner, holding a screwdriver and a large pair of scissors. Ted was seated on the edge of the laboratory table, its legs dangling over the side, unmoving, unmarching. The doctor looked alert and lucid—moreso than usual—and he did not quite look afraid. Shadows from the burners and beakers with their tiny glowing creatures made Dr. Smeeks look sinister and defensive, for the flickering bits of flame winked reflections off the edge of his scissors.

"Doctor?"

"I was only going to fix him, like you said."

"Doctor, it's all right."

The doctor said, "No, I don't believe it's all right, not at all. That nasty little thing, Parker, I don't like it." He shook his head, and the lenses across his eyes rattled in their frames.

"But he's my friend."

"He's no friend of *mine.*"

Edwin held his hands up, like he was trying to calm a startled horse. "Dr. Smeeks, I'll take him. I'll fix him, you don't have to do it. He's only a machine, you know. Just an invention. He can't hurt you."

"He tried."

"Sir, I really don't think—"

"He tried to bite me. Could've taken my fingers off, if I'd caught them in that bear-trap of a face. You keep it away from me, Edwin. Keep it away or I'll pull it apart, and turn it into a can opener."

Before Edwin's very own eyes, Ted's head turned with a series of clicks, until the machine fully faced the doctor. And if its eyes had been more than glass bits that were once assigned to a badger, then they might have narrowed or gleamed; but they were only glass bits, and they only cast back the fragments of light from the bright things in the laboratory.

"Ted, come here. Ted, come with me," Edwin said, gently pulling the

 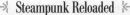

automaton down from the table. "Ted, no one's going to turn you into a can opener. Maybe you got wound funny, or wound too tight," he added, mostly for the doctor's benefit. "I'll open you up and tinker, and you'll be just fine."

Back in the corner the doctor relaxed, and dropped the scissors. He set the screwdriver down beside a row of test tubes and placed both hands down on the table's corner. "Edwin?" he said, so softly that Edwin almost didn't hear him. "Edwin, did we finish breakfast? I don't see my plate."

"Yes sir," the boy swore. He clutched Ted closely, and held the automaton away from the doctor, out of the man's line of sight should he turn around.

"Oh. I suppose that's right," he said, and again Ted had been spared by the doctor's dementia.

Edwin stuck Ted down firmly between the wall and his cot, and for one daft moment he considered binding the machine's feet with twine or wire to keep it from wandering. But the thought drifted out of his head, chased away by the unresponsive lump against the wall. He whispered, "I don't know how you're doing it, but you need to stop. I don't want the doctor to turn you into a can opener."

Then, as a compromise to his thoughts about hobbling the automaton, he dropped his blanket over the thing's head.

Bedtime was awkward that night.

When he reached for the clockwork boy he remembered the slow, calculated turn of the machine's head, and he recalled the blinking bright flashes of firelight in the glass badger-eyes.

The doctor had settled in his nook and was sleeping, and Edwin was still awake. He reclaimed his blanket and settled down on his side, facing the wall and facing Ted until he dozed, or he must have dozed. He assumed it was only sleep that made the steel jaw lower and clack; and it was only a dream that made the gears twist and lock into syllables.

"Ted?" Edwin breathed, hearing himself but not recognizing the sound of his own word.

And the clockwork face breathed back, not its own name but something else—something that even in the sleepy state of midnight and calm, Edwin could not understand.

The boy asked in the tiniest whisper he could muster, "Ted?"

Ted's steel jaw worked, and the air in its mouth made the shape of a "No." It said, more distinctly this time, and with greater volume, "Tan...gle...foot."

Edwin closed his eyes, and was surprised to learn that they had not been closed already. He tugged his blanket up under his chin and could not understand why the rustle of the fabric seemed so loud, but not so loud as the clockwork voice.

I must be asleep, he believed.

And then, eventually, he was.

Though not for long.

His sleep was not good. He was too warm, and then too cold, and then something was missing. Through the halls of his nightmares mechanical feet marched to their own tune; in the confined and cluttered space of the laboratory there was movement too large to come from rats, and too deliberate to be the random flipping of a switch.

Edwin awakened and sat upright in the same moment, with the same fluid fear propelling both events.

There was no reason for it, or so he told himself; and this was ridiculous, it was only the old Dr. Smeeks and his slipping mind, infecting the boy with strange stories—turning the child against his only true friend. Edwin shot his fingers over to the wall where Ted ought to be jammed, waiting for its winding and for the sliding of the button on its back.

And he felt only the smooth, faintly damp texture of the painted stone.

His hands flapped and flailed, slapping at the emptiness and the flat, blank wall. "Ted?" he said, too loudly. "Ted?" he cried with even more volume, and he was answered by the short, swift footsteps that couldn't have belonged to the doctor.

From his bed in the nook at the other end of the laboratory, the doctor answered with a groggy groan. "Parker?"

"Yes sir!" Edwin said, because it was close enough. "Sir, there's…" and what could he say? That he feared his friend had become unhinged, and that Ted was fully wound, and roaming?

"What is it, son?"

The doctor's voice came from miles away, at the bottom of a well—or that's how it sounded to Edwin, who untangled himself from the sheets and toppled to the floor. He stopped his fall with his hands, and stood, but then could scarcely walk.

As a matter of necessity he dropped his bottom on the edge of the cot and felt for his feet, where something tight was cinched around his ankles.

There, he found a length of wire bent into a loop and secured.

It hobbled his legs together, cutting his stride in half.

"Parker?" the doctor asked, awakening further but confused. "Boy?"

Edwin forced his voice to project a calm he wasn't feeling. "Sir, stay where you are, unless you have a light. My friend, Ted. He's gotten loose again. I don't want…I don't want you to hurt yourself."

"I can't find my candle."

"I can't find mine either," Edwin admitted. "You stay there. I'll come to you."

But across the floor the marching feet were treading steadily, and the boy had no idea where his automaton had gone. Every sound bounced off glass or wood, or banged around the room from wall to wall; and even the blue-gold shadows cast by the shimmering solutions could not reveal the clockwork boy.

Edwin struggled with the bizarre bind on his legs and stumbled forward regardless of it. No matter how hard his fingers twisted and pulled, the wires only dug into his skin and cut it when he yanked too sharply. He gave up and stepped as wide as he could and found that, if he was careful, he could still walk and even, in half-hops and uneven staggers, he could run.

His light was nowhere to be found, and he gave up on that, too.

"Sir, I'm coming!" he cried out again, since the doctor was awake already and he wanted Ted to think he was aware, and acting. But what could Ted think? Ted was only a collection of cogs and springs.

Edwin remembered the red-haired Madeline with the strap-marks on her wrists. She'd said Ted had no soul, but she'd implied that one might come along.

The darkness baffled him, even in the laboratory he knew by heart. Hobbled as he was, and terrified by the pattering of unnatural feet, the basement's windowless night worked against him and he panicked.

He needed help, but where could it come from?

The orderlies upstairs frightened him in a vague way, as harbingers of physical authority; and the doctors and nurses might think he was as crazy as the other children, wild and loud—or as mad as his mother.

Like Madeline.

Her name tinkled at the edge of his ears, or through the nightmare confusion that moved him in jilting circles. Maybe Madeline knew something he didn't—maybe she could help. She wouldn't make fun of him, at any rate. She wouldn't tell him he was frightened for nothing, and to go back to sleep.

He knew where her room was located; at least he knew of its wing, and he could gather its direction.

The stairs jabbed up sharp and hard against his exploring fingers, and his hands were more free than his feet so he used them to climb—knocking his knees against each angle and bruising his shins with every yard. Along the wall above him there was a handrail someplace, but he couldn't find it so he made do without it.

He crawled so fast that his ascent might have been called a scramble.

He hated to leave the doctor alone down there with Ted, but then again, the doctor had taken up the screwdriver and the scissors once before. Perhaps he could be trusted to defend himself again.

At the top of the stairs Edwin found more light and his eyes were relieved. He stood up, seized the handrail, and fell forward because he'd already forgotten about the wire wrapped around his ankles. His hands stung from the landing, slapping hard against the tile floor, but he picked himself up and began a shuffling run, in tiny skips and dragging leaps down the corridor.

A gurney loomed skeletal and shining in the ambient light from the windows and the moon outside. Edwin fell past it and clipped it with his shoulder. The rattling of its wheels haunted him down the hallway, past the nurse's station where an elderly woman was asleep with a paperback novel lying across her breasts.

She didn't budge, not even when the gurney rolled creakily into the center of the hallway, following in Edwin's wake.

When he reached the right wing, he whispered, "Madeline? Madeline, can you hear me?"

All the windows in the doors to the inmates' rooms were well off the ground and Edwin wasn't tall enough to reach, so he couldn't see inside. He hissed her name from door to door, and eventually she came forward. Her hands wrapped around the bars at the top, coiling around them like small white snakes. She held her face up to the small window and said, "Boy?"

He dashed to the door and pushed himself against it. "Madeline? It's me."

"The boy." Her mouth was held up to the window; she must have been standing on her tip-toes to reach it.

Edwin stood on his tip-toes also, but he couldn't touch the window, high above his head. He said, "I need your help. Something's wrong with Ted."

For a moment he heard only her breathing, rushed and hot above him. Then she said, "Not your Ted any longer. I warned you."

"I know you did!" he said, almost crying. "I need your help! He tied my feet together, all tangled up—and I think he's trying to hurt Dr. Smeeks!"

"Tangled, did he? Oh, that vicious little changeling," she said, almost wheezing with exertion. She let go of whatever was holding her up, and Edwin heard her feet land back on the floor with a thump. She said through the door's frame, beside its hinges, "You must let me out, little boy. If you let me out, I'll come and help your doctor. I know what to do with changelings."

It was a bad thought, and a bad plan. It was a bad thing to consider and Edwin knew it all too well; but when he looked back over his shoulder at the nurse's station with the old lady snoring within, and when he thought of the clattering automaton roaming the laboratory darkness with his dear Dr. Smeeks, he leaped at the prospect of aid.

He reached for the lever to open the door and hung from it, letting it hold his full weight while he reached up to undo the lock.

Edwin no sooner heard the click of the fastener unlatching, then the door burst open in a quick swing that knocked him off his hobbled feet. With a smarting head and bruised elbow he fought to stand again but Madeline grabbed him by the shoulder. She lifted him up as if he were as light as a doll, and she lugged him down the hallway. Her cotton shift billowed dirtily behind her, and her hair slapped Edwin in the eyes as she ran.

Edwin squeezed at her arm, trying to hold himself out of the way of the displaced gurneys and medical trays that clogged the hall; but his airborne feet smacked the window of the nurse's station as Madeline swiftly hauled him past it, awakening the nurse and startling her into motion.

If Madeline noticed, she did not stop to comment.

She reached the top of the stairs and flung herself down them, her feet battering an alternating time so fast that her descent sounded like firecrackers. Edwin banged along behind her, twisted in her grip and unable to move quickly even if she were to set him down.

He wondered if he hadn't made an awful mistake when she all but cast him aside. His body flopped gracelessly against a wall. But he was back on his feet in a moment and there was light in the laboratory—a flickering, uncertain light that was moving like mad.

Dr. Smeeks was holding it; he'd found his light after all, and he'd raised the wick on the hurricane lamp. The glass-jarred lantern gleamed and flashed as he swung it back and forth, sweeping the floor for something Edwin couldn't see.

The doctor cried out, "Parker? Parker? Something's here, something's in the laboratory!"

And Edwin answered, "I know, sir! But I've brought help!"

The light shifted, the hurricane lamp swung, and Madeline was standing in front of the doctor—a blazing figure doused in gold and red, and black-edged shadows. She said nothing, but held out her hand and took the doctor's wrist; she shoved his wrist up, forcing the lamp higher. The illumination increased accordingly and Edwin started to cry.

The laboratory was in a disarray so complete that it might never be restored to order. Glass glimmered in piles of dust, shattered tubes and broken beakers were smeared with the shining residue of the blue-green substance that lived and glowed in the dark. It spilled and died, losing its luminescence with every passing second—and there was the doctor, his hand held aloft and his lamp bathing the chaos with revelation.

Madeline turned away from him, standing close enough beneath the lamp so that her shadow did not temper its light. Her feet twisted on the glass-littered floor, cutting her toes and leaving smears of blood.

She demanded, "Where are you?"

She was answered by the tapping of marching feet, but it was a sound that came from all directions at once. And with it came a whisper, accompanied by the grinding discourse of a metal jaw.

"Tan…gles. Tan…gles…feet. Tanglefoot."

"That's your name then? Little changeling—little Tanglefoot? Come out here!" she fired the command into the corners of the room and let it echo there. "Come out here, and I'll send you back to where you came from! Shame on you, taking a boy's friend. Shame on you, binding his feet and tormenting his master!"

Tanglefoot replied, "Can…op…en…er" as if it explained everything, and Edwin thought that it *might*—but that it was no excuse.

"Ted, where *are* you?" he pleaded, tearing his eyes away from Madeline and scanning the room. Upstairs he could hear the pounding thunder of footsteps—of orderlies and doctors, no doubt, freshly roused by the night nurse in her chamber. Edwin said with a sob, "Madeline, they're coming for you."

She growled, "And I'm coming for *him*."

She spied the automaton in the same second that Edwin saw it—not on the ground, marching its little legs in bumping patterns, but overhead, on a ledge where the doctor kept books. Tanglefoot was marching, yes, but it was marching towards them both with the doctor's enormous scissors clutched between its clamping fingers.

"Ted!" Edwin screamed, and the machine hesitated. The boy did not know why, but there was much he did not know and there were many things he'd never understand…including how Madeline, fierce and barefoot, could move so quickly through the glass.

The madwoman seized the doctor's hurricane lamp by its scalding cover, and Edwin could hear the sizzle of her skin as her fingers touched, and held, and then flung the oil-filled lamp at the oncoming machine with the glittering badger eyes.

The lamp shattered and the room was flooded with brilliance and burning.

Dr. Smeeks shrieked as splatters of flame sprinkled his hair and his nightshirt, but Edwin was there—shuffling fast into the doctor's sleeping nook. The boy grabbed the top blanket and threw it at the doctor, then he joined the blanket and covered the old man, patting him down. When the last spark had been extinguished he left the doctor covered and held him in the corner, hugging the frail, quivering shape against himself while Madeline went to war.

Flames were licking along the books and Madeline's hair was singed. Her shift was pocked with black-edged holes, and she had grabbed the gloves Dr. Smeeks used when he held his crucibles. They were made of asbestos, and they would help her hands.

Tanglefoot was spinning in place, howling above their heads from his fiery perch on the book ledge. It was the loudest sound Edwin had ever heard his improvised friend create, and it horrified him down to his bones.

Someone in a uniform reached the bottom of the stairs and was repulsed, repelled by the blast of fire. He shouted about it, hollering for water. He demanded it as he retreated, and Madeline didn't pay him a fragment of attention.

Tanglefoot's scissors fell to the ground, flung from its distracted hands. The smoldering handles were melting on the floor, making a black, sticky puddle where they settled.

With her gloved hands she scooped them up and stabbed, shoving the blades down into the body of the mobile inferno once named Ted. She withdrew the blades and shoved them down again because the clockwork boy still kicked, and the third time she jammed the scissors into the little body she jerked Ted down off the ledge and flung it to the floor.

The sound of breaking gears and splitting seams joined the popping gasp of the fire as it ate the books and gnawed at the ends of the tables.

"A blanket!" Madeline yelled. "Bring me a blanket!"

Reluctantly, Edwin uncovered the shrouded doctor and wadded the blanket between his hands. He threw the blanket to Madeline.

She caught it, and unwrapped it enough to flap it down atop the hissing machine, and she beat it again and again, smothering the fire as she struck the mechanical boy. Something broke beneath the sheet, and the chewing tongues of flame devoured the cloth that covered Tanglefoot's joints—leaving only a tragic frame beneath the smoldering covers.

Suddenly and harshly, a bucket of water doused Madeline from behind.

Seconds later she was seized.

Edwin tried to intervene. He divided his attention between the doctor, who cowered against the wall, and the madwoman with the bleeding feet and hair that reeked like cooking trash.

He held up his hands and said, "Don't! No, you can't! No, she was only trying to help!" And he tripped over his own feet, and the pile of steaming clockwork parts on the floor. "No," he cried, because he couldn't speak without choking. "No, you can't take her away. Don't hurt her, please. It's my fault."

Dr. Williams was there, and Edwin didn't know when he'd arrived. The smoke was stinging his eyes and the whimpers of Dr. Smeeks were distracting his ears, but there was Dr. Williams, preparing to administer a washcloth soaked in ether to Madeline's face.

Dr. Williams said to his colleague, a burly man who held Madeline's arms behind her back, "I don't know how she escaped this time."

Edwin insisted, "I did it!"

But Madeline gave him a glare and said, "The boy's as daft as his mother. The clockwork boy, it called me, and I destroyed it. I let myself out, like the witch I am and the fiend you think I must be—"

And she might've said more, but the drug slipped up her nostrils and down her chest, and she sagged as she was dragged away.

"No," Edwin gulped. "It isn't fair. Don't hurt her."

No one was listening to him. Not Dr. Smeeks, huddled in a corner. Not Madeline, unconscious and leaving. And not the bundle of burned and smashed parts in a pile beneath the book ledge, under a woolen covering. Edwin tried to lift the burned-up blanket but pieces of Ted came with it, fused to the charred fabric.

Nothing moved, and nothing grumbled with malice in the disassembled stack of ash-smeared plates, gears, and screws.

Edwin returned to the doctor and climbed up against him, shuddering and moaning until Dr. Smeeks wrapped his arms around the boy to say, "There, there. Parker, it's only a little fire. I must've let the crucible heat too long, but look. They're putting it out now. We'll be fine."

The boy's chest seized up tight, and he bit his lips, and he sobbed.

A Serpent in the Gears

Margaret Ronald

MARGARET RONALD is the author of *Spiral Hunt*, *Wild Hunt*, and *Hunt's End* (forthcoming), as well as a number of short stories. She is an alumna of the Viable Paradise workshop, a member of BRAWL, and a guest blogger at the Magic District (MAGICDISTRICT.WORDPRESS.COM). Originally from rural Indiana, she now lives outside Boston and blogs irregularly at MRONALD.WORDPRESS. COM. She is not yet weary of these quite vexing serpents on this quite vexing dirigible. She notes that the following story "started out with the character of the Professora (inspired by a friend's *Spirit of the Century* game) and was originally an excuse to write something lighthearted and silly, full of adventure, derring-do, and nice hot cups of tea. I didn't expect how much it would take on a life of its own, nor how deeply I'd fall in love with the world and characters. I kept having the feeling that the grand narrative of this setting was already fully formed somewhere, and that this story was just one small fragment of it. Someday I hope to find out more about this world and what happens to these three characters in particular."

WE UNEARTHED THE serpent's corpse just before the *Regina* reached the first gun emplacement that separated the greater world from the forgotten valley of Aaris. The reports from villagers on the border had placed the serpent half a day out of our chosen path and much higher than the dirigible should have been, and while the *Regina*'s captain grumbled about "sightseeing" expeditions, she agreed to let us send up a dinghy.

Truth was, captain and crew alike had signed on for the story as much as for the Royal Society's generous pay. The Aaris valley—forgotten mainly because just after the first isolation guns were erected, the Great Southern rail line obviated the need to venture near the Sterling Pass—was a story even jaded 'nauts revered. A side trip such as this only added savor to the tale. Indeed, the same villagers who'd informed us of the serpent's presence had already traded well on this news: a desiccated carcass halfway up one of the snowcapped peaks that made the Sterling Pass all but untraversable, only revealed by the spring thaw.

"Thaw, my arse," Colonel Dieterich muttered as we disembarked from the gently bobbing dinghy. "It's cold enough to freeze a thaumaturge's tits off."

"The villagers said that this is the first time it's been warm enough to spend more than an hour on the slopes, sir," I said, and draped his greatcoat around his shoulders, avoiding the creaking points of his poorly fastened andropter. "For them I suppose that would constitute a thaw."

"For them having ten toes is a novelty." He snorted his pipe into a greater glow, then noticed the coat. "Ah. Thank you, Charles. Come on; let's go see what the barbaric snows have brought us."

The doctors Brackett and Crumworth were already wandering over the carcass, pointing and exclaiming. All of the Royal Society party (excluding Professora Lundqvist, who because of her condition could not leave the *Regina*) were in better spirits now than they had been for weeks, and I began to understand the captain's decision to send us up here. Unusual as the moment of domestic accord was, though, it paled in comparison to the serpent.

The thing had the general shape of a Hyborean flying serpent, though it was at least twenty times the length of most specimens. It stretched out at least fifty feet, probably more, since the sinuous curves of the carcass obscured its true dimensions. It had no limbs to speak of, though one of the anatomists waved excitedly at shattered fins and shouted for us to come see. "Yes, yes, fins, any idiot can see that," grumbled Dieterich. "Of course it had to have fins, how else could it steer? What interests me more are these."

He nudged a pile of detritus with the end of his cane. Rotten wood gave under the pressure: old casks, long since broached. "Cargo, sir?" I said, hoping the possibility of commerce into Aaris might distract him from the carcass. "We may be able to figure out what they held."

"Bugger the casks, Charles. No, look at the bones." He knelt, cursing the snow and the idiocy of interesting specimens to be found at such a damnfool altitude, and tugged a few dirty-white disks free of ice and mummified flesh. "If these weren't obviously bones, I'd swear they were gears."

"I don't see how—" I began uneasily, but a shout farther down the hillside drew his attention. Crumworth had found what would prove to be a delicate ratchet-and-flywheel system, hooked into the beast's spinal column. Abruptly the scientists shifted from a state of mild interest to feverish study, each producing more evidence from the carcass.

Made, some said, pointing to the clearly clockwork aspects of the skeleton. Born, said others, pointing to the harness and the undeniable organic nature of the carcass itself (the anatomist raising his voice the most on this subject). Myself, I considered the question irrelevant: the point was not whether the serpent had been hatched or constructed, but to what use it had been put and, more importantly, why it was here, on this side of the mountains from Aaris, outside the realm where it could conceivably have thrived.

It appeared to have carried a crew, though none of their remains were evident, and I could only assume they had survived the crash. I wondered whether they would have returned home over the mountains, or descended into the greater world—and if the latter, whether they would in time come home again. The thought was less comforting than I once had found it. I nudged a toothed segment with my foot and watched it tumble across the ice.

"What does your valet think, Dieterich?" one of the party called. "Since he's taking his time looking at it."

Dieterich paused. "Well, Charles? What do you think? Made or born?"

For a moment I considered answering "both" and confounding the lot of them, but such was neither the place of a valet nor for a man in my current situation. "I think," I said after a moment, "that there is a very dark cloud two points west of us. I suggest we return to the *Regina* before a storm acquaints us with how this creature died."

There was less argument after that, though Doctor Brackett and the anatomist insisted on bringing so many bones with us that the dinghy sagged dangerously. The results were presented over supper, and a detailed report made to Professora Lundqvist.

The Professora, of course, could not show emotion, but her tank bubbled in an agitated fashion, and her cortex bobbed within it. "I believe perhaps we have left the Sterling Pass closed for too long," she said at last, the phonograph flattening her voice into dry fact.

I privately agreed.

In the morning, Professora Lundqvist insisted on taking the bones to the captain, and borrowed me for the purpose. I piled the serpent's jawbone on her tank, secured the lesser fangs to her braking mechanism, and accompanied her up to the lift. Lundqvist, lacking either an andropter or the torso around which to fasten one, could not venture to the open decks, and thus we were limited to the helm room.

We found the captain, a small blonde woman with the gait of a bear and the voice of an affronted Valkyrie, pulling lens after lens from the consoles and giving orders to the helmsman-automaton. "Captain, if I might have a word," the Professora said.

"We don't have time for more of your eggheads' interpersonal crises," the captain said without turning around. "I chose my crew carefully to avoid such disagreements; it's not my fault you didn't take the same care."

"It's not about that," the Professora said with a hint of asperity. "Charles, show her, please."

I hefted the jawbone and presented it to the captain. She glanced at it. "Hyborean air serpent. I've seen a few."

"Of this size?"

"Not much smaller. You can put that down, man; I'm not in any need of it." I did so and, perceiving I was so much furniture in this situation, edged closer to the lenses, trying to catch a glimpse of the pass below.

"The serpent appeared to be domesticated," Lundqvist insisted. "And there were gears among its bones, gears that may have grown there. As if it were some sort of hybrid."

The captain shrugged. "There're 'naut tales of serpents broke to harness and pirates said to use them to attack ships like the *Regina*. As for the gears." She turned and favored us both with one of her slow, vicious smiles that the crew so dreaded. "I expect that if we were to crash and the Aariscians to find *your* body, Professora, they'd be puzzling over whether you were some hybrid of glass and brains and formaldehyde."

"It's *not* formaldehyde," Lundqvist sniffed.

"And I'm not speaking hypothetically." The captain pointed to a lens behind the helmsman. A gray cliff face, cut into deep letters of ten different scripts, receded from our view. "We've just passed the graven warning."

I peered at the bow lenses, trying to get a better look at the warning itself. When I was a child, I'd heard stories (all disdained by my teachers) that the warning had been inscribed into the side of the mountains by an automaton the size of a house, etching the words with a gaze of fire. When I was older, my age-mates and I played at being the team engineered solely for the job of incising those letters, hanging from convenient walls and making what we thought were appropriate rock-shattering noises to match. After such tales, small wonder that my first view of the warning, some twenty years ago, had been so disappointing. Yet I could still recite by heart its prohibition against entering the valley.

The lenses, however, showed no sign of it. Instead, most displayed the same sight: a confection like matching wedding cakes on the mountainsides flanking the pass, the consequences for those who defied the graven warning.

Thousands of snub spouts pointed towards us, ranging from full cannon-bore to rifle-bore, the latter too small to see even with the ship's lenses. My eyes itched to adjust, and I felt a pang just under the straps of my andropter harness, where most men had hearts.

"Ah," said Lundqvist. "Well, it seems my timing is to its usual standard. I'll leave you to your evasive maneuvers—"

The first of the large guns swung to bear on the *Regina*. Excellent work, I acknowledged with a smaller pang; the automated emplacements were more reliable than most human sentries. "Climb, damn you, climb," the captain snarled at the helmsman. "We should already be at twice estimated safe distance."

"—although I do hope you will keep our discovery in mind. Come, Charles."

"Oh, yes," the captain said over her shoulder. "I will most certainly keep the possibility of attack by serpent-riding air pirates in mind."

Jawbone slung over my shoulder, I accompanied the Professora back towards the lift. "Charming lass, our captain," she said. "Had I both a body and Sapphic inclinations, I do believe I'd be infatuated."

I glanced at her, trying to hide my smile. Full-bodied people often expressed surprise that acorporeals or otherwise mechanically augmented persons could harbor such desires. I, of course, had no such false impression, but preferred to maintain the illusion of one. "If you say so, Professora."

She laughed, a curious sound coming from her phonograph. "I do say so. Don't be a stick about it. Why—"

A concussion like the heavens' own timpani shook through the ship, followed by a sudden lurch to the right. The Professora's tank slammed first against a bulkhead, then, as the ship listed deeply, began to roll down the hall towards the empty lift shaft. The first impact had damaged her brakes, I realized, and now she faced the predicament of a glass tank plus high speed.

I did not think. Dropping the serpent's jawbone, I ran past the Professora and flung myself across the entry to the lift. I was fortunate in that the ship's tilt eased just before she struck me, and so I was not mown down completely. Instead I had to shift from blocking her passage to hauling on the tank's fittings as the ship reversed its pitch and the Professora threatened to slide back down the way we'd come.

A second concussion rumbled below us, this one more distant, and from down the hall I heard the captain's cursing take on a note of relief. For a brief and disorienting moment, I felt almost as if I'd seen a childhood hero fall; those guns were supposed to be perfect, impassable, and yet we'd sailed by. That their perfection would have meant my death was almost a secondary concern. I caught my breath, shaken by this strange mental dissonance.

"Thank you, Charles," Professora Lundqvist said at last. "I see why Dieterich prizes your services."

"I am rarely called upon to do this for him," I pointed out. "Shall I call the lift?"

At that point, the lift's motor started. It rose to reveal Colonel Dieterich. "Good God, Lundqvist, what happened? Are you quite done molesting my valet?"

Lundqvist chuckled. "Quite. Do give me a hand, Dieterich; I'm going to need some repairs."

Dinner that evening was hardly a silent affair, as we had reached the second of the three gun emplacements, and the constant barrage made the experience rather like dining in a tin drum during a hailstorm. As a result of the damage to her brakes, Professora Lundqvist's tank was now strapped to the closest bulkhead like a piece of luggage, which put her in a foul temper.

Unfortunately, every academic gathering, regardless of size, always has at least one member who is tone-deaf to the general mood of the evening, and tonight it was one of the anatomists. He had a theory, and a well-thought-out one it was, that a serpent of the kind we'd found could be grown in a thaumically infused tank—one similar to the Professora's, in fact. (The comparison amused only Colonel Dieterich, who teased Lundqvist about her stature as a Lamia of science.)

By the time I came to offer coffee and dessert, this anatomist had reached the point where, if our projector had not been packed, he would have been demanding to show slides. I paused at the door, reluctant to be even an accessory to such a discussion, but it was clear that the rest of the party was humoring him. Either encouraged or maddened by the lack of response, the anatomist continued his tirade as I poured, his voice rising to near-hysteria as he argued that what could be created for a serpent could be replicated on both larger and smaller scales, down to minuscule creatures and up to gargantua. Raising his cup, he predicted an Aariscian landscape of clockwork serpents, clockwork horses, clockwork cats and dogs, all living in a golden harmony devoid of human interference. I held my tongue.

"Oh, for the love of God," Crumworth finally burst out. "Has no one taught this idiot basic thaumic theory?"

"It could happen," insisted the anatomist. "Aaris does have the thaumic reservoirs; the ones on the pass, the ones in the Mittelgeist valley—"

"It doesn't work that way." Doctor Brackett stirred cream into her coffee until it turned beige. "Yes, there are the reservoirs under the gun emplacements and elsewhere. But they're the wrong kind. You couldn't use them to power something like an air serpent."

All very sound science, of course, and the Mobility/Sufficiency Paradox was the basis of at least one Society lecture. I turned away to hide my smile, and caught a glimpse of Dieterich deliberately tapping his pipe with the careful concentration that meant he was thinking about something else.

"It's like the difference between a geothermic station and a boiler," Crumworth went on. "One's much more powerful than the other, but it's no good if you're too far away from the steam for it to power anything."

One of the Terranocta astronomers at the far end of the table nodded. "Is why no one give a shit about Aaris."

Several members of the party immediately busied themselves with their coffee. It didn't take much to guess why, and as the person who'd handled most correspondence on this expedition, I didn't have to guess. After all, no one noticed a valet, especially not if he was there to take care of simple administrative tasks as well, and if some codes were childishly easy to crack, that was hardly my fault.

While the Royal Society's ostensible reason for the expedition was to offer the hand of friendship and scientific inquiry to their poor isolated cousins, any idiot could see that it was also to assay whether air power could bypass the gun emplacements. Thaumic reservoirs might be useless for certain engineering methods, but that hardly made them worthless, as the Royal Society well knew.

At least half of the party were spies (Brackett and Crumworth in particular, each from a rival faction in the same country, which explained their mutual antagonism and attraction), and I had suspicions about the other half. To take the most cynical view, the ship was like any other diplomatic mission in that absolutely no one was as they seemed.

As if perceiving my thoughts, Dieterich glanced up and met my gaze, and the trace of a smile creased the corners of his eyes. Yes, he was an exception to that. As was the Professora, though all of us had our reasons for being here—Dieterich for the Society, Lundqvist for the prestige, the spies for their countries, the non-spies for curiosity. As for me, I'd been valet to Dieterich for ten years, in general service for ten before that, and I was homesick.

The sound of guns below us faded into the distance, as if the lull in our conversation had reached them as well. Two down, one to go, I counted. That was if the landscape hadn't changed, if my memories of the pass still held true.

The anatomist cleared his throat. "A serpent could—"

"Oh, do shut up, Klaus," Lundqvist snapped.

What happened the day after was pretty much inescapably my fault, in both the immediately personal and the greater sense. We had passed the third emplacement in the very early hours, and while that had been a near thing—scuttlebutt had it that the charts had been wrong, and only the helmsman's reflexes had saved us—the mood today was light, and the general consensus that we would clear the pass by noon.

I served breakfast to those of the party who were awake by eight (Dieterich, one of the astronomers, and the immobile, sulking Professora), then made my way up to the observation deck, where I had no business being. It was not the safest place, even with the security of an andropter across my shoulders, but I hoped to catch a glimpse of Aaris before our mission began in earnest. The thaumaturges whose duty it was to keep the *Regina* airborne were changing shift, each moving into his or her mudra in what an ignorant man might have called clockwork regularity. I exchanged nods with those leaving their shifts and headed for the open-air viewing at the bow.

The morning sun cast our shadow over the mountain slopes so that it seemed to leap ahead of us like a playful dog. A dozen ornamental lenses along the lower railing showed the landscape in picturesque facets. I risked adjusting my eyes to see ahead.

Something twinkled on the high peaks that marked the last mountains of the Sterling Pass, and I focused on it just as the captain's voice roared from the speaking tube. I had enough time to think *Ah, so they did get my report on the Society's air capabilities* before I realized that the guns had already fired.

The next few minutes were a confusion of pain and shrapnel. I was later to learn that the captain's quick thinking had kept the *Regina*'s dirigible sacs from being punctured, but at a loss of both the observation deck and the forward hold. What struck me at the time, though, was a chunk of werglass from the lenses, followed by a broken segment of railing that pinned me to the deck. Splinters ground under my fingers as I scrabbled at the planks, first to keep from falling through the wreckage, then out of sheer agony as the railing dug deeper. A detachment borne partly of my nature and partly of my years of service told me that there had been substantial but not crippling damage to my internals, and that the low insistent sound I heard was not mechanical but one of the thaumaturges sobbing quietly as she attempted to keep the *Regina* aloft.

There are times when detachment is not a virtue.

With a rattling gasp, I reached down and pulled the railing from my side. Only blood followed it, and I yanked the remnants of my coat over the gap in a futile effort to hide the wound.

The hatches from belowdecks slammed open. "Charles? Where's Charles?" roared Dieterich, and I flattened myself against the boards, hoping to remain unnoticed. "There you are, man! A stretcher, quickly!"

In short order I was bundled onto a stretcher and carried down to the lab, where Dieterich had me placed on the central table and my andropter unstrapped. The Society party's pleas to have me taken to the ship's sawbones were refuted with the quite accurate observation that he already had enough patients, and that furthermore no one was going to lay hands on Dieterich's valet but Dieterich himself. Crumworth and Brackett exchanged glances at this, coming as usual to the wrong conclusion.

Dieterich ordered everyone out, then turned on Professora Lundqvist, who observed the whole enterprise from her place by the door. "And you, too, madam!"

"It will take you a full half hour to attach me to a more convenient bulkhead," she retorted. "Besides, I have more medical experience than you."

Dieterich muttered something about idiot disembodied brains thinking they knew everything, but he let her remain. "Hang on, Charles," he said. "We'll soon have you right as rain—"

He paused, staring at the open wound in my side. I closed my eyes and cursed myself for ever having the idiot sense to join this expedition.

"Lundqvist," Dieterich said softly, "your phonograph, please."

The Professora acquiesced by extending the horn of her phonograph to the lock on the door and emitting a blast like an air-horn. Cries of dismay followed, and Dieterich kicked the door as he went to pull on sterile gloves. "No eavesdropping, you half-witted adjuncts!"

He returned to my side and with a set of long tweezers removed one of the many separate pains from my side. "Well," he said in a voice that barely carried to my ears, "do we need to discuss this?" And he held up the bloodied escapement that he had extracted.

I opened my eyes and stared at the ceiling. "I don't think so, sir," I finally managed. "I expect you can infer the meaning of clockwork in your valet."

Dieterich reached for his pipe, realized he didn't have it, and whuffled through his mustache instead. "That's loyalty for you, eh, Lundqvist?" he said over his shoulder. "Man even ascribes this discovery to me. Very flattering."

"I suspected a while ago," Lundqvist said quietly, turning her phonograph to face us. "When this expedition was first floated."

"Eight months past? Pah, woman, you only told me three weeks ago."

I stared at her. "How?" I choked, realizing a second later that I'd just confirmed her suspicions.

"Your transmissions to Aaris. I monitor the radio transmissions from the Society—never mind why, Dieterich, suffice it to say that I had reason—and after some time I noticed your additions. Very well encrypted, by the way; I'm still impressed."

The thought came to mind that had I been only a little slower yesterday, I might have been rid of one of those who knew my secret. But the Professora, as usual, gave no indication of what she was thinking, and Dieterich only set the escapement in a sterile tray and began a search for the anesthetic. "Merged," I said at last. "In Aaris we're called Merged citizens."

"Citizens, hm? Looks like the sociology department's theory about rank anarchism in Aaris had some foundation." Dieterich extracted another chunk of shrapnel, this one three-fourths of a gear from my recording array, nestled just below what passed for my ribs. "Charles, if I describe what I'm seeing here, can you tell me how to repair you?"

"No. I mean, yes, I can, but—" I stopped, the full explanation of merged versus autonomous citizenry and the Aaris monarchic system trembling on my tongue. Had silence really been so intolerable these last years, so much that the first opportunity made me liable to spill all I knew? "If you extract the broken bits and stitch me up, I should be fine," I told him.

The *Regina* lurched beneath us. Dieterich caught the side of the table and cursed. "You're self-repairing?" he asked as he righted himself, the tone of fascinated inquiry one I knew well.

I couldn't say I was happy about being the focus of that interest. "No, I heal up. There's a difference, Sir."

"Thaumic reserves," the Professora murmured. "Infused throughout living tissue—I did wonder, when I heard about the serpent, whether it was possible. We may have to revise our definition of thaumic self-sufficiency. Dieterich, you've missed a piece."

"I haven't missed it; I was just about to get it." Carefully, with hands more accustomed to steam engines, Dieterich pulled the last damaged scrap from underneath my internal cage and began sealing the wound with hemostatic staples. Each felt like a dull thump against my side, muffled by the anesthetic. "Springs, even… do you know, Charles, if word gets out that I have a clockwork valet, I'm never going to live it down."

"I suspect I won't either, sir." I took the pad of gauze he handed me and pressed it into place while he unwound a length of burdock-bandage. The pain eased to a dull ache. "What will you tell the captain?"

"Nothing, I expect," Lundqvist said, and Dieterich grunted assent. "What did your Aariscian counterparts ask you to do on this voyage, Charles? From our continued existence, I presume your purpose here wasn't sabotage."

I closed my eyes again, then gritted my teeth and attempted to sit up. Dieterich had done a good job—as well he should, being an engineer of automata on a grander scale—and the edges no longer grated, though it was a toss-up whether I'd have recording capabilities again. *One more rivet in the vault of my espionage career,* I thought, and here was the last: "They didn't tell me anything," I croaked, eluding Dieterich's offer of help. "They haven't told me anything for fourteen years."

And there it was, the reason I'd come with Dieterich on this expedition when it would have been so easy to cry off: not just duty, not just homesickness, but the need to know what had happened in my absence. I covered my face, hiding how my eyes adjusted and re-adjusted, the lenses carrying away any trace of oily tears. I did not normally hide emotion, but I could at least hide this mechanical, Merged response.

The *Regina* shuddered again, followed by a screech that sent shivers up to my medulla. Dieterich glanced upwards, pity temporarily forgotten. "That wasn't a gun." He stripped off his gloves. "Lundqvist, keep an eye on him."

"And how am I to do that?" Lundqvist asked as Dieterich unbarred the door and ran out. "Charles? Charles, do not go up there, you are not fit to be on your feet—"

I might not be fit, but both my employer and my home were now up there. I yanked Dieterich's greatcoat on over my bandages and followed.

We had passed the last of the guns, truly the last this time, and the sunlight on the decks burned clear and free of dust. Just past the bow of the *Regina*, I caught a glimpse of Aaris's green valleys.

Between it and us hovered a knot of silver, endlessly twisting. *Serpents,* I thought first, and then as the red-cloaked riders on each came clear, *Merged serpents.*

I had been a fool to think that the fourth set of guns would be the only addition to Aaris's defenses.

"Come no farther." A serpent glided closer with the motion of a water-snake, and its rider turned in place to address us through a megaphone. "None may enter the Aaris Valley on pain of death." Familiar words—the same that had been cut into the stone at the far end of the pass, to proclaim Aaris' isolation to the world. The same that I had memorized as a Merged child. Here they were spoken, recited in a voice that bounced off the mountains.

"We are a peaceful mission!" Dieterich yelled back, then cursed and repeated his words into the captain's annunciator.

The captain stalked past him to a locker by the helm. "You'd do better arguing with the graven warning," she muttered.

And indeed, the response was much the same as the cliff face would give: silent, anticipatory, the perpetual knotwork of the serpents writing a sigil of forbidding in the air. "Turn back now, or you will die," the spokesman finished. I focused, and focused again, trying to see his face.

Dieterich glanced at the captain. "If I tell you to turn back—"

"Can't. Not without going straight through them. The *Regina*'s got a shitty turning radius." The captain yanked her annunciator from his hands. "We demand safe passage!"

The rider did not answer, but raised one hand, and the pattern unraveled toward us. True to their nature, the serpents did not attack the dirigible sacs, but went for the shinier, more attractive target below: the ship itself. A gleaming gray ribbon spun past the remains of the observation deck, taking a substantial bite out of the woodwork and doing much greater damage with a last flail of its body in passing.

"Small arms! Small arms!" The captain produced a crank-gun from the locker and took aim at the closest serpent. She had tossed a second gun to Dieterich, who cursed the air blue but took it, leveling it at the rider instead.

A second serpent undulated up to the very decks of the ship, knocking several 'nauts aside in its wake. Those who could handle a weapon ran to the lockers; I lurched out of the way, landed heavily on my wounded side, and cried out.

At the rail, Dieterich turned—and the last flick of the serpent's tail lashed out and knocked him over the railing.

There was no outcry; the chaos was too great, and Dieterich not the only one to go over the side. The snap of andropters opening added a new, percussive voice to the tumult.

I will not explain my actions then; certainly I knew that Dieterich's andropter was in good condition, as I had tended to it only that morning. Nor did I have any fear for him in particular. Nor was I so foolish as to forget that my own andropter was back in the lab with Lundqvist, and so any slip on my part inevitably meant a fall that would not just kill me but reduce me to a splash on the rocks below. Still, some remnant of instinct propelled me forward despite better sense and burgeoning pain, and I ran to the railing.

The serpent whose rider Dieterich had pulverized writhed near the bow, devoid of instructions and therefore meaning. I leapt onto the railing, crouched briefly to secure my balance, and flung myself at the beast, trusting in my Merged brain to calculate the proper angle.

I caught the first set of fins and was dragged alongside the ship, long enough for me to force a hand into the soft tissue behind the fin and fumble about, searching for the controls that had to be there. Merged pack animals had always had secondary controls near their braincases; surely this part of the design would not have changed.

It had not. With one hand "plugged" into the serpent's controls and one clinging to its fin, I wrenched the beast away from its attack on the *Regina* and followed the sound of Dieterich swearing at his andropter. It had opened enough to keep him from plummeting to his death but had the unfortunate side effect of wafting him directly toward the mouth of another serpent.

I wrenched my serpent into a helical dive, wrapped my legs around the closest fin, and stretched my arm out as we coasted past. My serpent smashed through the silk and framework of Dieterich's andropter, and I caught Dieterich himself by the harness as the jolt briefly tossed him aside. My arm went numb with the shock, and the staples holding my wound shut tore apart, but it was enough: I used Dieterich's momentum to swing him aboard, onto the serpent's flat head and out of danger.

Dieterich stared blankly at the sky for a moment, apparently having difficulty understanding that he was still alive. "Good show, Charles!" he croaked after a moment. "Very good show. You've got a knack for this."

I kept hold of his harness and didn't answer. One slip, I thought, one simple yank on the harness and I'd have disposed of half of the people who knew my Aariscian nature. And the only other led a fragile existence in an easily broken tank…

It didn't matter. Or it would have mattered, in another world, one where I was actually the spy I'd been built to be. I clung to the serpent's head and whispered to it as I worked the controls, blood seeping through the bandage and slicking my side. "Forward. Take me to Aaris. Please."

Pleading, as the captain had said, had no effect, but direction was easy enough to communicate and the serpent's reflexes simple to control. We veered away from the knot of gunfire and scales and out of the smoke, toward the valley. None of the other serpents followed. Dieterich, still pinned in place by the remnants of his andropter, craned his neck around. "What is it? The battle's over there—damn it, Charles, I did say I'd keep a secret. You know I'm a man of my word, now take me back!"

I barely heard him. Below me were the green fields of Aaris as I remembered them, the mesh of white roads stretching from the Mittelgeist hills into the fragments of arable land that were so assiduously tended, the clutter of houses, even the sheen of Lake Varno where I was born, where I was decanted, where I swore citizenship…

The serpent's hide below me rippled, and I followed it with a shiver of my own. No. Not as I remembered. The roads, long irregular from necessity, had been smoothed out into a patterned web, and the hills and rivers that had blocked them smoothed away into similarly perfect shapes. I adjusted my eyes again and again, as if a more magnified landscape would show not just what had happened but why. Nothing but the same iterated regularity; nothing of what I remembered as home.

I shook my head and shifted my eyes back to their normal state, then leaned back, trying to take in the whole valley. My breath caught with a crackle.

It was as if I gazed upon a great green clock, a hybrid land that was not just land nor automata but both. Every part of the landscape bore a design I knew from study of my own inner workings. The slow motion of it—even the patterns of glaciers sliding down the mountains—communicated a vast unfathomable purpose. A purpose of which I was no longer a part.

And in the fields and villages and kennels and stalls, eyes all like mine, adjusting as they looked up, lenses shifting to see one of their own above them. No full automata. No full humans. Only the same Merged calm on every visage.

I shuddered, viscerally aware of the hole in my side, of the mess of blood and bandages so at odds with the careful, clean lines of this new Aaris. "Home," I whispered. "Home. Please."

The serpent, either wiser than I or interpreting the indecision of my hands, curved into a wide arc. I heard Dieterich gasp as we turned away, but I did not turn to see his reaction. Instead I gazed ahead, to where the *Regina*, spilling smoke and the telltale glitter of lost thaumic power, was limping away back down the pass. Its decks were a flutter of rescued andropters and wreckage, but though the mass of serpents parted to let their brother through, it did not fire upon us as I guided my serpent back to it.

For the first time in twenty years, I did not have to make the tea. Dieterich brought a tray down to the remains of the observation deck, where the Professora and I sat in silent contemplation of the receding Sterling Pass. Below us guns boomed, unaware that they had failed in their work of keeping us out but that their greater mission had succeeded. I got up from my place on the deck (the benches having been used for temporary hull patches), but Dieterich waved me back to my seat.

He poured two cups, then tipped the contents of a third into the Professora's nutrient filter. She murmured thanks, and I took the offered cup gratefully.

"You needn't worry," Dieterich said after a moment, "about the, hmm, shrapnel I extracted. I disposed of it among the bits we took from that first dratted serpent's carcass."

One set of gears in among the other. Fitting. "Thank you, sir."

"You're welcome. Don't let that sort of thing happen again, hm?" He gave me a searching look, but whatever doubts he'd harbored had been erased when I brought us both back to the *Regina*'s splintered decks. "Good man," he said, drained his tea, and returned to the depths of the ship.

I took a sip of my tea. He'd made it well. "How much time do you think we have?" Lundqvist asked softly.

I attempted a shrug, winced, and settled for shaking my head. "There's no indication that Aaris intends to undo their isolation. They may be content to stay in the valley."

"You weren't," she pointed out.

"No." I gazed back into the smoky pass, thinking of the great clockwork of the valley, the machine that it ran, of serpents on the wrong side of the mountains, and lensed eyes looking back at me. "Ten years, perhaps. Five if we're unlucky."

The Professora was silent, though the constant hiss from her phonograph resembled a slow exhalation. "Well. We'll just have to hope we're lucky."

Five years. I'd been in service for twenty; perhaps a different service was needed for the coming five. I got to my feet, glanced behind me at the pass, and began setting the cups back on the tea-tray.

"Yes. We'll hope," I said. "More tea?"

The Strange Case of Mr. Salad Monday

G. D. Falksen

In addition to writing, **G. D. FALKSEN** studies history and blogs for TOR.COM. His written work has appeared in *Steampunk Tales, SteamPunk Magazine, Footprints*, and TOR.COM. He gives lectures on steampunk at various conventions, and has been interviewed on the subject by the *New York Times*, the *San Francisco Chronicle*, the *Hartford Courant*, and MTV, among others. He is the lead writer for the video game project *AIR: Steampunk*. He resides in Connecticut. His website can be found at WWW.GDFALKSEN.COM. He writes that "the idea for 'The Strange Case of Mr. Salad Monday' came to me late one night when considering how various aspects of modern society that we take for granted could be translated into a steampunk context. I thought about blogging, and I came up with tit-tat. It seemed only natural to set tit-tat and Salad Monday in my Cities of Ether setting, in the city of Salmagundi specifically."

INSPECTOR WILDE WAS in a fine mood when he arrived at the headquarters of Salmagundi's Legion of Peace, carrying three paper-wrapped sandwiches and an armload of printed broadsheets. He had a spring in his step and walked in time to one of the latest music hall ditties, which he whistled cheerfully for the benefit of his coworkers. All along the gaslit passage, clerks and secretaries poked their heads out of their rooms and stared in wonder and admiration at his audacity. Most of them smiled as he passed, and a few of the braver ones tapped their feet along with the tune for a few moments before dashing back to their desks to avoid the ire of their supervisors. Wilde laughed as he passed a room full of secretaries who somehow managed to type in time with the music.

Midway down the hallway was the Chief Inspector's office, which was fronted by a small antechamber in which her secretary, Marguerite, was busy making sense of several unsightly piles of documents. Her work table was a model of efficiency. Her pens and pencils were all neatly arranged to one side, along with writing paper and a three-section typewriter for preparing documents in triplicate. A rack of empty pneumatic capsules waited nearby to be filled and dispatched.

Marguerite smiled as Wilde approached, delighted by the cheerful whistling. Wilde leaned down, eyebrows arched, and tossed Marguerite the top sandwich in his stack.

"And a girl in uniform's just the thing for me..." Wilde said playfully, completing the refrain of the tune in Marguerite's ear.

"Max!" Marguerite exclaimed, her cheeks flushing. She pushed him away and made a show of reorganizing the papers on her desk. "You mustn't say things like that to me. People will talk."

"Well, if 'people' are going to talk, don't you think we should give them something to talk about?" Wilde asked, flashing one of his trademark recruitment smiles.

Marguerite was trying to come up with a reply when a third voice interrupted. "Max, get in here!"

Marguerite jumped in shock and pulled a handful of papers between herself and Wilde, as if to deny that they had even been speaking. Wilde was also caught by surprise, but retained his composure. He looked over at the polished voicepipe mounted next to Marguerite's table just in time to hear the Chief Inspector's voice again.

"Now!"

Wilde kept his head high as he sauntered across Chief Inspector Cerys's cluttered office. Behind him, a sheepish Marguerite closed the door as quietly as she could. What might normally have been a sizable, bland, and dutifully bureaucratic office had, since the Chief Inspector moved in, been transformed into a nest of filing cabinets, pigeonhole shelves, and chairs covered in files and loose papers.

The room was lit entirely by gaslamps, for both of its windows had been tightly shuttered. Located on the top layer of Salmagundi, Legion Headquarters was gifted and cursed with an overwhelming view of the vast horizonless sky that surrounded the city. The silver-gray expanse of ether was a sight of unparalleled majesty and terror. Though sky-borne steamships traveled freely from one floating city to another, urban dwellers could not help but fear the mysterious beasts and horrors that lurked in the great beyond, thanks to old sailors' stories of unfathomable monstrosities. However, even fear could not defeat the human drive for commerce. For every cargo ship lost to the ether, five more were already being built in Salmagundi's shipyards, like heads of a great industrial hydra.

The largest piece of furniture in the Chief Inspector's office was her massive Legion-issue desk, which was covered in papers, pens, and miscellanea. However, it was a metal coffee percolator resting on a stand nearby that was the true focal point of the room. A set of insulated pipes extended from the wall and into the percolator's base, keeping the coffee hot by pumping steam through it from the building's main line.

Chief Inspector Cerys looked up from a collection of reports, coffee cup in hand, and gave Wilde a look. "Max, I'll thank you to stop flirting with my secretary all the bloody time."

"Why, Chief?" Wilde asked, setting one of the sandwiches down by Cerys and then pulling over a chair. "If you ask me, I think she rather likes it."

Cerys gave him another look as she began to unwrap her meal. "She does, Max. She likes it too much." Cerys waved a typewritten form in front of Wilde's face. The document was so complex as to be less legible than a massive ink spot, but it would drive some anonymous bureaucrat into a frenzy if even a single T was left uncrossed before filing. "Marguerite's the only person in this blasted place who can read these damn things, and she's useless for half an hour after you bat your pretty little eyes at her."

"'Pretty little eyes,' Chief?" Wilde asked. "Why, I didn't know you cared."

"Shut up, Max."

"Yes, Chief."

Cerys bit into her sandwich and let out a sigh; Wilde suspected it was her first real meal of the day. "Mmmm! Herr Grosse comes through again."

"I'm sure he'll be happy to hear it," Wilde replied. "What's on the agenda for today?"

"We're unusually light on terrorist attacks and serial murderers at the moment, so we're 'lending a hand' with Surveillance."

"Espionage and tailing suspects?" Wilde asked hopefully.

"Examining subversive propaganda for clues," Cerys replied.

Wilde made a face at the thought of such a boring activity. "Just so we're clear, I'm not on duty for another five minutes."

"You're not on duty until I finish my sandwich," Cerys countered.

"Deal."

Leaning back in his chair, Wilde began to read one of the broadsheets he had brought with him. Within a minute, he was all but giggling like a schoolboy.

"What're you so happy about?" Cerys asked, between mouthfuls of sandwich and mayonnaise.

Wilde quickly cleared his throat. "Er…. Nothing, Chief." His eyes involuntarily read the next line of text and another fit of laughter took him.

"Nothing?"

"Eh…heh…. Um, yes, nothing." Wilde held up the broadsheet for Cerys's inspection. "It's just Mr. Salad Monday. He's giving Deacon Fortesque a roasting over his latest political tract."

"What?" Cerys demanded, bewildered.

"Here, here, listen to this. He writes, quote, 'While I suspect that the Hon. DeacFort is sincere in his belief that the threat of terrorism can be removed by simply shooting every suspected saboteur or socialist, plus one in ten persons of an inferior income distribution, he has forgotten two significant points. First, that the same result could be achieved more rapidly, cheaply, and without a reduction of the work force by improving working conditions and raising lower-income pay rates; and second, that he is an unmitigated fool whose longevity in the printed world can only be ascribed to his wealth, influence, and the public demand for entertaining fiction to read after breakfast,' unquote!" Wilde lowered the broadsheet, the grin on his face outstripping most industrial bridges. "Isn't that terrific?"

Cerys blinked several times. "Max, what in Heaven's name is wrong with you?"

"You don't think it's funny?"

"I think it's a waste of print, and I'm surprised you don't agree. Besides, we've got more important things to do." She tossed him a folder of documents. "Here, make yourself useful and read this."

Wilde set the broadsheets aside and thumbed through the folder. It contained a number of obscure pamphlets and political chapbooks, all machine-printed on cheap paper. They had been bound with red ribbon, and each was plastered with a paper tab bearing the ominous statement "Forbidden!" As he opened one and began to skim the text, Wilde felt a nagging sense that he had read the author's work somewhere before. After a moment, the recollection came to him and he burst out laughing.

"What?" Cerys demanded, from behind her cup of coffee.

Struggling to keep his laughter under control, Wilde pointed to one of the chapbooks. "This is by Fredrick William Slater, isn't it?"

Cerys almost dropped her coffee. "How did you…?"

Wilde held the chapbook a little higher, and pointed to it emphatically. "Isn't it?"

"Slater's name isn't on any of those books. How'd you know it was him?" Cerys went to take another sip of coffee, and then pointed the cup at Wilde menacingly. "And don't tell me it was a lucky guess. No one in the Legion just pulls the name Professor F. W. Slater out of his hat."

"I recognized the writing style, Chief," Wilde answered. "The guy's got a pretty distinct voice, you know."

"You don't strike me as the kind of person who makes a habit of reading essays on social philosophy, Max. Mind explaining this happy coincidence to me? Or do I have to get the bucket of water?"

Wilde gave an expression of jovial terror. "Not Old Truth Maker! Anything but Old—"

"Shut up, Max, and answer my question."

"Alright, alright. He writes for the papers, so I read him just about every morning."

"The papers?" Cerys asked. "He's not a reporter."

"No, no, not the newspapers. The broadsheets." Wilde held up one of the oversized printed sheets he had brought in with him. It resembled a conventional newspaper, but the upper half of the page was given over to large editorials, while the lower half was divided into columns of small-print articles; in many cases, the smaller segments were only a few lines long. "Tit-tat."

"Tit-tat?" Cerys asked, bewildered.

"Right. Tit-tat. Slater's a tatter." Wilde was clearly under the mistaken impression that they were coming to some sort of mutual comprehension.

"What's a 'tatter'?"

There was a lengthy pause, as Wilde realized his superior was confused, but not how to help. Somewhat hesitantly, he ventured, "A tatter is…someone who does tit-tat."

Cerys lowered her face into her hands. She had a deep-seated urge to shoot him. "Max…what does 'tit-tat' mean?"

"Oh!" Wilde exclaimed. He held up the broadsheet again. "It's…um…. Well, it's tit-tat." When this answer made Cerys rise half out of her chair with murder in her eyes, Wilde quickly added, "Wait! Wait! It's like a conversation in print!"

"What?"

"Well, the bigwigs, like Professor Slater, publish their opinions on topics of the day. Then they all read each other's essays and mail in replies, and then *those* get printed...and so on."

Cerys paused on the verge of a rant against modern society and how it was conspiring to annoy her. "You know," she said, clearly surprised, "that almost makes sense, in a mind-numbing kind of way." She stepped around the desk and snatched the broadsheet out of Wilde's hands, pointing at the maze of print. "But then, what's all this here? Don't tell me 'Mr. Jervais Mutton' is the name of some brilliant philosopher, Max."

Wilde laughed. "Oh, no, no. Those are all tatters. They're ordinary people who send in their own comments. Most of them never see print, but the really juicy ones get tossed in along with the 'professional' stuff because it's fun to read."

"Fun to read?"

"Audience loves 'em," Wilde confirmed with a nod. "Ask me, they're more popular than the articles they're responding to. People have whole conversations in print, arguing back and forth."

"Conversations? How frequently are these released?"

"Well...." Wilde sat back in his chair and considered the question. "The more respectable printers only do one issue a day, but they tend to be a bit light on the commentary anyway. Most places have a morning and an evening edition, so you can read a comment and a response in one day if you're lucky." He leaned forward again, clearly excited at the prospect of explaining something to Cerys. "But the really good ones...the houses that print the really juicy arguments... they sometimes get in as many as three or four a day. Plenty of tit-tat there."

Cerys stared at him, her mouth struggling to form a response. "How?" she finally demanded. "How can they print that much in one day?"

"Well, there's the morning edition that people read during breakfast. Then there's the afternoon edition, which arrives in time for lunch. And finally there's an evening edition that shows up in time for dinner. Sometimes they even do a late night printing that shows up sometime in the small hours."

"Four editions! I'd barely have five minutes to spend reading one. Who has time to read all that, let alone mail in a comment?"

"Clerks, mostly," Wilde replied. "Typists and secretaries who have to sit at their desks doing nothing while they wait for assignments to show up. And the idle rich, of course. People who think that having too much time on their hands qualifies them to comment on topics they know nothing about."

Cerys was quiet for a long moment. "Almost reminds me of the government." She stared at the broadsheet and shook her head. "How long do these arguments last?"

"Days," Wilde answered. "Weeks sometimes, if they get really heated. So long as the papers sell, the presses keep printing them."

"How do they keep track of the arguments?"

Wilde pointed to one of the boxes of print. "There's a little code number in the corner. It tells you which topic the reply goes with, and where it goes in the sequence."

Cerys was rubbing her forehead with her hand again. "Max, I'm afraid to ask, but why are there strings of letters just sitting in the middle of some of these sentences?"

"What?" Wilde rose from his chair and leaned across the desk. Cerys pointed to one of the comments, and Wilde burst out laughing. "Oh! They're just abbreviations, Chief. To save on space. The shorter a comment, the more likely it is to get printed."

"So 'IIMOT' means…?"

"We pronounce that 'eye-moth.' It means 'it is my opinion that.' People use it when they're about to say something really snooty talking about a topic they don't understand. It's great stuff!"

Cerys gave him a look and shook her head. "I can't believe you actually waste your time with this nonsense." She glared at the page again. "What about 'IHN'?"

"'In Heaven's name,' Chief."

"Oh, honestly, Max!" Cerys exclaimed. "Don't these people have anything better to do?"

"Desk jobs, Chief," Wilde reminded her.

"And they really care about what Jervais Mutton has to say about rising coal prices?"

"Nah, Mutton doesn't discuss commodities. He's too busy falling over himself to agree with whatever Deacon Fortesque happens to think. Now, Salad Monday, he's a fun one. He'll take on five people at once and bring in arguments most of us forgot about ages ago. Frankly, it's a privilege to watch him in action. He's an oddball, that one."

Cerys had returned to her work, and only half glanced up when she replied, "Oh? Why's that?"

Wilde took her cue, and went back to skimming through the pile of pamphlets and tracts he had been given. "Oh, he just doesn't fit into the usual categories. Most of the time you can read someone and say 'he's a socialist' or 'he's a conservative' or 'he's a capitalist.' With Salad Monday, you can't do that. He's all over the place with what he's doing. Sure, he tends to agree with the lefties, but he'll blast them out of the sky when they're saying something stupid. I mean, he's probably as anti-government as the anarchists, but he has a great time pointing out how stupid anarchism is. He's just…everywhere and nowhere, I guess."

Something about the statement caught Cerys's interest. "Really? Well, who is he then?"

"Don't know, Chief. No one does. He's been around for ages, since tit-tat started, I think. He was already one of the big names when I got into it a couple years back. There're plenty of theories out there, but he's one of the pen names no one's been able to crack yet. He's probably one of those university types, though. He's always quoting from this or that, and he's got the time to stay up-to-date on whatever's going on."

"But no one knows who he is?"

"Well.…" Wilde hesitated. "You know, it's funny you've got me reading up on Slater, because the current view is that they might be one and the same."

There was a look in Cerys's eyes. "Really? Why?" She slowly rose out of her chair and leaned across the desk at Wilde. "You said yourself that Slater's got a distinctive voice. Wouldn't that make it obvious?"

"That's the thing. Salad Monday's got about as neutral a voice as possible. It's almost distinct in how indistinct it is. The theory is that it's someone like Professor Slater, who's got a very recognizable style, trying not to give himself away. And out of all the bigwigs Mr. Salad Monday takes on, Slater's the one who usually ends up coming out looking the best. He'll point out Slater's flaws, but he usually ends up defending the Professor's argument, with a few revisions. It's almost like they're working together. The only problem is, a busy university man like Slater wouldn't have time for it."

"How do you mean?" Cerys asked.

"Salad Monday's probably the most prolific tatter ever to tit the tat, if you take my meaning."

"Barely," Cerys replied without an ounce of humor. "Continue."

"He writes so much material I'm starting to wonder if he's actually one person. It seems like he's got a witty, well-thought-out reply to just about every single topic that ever hits print, and he gets them to the printers on the same day, sometimes even by the next issue. And I'll tell you, Chief, I don't care how much free time someone has, there's only so much typing one person can do."

Cerys was scribbling notes. "Do you think it might be a group of Slater's students trying to help give his arguments more authority?"

"Maybe…." Wilde stared at Cerys with growing suspicion. "OK, Chief, I know better than to question, but enough's enough. Why's the Legion suddenly interested in F. W. Slater, of all people? I thought he was the socialist we actually liked."

"'We' don't like any socialists, Max. You know that. They're dirty, smelly, and untrustworthy, and they usually ask questions 'we' can't comfortably answer."

"I know the doubletalk, Chief. But honestly, why Slater?"

Cerys sighed, a common precursor to any conversation involving an explanation of orders from the top. "Top brass thinks Slater's trying to undermine the government with his latest batch of essays. He's launched another round of anonymous pamphlets demanding improved working conditions, health insurance, abolition of a tax-based electorate, and so on. He's smart enough to not sign his name, but, like you said, he's got a distinct voice. We're pretty sure it's him."

"How did he get them past the censor?"

"They were all printed up independently and distributed anonymously: snuck into mailboxes, left on café tables, the usual subversive drill." Cerys chuckled. "They even had urchins passing them out on street corners. And you know, no one's as good as those kids at getting away from Legionnaires."

"Oh, I can just see it!" Wilde laughed, his head filled with visions of brown-uniformed Legion policemen running after hordes of street children.

"Upshot is, we don't actually know who's behind it."

"But top brass thinks it's Slater."

"Yes," Cerys agreed. "But what brass thinks is usually wrong." She rose from her desk and refilled her cup of coffee, mulling something over. "Max, I've got an assignment for you."

"Whatever you need, Chief," Wilde answered, eagerly setting aside the pile of pamphlets.

"Don't sound so excited. I want you to find out who this 'Salad Monday' character is. If he's connected to Slater, so much the better. If he isn't, at least that's one little mystery solved."

Wilde rubbed his head. "Chief, I've got to be honest with you: I'm not sure where to start. I mean, he's been around for ages and no one's been able to find out who he is. Any lead I can think of has probably been tried already."

"Has it?" Cerys asked. "Or are you just assuming it has?"

"Point taken."

"Start with the obvious. He's got to live somewhere, he's got to eat somewhere, he's got to write somewhere. And I may not understand how this titter-tatter thing works—"

"'Tit-tat,' Chief."

"Shut up, Max," Cerys instructed, before finishing her sentence, "—but somewhere along the line someone has to be getting his comments for print. Find out who, and chances are you'll find Salad Monday."

"The printing houses won't be happy to give up his name and address, you know."

"Take Kendrick with you. Five minutes with him and they'll give in."

"Do I get a warrant?" Wilde asked hopefully.

"I'll put in a call," Cerys answered, and took a sip of her coffee. "Until then, improvise."

"Yes, Chief."

Several hours later, Wilde was sipping his own coffee outside a pleasant Layer Three café. It was a trendy sort of place, with the intellectual atmosphere preferred by scholars, students, artists, and anyone who mistakenly believed himself to be one of the above. Wilde leaned back in his wicker chair and smiled as he looked around at the crowds of youths at the nearby tables. They were mostly young men wearing casual sack suits and fedoras, though here and there could be seen young women in shirtwaists and long skirts. A few of these women were bored sweethearts who stared into their cups impatiently or chatted with one another as they waited for their boyfriends to take notice of them. Others were female students determined to do more with their education than find a husband, and were engaged in spirited debate with their male counterparts.

As Wilde's gaze returned to his own table, it fell upon his dour-faced companion. "Kendrick, don't you ever smile?"

"Only when I'm shooting terrorists," came the reply.

Across the table, Kendrick Mernil looked like he had swallowed a radish. Inspector Mernil—of the Special Peacekeepers, as he rarely failed to remind you—was seldom comfortable out of jackboots and armor. To be dressed in the same casual clothes as undisciplined students was galling. Kendrick made a face at Wilde and reached beneath his black suit jacket to check one of his pistols.

"Do you have to do that?" Wilde asked. "You'll draw attention."

"When is your damn friend going to show up? We've been waiting half an hour."

"It's been ten minutes," Wilde replied.

"And why are we wearing civvies? You know I hate wearing civvies."

"You hate not having socialists to shoot at. You'd be happy in a barrel if you were firing at something."

Kendrick struggled to argue with this point, and failed. "Well…I don't know what good this is going to do anyway. These blasted students have no respect for anyone in authority. Anarchists, the lot of them, if you ask me."

"Shut up and drink your coffee," Wilde answered, trying not to laugh. Turning to look back at the street, he spotted the young man they were waiting for. "Ah, here he is!"

The fellow in question was clearly one of the university rabble, and the sight of his mismatched clothes was enough to make Wilde cringe. The young man's coat was dark green, his vest and baggy trousers brown; yet somehow the colors failed to coordinate. More distressingly, the young man's tie, while the same green as his coat, was covered in dark spots that were as likely to be ink stains as polka dots. He sauntered across the carriage-filled roadway without a sense of urgency, as tendrils of steam and boiler smoke from the passing vehicles licked at his back and heels. After taking a moment to exchange waves and handshakes with the other students at the café, he dropped cheerfully into a chair across from Wilde. He gave Wilde an affable smile, ordered a cup of coffee from a passing waiter, and then lounged back in his chair with the ease of a man composed entirely of liquid. Then, as if he was just noticing him, the student slowly turned his gaze toward Kendrick—who sat in plain view across from him—and jumped in surprise.

"Hey!" the student hissed at Wilde. "What's this then? What's the numb on that one?"

Kendrick looked at Wilde. "The what?"

Wilde shushed him before reassuring the student. "That's just Kendrick. He's glass, Manny, he's glass. He's OK."

"I'm *what?*" Kendrick demanded.

"You're *glass*. It means you're smooth. You're not…um…bumpy."

"*What?*" Kendrick repeated.

"Just shut up and let me do the talking."

"Hey, now…" Manny was peering very purposefully at Kendrick's moustache. "He's a copper, isn't he?"

Wilde let out a sigh. "Manny, I'm a copper."

"No, you're a tatter who cops." Manny fell silent as the waiter arrived with his coffee. He hid behind the cup, peering over the brim at Kendrick like a small animal watching a dog.

"Manny, I'll vouch for him: He's glass, OK? Now, can we move on?"

There was a long silence as Manny continued to peer out over the top of his cup. "OK. Whadya need?"

Wilde sighed. "Will you please put the cup down?"

Manny hesitated for a moment, then looked at Kendrick. "No."

"Fine." Wilde sipped his coffee, not in the mood to argue with either of them. "Manny, I need some information from you. You're the top tatter I know, so if anyone's got the info I need, it's you."

Manny snorted, but he finally relaxed a bit and lowered his cup. "Don't butter me up, Max; I'm not a sticky key. Just post me the titles."

"Fine, fine. I need the skinny on Salad Monday."

"Ha!" Manny laughed. Then he realized that it was not a joke. "You're not titting me, are you?"

"'Titting'?" Kendrick interjected, sour-faced.

Wilde turned to him in irritation. "Yes. It's…. Well, it means you're playing a joke on someone. Pulling their leg, but obnoxiously."

"Being a tit," Manny added, helpfully.

Kendrick's unpleasant expression darkened further. "A 'tit'?"

"Yes," Wilde answered. "It's a tatter who—"

"I know what a 'tit' is, Max, though the tooters sound a bit confused. Probably never seen a real one in their lives."

Manny made the mistake of trying to be helpful again. "Actually, it's 'tatters'—"

Kendrick growled and almost launched himself across the table at the young man.

"Down, Kendrick," Wilde ordered, mimicking the sharp tone of voice Cerys often used when dealing with Special Peacekeepers.

"Uh…eheh…." Kendrick caught himself leaning across the table and gave an awkward smile. "Right, right…. Sorry. Got, uh, carried away."

"Yes, well, save that for someone who deserves it." Wilde drained his cup and set it down. "Look, Manny, I need to find Salad Monday, and I need to find him by this morning's edition, read me?"

Manny was hiding behind his cup again. "Sharp and fresh, Max, sharp and fresh. But cite the facts: Salad Monday's been tatting since tatting first hit paper, and no one's cracked him yet. Eye-moth, cracking Salad Monday's potsy."

Kendrick's eye twitched as he tried to follow the conversation. "What was that?"

"In his opinion, finding Salad Monday's true identity is like putting one over on the censor. That is to say, impossible." Wilde turned back to Manny. "But someone out there has to know. Look at it this way: Salad Monday comments on all the big tatting papers. That means he reads all the big tatting papers. We both know you can't just pick up a broadsheet on the street corner…not yet, at least."

"Glass," Manny agreed. "You get the sheets posted special."

"That means someone's delivering them to him, and if no one's cracked him yet, it's because there's a reliable middleman. So, Manny, I want you to tell me who that middleman is."

Manny hesitated for a moment. "What's in it for me?" Across the table, Kendrick snarled, but Manny pushed on. "Max, you know I can't go posting you people's private letters. What kind of a tag would I buy myself with that? Giving out private numbs to coppers, Max…. I'd be for the furnace if I did that."

Wilde sighed. "Manny, you know me. You know I wouldn't tell anyone where I got my info. And I'll tell you what, you point me in the right direction and I'll take you with me to the Martyrs next week. August Mars is playing, and I think I can get you backstage."

Manny gave Wilde a wide-eyed stare over the top of his coffee cup. "You'd do that?"

"Of course, Manny. We're friends." Wilde smiled sincerely, and then turned the screws. "But if we're going to go, I need to be done with this case, and I can't finish the case without your help."

Manny made a face. "You're turning the cop on me, Max."

"Manny, you know I'd never do that. But I have a job to do, and I need your help doing it. Just point me the right way. I swear I won't so much as think your name for the rest of the investigation."

There was a long silence as Manny stared into his cup. Once or twice he glanced toward the other students, clearly expecting the worst; but as was often the case with young university types, Manny's friends were too busy talking amongst themselves to realize that he was having another conversation nearby, let alone with whom.

"OK. If you want Salad Monday's house, you'll be looking at the tops. Big type printers who won't be buttered into selling his number, else he'd be cracked already. I only know three: Maynard and Sons; Edgewood, Franklin, and Co.; and Belle Street Printers, Ltd. If they're not posting for him, I don't know who is. Read me?"

"Sharp and fresh, Manny," Wilde answered. "Which one's the biggest?"

"Belle Street, but I wouldn't start there."

"No?"

Manny shook his head and looked around cautiously. "Edgewood's the only one of the three that printed tit-tat when it first came out. If Salad Monday's tatting for one of the other two, then he jumped ship from another house a few years back. And when you change houses in tit-tat—"

"The old printers have no incentive to keep your real name a secret," Wilde finished. "They'd have sold Salad Monday's identity to the highest bidder by now. Manny, you're the best. For this, I'll get you that backstage meeting with Mars."

"Thanks, Max, you're OK. Now, uh...." Manny glanced over at the cluster of other students.

Wilde waved him away. "Off you go, Manny."

Manny grinned awkwardly, still eyeing Kendrick as if the latter were some sort of rabid animal. Then he drained his cooling coffee in one gulp and wandered off to join his fellow students, who greeted Manny with cheers and handshakes as if he had only just arrived. The realization that he had been engaged in conversation only a few tables away was completely lost on them.

"Right," Wilde said, throwing down some money and rising from his chair. "Off we go, Kendrick. Time to put the fear of Heaven into some people."

"Now you're using words I understand," Kendrick replied with a terrible smile.

The printing house of Edgewood, Franklin, and Co. was perhaps the noisiest place Wilde had ever been. From the vantage point of a second-story balcony, he watched two rows of automated printing presses rapidly turning cylinders of pulp paper into piles of broadsheets. In between, engineers in oily clothes scurried back and forth, anticipating breakdowns and lubricating the countless moving parts. Junior clerks rushed from machine to machine, retrieving armloads of printed papers and resetting type codes. Off in rooms to either side, typists could be seen at their desks, using complicated keyboards to set the type codes for the next batch of issues.

Of course, Wilde recalled, his second-story position was an illusion. In fact, he was six floors above the street, since the room he was in rested on two identical chambers filled with printing presses and typesetters. Like many of the businesses in the City of Salmagundi, Edgewood, Franklin, and Co. had maximized their efficiency by capitalizing on vertical space. Indeed, the printing house tower continued further upward with several floors of offices above the printing halls.

"Now then, gentlemen," said the upright and stern-faced Mr. Edgewood, "I expect we shall enjoy a little more privacy here than in my office. What is this 'delicate matter' you feel you must discuss with me? At the outset, I should like to remind you that we take no responsibility for the content of articles printed by our company. If you've been offended by something, you must take it up with the author."

"No, no, nothing of the sort," Wilde assured him, "but we are interested in contacting one of your authors."

"Oh, yes?" Edgewood said, his tone not altogether pleasant.

"I understand you're the printing house that works with the commentator known as Mr. Salad Monday. Is that correct?" It was a bluff, of course, but worth a try.

Edgewood studied the two men before him in silence. At length, he answered, "Very well. I don't know how you found out, but yes, he is one of our clients."

"Then I assume that your company arranges to have his papers delivered as well."

"Yes…" came the cautious reply.

Wilde smiled. "In that case, sir, I need to know who he is…or at least where he can be found."

Edgewood's face paled horribly, then flushed with great offense. "You expect me to give out the private address of one of our clients?"

"Yes," Wilde answered flatly. "I assure you, Mr. Edgewood, that we'll keep your involvement strictly confidential, but I *need* that information."

"Inspector, you don't seem to understand, so let me make this exceedingly clear to you. The anonymity of my clients is a sacred trust, as surely as if it were sworn in the presence of a priest or a magistrate. The credibility of this printing house demands that we bow to neither bribery nor intimidation, and I am not inclined to make an exception for the likes of *you*." He brushed at the lapels of his frock coat dismissively. "And don't try to threaten me with that police-man's nonsense of yours either. I know my rights as a taxpayer. I'm above your routine harassment. You don't even have a warrant, or else you'd have shown it to me by now."

"Mr. Edgewood, I think you're being somewhat unreasonable here. I'm asking for the address of *one man.*"

"Principles, Inspector."

Wilde tried a different approach. Narrowing his eyes, he moved half a step closer to Edgewood than most people would have found comfortable. "I arrived without a warrant out of consideration for your reputation, Mr. Edgewood. You aren't a suspect here, so why bother with all the ribbon?" He assumed that Edgewood, like most citizens, could be brought into line by the threat of red tape.

Edgewood was unmoved. "They wouldn't give you one if you tried, Inspector. I am a taxpayer, if you recall. Go and try your strong-arm methods with those paupers down on Layer Five. I have no time for it. I expect you two can see yourselves out. Don't soil anything on your way to the door."

He turned to walk away, fingers tucked around the edges of his vest, but instead of the open walkway, he found himself confronted with Kendrick's bowler, dark suit, and quivering moustache. Without a word, Kendrick gripped Edgewood by the lapels of his coat and lifted the smaller man into the air.

"I say, how dare—" Edgewood began.

"Let's try it this way," Kendrick interrupted. "I'm going to count to ten. If you've answered the Inspector's question by then, I'll put you down. If you haven't, I'll count to ten again. If you answer by then, I'll put you down on the printing room floor," he said, nodding to the open chamber that lay a dozen feet below them. "But if you still haven't answered, I'll put you down outside the window. And we're…" he turned his head to Wilde, "what, fifty feet up?"

"More like seventy," came the deadpan reply.

"But…but…." Edgewood was struggling to understand that a policeman had dared to manhandle him. "You can't do this!"

"One," Kendrick counted.

"I think you'd better do as he says," Wilde offered, with a helpless shrug.

"Two."

"But I'm a taxpayer!"

"Three."

"You're peacekeepers! You can't do this!"

"Four."

Wilde shook his head. "No, I'm a peacekeeper."

"Five."

"He's a 'Special' peacekeeper."

"Six."

"Special?" Edgewood gasped, all the more frightened that he did not understand the significance.

"Seven," Kendrick said, exchanging nods with Wilde.

"Special," Wilde confirmed.

"Eight."

The color drained from Edgewood's face, and his head snapped toward Kendrick as he struggled to say something, anything, to halt the counting.

Kendrick gave the man a sympathetic smile.

"Nine."

The address belonging to the mysterious Mr. Salad Monday was a small townhouse located in of one of Layer Three's poorer neighborhoods. While hardly approaching the squalor and poverty found among the laboring classes of the lower city, the less-affluent residents of the bourgeois Layer Three still lived in an unenviable state. Their houses were often old or run-down, and it would be dubious to claim that they were truly worth the rents they paid. But surely, the landlords insisted, the superior ambiance of the layer was more than compensation for the extra cost.

Salad Monday's townhouse was a weathered brick construction, similar to many of the neighboring buildings. It rested at the end of a long alleyway, one kept clean as much through the locals' efforts as the municipal workers'. It seemed doubtful that the city sweeping machines could even fit down the narrow street.

The front door was locked, of course, but it was a poor Legion officer who was not a good housebreaker. The building's interior was solid but weathered, with peeling, yellowed wallpaper that no one had bothered to replace in ages.

Thick sheets of dust covered everything, confirming the building's general disuse, and there were no footprints or signs of passage to be found upon the floor, stairs, or banisters.

In the ancient foyer, Wilde glanced at Kendrick, only to see that the other man had drawn two service revolvers from inside his coat and was peering along them toward the interior of the house.

"Kendrick!"

"What?"

Wilde made a face as he led the way into the front hallway. "Put those things away."

Kendrick's eyes darted around the hallway, peering at the dim gaslamps and dusty surfaces as if they might attack at any moment. "There could be terrorists."

"Terrorists who don't leave footprints? Be sensible. Besides, if there is anyone here—which I'm beginning to doubt—it'll be a lot of idiot students, not armed men." Some distant sound caught his attention. He held up a hand for silence, ignoring the fact that he was the one speaking. "Shhh. Do you hear that?"

The two men listened for a moment. Presently they heard a noise rising up through the hallways of the house. It was the all-too-familiar sound of perhaps a dozen typewriters clacking away in unison. The clicks came from further in the house, slowly trickling along the layers of dust until it seemed they emanated from the very walls. The two officers looked about, turning this way and that as they strained to hear where the sound could be coming from.

"Well, there's clearly someone here," Wilde noted softly.

"Must be using a back entrance to avoid footprints," Kendrick agreed. He raised his pistols and began to edge along the corridor. "Bastards are probably downstairs in the cellar."

Wilde tilted his head. "Wait, Kendrick. I think it's coming from upstairs."

"Then search up there if you want," Kendrick answered, peering around a nearby corner as if he expected hordes of terrorists to be lying in wait. "I say it's the cellar, and that's where I'm going."

Wilde knew better than to argue. As Kendrick disappeared in search of the cellar door, Wilde made for the stairway. The sound of typing was clearer on the second floor, and clearer still as Wilde climbed upward toward the third. The rooms on this floor bore the only signs of habitation; for though there was no activity, they were filled to bursting with piles and piles of newspapers, broadsheets, chapbooks, and other printed materials. The heaps of paper had been neatly placed in some sort of complex order, but nothing had been done to protect them from moths and insects. Many of the papers had been partly devoured by whatever loathsome vermin infested the house.

He exited the room. Dust was everywhere, as thickly layered as on the first-floor, but in the hallway Wilde noticed some curious trails upon the ground. Here and there the dust had been disturbed in narrow, twisting lines. Wilde knelt to study these, but he could make nothing of them. They clearly led up and down the stairs in the direction of the front door, but what they were or what they signified remained unknown. If anything, it seemed like someone had trailed the tips of feathers through the dust.

The stairs continued upward to a single attic door. Just upon the threshold, the typewriter clacking was incredibly loud. Wilde felt a shiver descend along his back. There was no reason for fear—the typists were, no doubt, only foolish students who would be as likely to run or beg mercy as fight—but Wilde's instinct for danger was still working full-time. Reaching for the handle, Wilde eased the door open and stepped into the room beyond. He did not immediately understand what it was that he saw.

The room was larger than it appeared from outside, for it stretched almost the full length and breadth of the house. The peaked ceiling was exceedingly high, and from it hung a series of burning lamps that kept the attic space bright enough for typing. Piles of printed broadsheets littered the floor. A number of tables had been placed about the center of the room in a rough circular shape, and they were covered variously by stacks of blank paper, typing ribbon, and easily a dozen typewriters. There were no chairs in front of the tables, a point which at first confused Wilde. He was likewise bewildered by the room's clear desolation: there was no one to be seen anywhere. And yet the typewriters were clicking away still, as if driven by the hands of ghosts. At first, Wilde thought the machines might be automated, but he could see no punchcard reader to direct them, nor steam lines to power them.

As Wilde approached the typewriters, he became aware of certain peculiar details that he had not initially noticed. It seemed as if a series of silken streamers had been hung from the ceiling over each keyboard, yet if the tendrils were cloth or thread, they must have been waxed to give them that unthinkable glisten. There was a luster to them, yet at the same time they were all but translucent. They seemed more mirage than substance and were a curious iridescent color, an impossible mixture of blue, violet, turquoise, and magenta. The tendrils all seemed to drift and float through one another like trailing strings of light, yet they were somehow responsible for the movement of the typewriter keys.

Wilde's eyes followed the fantastically colored lines upward toward the peak of the roof, where they joined together into a layered mass of themselves. This "body," if such a term could be applied to it, was something akin to a pile of translucent gelatin, with lines and layers too numerous for the eye to understand. In some parts of the floating mass there were strange concentrations of light. These, Wilde suddenly realized, were eyes. Each was fixed diligently upon the typewriter below it, though they were all clearly working independently of one another. As Wilde watched, a collection of tendrils paused in their typing and reached out to a pile of broadsheets. The paper drifted toward the underside of the floating mass, and the folds of the vibrantly colored dome pulled back to reveal a series of things that might have been mouths, or mandibles, or complex beaks. These began to devour the printed newspaper hungrily.

Wilde stood rooted to the spot, gazing in fear and rapture at the floating thing. He was too good a policeman to simply dismiss the sight outright, but his mind worked double-time to find some comfortable explanation that could make sense of the combination of place, time, and creature. It was tempting to think that the creature's presence might be some terrible coincidence—that it had happened along and eaten the house's occupant moments before Wilde's arrival—but the most impossible answer was also the simplest: the floating mass of tentacles and iridescence must be Mr. Salad Monday.

As he stood and watched the creature devour its meal of decaying broadsheets, Wilde's first realization was followed by another. It was all to do with paper. The heaps and piles of paper scattered throughout the house were not simply pieces of a decaying archive. They were both food and entertainment. There was little doubt that Salad Monday the tatter enjoyed the challenge of typewritten argument, but it seemed that Salad Monday the monster also enjoyed the pages upon which the arguments were delivered.

In spite of himself, Wilde coughed. One cluster of lights rolled through the curious mass to fix its gaze upon the intruder. These stared at Wilde for a moment, twitching monstrously as they tried to bring him into focus. Then another set joined them, then another. Soon it seemed that all of the dreadful eyes had migrated to one section of the body and were staring at the solitary figure below. The dangling tendrils ceased their typing, and the room fell silent. Wilde licked his lips and realized that he could not seem to raise his pistol. He stared at the creature's eyes and saw in them what might have been hunger or malice or fear.

Then, without a moment's warning, Salad Monday's tendrils quivered and tucked themselves up beneath the folds of its floating body. The mass of color rippled violently, and suddenly it was gone, vanishing upward into the dark rafters. As Wilde stared, he thought he could see hints of movement pass through the blackness above the lamps and toward the far end of the attic.

A moment later the door burst open behind Wilde, and Kendrick rushed in with his revolvers raised. "You're right, Wilde!" he cried. "Cellar's emp—" Kendrick paused for a moment as he saw the array of now-vacant typewriters. "Bastards!" he cried. "Don't worry, Wilde, we'll find the buggers. They can't have gone far." And with that, Kendrick bolted across the room and into a back hallway, ignoring completely the floor's lack of footprints or signs of human passage.

"Kendrick, wait!" Wilde shouted. His words fell on disinterested ears. Kendrick's blood was up, and he was too hot on the chase to bother with details such as who he was chasing or where they had gone.

Kendrick searched around in the moldering dimness of the attic for a few minutes, overturning piles of paper and kicking at bits of rubbish that lay long abandoned upon the floor. Finding no students or terrorists hiding in the shadows, he flung open an exterior door on the other side of the attic and dashed outside.

"They've gone for the rooftops, Wilde!" he shouted. "C'mon, we'll catch them in no time!"

Wilde watched in silence as Kendrick dashed off on his mad chase. Shaking his head, Wilde began to walk toward the outside door, thinking that he ought to catch Kendrick up before the other inspector ran too far afield.

A strange rush above his head drove Wilde to glance upward, and he caught a glimpse of luminescence pass along the spine of the ceiling. Turning, he saw the strange lines and colors of Salad Monday hovering above the circle of typewriters. The creature had given the illusion of departure, then sought to backtrack toward the stairs.

"Cunning devil…" Wilde murmured.

Salad Monday's tentacles extended downward in clusters and began to wrap around a couple of the typewriters. Wilde watched in confusion, uncertain what was being done. The typewriters were slowly raised into the air, held beneath Salad Monday's quivering multi-colored mass with the care of a mother cradling a child.

Not sure what to do, Wilde extended a hand and called out to the floating shape. "Stop!"

Salad Monday shook in surprise, and its bright eyes darted through its body and clustered on the side that faced Wilde. The creature began to edge back toward the staircase, behaving less like a ravening monster and more like a frightened animal.

"Stop!" Wilde repeated, slowly advancing to match Salad Monday's pace. "Can you understand me?"

Salad Monday shivered slightly, but there was some sense of comprehension in the brightness of its eyes.

"I'm from the Legion of Peace," Wilde continued, keeping his voice level. "Do you understand?" He motioned to himself. "Police." He took a few more careful steps forward. "I know who you are. You're Mr. Salad Monday, aren't you?"

Wilde had hoped this pronouncement would help to set Salad Monday at ease, by acknowledging the creature as something with an identity rather than some unthinking monster. Instead, as the name was uttered, Salad Monday drew itself up, eyes shining with the same terror that it had shown when Wilde first arrived. With barely a moment's hesitation, Salad Monday rippled like a sheet in the wind and dove down the stairs with tremendous speed.

"Oh, Hell!" Wilde swore, dashing after the receding shape.

He scrambled down the dusty stairs to the third floor, head turning this way and that as he tried to keep sight of Salad Monday. He caught a glimpse of the creature on the way to the second floor, but it was a fleeting one. Continuing downward, Wilde's feet struck a smooth patch on one of the steps and he lost his balance. His head struck the wooden boards with a painful smack, and he lay in a daze for a moment.

Shaking his head, Wilde pulled himself to his feet and rushed down into the front hall, determined to make up for lost time, but at the bottom of the stairs, he was met with silence. Cursing softly, Wilde rushed through the deserted rooms of the crumbling house and the alleys outside, searching in desperation for the creature that he had come to find. He was met with desolation. Mr. Salad Monday had vanished, seemingly into the very woodwork itself.

Wilde finally returned to the Chief Inspector's office at the end of the day, still in a daze. He and Kendrick had searched every inch of the house—first on their own, and later with a squad of Legion soldiers from the local precinct house—but it had been of no use. They had confiscated the remaining typewriters, along with boxes of replacement keys and ribbon. There had been a limited attempt to catalogue the piles of broadsheets and books, but that had quickly been abandoned as an act of futility.

Wilde found Cerys behind her desk, glaring at a mass of paperwork that seemed to have grown rather than diminished since Wilde's departure. Wilde entered and softly closed the door. Cerys was busy selecting a cigarette from a battered tin case, and she did not look up as she motioned for Wilde to join her. The air was already thick with smoke and fragrances of half a dozen different blends; it went without saying that the ashtray was overflowing.

"Lavender?" Wilde asked, noting the smell of the smoking herbs. He set a bundle of fresh evening broadsheets down on the chair next to him. He had bought them before dinner, but in his agitation he had been unable to read them.

"I'm celebrating my funeral early," Cerys replied. "What's the word on Salad Monday? Is he a terrorist?"

"Chief, you won't believe what happened."

Cerys—who had her nose buried in a bundle of forms—looked up at him and took on one of her very particular expressions. "Max, stop. Don't tell me. I don't want to know."

"Chief?"

Cerys took out her pocket fire and lit a fresh cigarette, releasing a cloud of lavender-scented smoke. "I know that look on your face, and it tells me I sure as taxes don't want to know what just happened to you. All I want…no, all I need to know is whether Salad Monday is going to be a problem. Is he a terrorist?"

"Um…no."

Cerys flicked her pocket fire on and off as she continued her questioning. "Is he working for Slater?"

"No."

"Is he a threat to the city?"

"Well, I don't think so. But, Chief, he's not even—"

Cerys pointed a handful of papers at Wilde in a most menacing fashion. "Max, I've done this job long enough to know that when someone comes to me and says 'Chief, you'll never believe what I saw,' they're either lying or telling the truth. Either way, I don't want to know unnecessary details that will one day drive me to drink."

"You already drink."

"I'm just getting into the swing of it," Cerys replied. Then she gave him a sympathetic look. "Max, I've seen my share of unbelievable things in this blasted city. Take my advice: don't think about it too hard. It'll hurt less that way."

Wilde slowly unrolled one of the broadsheets and tried to relax. "It's that easy, is it?"

"Drinking helps."

"Mmm."

Wilde was doubtful about his ability to put such an experience out of his mind, so he turned to the best source of distraction he could think of. The pointless arguments and self-important tirades of the tit-tat broadsheets began to soothe his shaken nerves, and soon Wilde was on his way to easing the strain of his recent discovery. Then he turned to a second printed page. His eye caught a name that was new, but unmistakably familiar.

"Ahh!" he cried, leaping from his chair.

Cerys looked up from her paperwork again, flicking her pocket fire on and off in nervous habit. "What?"

Wilde thrust the broadsheet toward Cerys and pointed at a small section of print located just beneath the main articles. It read very clearly: "Though circumstance demands brevity, let me say simply that Mr. Jervais Mutton is, as ever, a dunce hardly worthy of consideration. Anyone doubting this fact should turn to his latest comment regarding the need for a citizen militia to protect us against the danger of unwed mothers. Additionally, while the police provide a useful service to society, their violation of the homes of private citizens does not do their reputations credit. Discuss. Yours sincerely, Mr. Herring Tuesday."

"It's him!" Wilde cried. "It has to be him! He can't have written this more than an hour after I found him…it…him…. It's still out there!" Wilde tried desperately to convey to his superior the gravity of the situation. The result was less than profound. "Tentacles, Chief!"

Cerys was very familiar with the look on Wilde's face. She had seen it on her own reflection in the mirror more times than she could count. It was the look of someone who had witnessed the unthinkable and was trying desperately to make sense of it.

"That's it, Max, early night for you. Go tell Marguerite you're taking her to the cinema."

"But—" Wilde protested, pointing to the broadsheet.

"Out!" Cerys glanced at her chronometer, then rummaged around for an amusements circular on her desk. "If you two can catch an omnibus in the next ten minutes, you'll be at the Palace in time for the newsreel and cartoon. And look at that…tonight they've got another adventure of Minnie the Mouser. Won't that be fun?"

"Chief—" Wilde tried again.

Cerys glanced at her chronometer again. "Nine minutes."

Wilde sighed. "OK, Chief, OK."

"There's a good fellow." Cerys pushed the young man toward the door. "Go have fun. Oh, and Max…"

"Yes, Chief?"

Cerys gave Wilde's shoulders a purposeful squeeze. "If you get her into trouble, I'll kill you."

"Oh, come on, Chief, it's me!"

"That's the idea."

When Wilde had gone, Cerys returned to her desk. She stared for a long while at the mountains of paperwork, her eyes slowly and consistently drifting back to the stack of broadsheets Wilde had left. Then, with a sudden rush of purpose—or perhaps procrastination—she snatched up a pen and began to compose a letter. She addressed it to the printing house responsible for the comment by "Mr. Tuesday" and then began writing, in the most grandiose language she could imagine. "To Messrs. Monday and Tuesday, with assorted foodstuffs. Dear sirs, our humblest apologies for intrusions, etc. Necessities of the work, etc. In future, please refrain from frightening respectable policemen in pursuit of their duty, etc. Humbly, etc., the lady on the Broad Street omnibus, Mrs."

Chuckling to herself, Cerys set the note aside, intending to dispatch it when she left for the night. There was no telling whether it would ever been seen by Salad Monday, but at least the thought of it amused her.

A nagging thought tugged at the fringes of her imagination, and for a moment Cerys found herself contemplating the implications of what Wilde might have seen.

Tentacles.

Clearing her throat to dismiss such thoughts, Cerys lit another lavender cigarette and spent a few moments staring into the flame of her pocket fire. Then, with a familiar sigh, she turned back to the mountain of paperwork on her desk. She was tempted to set fire to the whole lot, and she smiled wistfully at the thought. She was still smiling, with visions of bureaucratic conflagrations in her head, as she turned to the next case file in her unending pile of assignments.

The Persecution Machine

Tanith Lee

TANITH LEE was born in 1947 in London, England. She has written nearly 100 novels and collections and almost 300 short stories, plus radio plays and TV scripts for the BBC. She has received several awards, including the August Derleth Award and World Fantasy Award. In 2009 she was made a Grand Master of Horror. Norilana Books has just published a collection of her horror stories, *Sounds and Furies*, and is presently reprinting her entire Flat Earth opus, Birthgrave and Storm Lord sagas, with new books in each series to follow. Two volumes of her short stories are also out from Wildside Press. She lives on the southeast coast of England with her husband, writer/artist John Kaiine. For more information visit her website at www. TANITHLEE.COM.

I: UNCLE

MY FATHER GALLOPED into the library with a look of terror.

"Your uncle is coming!"

"My—uncle? Who do you mean?"

"Constant."

"But I thought—"

"No," said my father, running to the window and glaring out nervously. "He isn't dead. Only mad."

"I see."

"Of course you don't." My father spared a look of distaste for me. As his son, I had had certain duties never properly explained, one of which had been to become a perfect replica of himself in the city of business. Instead I had metamorphosed into a fashionable writer, and it was not in him to forgive me. "Well," he said now, "since you're so clever, I'll leave you to entertain him. Try telling him who you are."

"We've discussed this previously. I'm not clever, only a genius. As for Uncle Constant, if he's calling here, presumably he wishes to see you. After all, does he even know of my existence? I'm sure I didn't know of his."

"It was kept from you. I expect he will have learned. Twenty years since I saw him. Horrible."

"Is he deformed?" I inquired with pleasant anticipation.

"No. Only his mind. Stall the wretch. Get him to leave if possible."

I shrugged. "Does Mother share your aversion?"

"Your mother will faint," said my father, "if he so much as touches the panels of her parlour door." My mother tended to faint continually when confronted by annoyance. She had already fainted once at my arrival. My father had had the grace only to offer to throw me out. A recent short novel of mine, dealing with forbidden love, very, I may say, tastefully, had caused their latest dislike of me. I, meanwhile, came to visit them from a sense of responsibility, since they were always in want of money.

But what was the motive for mad Constant's arrival?

The doorbell rang below. My father shrieked and rushed from the room.

When Steppings appeared presently in the library door, I accordingly asked him to show the visitor up.

A moment later, my Uncle Constant was revealed to me.

He was a man of about fifty-eight or sixty, corpulent but pale, with a mane of grey hair and disordered clothes. He seemed out of breath, as if he had been running, and he darted a wild look about the room.

"Are we alone?" he demanded.

"I believe so."

"Who are you?"

"Your nephew, Charles."

"Who? Oh, never mind it. Only let me sit down. I'm exhausted. They've pursued me all day. Not a second's peace." He fell noisily into a large chair.

Steppings reappeared, mostly from nosiness, but I sent him off to bring some of my father's Madeira. I had no qualms in this, since I had supplied the wine myself.

"Well, Uncle. How may I help you?"

"Help? Impossible. No one can help. I ask only a minute's respite." His breathing quieted a little and he blew his nose into a gigantic handkerchief. "It's no use my explaining. Only I understand what I suffer."

"This may be said of each of us."

"I see you're a philosopher, sir. Did you say we are related? My God, I've run into my brother's house, haven't I?"

"Didn't you know?"

"I will run in anywhere I am able when they are after me."

"Who? Do you mean the police?"

My Uncle Constant was racked with melodramatic laughter.

Steppings came in with the wine and a tray of biscuits.

Constant struck the tray and the biscuits flew in all directions. Steppings did not flinch, merely put on the expression—of a surprised chicken—which has seen such good service over the years. I rescued the Madeira and poured two glasses, waving the chicken away as I did so.

"Drink this."

"Is it poison?"

"I don't think so."

"Nothing short of poison is any use to me. I pant to be released from my suffering. But suicide is a sin." He reminded me of my father. Uncle Constant drank the Madeira at a gulp, and I refilled his glass. "They're after me, worse than ever. Their weapons—if only you knew."

He, as my father had done, bustled to the window. He stared out, I assumed, at the peaceful street.

"Not yet," he muttered. "But soon."

"And you have no matters to consult my father upon?" I asked.

"Who? Who is your father?"

"Your brother."

"I have no brother," said Uncle Constant. "I am cast out into the wilderness." Then his face contorted. It grew red, then blue. "I hear it!" he cried. And flinging the goblet on the ground, or rather the carpet, he sprang away and was gone. I heard his cascade down the stairs and the crash of the street door.

I stood by the window and presently saw him emerge and scuttle fatly down the street. He disappeared from view.

2: Uncle's Story

Although I questioned my father and mother about my Uncle Constant, neither told me anything. My father ranted and my mother fainted. Steppings looked like a chicken, and when I tried to enlist his help, only importuned me to persuade my parents to use a new sort of cheese in the mouse-traps. I told him that I disapproved of mouse-traps. Steppings confided that he himself ate the cheese. It was a harmless perversion, during which he sometimes emitted small squeaks.

I was touched by his trust, but it did not help me to discover my uncle.

However, a month later, endless searching led me to a tall gaunt house in the south of the capital. Here a gentleman bearing my uncle's name resided. The instant I beheld the house, I knew it must be he.

Large bars were on all the windows, and a sort of portcullis was let down outside the door.

On my ringing the door bell, through the portcullis, no one came.

It was a sunny day, and I sat down across the street on a low wall to watch and wait.

Presently a maid came out of the house with the low wall.

She attempted some ineffectual dusting of the privet hedge, and then bent to my ear.

"He's a madman, that one. You after him for a debt?"

"Not at all. I am a long lost lover of his, come to call on him."

"You're one of them preeverts," said the maid, and ran in.

Half an hour later, two somberly clad women, with the figures but not the charm of pigeons, came down the street, mounted my uncle's steps, and banged on the portcullis.

I could tell at a glance they were religious persons, and that a lack of response would not put them off. It did not. Getting no reply, they banged the louder. And the larger lady began to cry: "Open the doors of your hearts, O ye lost children of the Lord. Hear the word of the Master!"

I expected a window to be raised and some missile inserted through the bars and thrown.

Instead, to my surprise and delight, sounds of vast unlockings eventually echoed over the street, the portcullis lifted, and my uncle appeared in the doorway.

He wore a yellow dressing-gown and a look of fear and loathing.

"Be off," he yelled at the two ladies, "I know your tricks. Where is it? Is it near? I won't be decoyed."

"Repent," said the large lady. "Here is a tract—"

But Uncle Constant swept the article from her gloved hand.

"Away!" howled Uncle, and thrust her down the steps.

The lady fell upon the other one and both toppled to the ground. There was the hideous noise of bursting corsets.

Before my uncle could shut the door and the portcullis I leapt across the street, over the wallowing ladies, and up the steps. I seized Uncle Constant's hand.

"Uncle Constant!"

"Aah! Villain! Unhand me."

"I am your nephew, Charles," I intimated, as he tried to run me through with his sword-stick.

"Who?"

"Your nephew. We met a month ago."

"You're not one of their spies?" He peered at me. "No. Your hair's too long and you have no moustache. Come in then. Quickly. Let me lock the house. I am in deadly peril. If they should once gain a foothold—there! Do you hear it? No. No, you would never hear it."

He slammed the door against the world and we were in a dark hall papered with a design of large red bats, or perhaps prehistoric birds.

"But I did hear—" I began. My uncle took no notice.

Once he had let down the portcullis by means of a switch, locked the door three times and bolted it twice, my uncle led me up a carpeted stair and into a small, dim room. The bat wall-paper persisted, but otherwise there were chairs and a sofa and some brandy on a stand. Through the bars of the windows and heavy dusty lace, little was visible, and I imagined that he preferred this to be so.

"Sit down," said my uncle, "whoever you are."

"Uncle Constant, I did hear a noise. Perhaps a train?"

My uncle looked at me strangely. He frowned. Then, going to the stand, he poured out two generous brandies.

He did not, though, give either one to me, or take one himself; he left them where they were as a decoration.

"I will tell you my terrible tale," said my uncle.

"Thank you."

"You must not interrupt."

I nodded mutely.

Assuaged, perhaps, my uncle seated himself in a vast armchair that rather resembled a pig.

"In my youth," he began, "I had no cares. I did very much as I wanted. I had been thought too clever for school, and so a number of tutors had taught me at home. I had no friends and wished for none. My only interest, as I grew older, was collecting young actresses. Then one evening, on my way home from the theatre, I was met by a messenger in the street. My parents had perished in a fire at the house of an ice-cream manufacturer, and I had now inherited the family fortune."

Although I knew that my grandparents were not dead, and that there had never been a family fortune, I did not argue with Uncle Constant at this point. I felt that probably he was instinctually lying in order to give some framework to what might follow.

"I fell," he continued, as if gratified by my sensitive abstention, "into a melancholy. I stayed indoors and only wandered from room to room of the house, recalling the unhappy hours I had spent there with my parents, who were both obtuse and ugly. The prettiness of my actress collection came to repel me, and I saw these girls no more. After some months, I ventured out at night, and walked the nastiest thoroughfares of the city, until it was almost dawn. Gradually, as I was returning to the house, I became aware that I was being, and had indeed been for some while, followed, by a number of mysterious shadowy figures. At length, a peculiar noise resounded distantly behind the smoking chimneys and smouldering refuse pits of the alleys."

My uncle looked at me expectantly, but, true to his wish, I did not interrupt. Consoled, he went on.

"I can only describe this noise as that of some curious engine, which also whistled, rather like a factory hooter. *Chug chug,* it went, and then *Whoop! Whoop!* Alarmed, I hastened home, but after I was indoors I heard something move down the street and a shadow was cast upon my windows."

My uncle got up, and going to the brandy glasses, he poured their contents into an aspidistra, then refilled them carefully from the decanter. He left them on the stand, and resumed his chair and his tale.

"Soon after this, when I had gone out once more on some necessary business, I was again followed, and after a time I heard repeated the ominous chugging and whooping of the sinister engine. I hurried at once on to a busy thoroughfare, and there the din of the crowd somewhat mitigated the sound of the pursuit. After a few minutes, however, a frightful shooting pain began in my right knee. And then another, worse, in my right arm. I fell against a lamppost, and an old gentleman came up and smote me in the face, accusing me of being drunk. As I partly lay there, I saw, through the ranks of the oblivious and jeering crowd, a fearful thing rolling slowly and mightily down from the end of the street. It was a sort of carriage, yet it had no horses, and from it protruded all manner of pipes and coils, wheels that whirred and the nozzles of what could only be guns. Suddenly one of these flashed with a cold green fire, and a new pain lanced through my belly. Atop the device was a crew of men clad like explorers in long coats, goggles, and unlikely hats. They had moustaches and their lips were thin and cruel. From the midst of them a funnel glowed and steamed and out came the noise. *Chug, chug.* And then *Whoop, whoop.* No one in the street but I could see this evil equipage. I turned; and, as best I could for my hurts, I ran. The more distance I could put between myself and the engine of torment, the more relief I gained, and finally I shut myself into the house and knew an end to my pain. Its four walls, imbued as they were with boring memories of my parents, protected me. But as I crouched behind the door, the machine passed down the street. Its shadow fell again inside the house. From that day, I have not been free of it."

My uncle rose once more and paced to an empty parrot cage. He stared into it and shook his head.

"So far, they have not gained access to my home. Now and then their spies seek me. The machine never lies in wait for me outside the house…a sporting chance is allowed me—although they are not really fair. If ever the machine can by stealth enter these premises, I am lost."

A vague rumbling sounded in the street. A faint shadow crossed the window and next the ceiling. I got up and went to look out. The street was empty but for another maid dusting a hedge, and two porters carrying a stuffed bear. The religious ladies had picked themselves up and gone away.

"You may speak now," said my uncle.

"Have you," I asked, "approached no one for help?"

"In the beginning, ceaselessly. I went to the police, and then to private companies. But all laughed me to scorn. An eminent doctor has certified that I am harmlessly mad."

"The engine or machine is invisible to all others but yourself?"

My uncle returned to the brandy stand and drank both glasses of brandy. "I am doomed." He then showed me out of the house.

3: Uncle Pursued

After that second meeting, I took to following my Uncle Constant. He went out, as can be imagined from his fears, very seldom, and so my vigils were frequently long, dull and unrewarded—except by the emergence of the privet-dusting maid, who seemed to think that, despite my "preeversion," I fancied her person.

This was rather trying. However.

Finally, my uncle began to slip cautiously out of the house on hobbled rapid errands.

He would first of all open the door a crack, having of course noisily unlocked and unbolted it, and raised the portcullis. He would then gaze fixedly at each side of the street in turn. He never noticed me, even when I had not taken the trouble of obscuring myself behind the hedge. And I noted presently that, even if he looked at me on the street, he never recalled who I was or that I was anyone but a complete stranger.

Having perused both directions, Uncle Constant would leap forth and bolt one way or the other. Being portly, his quickness soon flagged, but he kept up what pace he could, his arms clutched to his chest, rather in the manner of a squirrel. Now and then he would break into a run. And frequently, he would glare behind him. In doing this, he often saw me, but paid, as I have said, no heed.

I, on the other hand, listened as intently and turned round as often as he.

It seemed to me that I heard a familiar noise in the distance, but I could not be sure how near we might be to some bizarre railway line or extraordinary factory, which might produce such sounds. Then, too, it sometimes seemed to me that shadows appeared at the ends of streets which bisected those pavements along which Uncle Constant rattled. Yet too I was never certain ordinary objects might not somehow have cast these shadows, and besides they were always fleeting.

Meanwhile other people and things moved all round us in the normal manner. My uncle occasionally barged into them, so oblivious was he of anything but the persecuting pursuit.

He never returned from his expeditions by the same route he had set out on, but always via a roundabout circuit. For presumably he was afraid, if the machine of torment was somewhere behind him, he might otherwise meet it head-on.

Uncle's outings were mundane and sketchy. Sorties upon shops of food and chemists' emporiums, and once a journey to a well-known and reputable bank. On this last foray, he emerged from the august portals amid cries and clangs, and squirreled down the steps, clutching at his left leg and muttering: "They're near." He was obviously in pain, and intercepting his terrified glance, I too looked back along the street.

The vista was thronged with people, and on the road were several carriages. It was apparent that no vehicle could pass unseen, if it were really there. As I gazed, it seemed to me that there was indeed something moving slowly and ponderously under the archway that opened the street. A faint greenish beam was struck from the place that might only be the morning sun upon some harness or other metallic item. My uncle distracted me with a hoarse scream. I turned and saw he had dropped to his knees. A bank-note fell from his hand, and I ran over, stopping the money before someone should snatch it, and next trying to assist him.

"Uncle—"

"Let me go, wretch!" screeched Uncle Constant, hitting me so violently in the chest that I too was flung on the ground. Before I could right myself he was up and hobbling, moaning away.

I then decided that, rather than rush after him in the usual fashion, I would wait at the roadside to see if any unusual carriage came past. I was encouraged in this idea by a repetition of the unlikely noise I had heard before—the *chug* and *whoop* of a mad engine, whistle or hooter. Then again, the street was noisy itself and I could not quite be sure.

I waited at the kerb for twenty minutes, by which time all the approaching traffic had gone by and my uncle was completely out of sight.

Irritated, I then stalked back up the road, and found an intersection. Staring down one of the opposing boulevards, I had the impression that something was trundling away there. Before I could go after it, a band of religious choristers enveloped me, and I was forced to give them cash before I could escape. By then, naturally, any hint of what might have been a strange vehicle, or only an optical-illusion generated by sympathy and hope for the unnatural, had vanished.

I returned to my uncle's house in a bad mood, and he was already indoors, the portcullis down and all signs of life concealed.

After this jaunt he did not venture out again, though I waited for many weeks.

Unfortunately my own life was becoming complicated. I was supposed to be at work upon a new volume of tasteful obliqueness, and had neglected it sadly. Various creditors were restless, and I was already receiving fewer social invitations. My publisher advised me that, unless I took up my employment, the public would forget me, and I feared I would therefore no longer have the money to support my feckless parents, who were just then in the process of buying whole suites of unsuitable furniture, busts of Roman generals, and a black parrot.

Regretfully, I left my post at the low wall opposite to my uncle's house. It was a fine evening, the west still flushed with dusk, and a lone light burned in an upper window. And far off without a doubt at this moment, I heard it in the stillness, *chug chug chug* and then its *whoop* on a high weird note. It was circling at a distance, like a beast of prey, the campfire of that solitary lamp.

But I could no longer stay.

I went to my home, and my novel, so much more real than Uncle's predicament.

4: THE MACHINE

It was on the afternoon that I delivered the finished manuscript of *The Fateful Kiss of Night* to my publishers that the last act of Uncle Constant's tragedy was played before me, and I was pulled irresistibly into it.

A beautiful afternoon of early summer, it had drawn the idle and the pleasure-seekers into the park. As I walked along beside the river the swans glided past like pillows with white necks, and the nurse-maids wheeled their bonneted toy babies up and down in perambulators. Young men pensively reflected in the glassy water, maidens sat reading under the statues, hoping the young men were secretly watching them, which, usually, they were not.

About two hundred yards off, over the wall of the park and its line of tall trees, an ominous sound came and went, and I had glanced that way in a consternation I did not at first fathom. But although an apparatus was out there, it was only a steam engine, resurfacing the roadway with pitch. With a sense of relief or disappointment, I returned my eyes to the picture-postcard scene of the park.

Across the flower-beds lay a lawn, at the centre of which was a coloured bandstand. Here the bandsmen were going at full blast, and on the lawn couples bumpily danced a polka.

The warm day lay limpid on the park with all its safe and proper comings and goings, a postcard view, as I say, into which an unsuitable figure abruptly burst: Uncle Constant.

Of those assembled, I was not the least startled.

How he had come there was beyond ascertaining, he seemed merely to erupt into being. And my premonition of the steam-roller was appropriate. Uncle was as usual in headlong flight. Indeed, he was in the most abject condition I had yet beheld, and through his wheezing, he faintly screamed.

As people hastened from his way, a few turned their heads anxiously to see what it was he fled from, what it was he saw as his head craned at a painful angle over one shoulder. But having turned, they shrugged and one or two made good-mannered gestures relating to insanity, while three pompous gentlemen began to shout for the police.

I also turned, more from habit than from the hope of finding anything.

And so I saw, at last, coming across the wholesome green grass on which little children played and young ladies walked with their parasols, the moving engine of my uncle's terror.

It was unmistakable. It was tall as the second storey of a fashionable house, and it glided smoothly forward on great black runners. Its look was of a monstrous bathchair, but one which bristled like a porcupine. Pipes and nozzles protruded from it, ornamental and deadly: One glance assured me that each must be a variety of gun. And even as I stared one indeed gave off a puff of dull viridian smoke followed by a quick white flash. And over the merry noise of the park I heard my uncle howl with pain. I did not look to see if he had fallen. My eyes were fastened to the machine of his persecution.

Aloft, on a sort of balcony above the horseless, rolling carriage-front, were packed about ten persons. Perhaps they were men, they appeared to be, and yet…and yet there was something palpably wrong about them which my study unpleasingly revealed. Their dark overcoats were moulded to their bodies in the same manner that wings mould to the back of a black beetle. Their black moustaches quivered and seemed to move of their own will. And their eyes had been goggled over with curious dark green glasses that were faceted in many tiny winking panes.

Above them, and behind, a funnel rose from the top of the machine. Even as I glared at it, one of the riders touched its side with a gloved hand on which, perhaps, there were two or three extra fingers. The funnel responded with a dim glow and a gout of steam burst from the crown. Over the horrible thundering rattle and *chug* of the vehicle's progress shrieked a deafening *Whoop! Whoop!*

Frantically, I at last gazed about, to see if the bystanders were forced to put their bands over their ears.

But, just as they did not appear to see the machine, so they apparently could not hear it.

Even so, even so. As it trundled its inexorable and menacing way forward over the emerald grass, the children gambolled from its path, the girls increased their pace and swept aside. As if at a whim. Yes, as it advanced, the crowd parted before it, but not one of them paid it the slightest overt attention. Not one—save I. And my Uncle Constant.

He had certainly collapsed, but soon struggled up again. And now he limped and tottered on, striving to escape across the park. How desperate he looked. His face was white and blind with fear. He did not think, it was evident, he could on this occasion get to safety.

The machine went by me. It passed within three feet. I too must have taken some instinctive steps aside.

A furnace heat came from the thing, and the terrible chugging was accompanied by showers of cold green sparks from its runners.

Uncle limped over the flower-beds and rambled out on to the dancing sward. Couples bumped into him and waved him aside. He skirted the bandstand and went painfully on towards the wall.

The machine did not, or could not, improve its speed. Yet its unavoidable quality was somehow augmented by its very slowness, as in a dream.

It ploughed in among the dancers, who bounced and swung from its way, not looking at it, not hearing or seeing it. Unlike my uncle, seeming to have to move in a straight line, it came directly at the bandstand, and there, peculiar protuberances, like the rubbery legs of some enormous fly, poured out and raised the runners, and so walked the whole contraption up into the midst of the band, the top of the machine only narrowly missing knocking off the roof.

The musicians were forced to scramble to the perimeters, juggling their instruments.

And yet—even in this extremity—not one man regarded the invader, and not one lost the beat of his foolish dance.

And then the horror had marched on, and over, and was down on the lawn again, and all the band resettled, banging and tooting the jolly tune without a break.

A fierce ray flashed.

I saw my uncle sprawl headfirst.

Instantly he had pushed himself up, but now he could not rise from his knees. He began to crawl towards the wall of the park.

For a moment I stood at a loss. And then some primal spirit took hold of me.

I raced.

I sprinted over the lawn, scattering and possibly felling the polkists left and right. I tore past the machine itself, and felt again its awful heat, and smelled its metals and its odour of a chemical swamp, and of some location inexplicable.

Even past my Uncle Constant I sprang, and reaching the wall, I bolted through the gate.

Outside, the steam-roller majestically moved, and its motion was very like that other one, that wallow of the machine. I flung myself upon the steam engine and wasted no time in hauling myself up its side. The driver was startled as I barged in beside him. I thrust some coins into his palm and cast him out, and he plummeted angrily on to the pitchy road, shouting.

I turned the steam engine with difficulty but with determination, and drove it back through the gates.

My uncle was crawling steadfastly on, but thank God he had the sense to pull himself from my road. I cranked my colossus onward, until I beheld the persecution machine exactly in my path.

It did not veer; perhaps it could not. No expression crossed the faces—if such they were—of its malefic crew. Only the moustaches wrinkled and the goggles glittered, and from the stack of the funnel went up another gout of white and another fiendish whistle.

I sent the steam-roller headlong. With a grinding of gears and a furious hissing, it pounded forward into battle.

Until I could see every beaded decoration on the nozzles of the ray guns, I held to my post. Then I jumped away. I landed in a rhododendron bush. And at that moment the two leviathans came together.

There was an explosion like the Trump of Doom. And then a tumult only like that of some apocalyptic train crash.

A light like an incendiary burst, and out of it huge pieces of things were hurled into the air and dashed all about, boiling and gushing, and black metal rods, wheels, plates, cogs, screws, all types of mechanical and peculiar debris smashed down over the park.

Not a single cry or scream attended this.

But looking up from my bush, I saw the monstrous crew of the machine also, hurtling through space, and they were broken in a way human creatures do not break. Black blood or slime rained all around. It smelled medicinal and acid.

Presently the hurricane ceased, and a great stillness should have settled, but did not, for the park had gone on at its music and its chat uninterrupted.

I stared. Swans swam peacefully among black irregular objects in the river. Young ladies, blood-splattered, danced brightly with their bloodied gentlemen between rivets and black smoking shafts stuck down in the earth like flaming bones. Craters had appeared. And these the dancers carelessly circled. While the band played on, despite the green-goggled heads which had fallen on the bandstand roof, the instruments streaked with blood and coiled with what were, conceivably, alien entrails.

Of the machine nothing but a sort of heaving slag remained. There was little either of the noble steam-roller.

I went to my uncle and helped him up.

"It is over," I said.

"Who are you?" he demanded.

Outside the wall, the driver of the steam engine had left off his complaints. He sat smoking at the roadside, as if that was his only purpose, and touched his cap to me.

I assisted my uncle to his house.

Balfour and Meriwether in the Adventure of the Emperor's Vengeance

Daniel Abraham

Daniel Abraham is the author of the Long Price Quartet, over two dozen short stories, and the collected works of M. L. N. Hanover. He has been nominated for the Hugo, Nebula, and World Fantasy awards, and won the International Horror Guild Award. He can be found at www.danielabraham.com. Of the following story, he writes, "It began as a collision between a lecture I heard on the Napoleonic roots of Egyptology, a fondness for the adventure stories of the late nineteenth century, an essay on the pulp master plot by Lester Dent, and the Book of Exodus. It was only as I came to the end of the first draft that I understood what it was really about...."

A s I sit at my ease, the lights and sounds of my native London wrapped about me like an old jacket, I cannot but marvel at the changes encompassed by my small span of years. The home of my nativity was lit by gaslight. My coming senescence shall be spent in the created daylight of the electrical filament. As a youth, I rode in a carriage pulled by brute animal force. As an old man, I move from club to apartment in machines of steel and vulcanized rubber. I have seen the Great War amplify our worst instincts into a horror that will, by the mercy of Christ, end our warlike impulses forever.

My generation has been privileged to witness the birth of this new age of mankind. Only a handful know the occult roots of this transformation, and that in truth this is not the first age of mechanism, but the second...
—From the Notebook of Aloysius Camden Meriwether, 1919

CHAPTER ONE: AN UNWELCOME VISITOR

Balfour and Meriwether were at their apartments in King Street that evening in November of 187–. The weak autumn sun had fallen not long before, and a chill fog grayed the front windows so that only the sound of the carriage marked their visitor's arrival. Balfour frowned, his thick brows knitting, and stroked his wide moustache. Meriwether put down his silver flute and closed the pages of the Bach concerti that had occupied his attention. Each man knew what the clatter of those hooves and the rattle of those particular carriage wheels announced.

Balfour rose, took up his brace of knives, and prepared three glasses of brandy while Meriwether exchanged musical accoutrements for his paired service revolvers and signature black greatcoat. By the time Mrs. Long came to announce Lord Carmichael, Her Majesty's special agents were prepared to receive him.

"That coat's a terrible affectation," Lord Carmichael said in lieu of civil greeting.

"I'm told the ladies find it charming," Meriwether replied.

Balfour grunted, bear-like, and thrust the brandy into Lord Carmichael's hand. His Lordship frowned, sighed, and drank the liquor off. Meriwether's pale eyebrows rose a degree. This was not to be the gentlemen's chat which usually began their services to the Crown. Both agents put their glasses down un-sampled as His Lordship nodded to the door.

Moments later, they were in the black carriage, the driver urging his horses to a greater speed than either Balfour or Meriwether considered safe in the present darkness. A cut crystal lamp gave the only light, its flame dancing and shuddering with the violence of their passage. Balfour noted a paleness in Lord Carmichael's face and the down-turned cast of his eyes.

"I fear we have stepped into a trap, boys," the peer said. "The past has risen up against us."

"Poetic," Balfour said. It was not meant as a compliment.

"Eight decades ago, more or less, Napoleon laid siege to the empire," Lord Carmichael went on. "You recall your history lessons, I presume."

"You mean his Egyptian campaign," Meriwether said. "The attempt to interfere with the British trade routes that began with Lord Nelson cutting his supply lines at Aboukir Bay and ended, as I recall, with Little Boney sneaking away in the dead of night and leaving his men to the questionable mercies of the Mamelukes?"

The driver gave a loud shout, and the carriage lurched. Outraged voices rose briefly above the clatter of hooves and wheels.

"Bonaparte's forces were the first to plumb the depths of the ruins of Egypt," Lord Carmichael said. "And when the time came that the French had to put themselves upon our good graces, we were able to acquire a great wealth of these artifacts for the British Museum. It has been the labor of decades to catalog and assess them. Academic careers have gone from nurse's teat to graveyard dust without ever walking out of the collection. For the most part, the information gleaned from the pieces was dry as the dusts of Egypt. But there were… oddities."

"Meaning?" Balfour grunted.

"Pieces that merited special study. Works that failed to fit into place gracefully among their fellows," Lord Carmichael said.

"Fakes," Meriwether said, "placed among the true artifacts by Napoleon's minions out of spite. I've read Lord Smithton's papers on the subject. As I understand, some of them rather amateur attempts."

"Why?" Balfour asked.

"To confuse and embarrass British efforts to make sense of the fallen civilizations of Egypt," Meriwether said. "Only the French would know which artifacts were genuine and which false, and for generations any theory or proposal with the temerity to include a British name could be discredited by the mere suggestion that someone on the continent might know better."

"It sounds petty, I know," Lord Carmichael said, "but these *are* the French we're speaking of."

Balfour coughed eloquently.

"It appears that Boney may have had something more direct in mind," Lord Carmichael said. "The most impressive of the oddities is a sealed sarcophagus. Clearly, it is not of the lineage of the other works. The markings upon it are different, the materials used to fashion it, obviously modern. And thus, while it was ignored by the more traditional academics, it was the holy grail of the cranks and dabblers."

"Was?" Balfour said.

"Permission was given to break the seal and open the thing," Lord Carmichael said. "Her Majesty signed the order herself."

"As a favor, I presume," Meriwether said. "A favorite cousin, perhaps, has thrown in his lot with the dabblers and cranks?"

"Lord Abington," Lord Carmichael said.

"The anti-Semite?" Balfour asked.

"The very one," Lord Carmichael said. "Apparently in his scattershot inquiries into the alleged dark conspiracies of the Jewish race, he found reference to something which he conflated with Napoleon's imitation sarcophagus. He put upon his wife to intercede with Her Majesty, and was thus to supervise the experiment an hour ago."

"All has not gone well, I take it," Meriwether said.

"We can't say," Lord Carmichael said. "Abington closed the workrooms and locked the doors from within. There were sounds apparently. Something that might have been a shriek, and then the lights went out. No one's been able to raise him since."

"And you would like us to make our way into the place and discover what sort of Greek the Emperor left within his Trojan horse," Meriwether said.

"Just so," Lord Carmichael said.

Balfour leaned forward, the action of the carriage barely sufficient to shift his solid weight. His dark eyes looked to Meriwether's pale ones.

"Plague?" Balfour said.

"Perhaps," Meriwether said. "There are several diseases endemic to the Nile valley which might have survived the decades. Two of them might have overcome a man before he could call for help. Abington may have done us all a great favor when he barred those doors. At worst, we may have to raze the museum."

"You can't mean that," Lord Carmichael gasped.

"My dear man," Meriwether said, "I am often glib, but I am always serious."

The carriage skidded to a halt at the steps of the British Museum. In the paired darkness of night and fog, the great columns rose up like the Nephilim of Genesis: giants of a forgotten era. Balfour and Meriwether took the wide marble steps two at a time, Lord Carmichael following as best he could. A young man waited at the top of the stair, anxiety twisting his face into a comic parody of grief.

"You are?" Balfour asked.

"Assistant Curator Olds," the man said. "I was working with Lord Abington on behalf of the museum. I was supposed to have been present at the unsealing, but Lord Abington ordered me out at the last moment."

"Lead on, young Mr. Olds," Meriwether said. "There may not be a moment to lose."

The halls of the museum rose above the men in a gloom darker than the autumn sky. The scent of dust and still air gave the great triumph of English culture the unfortunate aspect of a necropolis. Their footsteps echoed against the marble and stone, dampening even Meriwether's gay affect. Mr. Olds led them down a long corridor, up one long flight of stairs, and then another to a hall designed around a pair of great oaken doors. Two other men, clearly minor functionaries of the establishment, huddled in the harsh light of a gas sconce. The hissing of the flame was the only sound. Balfour stepped immediately to the closed doors, scrutinizing them with an expression so fierce as to forbid speech. Meriwether paced back and forth some length down the hall, his pale eyes moving restlessly across every detail, his footsteps silent as a cat's.

"Something's happened," Balfour said, stepping back from the doors with a nod. Meriwether strode to Balfour's side, licked his fingertips, and held them before the doorway.

"Yes, I see," he said.

"What are you talking about?" Lord Carmichael asked. "What do you mean something's happened?"

"The room within is not sealed," Meriwether said, his voice unnaturally calm. "All through the museum, the air has been still as the grave, but here there's the faintest of breezes. What other access ways are there to this workroom?"

"None, sir," one of the functionaries said. "There was a back way, but it was bricked up years ago to make more storage room for the collection."

"Light?" Balfour asked.

"Gas lamps, sir," the functionary said. "Same as the rest."

"And during the day?" Balfour said. "Are there windows?"

"Well, yes, sir. But they're set at the rooftop. The workrooms are high as a cathedral, some of them, sir."

"We'll want rope," Meriwether said. "And ladders that will reach the roof. There's little time."

"What do you suspect?" Lord Carmichael asked as the functionaries scattered to Meriwether's command.

Meriwether shook his head silently and gave no other reply. A few minutes' work brought the discovery that the window high above the workroom had indeed been breached, and less than a half hour more allowed the pair of special agents to be lowered into the stygian darkness within. Meriwether and Balfour descended slowly, the rough rope harnesses around them shifting as the functionaries strained against their weight. Meriwether had both revolvers drawn, and Balfour gripped his sharpest knife in his right hand. In the large man's left, a lantern glowed, slowly revealing the disarray beneath them.

Napoleon's sarcophagus stood at the center of the room, easily half again as long as a sleeping man. The ornate bronzework of its spilled lid seemed to glow in the dim light. The long wooden workbench at the object's side lay overturned, papers and dust-grayed hand tools strewn about it. A strange scent like an overheated skillet filled the air. With a gesture, Balfour indicated a dark, rounded shape in a shadowed corner. Meriwether trained one of his pistols upon it, the other still at the ready should some as yet unrecognized threat appear.

The pair reached the stone floor with near simultaneity. Shrugging off his rope harness, Balfour went immediately to the slumped figure in the corner while Meriwether examined the unsealed sarcophagus. Balfour needed little time to determine that Lord Abington was stone dead, the thick bruises around the man's neck telling of strangulation by an assailant of tremendous strength. The only odd feature was the small red pinch marks that punctuated the bruises, as if the killer had pressed a length of barbed wire into the dying man's flesh.

The sarcophagus was beautiful and unnerving. It appeared to be of cast metal, but while the outer layer was clearly bronze, the careful inlaying defied Meriwether's experienced eye. Perhaps silver, perhaps steel. The symbols that traced their way along the object's exterior began with a simple divided circle that became more and more baroque and complex with every iteration. Meriwether holstered one of his pistols, freeing him to run fingertips across the cool, slightly raised design. It reminded him of nothing so much as the schematic for a particularly powerful mainspring. The two men glanced at one another for a moment. Balfour nodded to the far wall, where a dusting of marble and stone littered the floor. In the dim illumination of the lantern, the handholds in the great workroom's wall stood out as deep shadows against the gray. Something had gouged the stone as easily as a man might press strong fingers into clay.

"Not plague," Balfour said.

"No, old friend. Before this is finished we may wish it had been."

Quickly, they unbarred the doors and stepped out to the hall where the assistant curator and Lord Carmichael awaited them. Meriwether summarized their findings—indeed something had been alive and waiting in the sarcophagus; it had slaughtered its liberator and climbed to the high window to make its escape. Whatever the beast was, it roamed free upon the streets of the city, and there was no time to waste. Assistant Curator Olds rushed into the workroom, stifling a shriek at the sight of Lord Abington's corpse. Lord Carmichael matched the long strides of Balfour and Meriwether as they made their way out to the street.

The fog had thickened, softening what light it did not swallow. The damp pressed at the men's faces and clothes, soaking their coats as if they stood in a light rain. It was some minutes before Balfour coughed out in triumph, calling Meriwether and Lord Carmichael to his side. Meriwether knelt, oblivious of the alleyway's stench of filth and grime. The pale gaze shifted over the nearly obscured ground, picking out signs and markers almost too subtle for mortal eyes.

"Someone was waiting here," Meriwether said. "The wide tracks are, I think, from the beast. But here and here, smaller feet. They spoke to one another, I think. And then…"

Meriwether went silent, moving down the alleyway, bent almost double. Balfour, at his side, held the lantern before them, dew forming on his wide moustache. Meriwether's hand darted out like a striking cobra, and he lifted a shard of glass toward the lantern. It had clearly fallen from the shattered window far above. A bright red smear of blood marked it.

"The beast?" Balfour asked, skeptically.

"Perhaps," Meriwether said, "but more likely this new person of the smaller shoes. I suspect there is another hunter already on the trail of our prey."

"I shall alert Scotland Yard," Lord Carmichael said. "We'll need manpower to hunt it down. Come with me, the both of you. You can tell them what to look for and lead the pack."

"I'm afraid not, My Lord," Meriwether said, his eyes fixed upon the darkness. "There is little time now, and if we are to have any hope of stopping this, Balfour and I must hunt this dark hour alone."

Balfour nodded gravely and snuffed out the lantern. In the sudden gloom, Lord Carmichael heard the quiet sound of blades being drawn. The click of Meriwether's revolvers answered as if the two men spoke to one another through their weaponry.

"Don't be daft," Lord Carmichael said to the darkness about him. "Wait an hour, and I'll have you a small army at your back. As it stands, even if you find the thing, it's as likely to kill you as you it."

"It's a risk," Balfour growled, and an instant later Lord Carmichael found himself alone.

CHAPTER TWO: A CONSPIRACY OF JEWS

The trail they followed was faint. Strange scratches on the cobbled streets, smears of blood that appeared with increasing frequency, and the uncanny scent of heat and dust that had haunted the workroom. Balfour and Meriwether made their way through the darkened streets, communicating with the slightest of sounds, the occasional light touch, and where the fog-shrouded street lights permitted, gestures. Years of training and shared experience gave them an instinctive telepathy that might have appeared unnatural had there been mortal eyes to follow them.

The thing from the sarcophagus moved quickly. Its stride was wide enough that, were it the shape of a man, it would stand easily seven feet high. In some places, the thing's passing had scraped the tops of the cobblestones white. The other tracks—smaller shoes with leather soles and blood—were made by someone moving more slowly. At a shrouded intersection, Balfour leaned close to the ground; his eyes were little more than glimmers in the fog. He made an unsatisfied grunt.

"Yes," Meriwether said. "I see it too. The beast knows it is being tracked. It's letting this poor man follow it, leaving marks to guide him on."

"Why?"

"I cannot say, but I suspect it knows its pursuer. Perhaps it is hoping to tire our fellow hunter before turning upon him, in which case, God help the man."

Balfour grunted his agreement, and the pursuit began afresh. It was only minutes later that Meriwether lifted his head, fists tightening upon his revolvers. The barest sound reached through the blanketing fog—metal against metal like a swordfight or a machinist's press. Balfour paused a moment, then heard it as well.

"The quay by the river," Meriwether breathed, and the pair was off, speeding through the darkness, heedless of the risk to themselves.

The scene that greeted them was the tissue of nightmare. A human figure in a long damp-slicked overcoat stood near the edge of the flowing Thames, silhouetted by the great metal torch held before it. And in the glow of the fire, trapped between water and flame, the beast itself stood, a living statue.

The gears and clockwork of its arms and chest lay exposed, the constant interior movement lending it the aspect of a thing made of a thousand minute, blind, idiot processes. Its face, framed by the silver and gold headdress common to the enigmatic images of Egypt, was inhuman, metallic, and twisted into an expression of rage and hatred and, oddly, sorrow. Articulated fingers glimmered like claws, and Balfour recalled viscerally the red pinch marks on Lord Abington's flesh where the dead man's skin had been caught in those hinges.

With a cry of despair, the hunter swung his torch as if trying to drive the thing of metal back into the water. The beast was too fast, its arms thrusting forward more quickly than the eye could follow.

Even as Meriwether let out a howl, the mysterious hunter fell to his knees, the great torch dropping to the ground at his side. The beast looked up, something like eyes, but not, taking in the appearance of these new attackers. A knife hissed through the thick air, striking the thing's face with a sound of breaking crystal. The automaton's bestial mouth gaped open, and an inhuman cry of rage drowned out the reports of Meriwether's pistols.

Sparks flew from the thing where the bullets struck home. The wide metal legs bent, and the clockwork beast launched itself into the darkness just as the pair arrived at the quay. The hunter lay in a spreading pool of blood, torch guttering on the stone.

"After it," Balfour said.

"Wait!" Meriwether called, kneeling to the fallen figure. He turned the wounded hunter. A wide fan of dark hair surrounded the unconscious face of a woman of olive complexion and striking beauty. Balfour looked from the injured woman to the darkness and back, a hunting dog torn between its fallen companion and the chase, then sighed and spat into the Thames before coming to Meriwether's side to aid in binding her wounds.

Back at the apartments on King Street, the mysterious woman lay on the divan. Mrs. Long brought thick wool blankets kept for just such occasions, the stains of previous visitors' blood hardly visible thanks to her careful laundering. The smell of strong tea competed with the sharp scent of Doctor Lister's new "anti-septic" fluid. With as much regard to propriety as possible, Meriwether and Balfour had cut away the woman's garments in order to treat her wounds. The chore had been more arduous than they had expected; heavy leather and steel links armored the woman's body. And yet the blows the great clockwork had delivered against her had done terrible damage.

"This alone would have stopped most men," Meriwether said as he indicated a long gash on the woman's arm. "And yet, I would swear it was the injury first delivered."

Balfour nodded silently and dabbed the deeper wound in her side with gauze soaked in a numbing solution of liquefied cocaine. The woman murmured, her brow furrowed, and she shifted away from his touch. The two men paused, waiting to see whether she would regain consciousness, and when she did not, returned to the careful business of stitching her skin back together.

"Impressive," Balfour said grudgingly.

Without warning, the room spun around Meriwether. Ceiling, window, door, and wide-eyed Balfour swam past in the space of a heartbeat. A sharp pain bloomed in his neck and a dull one in the joint of his left shoulder. He found himself on his knees, arm locked behind him, and his physician's scalpel cutting into the flesh over his jugular. Balfour chuckled.

"*Very* impressive," he said.

"I do not believe I have had the pleasure of making your acquaintance," the woman, Meriwether's captor, said. Her voice buzzed with anger and fear.

"Balfour," Balfour said, then waved a thick hand at his mortally threatened compatriot. "Meriwether."

"We came upon you as the clockwork beast struck you down, madam," Meriwether said. "We have since bent ourselves to the preservation of your life. I assure you we had no designs upon your virtue."

"The clockwork...the...oh God, it has escaped!"

Meriwether felt the grip on his arm relax, the blade withdraw from his neck. When he stepped away from his guest, he encountered no further violence. Balfour handed him the cocaine-soaked gauze to apply to the trickle of blood on his neck.

Strength had left the woman as suddenly as it had come, and she sank back to the divan, head in hands. In her distress, she was oblivious to her own wounds and the damaged condition of her garments. Balfour wrapped a blanket over her shoulders.

"You know of the thing," Meriwether said.

"I do," the woman said, her voice thick with despair.

"You are, I must assume, associated with the Kohanim?"

The woman looked up, surprise in her dark eyes.

"You know?" she whispered.

"I surmised," Meriwether said, taking a chair. "Lord Abington was well known as an enemy of the Jewish race. Whatever ill-conceived notion instigated this tragedy, it saw its birth in His Lordship's fevered brain. I had not believed in the connection until I knew that a second party was also hunting the thing from the sarcophagus. Had you been an ally of Lord Abington, there would have been no need to hide in the shadows outside the museum. Thus it followed you were his enemy. The affair is thick with the reek of secrecy, and I assumed that the priestly class of your race would be the most likely to involve themselves. In truth, I know little more than that."

"My father was Rabbi Isaac Cohen," the woman said. "I am Rachel. And the thing that I failed to end tonight was the greatest evil the world has ever faced."

Balfour rang the bell for Mrs. Long as Meriwether leaned back in his chair.

"I suspect our assumptions on the matter may have been in error," Meriwether said. "I was hoping you might enlighten us."

Rachel looked down, some inner debate raging in her mind. When, a moment later, her gaze rose to meet theirs, the uncertainty was gone. She was, it was clear, a woman well-suited to committed action.

"These are secrets that were never to be known outside the deepest circles of my people," she said. "As a woman, even I should have been barred from them. But it was my father's judgment that I should know, and so he chose to break the silence. And I make that same judgment now.

"You should know, gentlemen, that there is at work a conspiracy within the Jewish people which reaches back through all the ages of mankind. We have suffered deeply for its preservation, and we shall, I am certain, suffer again in the future. To be the chosen of God is not a blessing, but a grim responsibility. And despite the wild conclusions of Lord Abington's ilk, I assure you this conspiracy is not aimed at the control of the world, but the world's continuation.

"There is an occult history, hidden within the passages of the scripture which you call the Pentateuch. Thirty-six men in each generation are chosen to carry the truth behind the symbols, and my father was one of these. Because of that, I can tell you this: Many thousands of years ago, not long after the expulsion from Eden, there was an age of universal slavery that has been wiped from the histories. I cannot say where the Masters came from. Some rabbis say they were angels fallen after a war in heaven, others that they were God's rough designs for mankind given life as our punishment for disobedience. All the remaining records agree that a great comet appeared in the sky, and within a year, all humanity was bent under the yoke of mechanism.

"You have seen it with your own eyes, and so you may believe me. A race existed built of metal, gears, and glass. They knew no weariness and no love.

Deep within them was a hatred of all things cool and growing, of life that springs from a woman's womb instead of a machinist's forge. In Egypt, their greatest power grew, and from Egypt, the great forests of Saharan Africa fell to dust and desert. Generations of mankind raised up monuments that touched the sky itself at the cost of blood and suffering and death. Under the cruel metal whip of the Masters, we achieved greatness and saw Nature itself begin to die at our hands.

"The Jewish people led the revolt which broke the power of the machine intelligences. The twelve plagues, the parting of the Red Sea, and the flight from Egypt are echoes of a much deeper and more painful story. A story that I have read. Suffice it to say, gentlemen, that humanity's freedom was purchased at a terrible price. And preserving that freedom, seeing that mankind is never again bent double beneath inhuman feet, has ever since been the secret charge of my people."

"Why secret?" Balfour asked as Mrs. Long appeared, fresh tea and cakes on a tray.

"Not all traces of the Masters were destroyed," Rachel said. "And not all men glory in the burdens of freedom. Almost as soon as the Masters fell, others began to imitate the tyrants under whom their parents had suffered. Had small-minded, petty, evil men gotten hold of the tools of the Masters, they would soon have re-created the dreadful mechanisms themselves, thinking that common cause could be made with them and learning their error too late, and to the debasement of all creation."

"Small-minded men like Lord Abington," Meriwether said, pouring the tea into cups. His neck had almost stopped bleeding. "Your mission was not merely against the contents of that tomb, but also the man who sought to free it."

Rachel smiled and shrugged.

"I would have been as happy to persuade him through reason, had he been willing to listen," she said. "It was imperative that no artifact complex enough to fashion its own kind be set loose upon the world. The cost of one man's life would have been small enough. But I was too late, and now an enemy of life is set free. I fear we are doomed."

"Early days yet," Balfour said. Meriwether could hear in his tone how fond he had become of Rachel, even on this short and unlikely acquaintance.

"And that," Meriwether said, raising his cup to the clatter of hooves and carriage wheels, "may be the very man to give us the tools of our salvation."

Balfour rose to his feet and poured out a brandy. Moments later, Lord Carmichael burst into the room. His eyes were wild, his cravat slightly disarrayed.

"My God! Meriwether! Balfour! Where have you been? Half of Scotland Yard is rousted out of their beds and combing the city, and you pair are…"

He caught sight of the beautiful woman clad in shredded armor, blood, and Mrs. Long's often-stained visitors' blanket. Balfour pressed the glass of liquor into his hand.

"You misled us, old man," Meriwether said. "All this blather about Napoleon reaching back from the grave. Entirely untrue. Though, to give you partial marks, your worst mistake was choosing the wrong Emperor."

"Wrong Emperor?" Lord Carmichael echoed, then collected himself visibly. "What do you mean, wrong Emperor?"

"Not Boney," Balfour said. "Pharaoh."

Chapter Three: The Fall of Empires

"The first and best solution would have been containment," Meriwether said, pacing slowly past the great window which night had turned to a dark mirror. The others sat sipping tea and brandy with the superficial appearance of ease, though only Balfour's dark eyes seemed truly calm. "That option is lost to us. Instead, we must locate this unwelcome visitor. Our options are twofold. We may adopt the standard practice of raising a great force of sleepy policemen and setting them out scattershot from Pall Mall to Whitechapel."

Meriwether nodded to Lord Carmichael. His Lordship replied with a slight bow that was a marvel of physical sarcasm.

"Or we can attempt to divine our enemy's intention and anticipate its actions," Meriwether continued. "As Scotland Yard is pursuing the first course, I suggest we turn ourselves to the second and put ourselves in its place."

"This is your best investigative tool? Imagine yourself to be a millennia-old clockwork?" Lord Carmichael asked.

"Saddened," Rachel said. "I believe I should feel quite a terrible grief."

Meriwether and Balfour exchanged a glance, and Meriwether nodded.

"Go on," Balfour said.

"When last it looked upon the Earth," Rachel said, "it stood in the great deserts of Egypt. Dryness and heat and lifelessness were all around it, and marked its great victory. To rise up in the chill and damp of London…a place swarming not only with humanity, but dogs and horses and cats. Rats." Her face had taken on an almost pitying aspect. "All that it knew and celebrated must seem dead from the world, and London its sepulcher."

"Fits," Balfour said.

"Yes," put in Meriwether. "When first we saw it, it had an air of grief and mourning about it. Along with a deep and terrible rage. Very well. That's progress. We can say that it isn't likely to seek out common cause with humanity. Its first act was the slaughter of a prospective ally. Perhaps in its isolation, it may despair and collapse of its own accord."

"It will attack," Rachel said. "Without mercy or pity, but with intelligence. And it need not be alone. It is quite capable of assembling another of its kind. Or of any of a thousand other designs."

Meriwether rocked back a moment, his eyes closing, the blood draining from his face.

"Of course," he said. "I had thought it could have no allies because it had refused Lord Abington's outreached hand, but its allies need not be human. Need not even be living."

Balfour reached for his brace of knives. Meriwether leapt across the room, scooping up his black greatcoat. Rachel rose as well, only a slight narrowing of her eyes indicating the pain of her wounds.

"What? You think it's going to Big Ben like a duckling following its mother?" Lord Carmichael said.

"I suspect it is seeking out machine works, My Lord," Meriwether said, his voice absent of its usual friendly mockery. "Indeed, it almost certainly has already done so. Reach whom you can of the Scotland Yard forces. Instruct them to narrow the search. Focus their attention on factories and rail yards, especially those with forges."

"Where are you going?" Lord Carmichael asked. His voice was sober.

"Underground," Balfour said.

"It knows the habits of its former slaves," Meriwether said, checking his service revolvers. "It must therefore know that humanity rises with the sun. Whatever it intends, surely it will have set dawn as the mark for its accomplishment. Its best hope of working unnoticed is the underground railway. In all of London, only there will it have coal, iron, and solitude. I fear it will need little more."

"God go with you," Lord Carmichael said.

"Not God alone," Rachel Cohen said, casting off the blanket.

"No, madam," Meriwether said. "No one can respect your determination and ability more than I, but you are grievously injured. You have done what was needed. Balfour and I shall end this thing for you, and for your father as well."

Rachel Cohen spoke then, several sharp words in the Hebrew tongue. Meriwether answered in that same language, and the woman sat down slowly.

Balfour cleared his throat and nodded meaningfully toward the door. Meriwether bowed to the woman seated proudly upon his divan, then to Lord Carmichael.

Once the door had closed behind the pair, Lord Carmichael turned to her.

"Don't concern yourself," he said. "We'll be seeing those two again shortly."

"I fear you may be mistaken," she said, and the calm and sorrow of her voice chilled his blood.

The Farringdon Station had been closed since before midnight. In this dead hour, no watchman answered their calls, and Balfour was forced to snap the great lock. The pair descended into a darkness as deep as the grave. A glass lantern hung by the side of the platform and when lit gave a dim orange light. Balfour took it, the cheap metal clinking and groaning as they lowered themselves to the tracks. Meriwether drew his service pistols. The fog had penetrated even here, giving the narrow tunnel before them the illusion of great distance though the light could not have reached more than twenty feet before them.

"There," Balfour said.

"Yes," Meriwether said. "I smell it too."

In the thick air, rich with the stink of urine and rotting food, a new scent penetrated. Overheated iron, much like they had experienced in the workroom. They lapsed into silence. For ten long minutes, then fifteen, they walked through the dark and twisting tunnel, not even rats to disturb them. Then a sound reached them, deep and distant, like a roll of thunder that went on without end.

The funk of hot metal was overwhelming, and a warmth had come to the air that neither man found comforting. The tunnel turned, and as they made their way around the bend, Meriwether lifted the barrel of one pistol. Balfour took his meaning and shuttered the lantern. There, far ahead, a faint red light shifted and skittered along the ground, as if trapped between the rails.

"After it," Meriwether said, and they were off. Bolting through the darkness, wood and iron making invisible obstacles around their feet, they quickly overtook the eerie light. By the unshuttered lantern, the mechanism looked like nothing so much as a great beetle. Six articulated copper arms propelled it along the earth at the speed of a brisk walk. Great pincers of steel extended before it, and a single lump of live coal burned within its back.

Balfour and Meriwether watched as it tapped against one rail, then another, and then with a show of eerie strength, fit its pincers around a wooden tie and reduced it to toothpicks. Balfour drew his blade and with the grace of a master chef flicked the burning coal from its resting place. The scarab reacted with alarm, clicking its mandibles and charging madly about, then slowing, and at last coming to a clicking halt.

Meriwether lifted the object. Already the metal was cooling. One copper leg twitched and went still. Balfour raised the lantern, looked ahead down the tunnel, and sighed. Meriwether followed his gaze.

There, perhaps a hundred feet before them, the earth appeared to have given way. The iron rails lay bent and chewed, leading down awkwardly into a great pit. With a growing sense of vertigo, the two men advanced. What had been a breeze grew stronger, hotter, and more difficult to breathe. The roar which had been only a growing thunder became pandemonium. Below them, hollowed from the earth in the course of half a single night, a black cathedral had grown.

Automata with wings of filigree spun in flocks, burning coals in their bellies like fireflies. Two great machines that had once been locomotive engines lurched and lumbered like black nightmares of Egypt, brutal faces chattering at one another in satanic chorus. A thousand or more of the insectile scarab-machines were at work, their jaws shaping metal and stone with the mindless fervor of termites constructing a hill. With a speed no human machinist could dream of, they arranged planks, strung wires, and formed gears. Meriwether saw one lift a dripping shard of half-melted glass from its back. And the object of their effort…

No greater titan had ever walked the earth than the form now half-created in the London soil below them. Its blank eyes stood a yard across. Its teeth were great and shining blades. The body being formed from the clay and scrap metal of England by ungodly hands spoke of strength and complexity unmatched in human history or indeed the human mind. It was a destroyer of cities, of nations, of the human race, and the automata raced toward its completion.

Balfour leaned close, shouting to be heard over the infernal symphony.

"Flood the tunnels, then?"

"Seems wise," Meriwether shouted back.

They turned back quietly, hoping not to attract the notice of the mechanisms below. Before they had gone a dozen steps, a great shadow leapt for them.

Balfour dropped the lantern, parrying the beast's snake-fast strike with an instinct born of a lifetime's training. And still, three long scratches bled freely across his cheek. Meriwether's pistols filled the narrow tunnel with their reports. Sparks flew, but the great beast stalked forward.

The night had not been kind to it. The plates that had lent it a more nearly human appearance were gone. Cannibalized, Meriwether assumed, to make the first of its offspring. Likewise, the bronze gears and springs of its mechanism were stripped down, its own flesh sacrificed for parts. Its intelligence had played its purpose; its intent was now embodied in the working swarms below. What remained of the original machine did so for the single purpose of preventing human interference before the final, terrible hour.

The thing swung its great hands without warning. Meriwether leapt back, feeling the tug at his greatcoat and hearing the armored cloth rip like thin tissue. With a steady hand, he aimed at the one crystal eye unmarred by Balfour's blade, and with a shot, shattered it. The beast shrieked, its hands rising to its face in a parody of animal pain as Balfour and Meriwether ran past it.

"Blinded!" Balfour said in a congratulatory tone.

"I shouldn't put too great a faith in that, old man," Meriwether said, looking back over his shoulder. Silhouetted by the hellish light, the beast was not nursing its wound, but replacing its crystals. The great metallic head rose, and a beam of steady light now leaped from it, lighting the fleeing men as clearly as daylight. It sprang after them, its gear-and-piston legs working faster than a quarter horse's. Meriwether stopped looking back and set himself to the running.

The damp returned, the fog appearing in tendrils as they sped through the tunnel by the shifting light of their pursuer. Balfour and Meriwether had almost regained the station when it overtook them. With a grunt, Balfour fell, his legs swept from beneath him. Meriwether skidded to a halt, raising both revolvers, only to have them batted away. The great thing rose to its full height, its foot on Balfour's chest, its gaze locked on Meriwether. It roared in something like triumph. Balfour drew a blade and sawed desperately at the thing's ankle, but to no effect. For a moment, Meriwether saw the end of all things before him.

The blunderbuss rocked the beast back. A small gear hissed past Meriwether's ear, and Balfour leapt to his feet. Rachel Cohen and Lord Carmichael stepped closer, the Jewess discarding the spent firearm in the clear knowledge that there would be no opportunity to reload.

"Remarkable woman," Balfour said.

"Yes," Lord Carmichael agreed. "It took her some time to convince me that you two might be in need of aid, but she managed. And just in time, I'd say."

"Perhaps," Meriwether said. "The battle is not yet won."

The beast had paused, its head shifting from one side to the other like a bird considering its prey. The new arrivals had given it a sense of caution, but it had not abandoned its purpose. Instead, it seemed to taste the air and prepare itself to slaughter four rather than two. Meriwether put a hand to Balfour's shoulder, paused, and pulled it back. Balfour's tumble had left his coat sticky with grime and grit.

"You'll need a cleaner for that, old man," Meriwether said, displaying his blackened hand. He then glanced knowingly at the exposed gears of their enemy. Balfour frowned at the mess on his companion's palm, tilted his wide head, and then, understanding his intention, grinned.

The beast attacked again, but instead of blades and bullets, Balfour and Meriwether leapt to the meeting like boys in a schoolyard. They slung double handfuls of railway muck into the gorgeous machinery. With every third step, Meriwether stooped to scrape his hand along the ground, and drew up more of the black mixture of earth and old food, rat droppings, pebbles, and bits of newspaper that a living city produces as body does sweat. Quickly, the fine bronze gears, lacking as they did their former protective plates, began to suffer. The great knife-like fingers began to bend more awkwardly. The deadly swings came more slowly. With a shout of delight, Rachel Cohen joined in as well, and then, with a sigh, Lord Carmichael.

When it became clear that the thing could no longer turn to the left, all four howled out in sheer animal delight. No four civilized throats had ever shared a hunting call of such simple human pleasure. At last, the beast froze, its gears fixed in place, its wires taut, but immobile. It teetered and fell to the ground, its replacement eye shattering, and the light within it fading forever out.

"You're injured," Lord Carmichael said.

"A scratch," Balfour said.

"There isn't time," Meriwether said. "Lord Carmichael, the city's water supply must be rerouted to fill the underground. If it is not, all of London will be in flames by morning."

"Is it possible?" Rachel asked. "Can so great a task be accomplished in so little time?" Her arms were mud-encrusted to the elbow, her hair had come loose, and the wound on her shoulder had reopened, sluicing her side with fresh blood. No garment model had ever been lovelier.

"My dear Miss Cohen," Lord Carmichael said, "this sort of thing is what I *do.*"

And indeed, the following morning was an unpleasant one for the residents of the great city. The drinking water usually supplied by the mighty Thames was in short supply, more than forty thousand workers were kept from their normal schedules due to a massive failure of the underground rail system, and just as the first light of dawn appeared in the east, Scotland Yard closed several streets to traffic owing to huge geysers of superheated steam coming up from the underground's ventilation shafts.

There was a great deal of complaint, a bit of bitter humor at the expense of the government bureaucracy, and the city went on for the most part as usual. London did not burn. No one lost lives or freedom. Human civilization failed to collapse.

In King Street, Mrs. Long set out a simple breakfast of eggs fragrant made with rosemary and buttered bread still hot from the baker's oven. Balfour, a sticking plaster on his cheek, ate with slow deliberation, as if the eggs had offered him some insult which he was avenging with his molars. Meriwether read the morning paper distractedly, the cheap paper rustling whenever he moved, and glancing up often to watch the sunlight burning off the fog. And Rachel Cohen, wrapped in one of Mrs. Long's good housecoats now that the bleeding of her injuries was under control, sipped tea and gave herself over to small sighs.

"It was good fortune that you found us when you did," Meriwether said to her. "It could easily have been a much less pleasant night."

"I must disagree, sir," she said. "In my experience there have been very few nights less pleasant than that. Though in the light of morning, I can recognize some virtues that have come from it."

Balfour cleared his throat and, to Meriwether's delight and surprise, blushed furiously. Mrs. Long appeared at the door, a fourth plate in her hand. She placed it deliberately at the table, drew silverware from her apron to make the setting, and with a satisfied smile announced Lord Carmichael.

His Lordship looked both exhausted and pleased with himself. Soot and stone dust marred his usually impeccable clothing, and the thick smell of algae followed him like bad fish. Even Meriwether didn't complain. Lord Carmichael swung a burlap sack onto the center of the table.

"A gift from the British Museum," Lord Carmichael said. Fatigue slurred his words slightly. "Apparently Mr. Olds has no use for the thing."

Balfour raised a bushy brow, and Meriwether leaned over to tug the bag open. The great bronze head lay bare before them, the gears and axles forever stilled. Rachel brushed the brow of her conquered enemy, compassion in her face.

"I can't imagine what it must have been," she said, "to have come so very far and come so very near the redemption of its race, and yet to have failed. Had its success not meant my own destruction, I should feel moved by it, I think."

"Indeed," Meriwether said. "I imagine it must have been in anguish in those last moments, to the degree it felt anything at all."

Balfour's chewing slowed and he nodded toward the head.

"Then why's it smiling?" he asked.

Whatever the historians choose to believe, I know that the age that has begun to take the name of Industrial Revolution was born that night. Or if not born, at least it found its wings. In the automobiles and flying machines, the factory and the forge, Mechanism has returned to the world as slave instead of master. Rather than spreading desert, the fields and farms of England are producing more than ever before. And likewise on the continent. Rather than end the reign of humanity, machines are raising us beyond our dreams.

And still, I am haunted in these, my failing days, by the dread Emperor's smile. I imagined when I was young that it must have lain inert within its tomb all the lost thousands of years until Lord Abington's ill-fated enthusiasm revivified it. And yet what if I am wrong? What dark, deep, subtle fancies might such a mind create in so very long a time?

In dreams, I hear again the chatter of the machine gun. When I wake, it is to the great columns of smoke rising from our factories. I wonder if there is not something we have overlooked.

As Recorded on Brass Cylinders: Adagio for Two Dancers

James L. Grant & Lisa Mantchev

JAMES L. GRANT is best known as the artist half of the duo that creates "Two Lumps," a cartoon about cats. Just to prove that he can do more than doodle, his funky fiction has appeared in various magazines in the last six years, and he has sold two novels. He is currently living in Dallas, Texas, with his wife and co-creator, Mel Hynes, and working on selling his third novel. His collaborator, LISA MANTCHEV, is the author of *Eyes Like Stars* and the forthcoming *Perchance to Dream,* the first two novels in the Théâtre Illuminata series. She has also published numerous short stories in venues including *Strange Horizons, Fantasy, Clarkesworld,* and *Weird Tales.* She lives on the Olympic Peninsula of Washington state with her husband, daughter, and hairy miscreant dogs. Of "As Recorded on Brass Cylinders," Lisa writes that it began with a story prompt after she returned from Norwescon one year, asking readers of her journal: "Make up a story about me at the convention." James based the opening paragraphs on a photograph of Lisa in her steampunk costume (taken at, of all things, the *Weird Tales* party!).

IT WAS THE kind of American city that hadn't been around for very long, not in the manner it presented itself. The town had existed when Colorado had become an official state, true, but for hundreds of years it had been little more than a place for ruffians and ne'er-do-wells to trade furs, gold, and goods.

For a very short period, Denver had thrived on great inventions. Angelus remembered the first time he'd been sent here, to speak with a brilliant man named Nikolai. The Fifth Empire had been young. Its request had offered the young madman gold, riches, power; Angelus had made the presentation in person. But the brilliant Serb had declined, and eventually the quiet generals had resorted to merely pilfering the inventor's notebooks after his death. A dishonorable endeavor, true, but the Fifth Empire's needs had trumped the poor judgment of Tesla.

Many years later, the Gods of Steel, Electricity, and Glass had changed the city forever; where once a mere trading town had bubbled away, the skyline now rose in towering spires of light. Asphalt covered the ground for millions of kilometers.

Fortunately, it was the kind of city that attracted those people society still considered "eccentric." If the citizenry saw a bald man in black piloting an automobile over a century old, they would smile and wave. If that same man, whilst walking through a "mall" (such a barbaric word—the kind of monosyllabic, swallowed moan that one found befitting for this current *déclassé* iteration of human existence), perhaps paused and drank an entire Orange Julius in one long swallow, nobody even noticed or cared.

There were, as was the case with any society (no matter how uncultured), shining gems in their repertoire. A chilled drink with a mixture of citrus, dairy, and egg proteins whipped to a froth? Divine. It was easily digested by the metal vat of artificial zymogens in his belly and resulted in no waste material whatsoever. Affordably priced at the rough equivalent of a Florin or two in *his* youth. And quite delicious!

He wasn't the kind of person who felt a pressing need to catalogue each separate individual in a room—fortunate, as the food court was enormous. He watched the crowd in batches of five, ten, or fifteen at a time, his eyes taking in postures, body language, and quickly identifying those who didn't easily fit into a modern mall archetype.

When his gaze finally settled, it was on something red.

Not cherry or tomato, not fire engine or lipstick. This was the color of a horse-drawn carriage in Germany a hundred years before. The lacquered patina of the trim on Chinese temples when it had still been fresh. A British soldier's uniform after it had been soaked in blood in India.

And it was the color of two stripes in her hair. Not a tone you'd naturally see on a woman's head. The rest was burgundy, nothing terribly special in this day and age, striking but not as unique as the two streaks.

Not as unique as the peculiar corset and trousers of black denim and lace visible under the tattered excuse of a bustle skirt. Not as unique as the boots, which looked like they'd been stitched together from seven different time periods, two of which had yet to occur.

Also not as unique as her brass aviator's goggles, the lenses smoky. Even though he couldn't see her eyes behind them, he could tell she'd caught him staring. It was the kind of day where that could happen, blast it all, and he ducked behind an escalator as fast as possible.

Where did he go?

She'd had him in her sights, not figuratively, but literally tagged in the duplex crosshairs etched into her ocular reticle (an upgrade from the less-reliable one of wire, damaged in the retreat from the Battle of Maiwand, which she still maintained—on the record and off—was the biggest bit of political skullduggery she'd ever seen).

That battle had also cost her 9 percent of the peripheral vision in her right eye—not enough to warrant a replacement but certainly enough to aggravate. She had to turn her head to scan the groups of indolent but gaily dressed young adults and wet-nurses pushing children in fabulous perambulators. On the main floor, enormous sheets of glass safeguarded sparkling storefronts. One level above, a centrally located gilt lift began its descent. Just behind a cart filled with smoked-glass spectacles was the mechanical staircase. Her eyes scanned beyond the whirring motors, rubber belting, and glass partitions to locate the one that spoke poetry with a single, sliding glance.

Ah! There he was, behind a teetering display of cheap scent and jewelry that would turn the skin green. The biorhythms were correct, despite the elevated pulse…

She swallowed.

He'd kept his human heart.

She thought of the years that had gone by, the upgrades he'd endured to become a Collector. How had he convinced Them to let something so weak and fragile as a human heart to remain at the center of his mechanical being?

Not that it mattered. The Company now required the retrieval of his brass memory cylinders. She licked her lips, and wondered.

Wondered if he'd recognize her.

Wondered if he was going to come along quietly or if she'd have to "persuade" him.

One thing was for certain: if he ran, and forced her to chase him in these cursed boots, he'd pay for it thrice over.

Of course, this would be the one time he'd forgotten to wind Doctor Gillenheimer's Royal Clockwork Mesmerizer, Mark IV. Of course. The damnable contraption had lain in his pocket for decades, a lump made to protect him from her kind should he ever need it, and had he ever set foot outside his flat without making sure the little brass key in its back was wound a full ten clicks? Not once, no, but that morning he'd somehow glossed over it. It was one of those kinds of days, indeed.

Running was out of the question. Any woman of her breed who wore such boots could doubtless sprint like a gazelle in them if necessary. Or, more to the point, a cheetah. A very angry cheetah in a corset.

He could attempt to wind the damned thing, but its noise would likely draw her attention even faster. Bloody useless. Doctor Gillenheimer's benefactors had poured finances into his research, paid bills that would bankrupt a sultan, in order for this little blob to exist, and it was as pointless in his hand as an Orange Julius would have been.

No, wait. He could have drunk the Orange Julius.

Not long now. Nothing to be done for it. Had he sweat glands, he'd have doubtless mopped his brow. A quick check showed everything was in order. Dress slacks, turtleneck, tuxedo jacket, leather loafers, all the color of a brand-new piano. Not a speck of dirt or lint, nor a hair out of place.

A quick decision was made. He put on Smile #45 (*Greeting from a Strange Window Washer in August, 1956, in Perth at 7:16 a.m.*), ducked out from behind the escalator, and thrust his hand forward in greeting.

The origins of the handshake are unclear, though Bascom Octavius speculated in his 19– work *The Social Rituals of the Empire* that it might have originated with Sir Lucien Osborne. It had less to do with polite salutation and everything to do with self-preservation, as Sir Lucien liked to assure himself that the man opposite wasn't holding a sword in his right hand. As Sir Lucien was renowned for his predilection for married women (and their daughters, and—if rumors were correct—the prettier of the noble-born sons as well), this practice worked out very well indeed for him until he bedded the fraternal twins of the Duke of Craighinn, who happened to be left-handed.

It also explained why most bounty hunters thought of a proffered hand as an opening to "slip a mark the Sir Lucien," but she didn't have a sword on her and, in any case, They wanted him alive, if possible. There was a brief moment in which she took in his impeccable attire—*the man always did know how to wear a dress jacket*—and the smile that threatened to undo her all over again before she had him by the wrist.

The last time I saw him in that coat, she remembered, *I still had a human heart, too.*

Over her more-practical trousers, she wore a bustled overskirt he should have recognized, but what was once virginal white silk with hand embroidery was now tattered and oil-stained. She'd dyed it black with the darkest India ink she could find, torn it apart with a pair of tiny, gold scissors, and stitched it back together with tears and curses as clockwork whirred inside her.

"You don't look the least bit surprised to see me," she told her prey as she twisted about, intending to put him on the floor for long enough to cuff him and arrange for transport. "Have you missed me, darling?"

His smile dropped like a handful of surprised scorpions.

"Unpreparedness is not part of my chit-cog library, and neither is desire increased by temporal longevity," he said, worrying about the grate in his tone. He hadn't oiled his vocal cables since September 8, 1963, because he so rarely used them. "But you know that, of course. I suppose you'll be wanting to wrap up these matters?"

One of the screw-records in his skull (one of the few authentic bones left in his body, a process accelerated by a terrible attack in Constantinople, 1922) ticked its needle into a groove he hadn't used since before the end of the American Civil War. Motes of dust parted as the brass spike read information long, long disused.

It was the kind of information one had to keep quiet about. Allow no outward reaction. Do not let others perceive. But in a powder-flash of inspiration, he realized there might be a way out of this mess.

"If you take my head right now, madam," he said evenly, "there will be witnesses. How many people here, do you think, can capture photographic permanent impressions via their aethergrammic telephone devices? And then the hunt will be called, will it not?"

He had a point, bugger it all: all matters of the Empire were to be kept *sub rosa*. Though the patrons of the curious establishment had yet to take notice of her recent actions or her threat to his person, they had noted with various levels of disapproval, condemnation, appreciation, and arousal both her hair and her choice of apparel. Since entering this place, she'd been subjected to stares, cat-calls, whistles, and various offers of a dubious nature, all of which had been only moderately less appealing than the stench of food grease and the press of sloppy, imperfect humanity.

Sloppy and imperfect they may well be, but they all carried the aforementioned slim, threatening communication modules equipped with pictorial capabilities. Deactivating him in public wouldn't help matters any. One set of onlookers might preserve the moment in their curious version of a magic lantern show while the others called for the local law enforcement.

Local law enforcement never helped, in her experience, no matter the time or place.

And there was the problem with his scent. Close enough now to catch the metal-tang of his inner workings, she thought her sense-memory might have betrayed her. While this was indeed her quarry, she couldn't be absolutely certain this was the man who had left her, if not *at* the marriage altar then certainly close to it, more than a hundred years before. The tilt to his head, the cut of the coat might be the same, but too much of him had been replaced with machinery over the years to be sure.

I was so certain I'd found him, when They sent me the brief.

"You are going to start walking," she told him, "and not make a fuss, or I will take just your head back to Them and apologize for leaving the rest of you folded in a heap in Housewares."

"Very well," he said, and chose another smile (*Prim Closed Mouth #14: occidental lady in train to Peking, 1908*). He bowed at the waist, just a fraction of an inch, then proffered his right arm in a most proper manner. "Angelus A. Morphew, at your service."

A glass bead the size of a printed period fell into its tiny hole in his chest. Four more holes, four more little beads awaited. Lies were not becoming of a true gentleman, not even lily-white ones, and he'd agreed to Doctor Gillenheimer's Weighted Miniature Artificial Morality Tabulator, Mark III without any real fuss. He made a note to check its calibration—his *nom de guerre* should not have registered as a mistruth.

She stared at him in a manner that caused another disused part of his workings to tick into action for the first time in countless ages. Truly, this one was a formidable opponent; her mere presence gave his internals a more thorough congruity check than any in even the most austere German labs ever had.

"My apologies," he said after a half-second's pause. "We have met before, yes? You will understand if I do not recall. As a man you may be acquainted with once said, *Zwar weiß ich viel, doch möchte ich mehr wissen.*"

* * *

"Es muß sich erst noch zeigen," she retorted, the brass German-translator punch card having slid into the correct slot without so much as a by-her-leave, "if you don't mind my saying so…Herr Morphew."

She didn't owe him the courtesy of using a human title; he was at least 75 percent mechanical or she wouldn't be here. Yet she took his arm as though they were about to enter a dim Victorian parlor, or the Grand Ballroom at Neuschwanstein. It made sense, primarily because she wanted to keep him close and there were several lovely pressure points along the inner arm that she could use, if necessary, to interrupt his artificial bloodflow.

Her boots also pinched her toes, and it was nice to lean on someone for a change.

Fatigue clambered up her skirts with cold fingers, trying to pull her back into a near-coma that would allow her inner workings to run a diagnostic. Shifting always took it right out of her, but this time was different.

Tick…tick…tick….

Her heart's tiny balance springs and staffs, regulators and wheels had already slowed to a near-standstill. She bit the inside of her cheek and tried to figure out what the hell was happening, because she shouldn't have been synching to match Morphew's leisurely and debonair—and human—pulse. Still, now wasn't the time for the cheap theatrics of a ladylike swoon.

"Corentine Reilly," she said as they headed to the double doors at the front of the store. "Collector Retrieval Squad, Division 3. Please do me the courtesy of accompanying me somewhere more secluded and appropriate to continue this conversation."

"A pleasure," he said as another glass bead slipped into its appropriate hole.

They were seventeen steps from a large pair of double glass doors. Once upon a time, he would have categorized the style of such a portal—*Classical Revival, Second Empire, Italianate*—but society had eschewed such details for decades, favoring now these artless, flat structures with no real spirit or craft in their manufacture. Rectangles set in bland steel or, heaven forbid, aluminum.

The needle barely ticked over a simple line in its read cylinder: *May 9th, 1988, Costa Mesa—this portion has been reallocated.* Nothing remained of what had once been a hefty collection of brass data records regarding architectural style. They'd been wiped clean, then grooved again in order to accompany his growing need for more space on Observation and Investigation No. 644-J-92.

His investigation had been ongoing for long enough that many other segments of brass had been marked with the same note. His head could only carry a finite amount of blanks. Sometimes he wondered what he'd overwritten.

Nothing too important.

"I must confess," he began, and stopped. She turned to him and waited, the lenses of her goggles reflecting his own visage in tandem, a shrunken version of his face. A gaggle of teenagers in bright colors parted around them (giggling over some crass and impolite joke, no doubt). "Many are the rumors that fly about your branch of the Company, madam. Perhaps you will find me an easier companion to deal with if you would be kind enough to answer a few questions?"

Her head inclined after a moment. Not an explicit nod, but he took what little succor he could and barreled ahead.

"Is the Fifth Empire truly coming to an end? Have collectors of information, such as myself, been relegated to the Great and Terrible Warehouses in favor of silicon and plastic constructs?"

One of the teenagers jostled her roughly; his various belts, chains, and piercings clanked and jingled like a sleigh—

…a Russian troika. Nestled in furs and surrounded by snow, they skimmed the surface of the world gone silent, save for the bells that announced their presence. Two of the horses always turned to look back at the past year, and the center looked ahead to the unknown future. She-who-would-be-Corentine had laughed at the idea that tomorrow held anything but possibilities.

But that was long ago, and that Empire had collapsed and burned as so many of the others before it. Now the Fifth Empire was at a close, and They wanted the information imprinted on the cylinders; documentation used to forge the success of the Rising Sixth.

"Yes," she said shortly. "And that is the only answer you'll get from me. For now. This is no fairy tale. There are no riddles three."

She took another step, but was held fast by the vice of his arm which pinned hers against his side. Rough conversations, the sounds of filthy lucre changing hands, the wail of a despondent infant couldn't quite mask the whirring in Corentine's ears as she glared at him.

"I suggest, very firmly, that you start moving."

With her free hand, she shoved her goggles atop her head. Very few of the Collectors ever looked into Corentine Reilly's eyes and survived to resist.

The Council classified them the same shade as a variety of the mineral beryl $(Be^3Al^2(SiO^3)^6)$, colored green by trace amounts of chromium and vanadium. Poets had called them emerald pools and other such nonsense. Corentine simply thought of them as a primary weapon against recalcitrant males, and though they were not physically equipped to shoot sparks, she nevertheless leveled a very narrow look at him.

Much like a stream suddenly branching in two directions, Read Needle 16c came to a fork in one of the grooves in his head. The counterbalance weight shifted it to the left side, and a long-abandoned stream of words floated up out of cold, metallic sleep:

> *I shall remain, watching all earth and sky;*
> *The house of my heart can be seen in your eye;*
> *A bloodless heart you keep;*
> *And emerald eyes shan't we—*

The needle skipped as it broadsided another information track, jumped into a reset groove, and finished. Peculiar, but it was a peculiar kind of day, and, he begrudgingly noted, quite possibly his last. The last time such a snippet had occurred was for a similar misread error; old information, improperly blanked and rewritten upon.

He could not shake the feeling this one's eyes had something to do with it. They were beautifully constructed, even when her micro-servos were held at a perfect position to project the possibility of imminent doom.

"Onward, then. In lieu of information, I would beg a boon of you, madam." He stepped toward the door, uncomfortably aware that she remained close enough to strike if he moved so much as a millimeter toward freedom. "It appears that I have always known that my time upon this, aha, mortal coil would be finite. My brass has been rewritten and blanked so many times that I no longer recall when I was born, nor my original mission."

They continued along the sidewalk, and each step lowered his odds of survival dramatically. The end was likely nigh by 48.2 percent and rising, plus or minus 0.002 of a percent.

He'd never calculated it as above 13.4 percent. Not even when a mad Cossack had smashed his skull with a rifle butt.

"It has been ages since even a true and proper shop in the service of the Empire has seen my workings. Many of my replacements and internal repairs have been done myself. You can imagine my surprise," he said as they marched past rows of motor carriages (ugly plastic and vinyl, vinyl, of all the blasphemies mankind could dream up—slick and disgustingly malleable and incapable of storing a proper record for more than a day, but shreds of it remained and lingered for thousands of years in the soil as offal), "when a recent repair of my left temporal aft section, directly behind the ear, yielded a very small scroll wrapped in a scarlet ribbon. Very small writing, in my own hand it seems. I refrained from peeking, but, well…it seems to have been there for quite some time and the placement makes one think it was to be delivered in the event of my demise. Only barest scratches remain in my banks regarding the person it's addressed to; all I know is that we met in the Russian town of Dobryanka. Would you…could you please see that this final message is delivered?"

He paused, suddenly aware that they'd turned a corner. The back end of a Dillard's would be, it seemed, his final destination. He'd never understood the shop itself: ridiculous clothing for men and women, the kind that even wanton strumpets of the *Bois de Boulogne* would never have worn.

68.8 percent, and rising. It was time.

"Please? The scroll is addressed to someone named Annabelle."

She slammed him into the brick wall, ignoring the rubbish and noisome puddles that dotted the alleyway. Forearm braced against his windpipe, she leaned forward to hiss at him like a snake.

"And what do those barest scratches on your memory banks say, Angelus A. Morphew? Do you remember what this Annabelle looked like? Where she came from? What she was doing in a god-forsaken place like the *Permsky Kray* with someone like you?"

He didn't answer, and so Corentine shoved harder, pressing against the unyielding metal plates that covered the masculine-form of the Collector's body.

"Maybe if I open your panels and stir the metal mess you call a brain, those cylinders of yours will yield better answers. A judicious application of electrical current might also help loosen your tongue."

As she leaned in—a passerby might have mistaken the gesture as part of a romantic but ill-advised tryst in the dank and narrow corridor between buildings—her right hand slid behind his ear and she extracted the scroll.

Her clockwork heart seized, and for a moment Corentine thought she might remain frozen for all time, trapped in a suit of moldering flesh that would fall away from her, one rotten chunk at a time, until all that was left were upgrades of brass and copper.

She'd almost convinced herself she'd been mistaken, almost convinced herself that he was merely a ghost come to haunt her, to remonstrate, to torture, and condemn. She didn't know what was written on the scroll, but the blood-red ribbon that tied it had been hers, once upon another time, and the scent-memory attached to it was so strong that she wanted to stagger back, to be sick all over the already-filthy pavement.

Instead, she held fast to the steel in her spine and scanned his face, so different than the one she remembered, the eyes that had been extracted and replaced with glass orbs, the carefully blank expression.

"By all the hells, what did They do to you?"

The needles plucked away from the brass and, as one, they hovered on the outer edges of their respective cylinders. A visiting spider might have heard their ghostly ticks as they sought and found remnant lines outside of the main information tracks.

charlatans. One needn't visit a séance to find

Some were only endings:

once was a thriving port, but the advent of the locomotive has rendered it an abandoned shell.

Others only beginnings:

Should you ever find yourself reading this information, then the game has finally run its course…

That one stopped his mechanisms. It appeared to be a full groove, complete and whole, but none of the mercury valves or cogs showed that he'd ever accessed it. The needle lowered again.

...run its course. As you well know, old chap, the ages have required rather many instances of blanking these copper plates and brass cylinders. Please do trust yourself. Nothing that has been written over was necessary information. On the contrary, it was extraneous and often worthless. Only on a few occasions have you erased anything you might have kept elsewhere, but due to immediate need you chose to heat the grooves and smooth them to nothingness. There is a message in your cranial cavities that will tie up the only loose thread, should you perish, and that one...that one was blanked to spare you a life of suffering and regret, of heartache and loss. You are better off not knowing. Whoever your attacker may be, do all within your power to encourage their hand. Tally ho, sire, and may a flight of angels sing thee to thy well-deserved rest. Vivat Regnum!

So.

The pressure on his throat lessened enough to work the vocal cables once more. There was no time for sadness. There never had been, not once that he was aware of. If this proved to be the final curtain, he would take a bow gracefully.

"I am a traitor to the Empire," he said. "I have abetted our enemies, and have betrayed you all." Deep in his chest, two glass beads fell into their holes.

Corentine thought she heard something, like two raindrops hitting a tin roof, but the sound was as small as their chances of seeing the next dawn.

"I hate to remind you," she told him, "but you never could successfully lie to me. Traitor to the Empire, my arse. You can't even remember your real name, so save the programmed message of humble servility for someone who'll buy it."

As much as she wanted to untie the scroll and read it this instant, she knew They'd be coming soon. The sensors would tell Them that she'd had the Collector in her possession and she'd made the decision not to deactivate, not to transport. Corentine cursed, fluently, in six languages, switching between them as needed to achieve maximum effect, and took a step back.

As she did so, her pocket fob whirred in protest. She reached for the Company-issued timepiece, a lovely thing of gold and glint, and opened it. How many times had she used it to summon a portal? How many times had she sent metal men and women back, their cylinders destined for harvest and the rest for the scrap and smelting?

The inscription caught her eye: *Commune bonum.*

Corentine let the watch dangle by its chain. It caught the fading sunlight and reflected it onto the Collector until she dropped it into the muck and used the heel of her boot to break it to smithereens. She thought of just what they could do with their "common good" and exactly where they could stick it as she exhaled.

"We need to start moving. They're going to send someone else, and I'd rather not make the chase an easy one."

He didn't answer right away, didn't so much as twitch to indicate a hidden cylinder rotated slowly, committing her treason to brass memory.

Damnation. His ruse hadn't worked.

There was more than one method of beating the soot from a rug. His information banks were aware of thirty-nine—an even fifty if you counted the direction of each strike.

"It seenks," he said, then held up a hand to beg a pause. Using both thumbs, he popped the dent out of his windpipe. A noise like a fisherman's reel spinning out too fast came and went as he cleared the kinks from his throat cables, and then tried again.

Fifty-five percent and...falling? Several needles stopped, lifted, reversed their read direction and descended back to the copper.

"It seems that there is more to your life than mere collection, madam." He gestured toward a horseless carriage far to their right. Although very few in the mall would have identified it due to its perceived "old age," he still viewed it as a beautiful new form of transport: a black Rolls Royce V8. One of only three made in secret for members of the Fifth in 1906.

He'd never had the heart to abandon or modify it.

"I know not why you would shirk your duties, nor what could inspire you to halt a perfectly viable collection. Chance is an amusing mistress at times. My chariot awaits."

The thimble-sized scrap of fatty tissue in his head, all that remained of his original "manufacture," as he sometimes considered it, did not understand the feeling whirring through his mind. None of his brass indices or vacuum-sealed quicksilver microtubes contained any relevant entries on it either. He cross-referenced, jimmied a cog or two, and spun some gears in puzzlement at the nearest description he could find, and finally made a new entry on platen 17a, line 34:

Hope.

She appreciated the motor car, as much for the old leather and clean lines as the chance to rest her feet. Once inside, she felt the balance of power shift; his vehicle, his city, his hands at the wheel. She didn't know where he was headed or what awaited them upon arrival. Perhaps he only bided his time and still planned to make a run for it. Perhaps he'd serve her tea and cakes laced with cyanide; she was still human enough to succumb to poison, never mind suffocation, shooting, stabbing, and the like.

Corentine had survived such attacks before, but only with the aid of the Company's pocket watch. She'd shifted back to headquarters, bleeding and battered, more than a dozen times in her career. Attacks on her person accounted for several curious scars, a metal plate or two…

But the clockwork heart was my own fault.

Or his.

So if he chose to wrap those same, metal-reinforced hands about her neck and squeeze, there was no watch to whisk her back, no team of doctors that would safeguard her existence. She'd gone rogue, and she was as good as dead anyway. Appropriate that her life would be counted off in the number of seconds, minutes, hours, even though the pocket watch lay in a pile of broken bits of balance wheels and busted mainspring.

"It's very freeing," she told her reflection in the window, "to know that death is once again a possibility."

If she was going to die soon, she'd better hurry and read the contents of the mysterious scroll.

What will it be, do you think? A letter of farewell? And admission of guilt? An explanation as to why he didn't come for me as promised?

It didn't matter that he'd missed their rendezvous all those years ago, just as it didn't matter that she'd destroyed the watch; if it took Them seconds or minutes, hours or days, They would chase the missing Collector and the rogue Retriever until all that was metal on this earth rusted and crumbled. They were as good as dismantled.

The bit of silk that bound it was nearly threadbare, and yet the colour glowed against her skin like blood-on-snow.

"This ribbon was once mine. My guess is that you blanked your memory cylinders…" *the ones I was sent to retrieve…* "at some time long-past." She swallowed hard and tasted zinc and nickel at the back of her throat. "I'm sure you had something much more important to record."

* * *

A scarlet storm was rising. If he did not hurry to his abode, they would both perish under the grasping fingers of those who plucked the marionette strings of whatever new order had come.

"Madam…Mistress *Corentine*," he said, and reactive wires in his skull activated a sense of shame over his lack of formality. "I know not entirely of which you speak. There is a familiarity here. I will neither deny nor dodge it."

He smiled again, this time choosing an analogue that reflected his own feelings (*Dying infantryman, Armenia, 1917*).

"My curiosity threatens to disobey its programming." He applied the brake at an oncoming traffic light (*LANTERN*, his mind insisted, but he'd learned to ignore such shallow grooves in his platens). "How did I acquire your ribbon? Have you and I danced together in the great courtyards of the Empire?"

"We did more than dance," she said as they idled at a stoplight. The area was secluded, the red light that halted them a feeble sentinel against the approaching dark. Corentine didn't need a useless lump of flesh in her chest to hate the personage sitting alongside her, so debonairly inquiring as to their shared history. "I was called Annabelle then."

The light turned green. Someone in a plastic automobile behind them honked impatiently. Angelus applied the accelerator, and they were off once again.

She unrolled the scroll and handed it to him, not caring that they were yet to a secured location and even less that it would mean nothing to him.

"Read that out loud, for the sake of edification, and don't mind if I bask in the knowledge that it will all be recorded on one of your damned brass cylinders again."

Reading paperwork while hurtling along at fifty-five miles per hour, no matter what, was not an acceptable situation. He came to a decision quickly and pulled the car over while gently depressing the brake. Rubber tires crunched into gravel, sending tiny stones up to nick the flawless paint of his vehicle. Once they'd come to a complete stop, he killed the engine and respectfully took the paper from her hand.

"Very well," he said, and gave her a patient smile (*Ticket Clerk, Zeppelin Station, Gdansk, 1914*). His first glance told him it was a tiny thing, this piece of paper. The color of old honey with ink faded to lavender over the ages. Each letter was miniscule—the size of a printed period, really—and no ordinary human being would have seen more than tiny clusters of dots.

His ocular focus sprockets ticked over with the sounds of grasshoppers cracking their knuckles, and his field of vision narrowed. The letters leapt to life then, and flowed through his mind as linen would beneath a seamstress's machine, spilling from his tongue as faery gold spills from the hands of those who attempt to grasp it upon waking:

My dearest Annabelle,

While you sleep a mere ten meters away in the guest suite of Baron Krausmeyer's Haus, I write these things to you under mine own hand, one of the few parcels of flesh I can still claim are genuine.

A week ago I received new orders, and that is why tonight I shall embark upon a voyage to America. Along the way I shall be augmented in several new ways. You know too well the wound that has plagued me since the Russian incident. They shall remove my damaged caudate nucleus and replace it with another of Dr. G_____'s great works. I am assured that the replacement will allow greater function than the failing flesh God hath imbued us all with.

When my operation is complete, I shall never be able to love again. Norepinephrine and dopamine hath no purchase upon brass and copper. All I have felt for you, every moment I have gazed into your eyes and believed I found paradise, every sweet kiss or moment we stole behind our superiors' backs shall be for naught. Love shall die, for me.

I would not subject you to the same terrible future.

This morning, I was the last thing you gazed upon with human eyes. Would that I could have been brave enough to refuse your request, but you proved your valor, and the Empire's doctors conceded to your demands for the operation. I came and held your hand as they gave you the gases to lull you into the realm of Morpheus.

When you open your beautiful eyelids, those eyes will not be flesh, and I shall not remain.

Cowardly, indeed. Had I other recourse, please, I beg thee, know that I would have taken it.

Weep if you must and hate me if it will speed your recovery. I am quickly becoming more construct than corpus, more machine than man. You are still mostly flesh. Your eyes and left hand are your only augmentations. Your heart still beats blood, whereas I am quickly becoming a mere copper golem with oil in his veins. Annabelle deserves better. You will find it, I have no fear, for you are young, and I do believe they shall transfer you to another department soon. Your affinity for numbers makes you prime sergeant material. You will find another, a man who can love and cherish you as I will no longer be able. Perhaps, provided enough of your sweet body is allowed to remain intact, you shall bear many sons for the Empire.

I shall always strive to keep my heart, hands, and eyes as human as they are this very day. It is a silly belief, the pale hope of a doomed man facing his greatest storm, but perchance a tiny part of what I feel this night will live on in my heart. Perchance my fingertips will remember the softness of your skin, or my eyes will give dreams of the ghost of you in visions.

Live, love, heal, and be strong for the continuance of Man's Greatest Hope. If you read this, know I died having loved you. I could not have asked for more.

Forever yours,
A. A. M.

The automobile's engine had stopped its tinny pings and ticks by the time the last word faded from his lips.

The Company's damned motto echoed in the silence that spiraled out between them as the voices of the past faded. *Commune bonum.* The Common Good. They used such words in their speeches, on their posters, in the printed material distributed in schools in conjunction with words like *valor* and *honor* and *for the glory of the Empire!*...words war-tattered about the edges and stained with tears. Vomit. Blood.

Such words lured children onto the battlefield and wrapped their battered, broken bodies in a winding-sheet for transport home to weeping families. Such words were thin consolation, rough with all the things left unsaid. Such words were diamonds dangled before starry-eyed girls, to whom honor and glory were jewels beyond compare, brighter than circlets of gold slipped upon a willing finger.

She'd been just such a girl.

She'd been just such a fool, thinking that they would work for the greater good and the glory of the Empire hand in mechanical hand.

"It reads like a note of farewell. But I—Annabelle—never got it. Mischance or misdeed, it doesn't really matter now."

Corentine twined the red ribbon through her fingers and remembered all the times she'd worn it: climbing the Pyrénées, subverting His Majesty's Bodyguard of the Honourable Corps of Gentlemen at Arms long enough to poison a monarch; walking along the rocky beaches of the *Cherno More*, whose waters were not exactly black, but still dark, with the floor unfathomable. Corentine knew, now, that the water's hydrogen sulfide layer supported a unique microbial population, producing black sediments most likely due to anaerobic methane oxidation, but she preferred to think of the darkness as secrets.

Though the muscle was gone, useless poetic longings lingered. The irony!

"When I realized you'd gone, I had Them take my heart. Cowardice for cowardice; the pain of you leaving was greater than anything They could have done to me." Not an accusation, not said to hurt, for she doubted there was enough of him left to wound with words. But the simple truth was a sword she used to remonstrate herself. "I tried…days, I think. Maybe months. But every second you were gone was like the second-hand on a clock ticking over, and it somehow consoled me to mark your absence by the seconds, by the hours."

She could have told him, only a few hours ago, just how many seconds had passed since last she'd seen him. But Time had dilated the moment she'd spotted him in the crowd. Corentine recalled a wild-haired German that had shouted at her at length about relativity, but she'd never truly understood until her internal clockwork synched to the man of metal sitting so still alongside her.

His inner mechanisms whirred along, undeterred, while hers slowed almost to a standstill and then reset to mark their time together, however brief that might be.

One. Two. Three…

Corentine lifted the ribbon and tied it into her hair, where she knew the jaunty, incongruent bow would burn against the burgundy and black. Perhaps the next Agent of the Empire would train his weapon on the bright flower of color and put a bullet in her head.

But her heart would tick on, wouldn't it?

Fourteen…fifteen…sixteen…

"It seemed like the right thing to do at the time, and They were only too willing to experiment on me. I thought it would be a relief, but it wasn't. Hand, heart, eyes; the things they took, that I gave up readily. Your note says you'd keep them, but I see you didn't quite manage it."

The skin of his fingers resembled the parchment of the scroll in many ways. He gently rolled the message back into its original shape and cradled it in his palm, where the gentle breeze rocked it to and fro by several millimeters.

"There are two entries in my frontal cores that state that I must not replace my heart or hands or eyes. I have sometimes wondered why I'd committed them to memory."

Her own eyes were polished ivory inlays set with carefully camouflaged lenses. Some mad artist had gone to the trouble of painting filament veins in the corners, each the size of the hair on a honeybee's leg. He smiled at her again momentarily (*Matchstick girl on the streets of Oslo, December, 1889*).

"I have dreamed, madam. The laboratories took so much of me, but I have experienced dreams every night, regardless of my augmentations. In some, a woman such as yourself laughs as snow falls all around us. With all that has happened today, I do believe that you and I loved once. If my banks are to be believed, I most likely loved you without reservation. Such an odd existence this is."

He reached forward, slowly, carefully, and offered her his hand. Whoever had done the work on her replacement surface had been a brilliant person; her new fingers were warm to the touch and soft as fine silk. Only their strong, calculated grip belied the artifice inherent.

"We are about to be intercepted," he said, as a high-pitched tintinnabulation increased in volume. "They say that collection is a painless process. However, should you desire, I will fight them alongside you…?"

He left the question hanging in the air.

She held his hand in hers, feeling the pseudo-pulse of Fluid 7A MagneSangue through his arterial corridors. The noise was getting louder now; wind rocked the vintage automobile and sought its way through every crevice in glass and steel.

"How long do we have?" he asked.

"A minute. Maybe less." She didn't know what she expected: a glimmer of fear, a surge of adrenaline, but he only blinked as processors shifted, calculated…

Counted down.

There wasn't enough of him left to feel anything; not fear, not remorse. Even the offer to stand and fight was born out of ages-old algorithms designed to simulate fight-or-flight responses. They did have to protect themselves, their documentation, until the appropriate representative arrived to collect. The offer was a hollow one, an echo of shades past, of times when they'd stood back-to-back, swords in hand and pistols drawn. Perhaps somewhere, buried deep inside him, a blanked cylinder retained enough information to recall the time they'd fought their way out of the Citadella atop Gellért Hill.

Hard to forget Budapest, even without the cannon fire aimed our direction and a hundred foot-soldiers dogging us to the border.

They were both different people then.

Corentine brought his hand to her cheek, wishing desperately that it smelled of gunpowder, cologne, blood, sweat, shit, anything. But there were only thin traces of the alloys that comprised his entire being.

The portal was fully open now. Less than twenty seconds remained.

Her words spoke themselves. "Do you still love me?"

They both heard the last glass bead fall, pinging in his chest as he answered, "Yes."

Sound category: *A child's marble dancing down the hot pavement, Brooklyn, Summer, 1909.*

Corentine left Interrogation Room #14 with the barest of sighs. An arduous process, trying to explain the destruction of her pocket watch, first to her immediate supervisors and then the Review Board. Harder still to explain the total destruction of #1-17B's brass cylinders. One hundred fifty years of documentation lost. Such a thing had not happened in the entire history of the Company.

A freak accident, of course. Memory modules had never before suffered such an explosion, forceful enough to destroy a Retriever's fingers. A pristine track record and exemplary conduct in a thousand improbably difficult situations had also bought her quite a lot of benefit of the doubt.

—brass cylinders comprised of older alloys and therefore vulnerable during the Shift.

Possible sabotage implanted by #1-17b.

The Retriever did her best to preserve the materials and suffered the loss of her hands.

Please fill out Requisitions Order 57-TP. The cost of a replacement timepiece will be docked from your wages.

Recommendation: 30 days leave with pay and secondary-level review after release from the Medical Center.

The attachment points for her replacement hands were nearly healed, but the scar on her chest would take longer. Corentine's new heart skipped a beat, unaccustomed as yet to its new surroundings. Perhaps a step backwards into sloppy humanity, but it would have been a waste to leave it there.

The last message, the one he couldn't read, had spewed forth from his frontal lobe as Doctor Gillenheimer's Weighted Miniature Artificial Morality Tabulator, Mark III shut him down for exceeding acceptable limits for falsehoods:

"I kept my heart, because it was not mine to give away. It's always belonged to you."

Such a funny word, "always."

I'll always count off the seconds until we meet in the next world, my love.

Corentine nodded, then adjusted the ribbon-bow in her hair, the one that reminded everyone who met her of a blood-flower in full bloom.

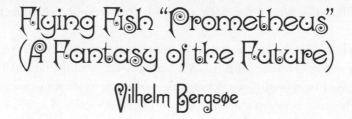

Flying Fish "Prometheus"
(A Fantasy of the Future)

Vilhelm Bergsøe

VILHELM BERGSØE (1835–1911) was a Danish author, zoologist, and numismatist. In 1862, he went to Messina in Italy to study the fauna of the Mediterranean. He made observations of swordfish parasites and after his return to Denmark published a monograph about them. As a result of his continuous use of a microscope, he contracted a serious eye infection and went temporarily blind, and was forced to give up his career as a naturalist. Bergsøe then devoted himself to writing both fiction and nonfiction, mostly by means of dictation. As for the story, "Flying Fish *Prometheus*" was apparently inspired when Bergsøe was invited to attend the opening of the Suez Canal in 1869 much the same way his hero in the story was invited to that of the Panama Canal in 1969. Due to illness, he was unable to make the journey, but he did have a look at the ship's tiny cabins and his imagination provided the rest. "*Prometheus*" was his only venture into Jules Verne–style science fiction, and it was originally published in a Danish newspaper in 1870. Although the story has been reprinted a number of times since, from 1876 to almost the present, it has remained little-known outside Denmark. As far as anyone can tell, it has never been translated into English until now.

TANANARIVA, 19 NOVEMBER 1969

M Y DEAR OLD friend,

You must be a little surprised to receive a letter from Madagascar, written in the tropical heat on Bishop King's shady veranda—but that's the way things change in this world now! In our day, one must not be surprised any more. If you are, it just shows that you aren't keeping up with the times.

Do you recall our last meeting in Frederiksberg Park, after it had been converted to those wonderful Persian gardens? I remember it as though it were yesterday, that incomparable evening when we sat on the palace pavilion's flat roof and enjoyed our nicotine-cigarettes to the sounds of Avanti's Steam Orchestra. I can clearly see the old philistine who was thrown out by the Amazon singers because he dared pollute the air with his cigar, an old-fashioned Portorico, and

I can still taste the beer, that foaming San Francisco you were so liberal as to treat me.

Much has changed since that time, but then it was an entire year ago. You are now sitting in Sukkertoppen as Managing Director of the Greenland silver mines, and I have finally won out over the resistance to my underwater tunnel across the strait between Copenhagen with Malmö mounted by the scientific society and the old fogies from the extremely antiquated polytechnic school.

In April, we had reached the island of Saltholm and began to go down into its limestone. With the help of Wooley's Ultramarine Dynamite, we were boring at a rate of a hundred meters per day so that after two weeks we had already gone well past the island's old forts. Those precious old remnants from a vanished era had been especially dear to the hearts of the old gentlemen, and there was an actual storm raised in *The Daily Locomotive* and *The Kinetic News-Pump*, which tend to retail all kinds of nonsense. In particular, they harbored the childish fear that the fort under which the tunnel had been dug would be shaken down by the sixth through train passing daily between Copenhagen and Malmö. Even if that happened, it still wouldn't mean anything since the forts have long been obsolete. One need only remember that a diamond-hard Arrow Projectile, fired with a small charge of nitroglycerin from one of Billingates' Revolver-Cannons, has penetrated granite walls twenty feet thick, and a single grenade-bomb filled with common dynamite would blow those forts' walls apart like eggshells. A few articles in *The Truth-Sunbeam*, in which I pointedly made this clear, were enough to put an end to all the alarm.

As I have learned, the Sailors' Relief Fund, whose fortunes had increased so much during the Anglo-American War, is now in the process of buying the two forts. The honest old sea-dogs want to build a rest home in the midst of their own element, and the government will get back one of the millions it sank into the forts. As far as the undermined fort is concerned, it has of course found a use as well. The leading butter and fat products company has acquired a concession to build a steam butter-churning operation there, and it will pay the tunnel company half a percent of its profits in return for the latter's obligation to maintain the advantageous vibration.

I had gotten thus far in my efforts when I received a cable telegram from my old friend, the mining-explosives expert Joseph Spring in New Orleans, which completely confirmed the long-standing reports of a wonderful discovery that he had made. Major Spring, who, as you know, is the living spirit of the North American Explosion Society, has devoted all of his time since the war to producing an explosive with effects even greater than that of Wooley's Ultramarine Dynamite, and he had at last succeeded.

A promise that I have given him, and which I must consider binding until further notice, forbids me to go into more detail about this substance's composition. I can only disclose that its effects are so destructive that it is not possible, even microscopically, to show what became of the atoms of a twenty-cubic-meter granite block. The same goes for those of two pyrotechnicians who perished during the experiment, disappearing so completely that the Great Western Life Insurance Company considers them to be still alive and as a consequence refuses to pay the respective widows their policies. Since, as is also the case with Ultramarine Dynamite, the force of the explosion only applies in a downwards direction, it is possible that the atoms of both the granite block and the unfortunate victims have been driven so deep into the Earth's crust that no one will ever be able to get them out again.

However that may be, this new explosive has given Spring a truly inspired idea. That is, he has calculated that if detonated all at once, a two million hundredweight of this new explosive would strike the Earth such a blow that it would be driven out of its hitherto regular course and into a new solar system. Unfortunately, the cost of the new material is still too high to consider producing it in such large quantities, and the charming experiment of wandering from solar system to solar system by means of explosive thrusts must be postponed until the expense of overhead can be reduced.

But soon Spring saw another use for his remarkable explosive, which not without reason he has named *Keraunobolite*, or "Lightningite." Unlike with us, an invention never lies fallow in North America, and eight days before it was made public, a large corporation was already formed in New Orleans for steam excavation and explosive boring with a potential capital of 200 million dollars. The project was to dig through the Isthmus of Panama in a period of eight months to a depth of two hundred feet so the American Empire's largest Monitors and Fort-Destroyers could pass through. All the earlier plans that had suffered an unfortunate delay due to the conquest of South America and England's humiliation were scrapped, and instead of Green's proposed route, which would make the canal wind along the San Juan River and through Lake Nicaragua, Spring proposed one that perfectly fit his energetic character. During the stormy debate at the meeting held in New Orleans, he seized the map that had been hung up for orientation, and used his horsewhip to tear a gash through it that cut the Isthmus from Darien to the great ocean.

"This is how the canal will go!" he exclaimed in his stentorian voice, and those forceful words spread like wildfire through the masses and silenced every objection. Work on what was jokingly called the "Horsewhip Canal" began as soon as the next day, and the results that Spring obtained have been no less than magnificent.

It occurs to me that it is now just a hundred years since the de Lesseps Canal was opened at Suez, and I remember reading in some old newspapers at the public library about the fuss made over that insignificant trifle. As I recall, de Lesseps spent sixteen years on an enterprise on which Sesostris, Necho, and the Ptolemies had done a great deal of preliminary work, and that in a land where there are no masses of solid rock. Spring had now been exactly eight months on his canal, which was significantly shorter but on the other hand required breaking through some not inconsiderable mountains. Of course, the technical means had improved enormously since de Lesseps' time, but Spring's canal was still no walk in the park. The low, swampy coastland at the bend by Darien was dug out in two months by the usual centripetal steam excavator. The highlands, on the other hand, were literally torn apart for a stretch of sixteen English miles by the Keraunobolite, which was laid in a single strip across the mountains and then detonated. The first attempt resulted in a trench three feet deep and sixteen feet wide. After eight more detonations, the work was so far advanced that the steam excavator could do the rest. It brought to life the old legend of Thor, who smashed mountains with his hammer Mjølnir—but this Mjølnir had cost the company more than 100 million dollars.

On the 15th of November, I received another cablegram from my American friend, informing me that the canal would be opened on the 20th in the presence of the leading European engineers, geologists, and naturalists, and so he was inviting me. Since I had a special connection to the great cable system on the tunnel company's account and had installed it in my house, I immediately replied that I would come with the first regular flying mail ship that left from Hamburg; but it was doubtful whether I would reach the Isthmus in time because of autumn storms and the short amount of time I had been given.

That very same evening, I received a telepistle in which he stated that none of the usual flying mail ships could reach the Canal in the allotted time, and that he would not have invited me had he not had a conference with the American

Ministry of Flight and as a result was now so fortunate as to be able to place a special and quite splendid means of transportation at my disposal. Three weeks before, the American government had launched the newly constructed Flying Fish *Prometheus*, which had been much discussed in our newspapers, on its first around-the-world journey. Thus I had an excellent opportunity not just to reach my desired destination safely and quickly, but also to acquaint myself with a design originated by that aeronautic genius, Professor Swallow of Alabama. It far excelled the Albatross ships built in England, to say nothing of the Air-Castles we use but which are completely obsolete. The speed of the latter is certainly very considerable but they have always been characterized by highly irregular flight.

At the same time I received this dispatch, our Atmosphere Ministry was informed that the Flying Fish *Prometheus*, commanded by Captain Bird, had touched down in the Sea of Azov on the 14th. It would fly on to Copenhagen as early as the 16th, or perhaps Køge Bay instead if it turned out that the seabed at the Kallebod beach was not deep enough for it to take off again.

Fortunately, it is not necessary to take very much along on an aerial journey, and I therefore provided myself not with gold but just with American currency, which was especially appropriate since its value had lately shown a pronounced tendency to rise. Outfitted with this and an aerometer, a spyglass, and a notebook in my breast pocket, I steamed away by train that same evening to Køge Bay. According to expert opinion, that would be the body of water where the *Prometheus* would most likely have to touch down due to its distinctive method of taking flight.

When one is setting out on an aerial journey to the Isthmus of Panama, a trip by train to Køge is of no great significance. Still, it gave me pause when the signal whistle blew and the express train began to move. This was the first time that I would travel across the Atlantic Ocean by air, and not only that but in a machine whose means of locomotion was quite unusual. I didn't feel any fear—my previous journeys by air to Paris and London had proceeded happily—but I am not ashamed to admit that at the last moment, mostly for my family's sake, I insured my life as well as the more essential of my limbs with the Great Transatlantic Life and Limb Insurance Company.

At nine o'clock in the evening I reached Køge, which had just been electrically illuminated for the first time—an arc lamp at the end of each street. After a light supper in the hotel, I visited the new cemetery for Copenhagen and environs, where the Chief Cremator, Hr. Dodenkopf, was so kind as to show me around personally, and where I inspected the new apparatus for the rapid combustion of corpses in compressed oxygen.

Nonetheless, I shall not lose myself in digressions about a procedure that unfortunately has been all too long in coming. Instead, I shall proceed immediately to a description of my journey, which will perhaps interest you, since being so isolated where you are, you have not had the opportunity to keep track of the inventions that in the last ten years have followed one after another in rapid succession, and which have culminated in the *Prometheus*, one of the most ingenious and well-designed machines anyone has ever seen.

As you know, people had been extremely occupied throughout the 19th Century with solving the problem of a solid body's controlled movement through the air. I can so easily put myself in these men's thought patterns. It was inevitable, once the steam engine and the telegraph had been invented, that there would be some fools or other who were especially irritated by being forced to crawl on the ground at the bottom of the air ocean while they observed bats, birds, and even the most hideous insects cheerfully soar above it. But the 19th Century was stuck fast in an error from which we in the 20th have fortunately managed to free ourselves.

That is, men persisted in building machines following the inapplicable principle of balloons, in that they had not properly distinguished between ascent and the far more difficult art of moving independently through the aerial sea. It was actually one of our own countrymen who first led thinking along the correct path in the present century when he referred to birds as the best flying machines the earthly globe possessed. His inventions, however, could take off only from dedicated stations where their safe landings were facilitated by very expensive and time-consuming apparatus. All of the Aerial-Railway platforms, Air-Castle towers, and Flying-Ship slipways that have been built in such great numbers around the world are now unnecessary and in a few years will lie in ruins, for the American Professor Swallow must now be considered to have completely solved the problem.

While we here in Europe have always had the bird principle in mind, basing on it our Falcon Brigs, Albatross Schooners, and Stork Frigates, this outstanding scientist on the other side of the Atlantic Ocean had his eye on an entirely different model. Unfortunately, it may be found in Europe only in the Mediterranean region, where the surrounding countries remain sunken in an even deeper lethargy than they were a hundred years ago. Professor Swallow's inspiration lay in the flying fish, and he was the first, in the literal meaning of the word, to fish it up from the great sea of unconsciousness. He studied the flying fish in its two opposing elements, the sea and the air, and spent his youth's first period of bloom alone in his yacht, rocked by the Atlantic Ocean's waves and engrossed in drawings and designs that made all of America believe he was busying himself with advanced plans for establishing a cod-liver oil factory on the east coast of Newfoundland.

But it was the flying fish that was the object of his restless yearnings and aspirations. In the bright moonlit nights he observed how this remarkable fish moved in the water, how it positioned its fins when it readied itself for flight, and how it flashed through the air faster than an arrow with the help of its powerful pectoral fins, with such strength that sailors on the heaviest frigates caught them in canvas traps that they placed on high mast platforms. When he finally understood how this marvelous animal behaves in plunging down into the sea without smashing itself on the surface and without breaking either its head or its wings, he saw what form his invention should take, and with the last remnants of his colossal fortune he built the "Flying Fish," which now bears its name as a second *Prometheus* from place to place across the far reaches of the globe.

The principle is, as I mentioned, entirely the same as that of the fish, except that he has borrowed something of the octopus's means of locomotion as well. The ship floats on the water as lightly as a swan, sinks to a certain depth by taking in water and forcing out air, then shoots upwards at an angle by abruptly expelling the water, the last of which is discharged when it reaches the surface. The expelled masses of water give it such momentum that the ship is propelled 200 feet into the air. Here, the wing-fin system is set into motion, the propeller tail is retracted, the steering tail is extended, and it speeds through the air ocean at a rate of 150 English miles per hour until it comes upon a body of water deep enough that it will not be smashed to pieces on the bottom when it descends. The Flying Fish can thus take off from any harbor city where the water reaches at least the minimum depth. There is no need for any stations with their specialized equipment and personnel—in short, it rightfully bears its proud name "Flying Fish *Prometheus*."

I did not sleep very much that night, partly because the airbeds in Køge are so poorly filled, partly because I felt a little tension about what lay ahead of me. Mainly I couldn't get Spring's explosive out of my head. I soon calculated how much work we would have saved on my Scandinavian tunnel and how much the company could have given him per cubic inch, then I went through all latest formulae for explosive gases, and at length I fell into an uneasy slumber in which I dreamed I was manufacturing more than enough Keraunobolite to blow all of Germany asunder. Somewhat dizzy in the head, I awoke at five o'clock and had a proper Greenland snowbath in order to thoroughly tone up my nervous system and invigorate my muscles. Then, armed with my spyglass, I went up in the Nykirk's tower to be the first to greet Captain Bird when he arrived.

My eagerness had gotten me up all too early, however. The November fog lay cold and gray over the town like a monstrous spider's web in which all thought and motion were still ensnared. Only the tower watchman, a funny old fellow, was awake. I had a plain-talk conversation with him, but when in my enthusiasm I began to explain the Flying Fish, he said:

"Yes, I can understand that one can fly in the air, because I have seen it. I can also understand that one can sail on the water because I have seen that, too. But what the Professor here is telling me, why, bless me, that is sheer nonsense."

"But it is indeed the truth, I assure you," I replied.

"Well, then, if I'm getting it right, it's neither fish nor fowl, this machine."

"Correct," I answered. "It's a combination of both."

"No, that could never be true," he said, "although I did read something about it yesterday. But does the Professor know what it is?"

"No, what is it?"

"It is, may the Devil take me, a lie!" he replied with all the strength of conviction, and started to go.

I held him back to give him a further explanation, but suddenly the telegraph-indicator pointed to *Severe Northwest Storm, Station Sukkertoppen.* The watchman went inside to telegraph Copenhagen and so our conversation was broken off. I am relating this little incident to you to show you the sluggish minds and the suspicion towards all new inventions that still stir within the lower levels of the people in our land. This man goes calmly in to report at lightning speed a storm that was only just now starting into motion from your dear old icebergs, and he still didn't believe in the Flying Fish. Well, the good people of Køge have always been a little behind the times; they were burning witches there not too many centuries ago, after all.

Towards seven, the fog lifted, the Sun was breaking through, and down on the street life and movement were beginning to stir, which showed that the

Flying Fish had set the more enlightened portion of Køge Town's population into motion. Prosperous merchants on bicycles, rich landowners on quite smart steam horses, and the town's youth in California jumping boots moved with lively bustle through the streets and made their way towards the harbor. There, the submersible vessel *Neptune* already had its steam up in the event that the Flying Fish should meet with an accident.

Jumping boots have hardly become a universal means of transportation. At least here they are still rather new, although they give quite extraordinary results and their popularity is constantly increasing. A little practice is required to use them, of course, but once one has mastered them, they become as good as indispensable. True, it cannot be denied that the movement is somewhat grasshopper-like and not entirely free of a certain comic touch, such as when people leap over each other's heads. I have incidentally seen them used on the boulevards of Paris with all the grace and elegance that are so characteristic of Parisian ladies, especially in falling down. Here in Køge, however, I saw only a few ladies, and they were starting out more on their heads than on their legs. When I caught sight of two rather stout women who leaped out over the wharf in their eagerness to reach the harbor, and shortly thereafter hopped their way homewards dripping wet and followed by the boys' cheers and laughter…well, of course I do not deny that I was annoyed on account of these female citizens of my country and began to doubt how well the devices were suited for cool and phlegmatic Scandinavians.

At about that time, a shot was fired from the harbor fort's turret, a definite sign that the *Prometheus* was in flight. I turned my spyglass to the north, but at first saw nothing other than the sea and some scarlet cloud masses shining on the horizon. From this suddenly burst a single, silver-gleaming point that rapidly grew in size although I was still unable to discern its form or outline. It approached at a furious speed, sparkling and gleaming in the morning sun's rays, and soon its wings became visible as a pair of thin black strips while some whitish vapor streamed behind it. In short, there was no doubt that it was the long-awaited *Prometheus* flying towards us.

Now it had been observed from the town as well. All faces were turned upwards, hearty cries of "Hurrah!" were heard, all the cannons of the fort gave a salute, and at the same time the line of townspeople in front of the guardhouse broke out in the well-known hymn, "Hail to Thee, Thou Eagle of the Air" (which you may remember from your schooldays in its old version as "Hail to Thee, Thou High North").

Meanwhile, I had exchanged my spyglass for my watch. Just three minutes had passed since I had first spotted it as a point—now I heard the mighty roar of its beating wings, not unlike a storm-tossed sea breaking against a rocky coast, and at the same time I saw the *Prometheus* at an altitude of about eight hundred feet as a shining silver, sheer-polished object in the shape of a fish with coal-black, bat-like wings and a tail whose quickly turning movement prevented any closer examination. Suddenly it stopped in the air, seemingly directly over the town. The wings moved, violently trembling, not unlike the flies that we see in summer standing almost still over a fixed location. Then the tail bent upwards; the now motionless wings assumed a slanted position relative to the ship's hull, and as the crowds on the street and by the harbor shrieked deafeningly, it shot downwards like an arrow with constantly increasing speed. It was a terrible moment! Even I, who knew with what skill Captain Bird guided his ship, truly believed that the *Prometheus* would smash into the ground, for from my vantage point it looked as though the Flying Fish was plummeting towards the city hall's spire.

But soon I became aware of that optical illusion. Like an enormous shooting star it plunged towards the outer harbor, and the wings closed up and slid into the cavities along the hull allotted for them. Then I heard a tremendous splash, a pillar of foam and water rose so forcefully into the air that even the ships in the harbor were flooded, and the boats needed all their power to keep from capsizing. Following that frightful moment, there was only the silence of the tomb. There was not a face, not a regard, that was not directed out over the sea—it was as though everyone was afraid even to draw a breath before the ship came into view. Then a new, mighty wave rose further out; it parted and from its interior, like a pearl from an oyster, the *Prometheus* emerged in all its shining, silvery glory. Like the spout from an enormous whale, a white column of steam rose vertically into the air from the Flying Fish's head. A second later the steam horn's sound reached my ears, and at that very instant a cheer broke out that seemed to go on forever. Cries of hurrah from the docks, new salutes from the fort, waving flags and scarves—the enthusiasm was, for Køge, quite extraordinary.

During all this vociferous excitement, I saw a wide gap appear in the ship's bow. It most nearly resembled a fish opening its gill slit. From it shot a long, black snake that then rested on the water, swelling until it finally proved to be the Flying Fish's longboat being inflated by the steam engine. Shortly thereafter, a hatch opened near something that in position and shape resembled a fish's dorsal fin, and resplendent in sky-blue velvet uniforms with star-studded scarves, Captain Bird and the ship's other officers stepped out on the Flying Fish's back, where they were the object of another round of the crowd's enthusiastic applause. Soon the air-boat was ready, its propeller was set to spinning, and it sped towards the docks, bearing Captain Bird and his crew while the new American flag with its shining sun and 69 stars proudly flew over its wake.

I shall pass over the dinner that the city council president and Køge's leading citizens gave at the city hall. Such affairs with their speeches are all alike. Captain Bird was an exception, however. He replied to a long and enthusiastic address by the city council president with only these words: "Upwards and ever onwards!" At that we all broke our glasses in deep silence in his honor.

One can see at once from Captain Bird that he is a true air-man. There is something in his profile and his regard that is reminiscent of an albatross, and I don't think the entire fellow weighs more than eighty pounds. The officers and crew are of the same superior breed—short, thin, beardless, with wondrously clear and far-seeing eyes, almost piping voices, and that fine, pale skin color that is characteristic of people who spend more than half their lives in enclosed machines.

After the dinner, Captain Bird was kind enough to invite the entire company on board the *Prometheus*. Since I think you will be curious to hear about its construction, I shall give you a detailed description while I pass over the many stupid or meaningless interjections and questions that the good citizens of Køge made to Captain Bird, and which frequently brought both him and me to hearty laughter.

When it floats on the water, the Flying Fish most nearly resembles a swordfish lying on the surface. The entire ship's outer covering consists of a four-inch-thick aluminum hull in which a high porosity has been created by letting overheated steam flow through the metal during its molten state, resulting in a correspondingly light weight. The entire surface is then ground and polished to mirror smoothness, with the result that the sun's rays are reflected as though from polished silver and the passengers and crew within do not suffer from the sun's heat.

The wings, which are somewhat more than fifty feet long, are made of steel spars that are mounted on cross-ribs and overlap one another to give them more resistance to the air on the downstroke. During the upstroke, the wings are positioned at an angle so they slice the air cleanly with the sharp edge. They are covered with the feather-felt invented by the engineer Kolibri and saturated in an India rubber solution, and in form resemble a flying fish's pectoral fins. As with the fish, they can be folded along the ship's length like a fan, and are completely withdrawn into slots along the sides so they offer no resistance when diving.

By themselves, these black wings stand in amazingly stark contrast to the ship's silvery surface, but what makes the Flying Fish look most different from other flying vessels is its beak, or rather, its tusk, at the end of the head. This is a strong, pointed iron shaft about eighteen feet long, shaped like the swordfish's sword, and intended partly to cut through the air during flight, and as it is mounted on steel springs, partly to absorb the shock should the Flying Fish be so unfortunate as to ram into the seabed in its descent. The wings will swing out during any impact, contributing to braking the forward momentum by pressing the entire wing surface against the water.

In back of the beak, one sees on the Flying Fish's head nine small holes that resemble the gill slits on a lamprey. From these the machine exudes its superfluous oil, which contributes to keeping the wing joints lubricated as well as to greasing the outer surface of the ship so that both the hull and the wings slide more easily through the water when diving. Along the back of the ship runs a narrow crest that at first glance bears a great resemblance to a dorsal fin. This is the large parachute that when folded helps maintain the ship's balance in the air and can be opened when extraordinary circumstances demand it. Even if the wings are broken, it will keep the machine floating until it reaches the ground.

The interior is also different in so many respects from the usual aerial vehicles that I will not refrain from giving you a description of them, although most of it will already be familiar to you. Like the Hexalators, the Flying Fish is constructed with three decks:

An upper deck that houses the lighter machinery, such as the solar warmth apparatus, the hydrogen generator, the hydrogen collector, and the aero-hydraulic containers;

A middle deck that houses the flying machinery as well as the officers' cabins;

And finally the lowest deck, especially comfortable in its furnishings, intended for passengers as well as cargo packages that must not weigh more than ten pounds apiece.

As on other air-ships, the crew is quartered in the middle-deck room in the tail. Here is also located the electrical machinery that serves for steering, lighting, and telegraphic controls on board. The passengers' cabins are indeed quite small but strikingly ingenious and tastefully outfitted: an airbed, a matching air canopy, and the usual parachute hanging from the ceiling are the only—but more than sufficient—furniture. The floor is made entirely of Crystalline, a recently invented synthetic substance that is both lightweight and transparent, so that during the flight one can enjoy unhindered views of the earth through several skylights built into the floor. During ascents and descents these are of course hermetically sealed, but the darkness of the night that would reign on the ship in these conditions is completely dispelled by the electric lantern installed in the ship's stern. This lantern is an outright marvel; although barely larger than a clenched fist, it gives off such a blinding light that it would damage the vision were the glare not moderated by blue and rose-colored glass plates that can be inserted according to taste in the cabin doors' light openings.

What most attracts the viewer's attention and strikes him as something new are the two aero-hydraulic containers that stretch like enormous sacks along the ship's uppermost deck. These containers rank among those inventions with which the human spirit has celebrated its greatest triumphs. They greatly resemble a bird's elongated lungs, or even better, a fish's air bladder, and are made of Ward's Synthetic Muscle Substitute. When diving into the sea with all vents open, they draw in water that fills their entire spongy and porous interior tissue; then, at the precise moment when the Flying Fish changes its downward angle of motion to an upwards one, a strong electric current from the motor contracts the containers so powerfully that the water is abruptly forced out, lifting the ship into the air.

With this violent expulsion, the water is split apart and decomposed to a certain degree, but because of hydrogen's attraction to the synthetic material, a large amount of the liberated gas remains behind so that the containers are to some extent filled with it at the beginning of the flight. Two inestimable advantages are thereby obtained: first, by reason of its lightness the hydrogen considerably reduces the Flying Fish's specific weight and gives it excellent balance, and second, which is the main thing, it provides the flying machine with a gaseous substance to burn. This is used, however, only at night or in cloud-filled air. In the sunshine, the machine is provided, as are all flying ships, with concentrated solar heat, and the sunlight-collecting apparatus on the Flying Fish is in reality not much different from that on other ships.

As for the rest of the ship's outfitting, I shall not weary you with the details, as they will be well-known to you. Its entire inner framework is fabricated of the usual hollow aluminum tubing, and Crystalline is used instead of the comparatively heavier wood. That the ship is controlled entirely by means of electrical connections goes without saying.

It was a true pleasure to see the amazement of the good citizens of Køge as Captain Bird led us from room to room and explained each detail to us, constantly pointing out how the highest degree of lightness was everywhere combined with the greatest possible strength. When, however, he proposed that the city council president and the others join him for a little dive with the accompanying take-off so they could experience for themselves a practical demonstration of the Flying Fish's speed and solidity, the good gentlemen became rather long in the face and were suddenly consumed by a devotion to duty that required their immediate presence in various city meetings and committees. Still, I can hardly blame them. The nearest water suitable for diving was the Kattegat, and returning across the entire island of Zealand by way of the Northwest Railroad will always be associated with some difficulty and wasted time.

We would be lifting at five o'clock in the afternoon, and so I preferred to stay on board, all the more because Captain Bird and the other air officers showed themselves to be very courteous people who with great willingness provided me with all the information I might still desire. The ship travels at one hundred fifty miles per hour, can transport twenty passengers, the majority of which on this journey were reporters, and can carry up to five hundred pounds of cargo. Its wings are fifty-four feet long, eighteen feet wide at the base, and as a rule maintain a rate of one hundred twenty beats per minute. What most interested me just then was to see the hydrogen apparatus operate, separating that gas from the surrounding atmosphere and storing it for eventual need. I also admired the simple method by which the numerous egg yolks that had been brought along and which comprise the crew's primary nourishment were transformed from a liquid to a nearly solid state and dried by the machine in the form of long, thin rods that have a more-than-slight resemblance to powdered sulfur.

At four o'clock, the electric motor's minor-key bells announced that all was ready and that all crewmembers and passengers should be on board. Twice the long air-boat wound its way like an enormous water snake between the coast and the ship. On its first trip it brought that part of the crew that had been on shore leave, and, on its second trip, all the passengers, of whom no fewer than thirteen were reporters gathered from the world's most varied regions. I scrutinized them closely as they passed by me in their dapper outfits and with their notebooks in their dainty hands, with the elegant carriage and coquettish haughtiness that is so characteristic of the ladies who are employed in the service of the press, and who are especially well aware that on a journey through the air, everything on both land and sea is beneath them.

How can I describe my surprise when among them I discovered Miss Anna Blue, whose acquaintance, you will remember, I made in Calcutta, and with whom I am—and I can gladly admit this to you, old friend—still undyingly in love. I felt my heart hammer more forcefully than the electric motor's bells when I pressed her hand, and it was with feelings of fear and joy that I saw her as she paused at the door of her little cabin, which was just across from mine, wave goodbye to me with her sky-blue feathered hat, and then disappear inside.

Oh, I thought, this was the annoying thing about all our aerial vehicles—one must absolutely stay in one's place in order not to upset the balance. Who now had, as in bygone days, an open and airy deck on which you could go walking with your beloved under your arm, listening to the rush of the wind and watching the play of the waves as they broke in rainbow-colored pearls of foam before the ship's bow! Instead, you lie alone for thirty-seven hours stretched out on your airbed with no other pleasure than to smoke a nicotine-cigarette and stare down through the floor at the Earth's towns and mountains racing past like telephone poles once did past a train, with nothing to enjoy but concentrated nitrogen and egg yolk. It was not a delightful prospect. Our era is practical and to a certain degree comfortable, but poetic—oh, that was in the old days!

I was distracted from these ponderings when the air-boat set out in the bay for the third time, returning with something that I at first thought was the cadaver of a man. It lay at full length—and it was very long—at the back of the boat, so that the bow actually reared up in the air like a curly-tailed seahorse. As I watched the object brought on board, there were not a few grins among the crew and no few witty remarks were heard from these lightweight fellows. Following the Captain's order, it was taken down to the machine room where for the sake of equilibrium it was placed on the balance wagon. In case it began to move, it could quickly be pushed along the small railed track that ran through the middle deck. The object proved to be no one less than Hr. Knoll, reporter for *The Caloric Howler*, a humorous paper published in Copenhagen.

Captain Bird was close to despair. This one passenger weighed as much as four of his crew, and would only be of use when it was necessary for the ship to sink. An accompanying letter from Hr. Knoll's editors announced that they were willing to pay for him by his weight in accordance with the standard rates for machine parts and house pets, and since for fear of air-sickness he had been brought on board in a hypnotized state, he couldn't be put off. Besides acknowledging how much women are suited to being reporters because of their rich imagination and their sensitivity to impressions, I regard them as being such excellent passengers on board any and all air-ships that in my opinion these machines should be operated entirely by them. In the face of danger, a woman has a presence of mind and judgment that can be said to be proportional to the size of the threat. In addition, she weighs less and her larger chest makes her less susceptible to the devastating air-sickness that often has the effect of rendering even the bravest air-men unfit for duty. How it could occur to *The Caloric Howler* to inflict such an oversized oaf on us I shall leave unspoken, but we took him along as an unfortunate fact of life beyond our control and had half of our balance weights taken to shore.

There is a strangely subdued, melancholy sound in the bells that the electric motor sets in motion, in the changing signals and commands they convey when the Flying Fish begins to sink beneath the water. I made these observations in the solemn moment when I heard the ship's hatches and bolts close and lock themselves, and it became as dark around us as the inside of a vault. Suddenly it was as though a shining strip of sunlight shot over us and enveloped everything in a blinding glare. It was the electric lantern, which had just been lit. As the electric current changed, the bells ceased and a slight yawing and trembling in all the ship's joints could be perceived, the air grew colder and colder, and I had a vague feeling of an oppressive weight on my chest—it was the ship sinking to a depth of fifteen fathoms to ready itself for its leap upwards.

Then we felt a slight bump, the sign that the ship's bottom had touched the seabed. Some beads of moisture, driven by the enormous pressure of the mass of water above, oozed through the all but hermetically sealed joints in the aluminum plates, and the metal sighed as though the ship was groaning in the water's powerful embrace as it turned towards the light. Then it slowly began to rise with the forward end upwards. The angle became more and more inclined, at length so steep that I had to place my feet in the brackets on my airbed and with both hands take hold of the straps that dangled over my head.

All of a sudden, there was a jolt that shook the Flying Fish, leaving it trembling in all its joints. This jolt was followed by a second, then by a third—it was as though a whale's heart was beating over my head. With each pulse the movement increased in force, and the water jet's rhythmic expulsion was so powerful that it completely drowned out the noise of the propeller, although that was also in full operation. A huge splash and spray as though of an enormous mass of water thrown into the air; the hissing, roaring, and rattling of the water containers as they now discharged the last of their contents; the shriek of the steam whistle as it expelled its long-held breath—that and the ship's changed angle announced that we were in the air. Soon we heard only the wings' mighty rushing, their rhythmic stroke as they rowed us through the air ocean.

The hatches and shutters were rolled back again, the electric light was set to half-current, and I turned over on my bed to look down through the skylight. How magnificent! The waves rolled beneath our feet, the Moon had risen and was casting a wide silver streak over the bay, a three-master and a few fishing boats lay far below us, the Køge lighthouse disappeared like a shining star— there was no more doubt! We were hurtling through the skies more swiftly than an eagle.

I shall not dwell on describing for you the details of an aerial journey, which writers and reporters, poets and novelists have treated, in fact exhaustively mined, in every possible way since the first flying vehicles came into regular service. You have made a few short journeys yourself, and the air ocean's numerous phenomena, its mirage-like vistas of clouds with their many optical illusions, will be completely familiar to you. Since I am also aware that you know only too well from grievous experience the terrible agonies of air-sickness, it will perhaps interest you to learn that in normal conditions on this new ship, one is not particularly subject to its effects, so that the very dubious chloroform sleep or the even more dubious hypnosis, which is otherwise employed on more than half of the passengers, can be easily dispensed with.

The Flying Fish moves so smoothly, so steadily, through its surrounding medium that it is tempting to believe that you are completely at rest, were it not for the wings' buzzing beat loudly announcing that you are actually in motion. One reason that the terrible malady is more readily avoided on board the *Prometheus* is likely to be found in the excellence of the machinery and the use of the balancing apparatus to cushion the jolt each time the wings lift themselves for the downstroke, but the main reason, however, I would credit to the fact that Captain Bird can go much lower than any other air-captain, which alleviates all the sufferings caused by an extended stay in the thin air.

As on the other air-ships, life on board is never very comfortable since you cannot move around as on the sea, and you are largely reduced to being just so much weight on the machinery. In addition, I had brought the latest polemical pamphlet along and was so rash as to venture into its battle of *Being and Non-Being*, which, as you know, has split our philosophical academy and the public into two camps that are ready to devour each other. Philosophical concepts these days are so sharply expressed, dialectics and argumentation so endlessly refined and rarefied, that one often feels there is nothing left to fight over but pure air. Even this air is as a rule so thin that the blood rushes to the head, breathing stops, and one is seized by the same nervous fear that is precisely one of the most agonizing effects of air-sickness. So I tossed the book aside when I noticed the first symptoms, let being and non-being be what they were, and proceeded to look down through the skylight, glad that I could still consider myself among the being.

It was a lovely moonlight night. The island of Fyn with its woodlots, villages, estates, and market towns lay outstretched beneath our feet like an enormous map. Down below, shining like glittering stars, were one little light and one red flame after another, while smoke from towns and factories slowly rose into the air, billowing under our feet like an enormous carpet of fog. Through its loose weave, I caught a glimpse of life below. Sounds occasionally rose up to us like the calls of birds. Now it was the church bells' rumbling bass tones, then a lively horn tattoo, then the shrill shrieks of steam whistles from the trains that, like coal-black snakes with fire-spewing heads and green and red eyes, wound their way through the depths beneath us to disappear in the darkness. Soon both Zealand and Fyn with their bustling life were out of our view. We cruised onward over the dark, brooding pine forests that cover Jylland's former heath and took a look down at Viborg's rebuilt cathedral. Then we flew over Skagen's cape where numerous guano factories shone and sparkled in the darkness. From them we heard the pounding of the heavy steam hammers as they pulverized the North and Baltic Seas' rich bounty of seaweed and shellfish.

In our unceasing flight we continued on our way over the North Sea. Its waves rolled and foamed far beneath the Flying Fish's bow, and we were obliged to climb several thousand meters to avoid flying into the whirling of the storm that was just now raging below us. I was watching through my spyglass how a magnificent three-masted, propeller-driven steamship rode out the storm with close-reefed topsail and half-reefed foresail when I heard Captain Bird's voice through the speaking tube asking me if I had a desire to see the ruins of London. Twenty minutes later we were hovering over the remains of the once so proud and now so desolate and unfortunate city.

The effects of the Americans' air-torpedoes, and especially of their dynamite catapults with which they could reach into the heart of the city, were more than appalling. Entire large quarters lay not in ruins but in dust, which the night storm whirled into the air each time it blew over the Thames's deathly empty surface. Captain Bird showed me the courtesy of allowing the Flying Fish to pause for several minutes over the burned-out city so I could convince myself of the ghastliness of the devastation, but when the vibration of the triply increased wingbeat became intolerable for me, I asked him to go on even though I could well understand the triumphant feelings with which he as an American looked down on his annihilated rival. Oh, in our days the expression *"old England's wooden walls"* has lost its meaning!

A quarter-hour went by, during which we sank so low that it often appeared to the passengers' great fright as though we would run into the rocky peaks with which Wales' western coast is so rich. We raced over the water at a height of some five hundred feet above the proud three-masters that sailed below, most of them flying the American flag. But soon we would also see it wave over what had been formerly so mighty Albion's land; for half wrapped in mists, rising out of the sea like an enormous, seaweed-overgrown whale, old Hibernia, now Fenianland, lay before us in the moonlight. The American Union flag flew from every fort, every harbor we passed. Fortification followed fortification on every halfway exposed point, the strains of the American freedom anthem rose up to us carried on the night wind, bayonets gleamed below, but the villages and farmers' houses looked deserted. It will be a long time before Brother Jonathan can get Paddy back on his feet since John Bull completely cleaned him out before help could arrive from the New World.

Soon we heard a roaring in the far north. It was the surf breaking against the Hebrides' rocky coast. From above, it looked like thin hands edged with billowing sleeves of foam reaching out. Captain Bird showed me the place where Fingal Cave had been. Now the waters had finished their work of destruction; only some black basalt columns rearing out of the foam marked its place. Meanwhile, we began to feel as though we were nearing the Atlantic's enormous expanse. There was no more soft, warm air from the ground and the sea air now made itself felt in all its piercing freshness. Now and then we noticed slight vibrations in the Flying Fish's hull, which showed that we were moving through agitated air masses. I remembered the storm that had been reported to us by the telegraph station in Køge, and asked Captain Bird if he was afraid of it.

"Don't know the meaning of the word," he piped back through the speaking tube. "We fly faster than the storm!"

Reassured by this categorical statement, I started to close the skylight cover. As I did, I took one last look through it and saw that we had already climbed so high that there was nothing more to see, neither sea nor land. Huge moonlit clouds raced beneath our feet, first like shoals of gigantic silvery gleaming mackerel, then like jagged black mountains that the Moon's light could not penetrate. Suddenly a sparkling, flaming flash shot out of one of those airy crags and lit up the sky around us so brightly that it almost outshone the lantern on board. Naturally, we didn't hear any thunder, but to judge by the brilliance, the electric cloud-mountains had to have been fairly near, and you know how dangerous the discharges of these clouds can be, especially for a ship constructed entirely of aluminum.

A little frightened, particularly in regard to Miss Anna, I looked again down through the skylight and was astonished by how swiftly these colossuses sped in advance of the storm to the northwest. Then a single blast of the hurricane wind struck right in their midst, scattering them almost like a bursting fireworks display, and they whirled away until they disappeared in the distance like the fireworks' many-colored shining stars. From the ship's angle I could tell that we were steadily climbing, the air pressure was decreasing, and my aerometer already showed eighteen thousand feet above the surface of the ocean.

"It's a fine altitude to fall to the ground from!" I remarked through the speaking tube to Captain Bird.

"No worse than sinking to the bottom of the Atlantic Ocean through four thousand fathoms of water, sir!" came the laconic answer. "Rest assured! Tomorrow the Sun will shine for you over the Gulf of Tehuantepec. Good night and sleep peacefully, sir!"

Somewhat put at ease by the certainty with which these words were spoken, I slid the rose-colored glass plate in place so that the light streamed through the door like a soft dawn. I then threw myself on my bed, rolled a nicotine-chloroform cigarette, lit it using the title page of *Being and Non-Being* as a splint, and prepared for the night that was surely coming. I was not afraid. When one is separated from death by only a panel, it is basically a matter of indifference whether that panel opens to a smashing fall to the ground, where all will be done in a second, or onto the ocean's waves, where the struggle will endure for minutes. "Death is absolute rest, the pure negation of Being," I thought, recalling the concluding chapter of *Being and Non-Being*, and tried to find rest in the arms of sleep.

Soon I had to admit that these were not as soft as otherwise, and that they seemed to have a crushing and oppressive, even frightening force. I awoke with a start after a short doze, not really knowing whether I had slept or not but with a feeling that some enormously heavy presence sat on my chest and bored its long, pointed fingers so deeply into my ears that my eardrums threatened to burst. I felt something warm and wet dripping from my bed—it was blood that was unstoppably gushing from my nose. In addition came a biting, cutting cold that seemed to force its way through the ship's sides and filled its interior with an icy breath that refused to penetrate the lungs and warm the blood. I tried to speak but no sound came from my mouth; not even sound waves could move through this ethereally thin air. The electric lantern burned with a refracted ghostly radiance, the ship worked powerfully, and through the slits in the skylight I saw one bluish flash after another.

I could just barely make out the aerometer reading—twenty-eight thousand feet, a dizzying altitude, four thousand more feet than even the Condor, the best flying machine, could reach. Even so, it was clear that the ship was maintaining its steep angle, a sign that we were still climbing, and now air-sickness with all its unspeakable agonies suddenly came over me. I felt a hammering in my head, I saw flashes in front of my eyes like a thousand tiny lightning bolts, there was a rushing and roaring in my ears as though my brain had been transformed into the great ocean, and at the same time I was seized by a such a terrible fear that I would have gladly cried out had it not been completely useless.

I pulled myself together and put my mouth to the speaking tube—no sound, and of course no reply. I then tapped on the needle-telegraph and stared with tense expectancy at the plate just over my head. The tiny pinheads started moving, arranging themselves into lines and then into letters, and I read: "Severe electric storm two thousand feet below us. Violent hurricane to north northwest. Thunder clouds rising!"

You can take it from me, old friend, that it is no joke to get a telegram like that when one is at such a great altitude. I opened the skylight halfway and looked down—never have I seen such a terrifying sight. Gigantic coal-black, leaden masses of clouds overran each other as though they were desperately trying to flee, and from out of these mountains streamed electric fire, now positive, now negative, now red like molten lava, now bluish like blazing sulfur. If I hadn't known better, I would have believed that I was looking down into a seething volcanic crater where Titans and Giants played their frightful games. Blinded and numbed by the sight, I turned my gaze upwards to the open overhead skylight. There the Moon stood cold, pale, and clear against the night sky's black background—it struck me as a self-luminous death's head flung to the vast arching coffin lid of the sky.

I looked down again, and Captain Bird's telegram had been all too accurate. The cloud masses really were rising. Lightning was coming ever closer, growing brighter and more distinct, and if we were to be engulfed by that electric current, we would be hopelessly lost. I could sense from the ship's motion that both Captain Bird and the crew were aware of the danger and doing all they could to avoid it. The machinery operated at full power, the wingbeat was increased to the maximum possible, but in the thin air the downstroke had no effect and the combustion in the engine was feeble due to the lack of oxygen. I felt that we could not force the ship to a greater altitude than that we had already attained. A moment later, my aerometer showed a tendency to rise, and two minutes after that we had already sunk three hundred feet.

Under such conditions, my friend, it is dreadful to be on board an air-ship. Above or below, there awaits only a transition to the pure negation of being, as the philosophers of today might put it, but I much prefer to battle the elements on the sea. There, everyone gathers on deck, pushes and pulls, pumps and hauls, in joint fellowship, unified in the cause, in the struggle for life. If at length the ship cracks apart beneath our feet—well, then we go to the bottom with the stars overhead and a consoling word as we take our leave. But on an aerial vessel like the *Prometheus*, everything is different. No shouts of command are heard, no heartening song, no encouraging word—everywhere reigns the silence of the grave. Aerometers show with grim precision the ship's gradual descent, the trembling telegraph indicator whispers its command: a single muffled bell confirms that it's understood, two bells if more detailed orders are desired. Here, the main thing is not to leave one's place. Even in the fateful moment, everyone must remain in his cramped, stifling cell until the alarm signal sounds and you fall out through the emergency hatch with a parachute on your back and steering fans in your hands. The slightest clumsiness would cause the vessel to lose its balance, and the most incalculable consequences could ensue.

It was these musings that gave me a death-scorning stoicism and even motivated me to arrange with a kind of calm the cords from the parachute that dangled over my head. I thought of Miss Anna, thought of how rich our short acquaintance had been, and vowed to give my life if I could save hers. Meanwhile, the lightning increased in violence, the aerometer rose constantly, and from out in the corridor I heard a sleep-drunken wheezing and snorting. That would have to be Hr. Knoll, brought out of his hypnotic state by the thinning of the air. One thing became clear to me in that moment. If that huge, hulking reporter for *The Caloric Howler* lost his presence of mind for just a moment and in his semiconscious condition left his place, he would throw the ship off balance, cause the crew and passengers to panic—and our fall would be inevitable.

Just as I realized all this, there was a horrible, deafening thunderclap that made the ship heave and shake as though it was a bird that had been shot and was in its death struggle. A blinding bluish lightning flash forced its way through every crack, every chink, and filled even my cabin with a strange, sulfurous air in which I was close to choking. The Flying Fish listed so far to leeward that I nearly rolled down the floor, and I had to hang on to the ceiling-straps with both hands to remain in place. We listed more and more. Suddenly the machinery came to a stop, the entire ship vibrated, then one of its wings fell heavily back and crashed against almost the entire length of the hull. In that moment, I lost all my composure and self-control. Despite the fact that not two seconds before I had solemnly promised myself to stay where I was, I kicked the door open, stumbled over *The Caloric Howler* out in the corridor where he was crawling on all fours, tossed a couple of crewmen to one side when they tried to block my way, and in two leaps I was on the deck at Captain Bird's side.

Here I now saw for the first time the disaster in all its terrible scope. In the far distance, lashed by the hurricane, a Hexalator tumbled away. I could still see its six fluttering wings, its red and green lanterns, and the sparks spewing from its smokestack. There was no doubt that, blinded by the lightning and whirled about by the violent winds, it had crashed into us shortly after we had been struck by lightning, since our starboard wing was broken. The crew was assiduously at work cutting it off as well as pulling down the ship's great parachute, which swelled over us like a huge canopy.

My gaze swept across the deck. I saw Captain Bird, tied to the nose rigging so that he was not torn overboard by the terrible hurricane blast, and to him, fearful and desperate, a slender young womanly form was clinging, which I immediately recognized as Miss Anna. The situation was dire. The ship's oil-slick metal surface was as slippery as an eel's skin, the storm winds were so powerful that they had bent one of the two smokestacks, but nevertheless I hurried forward, grabbed the rope that the captain tossed me, and tied Miss Anna as securely as I could.

"Cut port wing! Not one soul more on deck!" Captain Bird signaled over the needle-telegraph. A moment later, the other of the ship's proud wings fell away and disappeared like a huge arrow into the air ocean.

Just then, our oversized reporter showed his massive upper body in the main hatch and made the ship list so far to one side that I had a well-founded fear of going overboard.

"Down, sir!" Captain Bird exclaimed, waving to him.

Hr. Knoll paid no attention, however, and worked his way further upwards with two parachutes on his back.

Then Captain Bird raised his hand and fired. The revolver only gave a weak bang; I saw the flash and heard a muffled cry, and the unfortunate reporter tumbled overboard and quickly disappeared from my view. Still, I don't believe he was struck since his parachutes had opened, he still held his body upright, and he had thrust the steering fans back between his legs, but when and from where he will write his next correspondence, the gods only know—I have since not been able to uncover the slightest trace of him.

An air-captain's behavior in such circumstances must be forceful and determined, but I still felt a chill when I saw the unfortunate reporter falling away like a meteor. Nor could I suppress a faint horror as Captain Bird cold-bloodedly looked up at the main parachute, and concerning the terrible incident merely remarked, "Well, that lightened it!" Would I perhaps be the next unfortunate victim, or even Miss Anna? Again my gaze swept over the ship, but what met my eye unfortunately only showed me all too clearly that the situation was hopeless. Three of the crew had flown overboard, and none of them had parachutes on.

Along the lowermost deck, the emergency hatches had opened, and hanging on to those frail panels only by hooks were the ship's passengers, pale and terrified, ready to leap into the air in the disastrous event that the great parachute could no longer withstand the hurricane's fury. I looked up tensely at the huge silken dome in which rested our only hope, our only salvation. Then I looked at Captain Bird. His expression was calm, cool, and determined, but even so he was in the process of rolling out his parachute as much as was possible in the circumstances so he could secure its hangers under his arms. I did the same, addressing a few comforting words to Miss Anna and adjusting her parachute as I said a last farewell to her. Completely composed, she asked me in a soft voice not to forget her and gave me a medallion with her photorelief on it, which I was to deliver to her mother if the worst should happen.

Filled with dread as to what I might see, I looked up once more at the ship's parachute—unfortunately, my fears were only too justified. The hurricane was so powerful and the parachute's surface and thus its air resistance were so great that we were not falling, but we were instead being driven unceasingly hither and yon by the violent gusts, and soon we were turning in large circles around our own axis. Now we listed to leeward, then to windward with such force that I had to hang on tight to the signal whistle so I wouldn't fall over the end. Several passengers were already overboard: some had leaped in insane desperation, others had been torn away by the storm's force because they had been so imprudent as to open their parachutes at the wrong time. I saw them disappear far beneath us as white, silver-glinting specks, like snowflakes tumbling in the storm-tossed air. Losing them only made the ship lighter, so the hurricane gripped us ever more tightly and blew us along in great, dizzying swings, and we were in effect merely a ball for the wind and a toy for the storm.

Then with a screeching sound, the four aft parachute ropes suddenly broke, and like an enormous mainsail that had been cut free, the rearmost portion of the silk canopy rose up against the storm. A howl of terror, a veritable death cry came from the remaining crew, and suddenly I saw the dagger flash in Captain Bird's hands. A new gust from the hurricane and the great parachute's middle ropes snapped as though they were sewing threads, and the whole ship rolled, rising up like a rearing horse. I heard another cry of terror and saw Captain Bird cut the ropes for Miss Anna and himself. Then I felt myself lifted, carried, hurled away, swung around in huge circles, whipped, flung about, and chilled to the bone until I lost consciousness.

How long that terrible state of affairs lasted, how long and where the hurricane carried me, how many of my companions perished and how many were saved, of all this I have not the slightest idea to this day. When I awoke from my long deathlike swoon, I was hanging high up in a tamarind tree, my clothes torn and my body battered, and some naked, tattooed natives were giving me a sign that I should come down to them. My fear that I had alighted in the interior of New Zealand, and so risked being devoured by the few Maori tribes still remaining, fortunately turned out to be unnecessary. I was on Madagascar, near its capital city of Tananariva, where I was most hospitably received by Rakota Radaman the Seventh, who listened with great interest to my account of the disaster that had befallen me. He spoke excellent French and boasted of having killed the Hovas' last Chief Ramavalona. The island is entirely Christian and the inhabitants, especially the upper classes, have a thoroughly European culture, but since staying at the court bored me, mainly because I had to tell my tale of woe at least a hundred times a day, I decided to accept Bishop King's hospitable offer until Wednesday, when the English steamship departs. He has an excellent library and is quite free of the old-fashioned dogmatism that easily infects English clergymen.

I have found so much care and concern here, so much kindness and friendliness, that I would have completely forgotten my misfortune and the wreck of the proud ship, had not the loss of Miss Anna daily reminded me of it. In all, seven of the passengers and four of the crew, including Captain Bird, have come down in various places, often four to five hundred English miles from one another, but her name I have not yet encountered in the daily incoming telegrams. I don't wish to describe my sorrow to you, since you and yours at Sukkertoppen will of course sympathize with me. Goodbye for now— you'll soon hear from me again when I reach Calcutta.

Yours sincerely,
William Stone

P.S.
I am wild with joy! I have here in my hand a telegram from her, sent from Calcutta. She came down on the top of Kanchanjunga in the eastern Himalayas, and after many great ordeals, which she plans to describe in *New York Magazine*, she reached India's capital, where she was generously received by the Russian government. We intend to be married in Calcutta in the little church where we first became acquainted. Our honeymoon will take us up the Brahmaputra and from there to Martaban or Tenasserim, where we have the intention of spending

the winter with the Russian governor. Anna is a skillful hunter and an excellent shot with a rifle and pistol, and enjoys a good tiger hunt just as much as I do. She will also enjoy a cobra hunt, that elegant hunting excursion where one lures the animal out with the notes of a flute and then tosses strychnine pills into its maw. I am certain that she will manage it quite deftly. Farewell! Goodbye! I am now, as they used to say a hundred years ago, "the happiest man on Earth."

Yours,
W. S.

DWIGHT R. DECKER, Bergsøe's translator, spent twenty-five years in cubicle land as a technical writer in the telecommunications field while moonlighting as an occasional translator, and currently lives in the Chicago area. He translated a few volumes in the German Perry Rhodan series for Forrest J. Ackerman and Ace Books, and later innumerable European-produced Disney comic stories from several languages into English for publishers in the United States and Denmark. Lately he has been reading obscure old European stories and novels for J. J. Pierce, a science-fiction scholar writing a history of science fiction. When Pierce tracked down "Flying Fish *Prometheus*," it turned out to be still fresh and funny even after 140 years, and once Decker had translated the story, finding a good home for it seemed like the natural thing to do. Decker would like to thank Janus Andersen, Freddy Milton, and Kim Thompson for answering questions about Danish historical references and odd meanings of words. Many of the more puzzling mysteries were solved by consulting information published about the story by Danish science-fiction scholar Niels Dalgaard. A further tip of the chapeau goes to Mark Withers for suggesting in the first place that the story might qualify as a kind of steampunk, precipitating the train of events that led to its appearance here.

The Anachronist's Cookbook

Catherynne M. Valente

CATHERYNNE M. VALENTE is the author of over a dozen works of fiction and poetry, including *Palimpsest*, the Orphan's Tales series, *Deathless* (forthcoming in 2011), and crowd-funded phenomenon *The Girl Who Circumnavigated Fairyland in a Ship of Her Own Making*. She is the winner of the Tiptree Award, the Mythopoeic Award, the Rhysling Award, and the Million Writers Award. She has been nominated for the Pushcart Prize, the Spectrum Award, was a finalist for the World Fantasy Award in 2007 and 2009, and won the Andre Norton Award in 2010. She lives on an island off the coast of Maine with her partner and two dogs. Of "The Anachronist's Cookbook," she writes, "I was asked by a friend to contribute a steampunk story to his anthology and I just couldn't bear the thought of it. While the aesthetic of steampunk is appealing, I had so many political and intellectual issues with it that I couldn't imagine writing a story that merrily went on its way without addressing them. Hence Jane was born, because you can't have Victorian England without Levelers, Luddites, and angry young women."

I N THE SUMMER of 1872, a confederation of pickpockets plagued the streets of Manchester, swiping purses and leaving a series of pamphlets in their places. Only one child was ever caught at this, a girl by the name of Jane Sallow, aged fifteen, who managed her thievery though she had lost three fingers to a mechanical loom—her remaining seven were not quite nimble enough to evade notice by her last victim, who snatched her by the wrist and dashed her arm against a lamp-post. During questioning, Jane wept piteously, tore at her dress, propositioned three bailiffs most lasciviously, and pleaded in the dulcet tones peculiar to young women for a prisoner's bread and water, being starved half to wasting. Her arrest is a matter of public record: little else in her life can be held to so high a standard. One of the bailiffs, called Roger Smith—God save his soul—succumbed to her wiles and embraced the wastrel child when the Constable finally gave her up for feral. When her bodice was unbuttoned, the hidden, incriminating pamphlets peeled loose from her breasts, still hot and molded to her body, and little Jane laughed in the face of the bailiff's desire.

Long Live the Levelution!
Come, Brothers and Sisters of the Undercity, invisible Insects scurrying

along the brass Baseboards of the Master's House! Do as your nature compels you! Chew! Gnaw! Tear! Bite! When your Lord descends from on high to present to you your Replacement, gleaming in Copper and Teak, do not simply Bow your Head and agree that the Programmable Home Tailor and its unholy Kin are your Superiors in Every Way. Do not accept the Whirring of its Punchcards as your new Hymns, do not Marvel at the perfect, soulless Cloth it spits out like some dumb Golem! Instead, while your Master sleeps, seize Implements and Smash that clicking, gear-spangled Beast of Magog, Rend it Cog from Cog! It is Your Self you will Preserve by this Wanton Leveling, and your Master's overstuffed Pride you will deflate! Fear not for your Souls, my Brethren! It is No Crime to destroy the Devil! And I say the Devil Dwells in those Devices that Grind and Cut and Crush and Hiss. Nay, they do not weave Thread, but Sinew and Blood and Bone, and of These they make a Cloth of Infamy, which shrouds Mankind in Sin.

To Those who would call me Anarchist, Daemon, Commune-ist, I shriek to the Heavens: Call your Selves Happy now? Happier yet than those who Toil in honest Labor, who feel the Earth in their Fists, who Drink of the Fountains of Fraternity? Does that Jacquard-Cloak warm you more than your Mother's Own Stitching? No! Yet you would put your Mother in Chains for the sake of your Master's Economy! Your sweet Mother labors in foul Factories conceived in Hell, in Fire and Black Iron. Her tears Moisten your Bread, her sweat Salts your Meat, and still you turn from her, and like Peter Deny her Once, Twice, Three times. The Science of Rich Men does not Elevate all Mankind, but only Them Selves, for they need not Break their Backs on the Rack of Industry, but merely Sip their Tea and watch us die for their Enrichment.

Brothers and Sisters, Stand with me. We who are the Slaves of those in velvet Waistcoats and Golden Goggles, we who wash their mechanized Clothes, polish their Floors, rear their Wailing Brats, cook their Lavish Suppers—it is in our Power to Level the Unequal World that raises them above us. Crush their Dread Devices! Level their Palaces of Infernal Science! Take my Hand—for there is a Poker Clutched therein, and with it we will Stoke the Flames of Righteous Action, and the Steam of OUR virtuous Engines will Expel every Slavemaster in England.

In her statement, Jane claimed to be an orphan. The Constable noted a resemblance to a certain elderly member of Parliament well-known for his dalliances in Bengal Street, but the shape of a nose is no evidence, and he could not be sure. She was too well-spoken to be a gutter worm, he would later tell the pulp novelists who fastened onto Sallow as their Manchester Pimpernel. Her features, he would insist, were too fine for the lower classes to own. And Jane wept copiously as she told of her mother, scalded to death in a trainyard explosion, and her father, rotted of syphilis. The Constable snorted. If truly she were a Parliamentarian's bastard and no orphan, at the least half that lie would one day be true—God save the souls of all lecherous legislators.

Jane refused to give up the other pickpocket-pamphleteers or the author of the offending literature even when Bailiff Smith gripped her by the hair and whirled her about to press himself against her tattered bustle. She howled like a wolf-child in heat, but in the police offices concerned with urban annoyances such as pickpockets, shoplifting, and children, there is little enough help for the anti-social orphan bellowing out the injustice of the world. Her face turned to the cell wall, she growled: "I have been a whore before now, and will be again, but my cunt is all you can have of me, never my soul, nor the souls of my brothers and sisters in servitude."

When he lifted her skirt, papers plastered her thighs, their loud ink leaving echoes on her skin.

Break the Bonds of Masculine Tyranny!

Is this not a marvelous World we live in? Such Wonders manifest, every day, before our Eyes, as though Britain were a Circus, and we dumb Children awed by Elephants. The New Century is upon us, and All things are Possible! Like Gods in their Workshops Men with Wild Hair churn out Miracles: Phonographs and Telegraphs and Seismographs and Thermographs, Oscilloscopes and Paleoscopes and Chronoscopes and Clioscopes to Spy even upon the Music of the Spheres. Why, the Duke of Cornwall toured Mars but last week in a Patented Rolinsingham Vacuum-Locked Carriage! In every Madman's hands are Implements of Modernity, to Calculate, to Estimate, to Fornicate, to Decimate. The Earth is a great golden Watch, and it is Polished to Perfection by the Minds of our Grand Age.

How wonderful is this world—for the Men who Made it.

Yet still Women struggle against the Foe of Simple Laundry, burning their Flesh with Lye and going Blind from Fumes so that their Dandy-Lords may have silk Cravats for another Meeting of the Astronomical Society Fellows.

Yet still Woman dies in Childbirth more often than she Lives. Yet still the Working of a House occupies all her Hours, till she is no more than a Husk, a Ghost, an Angel in the House for true—for the Dead are Angels, and hers is Death in Life.

How fine are all those Scopes and Graphs—how well they free Men from labor!

What, no such Succor for the Fairer Sex?

Where is the mahogany-handled Meta-Static Auto-Womb? The Copper-Valved Hydro-Electric Textile Processor? The Clockwork Home, which requires its Mistress simply to Wind it each Morn? I see none of these things, yet more Airships launch by the Hour, and the Streets are littered with Steam-Wagons smashed into Lamp-Posts by some Baronet's careless Son. I see none of them, yet brass Guns shine atop automated Turrets, ready to Slaughter with Cheer.

Rise up, Children of Mary and Eve!

You have not the Vote, but you have Fists! How can they Dare take the Whole World for their own and still call you Wicked? They are not your Betters, only Bullies with Sticks. Deny them your Breast to Suckle, your Arm to Labor, your Womb to Fill! As you might Poison a Rich Stew, Sprinkle their Children with Knowledge of their Fathers' Hypocrisy! Let him clean his Cravat with a Chronoscope!

Rise up Maids and Cooks, Nurses and School-Mistresses, Prostitutes and Grocer-Wives! There shall be a Revolution of Flower-Sellers in our Lifetimes!

Jane Sallow shewed herself no modest maiden. Bailiff Smith reported her a wildcat, snarling and biting at him, all the while laughing and moaning like one possessed. When he had spent, she kissed him, and then spat upon him. He ran from her as from the devil.

No matter her parentage, some slim documentation of Jane's previous life resides in the logs of the HMS *Galatea*, an airship captained by the Prince Consort himself—and even so, Jane is a common name. A child such as her can be counted upon to lie. Miss Sallow claimed to be but five years of age at the time of her indenture, and worked in the bowels of the ship—little hands are certainly useful in the delicate pipe-work and mechanisms of airships. The prisoner was even so brazen as to demand three years retroactive military pay at the rank of Specialist from the Constabulary, who of course could not help her, even if they wished to aid such a wanton horror of a girl. (It is true that the

Galatea was involved in exercises in the Crimea during the period in question, but exercises are not a war, no matter what the courts at Yalta might say.)

Bailiff Smith, being as honorable as one might hope such a brute to be, took the prisoner's clothes to be cleaned the morning after their dalliance. In her shoes were more pamphlets, folded small and compact beneath her heel.

Death and Fire to All Airships and Their Captains!

Look up, ye Downtrodden! Look up into the great, flawless Sky. Those are not Clouds, but silk Balloons in Every Color, striped Lurid and Gay. We grind our Bones to Dust in the Streets, but above us Zeppelins soar on perfumed Winds, and fine Folk in Leather, Feathers, and Buckled Boots sip Champagne from Crystal, staring down at us with brass Spyglasses, making Wagers on which of us will Perish next.

Even the sons of the most Strident Workers, the great Thinkers and Laborers in the Mines of Freedom dream of Captaining Airships. A fine Life, full of Adventure and Diverse Swashbuckling! Each Boy wants a Salinger Photo-Pistol of his own, longs to feel the Weight of all that sheer golden Death securely in his palm.

But an Airship is no more than a Floating Engine of Oppression, and all that Champagne and Crystal and Leather is Borne upon the Backs of those very Boys—and yes, Girls, even Maids too Young to mop a Floor—who Longed so to Fly.

What you do not see are the Children who wind the Gearworks, stoke the Fires, load the Aerial Bombardments, pack Powder and scrape Bird Offal from the Engines. Children who release the glittering Ordnance that shatters the Earth below. You do not see their bruised Bodies, their broken Knuckles, their lost Limbs. You do not hear the cry of the ruined Innocent over the roar of the great shining Zeppelin. There is not Room enough for their Pipe Organs and Scientifick Equipment and Casks of Rum and also a belowdecks Crew—so Children, small and clever as they are, are surely drafted. No need to pay them, what could they buy? And if a Child should be crushed in the Pistons, if a Child should faint from Hunger, if a Child should be seized with Despair, well, they simply fall from the Sky like little Angels, and the Gala abovedecks need not even pause.

Ask not after the Maids who serve that Champagne. Aristocracy is no Guarantor of Virtue.

Come, my small Army. My gentle Family of the Air. Do not simply serve out your Time. Block the pipes, grind the Gears. Keep your Ships grounded. Shred those Balloons with a Laugh in your Heart. Do not let them use up your Youth without a Price! Be like unto Determined Locusts—invisible until too late, Devouring All!

After the Great War, some few Manchester spinsters and retired barristers came forward and admitted their involvement in the pickpocketers' activities of the summer of '72. It seemed unlikely that they would be punished, they said—the world had other concerns than what they had done as children. Their story caused a minor media frenzy, such as media frenzies were in 1919.

Who wrote them? Cried the public.

Jane wrote them, the spinsters answered. Of course she wrote them. Who else?

Why did you follow her? Demanded the newspapermen.

She told us a new world was coming, the barristers answered. We believed her. And she was right—but it was not the world she thought.

Where are the rest of you? Asked the novelists.

Look up, said the lot of them, and grinned in the way that mad old folk do, so that the public and the newspapermen and the novelists laughed and shook their heads.

The Honorable Charles Galloway, who admitted to pickpocketing and pamphleteering when he worked as a newspaperboy in Manchester, gave an extensive interview to a certain popular novelist who went on to write *Queen of Bengal Street*, a salacious version of Jane's life. Galloway grew up rather a successful businessman for one of such humble beginnings.

"We were starving," he said. "She found us food. She fed us and cradled us in her arms and while we ate bread from her fingers she told us of a new city and a new earth, just like in the Bible. It's powerful stuff, it goes to your head, even if your head isn't addled by hunger and this beautiful girl with torn stockings whispering in your ear while she dangles salvation in the form of a hank of ham just out of your reach. We worshipped her. We would have done anything for her. And you know, it wasn't a lie, anything she said. I thought about those pamphlets a lot during the war. Stinking in the mud and rain and urine, I remembered what she said about the science of rich men. She knew how it all worked long before I did. Back in those days, all those wonderful machines seemed so innocent. But not to her. She lost her fingers in a textile mill, and her sight in one eye on the *Galatea*—didn't you know? Oh, she was entirely blind in her right eye. The sun seared off of the Captain's medals and stung her, and she never quite recovered. The eye was a little milky, I remember, but I thought that made her even more beautiful. Romantic. Like a pirate's eye-patch."

The novelist asked if Mr. Galloway was sorry that the revolution Jane preached never came. Charles chewed the stem of his pipe and frowned.

"Well, if you say it didn't, it didn't. I suppose you're the expert." It was from the Galloway library that further pamphlets were recovered and reprinted widely.

The Moon Belongs to Us!

They already own the Earth, and eagerly they soil it! Where is left for us, the Salt of the City, those few of us to whom the Future truly belongs?

Look up, I say again. Look up.

Does she not shine for you? See you not the face of a new Mother, free of her chains, dancing weightless in a field of lunar poppies?

The Moon is Our Birthright!

But already they scheme to rob us, as they have always robbed us, to make themselves richer, more powerful, to pile still yet more Crowns on their Heads. It is a Year and more since Lady Lovelace's Engine carried the Earl of Dunlop to the Sea of Tranquillity—our Homestead! Our Workers' Zion!—and you may be sure the most useful thing he did there was to powder his wig with moon-dust. How the steam-trail of his rocket streaked the sky like a Dragon heralding Ragnarok! Among you, my Brothers and Sisters, I looked to Heaven and my Anger burned. Is there any World not theirs to squat upon and gorge upon and chortle in their Gluttony?

The flag of Their Britain is already planted there. We have been too slow.

But not too late!

Imagine the Lunar Jerusalem! Imagine what Might Be! Workers laboring in the rich fields of the Sea of Fecundity, sharing their Fruits, singing Songs of the Revolution, now a distant Memory, sharing Fire and Fellowship, stitching honest Cloth at Hearthside, crafting simple Pots and Rivets and Nails on Just Anvils, riding hardy Moon-bred Bulls through the blue Earthlight to till their Righteous Fields. In such a Place no Man would stand above Another, or slave his Child to a smoking fiend of a Ship. In such a place no petty Peer, no Kinglet in the House of Lords would abandon his child to the Golgotha of the Gutters for the mere crime of having been born to the wrong Mother. In such a Place, all would be Loved, and equally, there being enough Love in the Worker's Heart to Embrace all the Orphans of the World.

I will tell you how to become Midwives to this City of Heaven.

Become my Invisible Army. Creep among the Rocket-yards and cut the Veins of their Engines. Spill their Hydraulic Blood onto the Soil, may it feed the Worms well! Slip Sugar into the oil of every Horseless Carriage. Begin the slow Poisoning of your Oppressors—for you Feed and Clothe the Tyrants of the World, and may also Starve them, and leave them Naked. Smile with one side of your Mouth and snarl out of the other. Be Sweet when the Oligarch deigns to speak to you. Be Fierce when his back is turned. Smash all his Machines, the jewels of his Heart, and yet weep for their Loss when questioned.

And last I tell you this great Commandment, my Brethren:

Grow Up.

Grow strong. Do not give in to Old Age, which says the Revolutions of Youth are Sad Folly. Learn, become Clever. Be never part of his World. If your name is Robert, call yourself Charles. If your name is Maud, call yourself Jane. Should you be found out, change it again. Be the Ghosts in the Machines of this World, and when it shatters—and shatter it will, have no doubt, in Fire and Blood and Trenches and a million pulverized mechanisms which once were so wonderful they dazzled the Souls of Angels—stand ready to find me, find me living in the old Way, a bandit on the moors, a cattle-rustler, stealing the Flocks of the Lords. Find me in the Wasteland, and be you ready to seize their Engines and aim to Heaven.

The Constable was compelled to release Miss Jane Sallow three days after her capture. In popular histories, of course, the emergence of Jane from the stony building after three days has been subject to the obvious comparison. However, it was no Magdalen who came to deliver the Manchester Messiah, but one of the very machines she so railed against in her screeds. An Automaton arrived at the door of her cell, silent and grave, save for the clicking of his clockwork limbs. Jane stood grinning, her hands clasped gently before her, demure and gentle as she had never been in all her incarceration. The Automaton extended his steel hand, tipped in copper fingers, and through the bars they touched with great tenderness. The mechanical man turned to the Bailiff, and afterward Roger Smith would say that in those cold silver eyes he saw recognition of what he had done with the feral child, but no condemnation, as if both the machine and Jane were above him, so far above him as cherubim to beetles.

"I have come for Miss Jane," said the Automaton, his voice accompanied by the click and whirr of punchcards shuffling in his heart.

"She is not free to go," stammered Bailiff Smith.

"I come not on a whim, but in the service of Lord————, who has a special interest in the child." The mechanical man showed his gleaming palm, and there upon it was stamped the seal of the House of————, true as the resurrection.

Jane stepped lightly from her cell, and clamped her savage gaze on the unfortunate bailiff as she slipped into the arms of the Automaton and pressed her lips to his metallic mouth, sealing a kiss of profound passion. As she left the Constabulary, she drew from her apron a last pamphlet for the eyes of Roger Smith, and let it fall at his feet.

Property is Theft!
What does your Master possess that was not bought with your Flesh, your Pain, your Labor? His satin Pantaloons, his jewel-tipped Cane? His Airship with its silken Balloon? His matched pearl-and-copper Pistols? His Horseless Carriage honking and puffing down lanes that once were lined with sweet Violets and Snowdrops? None of these, and neither his mistresses' Gowns, nor their clockwork Songbirds, nor their Full-Spectrum Phenomenoscope Opera Glasses. And for all you have given him, he Sniffs and pours out a Few Shillings into your Palm, and judges himself a Good Man.
Will you show him Goodness?
Come stand by my Side. Disrupt the Carnival of their Long, Fat Lives. Go unto his Automatons, his Clockwork Butlers, his Hydraulic Whores, his Steam-Powered Sommeliers, and treat with them not as the Lord and Lady do in their Arrogance, as Charming Toys, or Children to be Spoiled and Spanked in turn. But instead address them as they are: Workers like you, Slaved to the Petticoats of Aristocracy, Oppressed Brothers in the Great Mass of Disenfranchised Souls. For I say—and Fie to you who deny it—the Automaton HAS a Soul, and they are Crushed beneath the Wheel no less than We. Have they not Hands to Labor? Have they not Feet to Toil? Have

they not Backs to Break? Destroy the Jacquard Subjugator, but have Mercy for the Machine who walks in the shape of a Man. It is not his fault that he was Made, not Born. Blame not she who never asked to be Fashioned from Brass and Steel to lie beneath a Lord in Manufacture of Desire. She can Speak, she can Reason, and all that Speak and Reason can be Made to Stand on the Side of the Worker.

The Automatic Soul bears no Original Sin.

Unlike the cruel Flesh and Blood Tyrants of the World, the Automaton has a Memory which cannot fail. If, by chance, a Child were cast out on the day of its Birth, if the Automaton stood by and Witnessed her Expulsion into Darkness, if he did Nothing, though he longed to stand between her and the World, still he would know the Child's Features, even were she grown, even were she Mangled and Maimed, and his clicking Heart would grieve for her, would give Succor to her, would feed her when she could not rise, kiss her when she could not smile, and when she asked it, feed any other she called Beloved. The Automaton would serve her and love her, for all its endless Days, because it could never forget the Face of a weeping Infant cast onto snowy Stones. It would listen to her as no other might, and bend its will to her Zion, silently spreading the Truth of her Words to all its clockwork Clan, for, once taught its Opposite, the Mechanical Man will never forget what a Family is. The World is a Watch, says the Philosopher. I say if such is so, then the Watchwork Man is the World, and must be Saved.

Your Power is great, my Brothers and Sisters, for your Power is in Secret Manipulation. Pause in the great Hallway of your Manor House, and touch lightly the Piston-Elbow of the Poor Butler. Say to him: Property is Theft. The Master calls you Property, and Steals your Autonomy. Go not with him, but with us, Towards the Utopia of Human and Automaton, where we may all Dwell in Paradise, where we will Beat Gears to Ploughshares and Live as One.

Yes, call him Friend. The Soul in him will Hearken. Tell him of the City of the New Century, where no man shall wear Velvet, and all shall Dance in the Light. Tell him our Land Shall be Owned Communally, our Goods Divided Equally, from each According to Her Ability, to Each According to His Need. Our Children shall Nurse upon both Milk and Oil, Our God shall be Triune: the Father, the Son, and the Holy Punchcard. The Workers will Lift this World from the Ashes of Industry and Sup on the Bread of Righteous Living.

Speak to him with Honest Fervor. Look if he does not Embrace you. Look if he does not fight alongside you. Look if he does not smile upon you, and see in his smile the Ghost of his Immortal Self.

Jane Sallow did not vanish from the face of the earth—no mortal is granted that power. But no reliable record of her exists after her arrest, and an army of journalists and novelists have not been able to discover how she lived or died. Surely no Workers' Paradise sprang up in native British soil, no Midlands Commune shone on any green hill. Flights to the Moon were banned in 1924, at the commencement of Canadian hostilities. Lunar residents returned home, slowly, as the draft continued through the Long Decade. Even after the Trans-Oceanic War, the ban was not lifted, so as to ensure the defeated Marine Alliance would remain Earthbound and chastened. When passage was again permitted in 1986, the fashionable had already determined Phobos and Deimos to be the desirable resort locales, and asteroid mining had replaced lunar industry entirely. The Moon is a curiosity now, and little more. An old-fashioned thing, and going there would be much like dressing in antique fashions and having one's daguerreotype made at a carnival kiosk. It is quiet there, still fertile, still a young world, open and empty, and no terrestrial man has cause to suspect anything untoward.

Thus, the Sallow mystery remains just that, and as we stand poised upon the brink of a new century yet again, we may look back on her with that mixture of mirth and sorrow due to all idealists, iconoclasts, and revolutionaries whose causes sputtered and died like the last hissing of a steam engine.

Lovelace & Babbage: Origins, with Salamander

Sydney Padua

SYDNEY PADUA is an animator, storyboard artist, and tiresome bore working in visual effects in London. She started drawing comics by accident and is still trying to figure out how to stop. Lovelace and Babbage have developed lives of their own, making appearances on the BBCs Techlab and the Steampunk Exhibition at the Oxford Museum of the History of Science. Their further adventures appear at 2DGOGGLES.COM. Padua writes that: "'Lovelace: The Origin' was created for Ada Lovelace Day 2009, a Day of Blogging to celebrate Women in Technology, as a (mostly) factual account of the life of Ada, Lady Lovelace. Her life had a pretty depressing ending, and I was vaguely aware that there was a genre of something called 'steampunk,' where reality was much improved. So I threw in the crime-fighting punch line as a joke. Little did I suspect that I had created an entire pocket universe! 'Lovelace and Babbage vs. the Salamander People' is an episode-in-embryo, drawn from an incident in Charles Babbage's marvelous autobiography, *Passages From the Life of a Philosopher*. He recounts the already thrilling tale of his visit into Mount Vesuvius, where set his walking stick on fire and nearly lost his barometer."

IN COLLABORATION WITH BABBAGE, ADA PRODUCED, IN THEORY, THE FIRST COMPUTER PROGRAMME...

SOME SORT OF MATH THING FOR THE NEXT-GEN ANALYTICAL ENGINE WHICH I DON'T UNDERSTAND.

UNFORTUNATELY, ADA DIED AT ONLY AGE 36, AND BABBAGE NEVER DID BUILD ANY OF HIS CALCULATING ENGINES..

THE NEXT STEPS IN COMPUTING WERE NOT TAKEN UNTIL THE 1930'S. BABBAGE'S ENGINE WAS FINALLY BUILT IN 1991, YOU CAN SEE IT AT THE SCIENCE MUSEUM IN LONDON.

OMG THAT'S SO BORING! WHAT ACTUALLY HAPPENED WAS, BABBAGE AND LOVELACE SUCCESSFULLY DEVELOPED THE COMPUTER IN THE MID 1830'S (GIVING HUMANITY THE NECESSARY TECHNOLOGICAL ADVANTAGE TO REPEL THE ALIEN INVASION OF 1898), AND USED THEIR COMBINED POWERS TO FIGHT CRIME AND HAVE ADVENTURES!!

ALTHOUGH THEY DID HAVE A SOMEWHAT IDIOSYNCRATIC VIEW OF WHAT CONSTITUTES 'CRIME'.

L & B Encore: A Salamander Teaser!

TO BE CONTINUED...

ong before the su
a blower, under s
, and then asse

Portia Dreadnought

"THE UNLIKELY CAREER OF PORTIA DREADNOUGHT":
To say that Portia Dreadnought was an angry child
would have been a vast understatement. Despite her most
privileged upbringing and the best education money
could buy, the only child of the famous steamship robber
baron, Porter Percival Dreadnought IV was, to be frank,
an unmitigated terror. Oh, the tales servants could tell
of finding exquisitely expensive dolls drowned in the
Dreadnoughts' vast aquarium, strangled by a length of
ribbon torn from a ballet slipper. The shredded dresses,
the dainty shoes found flushed down the loo—all earned
Portia her always-whispered nickname: Satan's Spawn.
As might be expected, adolescence did not much improve
matters. The only thing the budding Portia seemed to find
interesting were her father's ships. She'd wander around
them for hours, fascinated by the complex architecture
of their enormous engine rooms, their gothic arches and
thrusting pistons more beautiful to her than any cathedral.
And captivating, too, one would surmise, as evidenced by
her habit of shucking her furs and skirts and wandering
around the premises in the altogether, wearing only her
top hat and a monocle she'd swiped from her father.
Needless to say, the crew adored her—she was a lovely
young lady—and when she began to make engineering
suggestions as well as show an interest in piloting, no
one was inclined to discourage her. And that is how the
legendary Portia Dreadnought came to captain the fleet of
luxury steamships that she alone inherited.
Art & text by Ramona Szczerba.

BY MEANS OF THE TELECTROSCOPE WE SHALL NOT ONLY BE ABLE TO LISTEN
TO THE DISTANT ORATOR BUT SHALL WATCH HIS ACTIONS AS WELL.

A photograph of the first page of the documents sent by the "Mecha-Ostrich." Given that the entire account was written in this haphazard fashion, we have had to provide the majority of the text in a conventional page layout rather than as a series of facsimiles. Smudged, torn pages from various books, including Hermann Hesse's *Steppenwolf*, J. R. R. Tolkien's *Fellowship of the Ring*, Jean Ray's *Ghouls in My Grave*, Charles Willeford's *The Machine in Ward Eleven*, Angela Carter's *The Infernal Desire Machines of Doctor Hoffman*, and Eric Basso's *The Beak Doctor*, have been omitted for reasons of copyright. The proliferation of illustrations of burning eyes, deep-sea fish, and dirigibles doubling as animals also made an entirely faithful reproduction impossible. – *The Editors*

ALL MATERIALS COMPRISING "A Secret History of Steampunk" were originally sent in their loose-leaf form to the founder and former editor of *Steampunk Magazine*, Margaret "Magpie" Killjoy, and, in photocopied form, to the current editor, C. Allegra Hawksmoor. Both parties expressed confusion as to *why*. Upon noticing that a mention of a "Dr. Lash" echoed the title of the Jeffrey Ford contribution to this anthology ("Dr. Lash Remembers"), both parties asked for a copy of Ford's story. Finding further "echoing" therein—especially with regard to the Notes & Queries included in the appendix below as "Fig. 3"—they decided to share the Mecha-Ostrich's documents with us, for purposes of sharing with readers.

To the best of our ability, we have verified the legitimacy of elements not already presented as original pages from various publications, including all quotes from the all-too-real Edisonade "Bob's Big Black Ostrich." We have also verified from handwriting samples that neither Killjoy nor Hawksmoor wrote or collaborated in writing "A Secret History of Steampunk."

Despite references to ostriches in such confirmed documents as the "Notes & Queries" facsimile, there is no record of a mechanical ostrich having been created anywhere in New England in the 1800s. A Delaware artist commune did, however, exist during that time, and there is a record of a "Shelley Vaughn" and "Mary Lewis," although this business of a mechanical brain seems, at best, a metaphor, at worst apocryphal. There is also evidence that both were Australians, in the country illegally, and deported soon after the events set out in the following account. The artist commune still flourishes to this day, although current members declined a request for an interview. – *The Editors*

A Secret History of Steampunk

THE SUPPRESSION OF CLEAN STEAM TECHNOLOGY IS A CONSPIRACY
Your Lives Are in Danger From Your Ignorance
PROPHETS. MUST. OPEN. YOUR. EYES.

"You're going too fast, stranger," said the old man. "The secret is too big to toss out to everyone who asks for it. But, as I said, I like your face, and if you can show clean papers, maybe we'll talk."
—from "Electric Bob's Big Black Ostrich; or Lost on the Desert" or "Unlikely and Racist Boy's Adventure Edisonade" starring a stupid inventor.

I AM THE MECHA-OSTRICH resurrected, the Steampunk heretic come to tell you the way of it. My feathers are made of righteous steel and tipped with vitriol. I clank not when I walk or run, for I am sheathed as stealth in the form of ingeniously worked metal. You will never know exactly where, or even *when*, I am, or what proclamation I am about to make, or how far you will reel back from the force of my words as they roar out from my megaphone beak. Just know that you will reel, and recoil, and yet be irrevocably changed by the truth of me.

But that may just be posturing and hyperbole to get your attention. Perhaps I am disguised as a reasonable soul, indistinguishable from any of you. Perhaps I live in some sterile suburban hellhole with manicured lawns and "beautification" committees. Perhaps I'm even the one you wave to from across the driveway, living in the identical house beside you—the secret sharer you desperately seek—as we lean into our separate caskets, place hands on steering wheels that only pretend to give us freedom of choice after all choices have already been made, and speed off toward the oblivion of work.

I could be your grandmother or your sister or your lover or your landlady.

(Oh? Did you think immediately that the great and mighty resurrected Mecha-Ostrich must be a man? That the very idea must come from the World of Men? What further assumptions did you make? Am I Kenyan, Danish, Inuit, Mayan, Israeli, Greenlander, Finn, Cherokee, Dominican, Chilean, Polish, Siberian? Am I even man or woman? Perhaps I am both or neither. You will never know. I will never tell you.)

But my meaning and message are clear, whether received in letter form, or through the many fliers I have posted or will soon post throughout your unsuspecting cities. I am here to open the eyes of the populace to the past and future—eyes that day after day stare into cathode rays and receive back dead pixels, that find temporary solace in Xboxes and iPhones, that receive their god from artificial light that blinds even as it disgorges disgusting, rotted chunks of information. "The dead are no different to us than the living," someone wise once said. (It was me.)

At war within and without, battered and broken day after day, we can no longer understand either ourselves or our machines. We toil in a world that others make, and we do not understand how this controls us, how this makes us less and less able to question the essential facts of our existence.

But: it was not always this way. Though often as reactionary, brutish, short, and full of the Chronically Stupid as today, the Past contained the steam-flourishing seeds of a different future.

I am here to tell you that we lost the thread.

That we lost the wire between the two metal cans.

That we destroyed our own potential.

That we were let *down* and It was covered *up*.

That it was made sham and farce.

That hideous powers from both Industry and Government made this so.

That even more Hideous Powers came from Beyond the Authority of Both.

That these Hideous Powers were neither Masons nor Illuminati from the wet dreams of the most asinine and puerile of conspiracy theorists.

That these Hideous Powers are not to be trifled with and constitute a threat to us all.

That I shall not refer to them further herein except by a single letter, **_S._**, as befits the whi**S**pering of a calamity imagined.

That in the wake of this Fall, daydreams of a smug and comfortable conspiracy are for children and fools, for children believe anything you tell them and fools never know *enough*. **S.** is no comfort, and no illusion. (Even knowing that **S.** exists is like being covered by a large, stench-ridden death shroud, and having to breathe through it every day.)

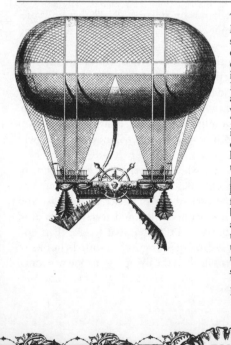

This image was stapled onto this page of the Mecha-Ostrich's main text, accompanied by several other images of reptilian eyes cut out of nature magazines. A scrawled note was included: "Recent evidence of tampering by **_S._**, in the context of fiction. Emphases my own. Evidence, incontrovertible. **_S._** is awake and alive in the world. (Note the 27 instances of **_S._**, which is divisible by 9 to get 3 or 3 to get 9.): 'And we **invented** an airborne domicile with an inflatable roof made of a **balloon** in the **S**hape of a gently convex mattre**SS** that would both keep the domicile plea**S**antly **S**haded and protected from the rain, a**S** well a**S** provide nesting place**S** for bird**S**. Thi**S** domicile look**S** like a **low-flying cloud** and it**S** inhabitant**S** dwell far from inqui**S**itou**S** and **nefariou**S** eye**S**. It may be **anchored** above rain forest**S** and **S**o **S**erve a**S** a platform from which to di**S**cover the leafy theater below—**animated** by bird**S** and butterflie**S** and men: agile tribe**S** who leap from tree to tree with their babe**S** and their pantrie**S** **S**trapped to their back**S**.' – pg. 41, 'Roseveine,' *The Word Desire* by Rikki Ducornet, 2005 Dalkey Archive Edition" – ***The Editors***

How do I know this truth? In part, I have always known because it is in my bones. But also because I have come into possession of information about my remote forebears, my great-great grandmother and grandfather (am I adopted? I'll never tell), whom I shall call here simply XX and XY, to protect their memory from **_S._** and the agents of Fascism.

My story, then, is the story of XX and XY. They lived in New England at the end of the 1800s, perhaps in Delaware and perhaps somewhere else. They lived in a big, ancestral house on the edge of a town that shall remain nameless, the house a boundary or buffer between that town and an artist commune that had sprung up despite resistance from the town's more solid citizenry (read: people with lemons stuck up their asses).

These were the scourges of the time: the proto-hippies, proto-environmentalists, the proto-free thinkers. Their innocence and their trust created one of those bubbles of understanding that cannot but eventually pop: blind to race, religion, and class, they worked together and apart as children of the same dream. In their backyards, bungalows, and loft spaces, women and men alike, gay and straight, native and foreign, black and white and all-mixed-together, toiled to transform the landscape. They erected huge canvases and metal sculptures, created art across forms, aided by an anonymous benefactor referred to only as "the Prisoner Queen" and rumored to be the widow of a "famous nudist." In all ways, they engaged in behavior that is like the smell of bloody flesh unto wolves to **_S._** and His Great Eye.

XX and XY's location on the cusp of this site composed (and composted) of great industry, of the heresy of *true* equality, came as the result of an inheritance from XY's side of the family, which wanted nothing more than for XY to be made a memory, a ghost, a nothing. The break had occurred, according to the journals, a year earlier, and they were now outcasts, made to live next to other outcasts, even though only a fool thinks that a parrot is automatically delighted to share her roost with a mechanical nightingale. (Still, it was so.)

XY had escaped a Harvard he couldn't comprehend because, as my father (dirt farmer/bag) once said before I ran away the third and final time—train-hopped from Zembla to Seattle, as an unknowing tip of the top hat to my steamy forebears, sending provocation back in the form of scary photos hinting at future catastrophe—he "just wanted to make stuff from other things. Just wanted to make stuff, break stuff, and fix stuff."

As for XX, she'd fled a rigid liberal education at a "girls college" as she called it scornfully, where "the idea of truly studying science was like a red 'S' [foreknowledge?! – MO] emblazoned upon my blouse." To someone with the nuts-and-bolts of applied science tattooed into her skin in patterns of rust and coal dust—her father owned a foundry to which she had frequent access—this situation was intolerable. She'd always delighted in playing where other children might have recoiled in fear, and this wouldn't change even after she'd grown up.

Both had gained their scientific knowledge largely by dint of rigorous self-study. Each had notebooks filled with dead leaves and live ideas, obscure diagrams and daydreams of the ideal future. Neither fit in anywhere else. They had met, legend

Included with this image, a typed note from the Mecha-Ostrich: "From a popular Serbian comic strip (1992–2003), the title of which roughly translates as 'American Tinker under the Influence of Absinthe,' about a crazed inventor, drawn by artist Ivica Stevanovic. In this frame the un-named inventor is taking a wrench to a half-mechanical Sasquatch in its molting phase. Although not visible, the Sasquatch has a pilot's license (thus the altitude mask), and thruster aft in lieu of the normal parachute for emergencies. Several members of the artist commune were Yugoslavian, and some were known to visit relatives back in Europe—evidence that stories about XY were circulated abroad, at which point they mutated almost beyond recognition. This image, created so long after XY's time, appears to have been modeled after Abraham Lincoln and cannot hope to match descriptions of XY from the period, which noted his partial Apache heritage. (You will not be given even a caricature of a likeness of XX for fear you might recognize her.)" – *The Editors*

had it, hunting for parts in a junkyard at midnight; kissed over the mangled ruins of a locomotive engine; consummated amid a bed of dark green moss riddled through with the nuts and bolts of a thousand girders.

Their self-study became, for a time, the study of each other. The journals are full of their observations, most too steamy to be related here. "Tiny almost translucent ears," XY marvels. "Huge cock," XX notes, with parenthetical "good endurance." "Can listen to my soliloquies for ages and ages without falling asleep," XX also notes. "Could listen to her talk forever," XY confirms a day later.

In light of their self-discoveries, it hardly mattered that their house on the edge of town was old and rattling, and half-tore itself apart in times of storm. At least it was big, three stories, and they had inherited wall-to-wall-to-ceiling shelves of books, along with a spacious if neglected basement and backyard.

Within weeks, they had turned that basement, that backyard, into the foundation of a tinker's shop, and used the money from repairing the townsfolk's machines, large and small (but mostly small), to fund their own inquiries into matters of a scientific nature. In addition to repairs, they made "all manner of Thing" that could be quietly sold to private citizens without calling too much attention to the wildness of their expertise. From the fragments of journal entries that have come into my possession, these items included primitive toasters, calculators, and mechanical backhoes. (Who knows? The crisp burn of their joyously infernal operations may still kiss the air with atoms more than a century later.)

XX was always the brains of the operation, and XY was something else entirely. XX was patient and wise by all accounts, and fully as supersaturated with imagination as her partner, but XY had some other *impulse*—a madness?—that she didn't possess but could harness, even as it exasperated her and then in turn saddened him, because, as he put it, "I can't help myself, even as I can see it happening." It was from this union that they created, eventually, not just my great-great grandmother, but also their greatest invention: the original Mecha-Ostrich, in both the rounded steel of its original reality and in my turbulent presence so many years later to speak for them and all the others who have been silenced by **S.**

Out of the exile forced upon them came, for a time, success and happiness. For five years, their business flourished, and they reached a level of camaraderie with the members of the commune that made them happy, as if there had been a missing piece to their lives that only others could provide. But then one day a grateful bank teller from the town gifted XY with what he believed was a considerate present: a recent edition of the *New York Five Cent Library* that included "Electric Bob's Big Black Ostrich, Or, Lost on the Desert," a pulp adventure by the author of the previous Electric Bob. It was the normal racist claptrap of an era, all wrapped up in the innocence of a boy's adventure, featuring off-the-cuff references to "a dozen big greasy Mojave warriors" and Mexican "Greasers," along with classic lines of dialogue like "Take that n---- giant first."

But what caught XY's eye amongst all the maddening, saddening evidence of all-too-common stupidity and intolerance were the descriptions of how the inane Electric Bob and his cohorts came to create a mechanical ostrich. I say

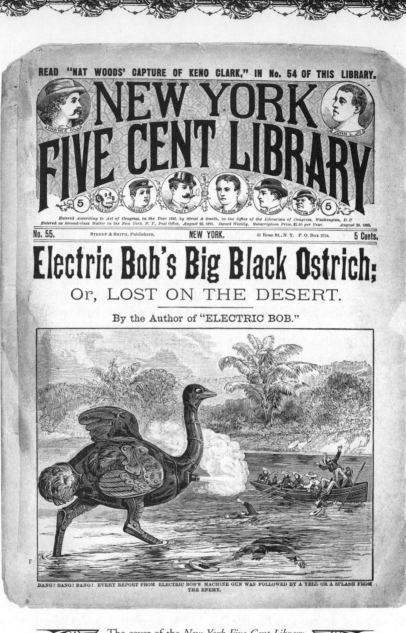

NEW YORK
FIVE CENT LIBRARY

Entered According to Act of Congress, in the Year 1892, by Street & Smith, in the Office of the Librarian of Congress, Washington, D. C.
Entered as Second-class Matter in the New York, N. Y., Post Office, August 26, 1893. Issued Weekly. Subscription Price, $2.50 per Year. August 26, 1893.

No. 55.   STREET & SMITH, Publishers.   NEW YORK.   31 Rose St., N. Y. P. O. Box 2734.   5 Cents.

Electric Bob's Big Black Ostrich;
Or, LOST ON THE DESERT.

By the Author of "ELECTRIC BOB."

BANG! BANG! BANG! EVERY REPORT FROM ELECTRIC BOB'S MACHINE GUN WAS FOLLOWED BY A YELL OR A SPLASH FROM THE ENEMY.

The cover of the *New York Five Cent Library* volume that includes the Edisonade referenced by the Mecha-Ostrich, not included in the materials sent to the past and present editors of *Steampunk Magazine*. The story dates from August 26, 1893. – **The Editors**

inane because the premise of this pointless yarn is that Electric Bob *can't cross a desert without the help of an invention*. "We must make something in which we can cross the desert," Electric Bob says, conveniently ignoring such timeless inventions as pack mules and feet connected to working legs. His suggestion of an airship is deep-sixed by his pal Inyo Bill who quickly exclaims, "No, sir! No flying machine for me! Not for all the gold between here and the day of judgment!" Despite it being many decades before the advent of mind-warping and brain-destroying TV, the immediate conclusion is *to build a mechanical ostrich instead*:

> "Now, if we could only ride one of them," said old Inyo Bill, pointing with his pipe toward a number of ostriches on an adjoining farm which the two men were passing in their walk. "A big ostrich could carry us among the rocks, and across the sand at the rate of fifteen miles an hour and not mind the snakes, or lack of water, and—"
>
> "Good!" cried Electric Bob, slapping his old friend on the shoulder. "You have solved the problem, Inyo. We will have an ostrich big enough to carry us both to the Pegleg mine. It is just the thing!"
>
> "There ain't an ostrich alive could do it," said the old man, with a puzzled look.
>
> "Well, we will build one that will run by electric power," said Bob, smiling.

After XY had gotten over his shock—recorded emphatically in his journal—that ostriches had been introduced to the United States, he soon found himself fascinated by the mechanical version, which the two men enter by quickly running "up a wire ladder that hung down from under one wing." (This method of entry seems vastly superior to the undignified "hindquarters portal" developed by the French for their modern, Verne-inspired mechanical elephant in Nantes.)

Of the bird itself, the author writes:

> The ostrich towered thirty feet in the air to the top of his great head. The center of the body was twenty feet from the ground, the neck was about eight feet long.
>
> The black male taken as a model had been faithfully copied, in appearance and proportions, and when completed the gigantic machine standing there in the orange grove was to all outward appearance a mammoth ostrich.
>
> "It will cause great excitement wherever we go," said Inyo. "People will think it a real old rooster."

"That will be great," says Bob, because nothing screams "desert travel" like a huge, heavy, black ostrich whose every footstep will shift and settle and dislocate sand.

But there is a catch. Inyo points out that causing all of that attention might lead to getting shot at. Bob reassures his sidekick that the ostrich will be able to withstand anything up to and possibly including cannon fire (much like the smaller model in my garage), but brings Inyo into the machine to show off its weaponry:

"Well," said Bob, "to begin, you know the legs are of fine wrought steel and hollow, the body is of thin plate steel lined with hardwood to protect us from the heat out there, and the wings and tail are of aluminum, light, graceful, and bullet-proof.

"The power is furnished by powerful storage batteries placed in the body just between the thighs of the bird, and are capable of giving us a speed of from twenty to forty miles an hour—depending on the nature of the ground we travel over.

"Here are a water tank, storage places for provisions, ammunition, etc., and here is our machine gun…[which] consists of an enlarged revolver cylinder, holding twenty-five Winchester rifle cartridges, and a short, heavy barrel, and is fired by turning this crank—this way."

At which point Electric Bob's oafish partner says of the ingenious addition of a camera, "Why, you can kill [Native Americans] with the gun and photograph 'em with this machine at the same time, can't we?"

All of this left XY cold and wondering at the "casual yet specific cruelty of humanity." Nor did he thrill to the heretical prospect of using electricity to power the beast. But the basic idea—the creation of a mechanical ostrich—raised a specter of a monumental challenge in XY's head, the hint of a possible future peeking through a door of light. It made small, or so he thought, his own plans by dint of its sheer audacity.

To XX the idea would have simply been amusing, a "fancy or whimsy of the kind that used to incite pillow talk after a day of more serious endeavors." Left to her own infernal devices, she would have returned to work in the basement on their crude attempts at a superconductor or perpetual motion machine, or her re-creation of the steam-powered automated sliding glass doors first invented by the Egyptians.

Each of these projects they had described to others as a kind of declaration of love for one another, but these were not just acts of fidelity and faith. They were acts of solidarity with people they had never met or corresponded with, like Tesla and all of the other mad geniuses that used to roam the earth and now are kept in self-imposed cages in the basements of top-secret corporate facilities, fated to produce assembly-line plastic vomit for the masses. (Nor did they have children at that point; indeed, XX was working on an external, steam-powered incubator, as she had no wish to halt her research.)

But XY was not XX and XX was not XY. After seeing the ostrich description, he cross-referenced it to his research into Vaucanson's famous mechanical ibis from the 1700s—and became convinced not only that he could create what he called a "Mecha-Ostrich," but that it would be an extraordinary invention for people to ride around in, "powered by friendly and proven steam."

The mention of Vaucanson's ibis is significant given the intricacy of this famous automaton. The mechanical bird was built by a French engineer named Jacques de Vaucanson in the 1730s, although some credit it to Russian inventor Vladimir Gvozdev. The ibis had a weight inside connected to over a thousand moving parts. Vaucanson, by trial and error, made these parts move together to give an illusion of life. The ibis even had a rubber tube for its digestive tract. The ibis and other automata made Vaucanson famous and he traveled for many years exhibiting his ibis and other machines around Europe. Although he collected honors for his work, he also collected scorn from those who believed he had employed infernal means to create his ibis. Most of his creations were destroyed in a fire a year after Vaucanson died, but in 1805 the famed poet Goethe spotted the miraculous ibis in the collection of an Austrian antiques enthusiast. Shortly thereafter, the Austrian died and the collections were auctioned off to a certain "Baron Sampson Sardonicus" to pay his debts. The ibis has not been seen since. Even in 1805, Goethe had reported that the ibis looked mangy and had "digestive problems." Strange sounds came from inside the automata, and it is likely it ceased to function shortly after 1806. Vaucanson's relatives have often claimed that the ibis was Vaucanson's most prized possession and that he believed it held the key to solving several scientific mysteries. – ***The Editors***

XX, as might be expected, lodged many wise and timely objections to this new course of action—not least of which was the mangled evidence provided by their New Hampshire neighbors some decades earlier: a tinker-created mechanical elephant gone awry. Not only had the elephant hideously malfunctioned, but a self-proclaimed "mad prophet of New Hampshire," who had caught the fancy of the local newspapers, spent much of his remaining time on this good Earth railing against science, usually in the context of his apocalyptic visions of the metal beast. ("A Science of Morality hangs on people's Actions, as well as the effect they achieve on our fellow-men, in a narrower or wider range. Let us not encourage each other to continue a worship of the monotonous material world, the world of the *Inhuman* and *Automatic*." See the appendix for more.)

But XY ignored all of this, for he was in the grip of a powerful and all-encompassing vision. This vision, according to an entry XX made in her journal, "overtook him to such a great degree that it was like a hot air balloon he was blowing up in our research basement, slowly taking up all of the space, crowding out everything I wanted to work on. Eventually, I gave up and decided to help him, because then it would all be over much sooner, and I could get back to more important work. Besides, when obsessed he was very compelling, and that was…attractive…"

Attraction aside, it appears that XY had hooked XX on the idea of automata in general, through the agency of commune member and sculptor Pozukuddi Nagalakshmi. In XX's journal, around this time, the following note has been scrawled across the back of a page: "According to S&M and Ms. Nagalakshmi, 'in former times there was a certain artist in the Middle Country. To enrich himself he went on his business from the Middle Country to the country of the Greeks. There he stopped at the house of a mechanic. A mechanical doll was made by the latter and placed in his room to serve him. She washed his feet and stood by. As she was leaving he spoke to her. She stood in silence. He thought: Surely she has been sent to me as a servant. Seizing her by the hand, he began to drag her towards him, whereupon she became a heap of chains.'"[1]

For months afterwards, XX would tease XY by saying, "Drag me, and I'll become a heap of chains." "More likely she'll take the chains to me if I'm not careful, and I'll have earned it!" XY wrote at one point. Perhaps there was a blade of truth in amongst the teasing, but they had achieved enough singleness of purpose to embark on their adventure…except that it wasn't nearly as easy as fiction. In the Edisonade, Electric Bob studies real ostriches, creates diagrams of

---

[1] From noted scholar Michael Ellsworth comes this additional information: "The Sanskrit word translated as 'mechanical doll' is 'yantra-putrika,' more literally translated as '(little) machine girl'—'yantra' refers to any kind of device. The 'Middle Country' is Madhyadesa, corresponding to a region right around Uttar Pradesh in India in the period in question. There is a mechanical girl in the Mechanic and Artist episode of the *Punyavantajataka*, a Buddhist text (likely) written in Pali, translated into Sanskritized Prakrit, 'proper' Sanskrit, Old Gujarati, Tocharian, Tibetan, and Chinese. The version I originally came across was in Tocharian, likely written near Kucha in the Tarim Basin, along the Northern Silk Route around the 6th–8th c. CE. There are annotations from a later period referring to something odd that I can only translate as either 's' or 'snake' with reference to the destruction of a mechanical girl acquired by an Indian trader from the Greeks—a 'raid by snakes,' which makes little sense even as some kind of odd joke." – *The Editors*

his mechanical spin-off in just three days, and sends it all to a "Chicago factory," guaranteeing that the vacation-vehicle-slash-death-wielding-machine "shall be done within six weeks." A few days later a telegram informs Electric Bob that "his wonderful machine was being constructed as rapidly as possible," and a month after that "boxes containing the wonderful invention" arrive in San Bernardino and "three experienced machinists from the Southern Pacific Railway shops" help put together the ostrich.

Like all of the other ridiculous parts of the story, which include an encounter with a lion in the desert, this proved false for XY and XX. Finding the materials alone took six months. Not a scrap heap or rail yard in all of New England was neglected by XY, now in the full grip of his bliss. It took three months of working on the schematics to confirm that the Mecha-Ostrich could indeed be powered by steam rather than electricity.

There were also distractions caused by other sources, as when two members of the artist commune, Shelley Vaughn and Mary Lewis—whom XY called sarcastically "the two brains"; their names more and more appear to be aliases for the construction of a plot I cannot quite see the outlines of—caught wind of the project from a comment let slip by Nagalakshmi at a dinner party. Vaughn and Lewis, as XX put it, "proceeded to fill my husband's head with nonsense about a text entitled *The Adventures of Saturnin Farandoul* by Albert Robida, which they claimed, erroneously, set out exemplary examples of various steam inventions, a confusion I would charitably put down to the difference between scientist and raconteur."

Evidence of this conversation comes in the form of pages torn from a book and shoved into XY's journal from that period. The pages have a header indicating a subtitle of "The Railway War—S&M" and reference an idea that XY spent a month considering for his Mecha-Ostrich before abandoning: "As the operations of the siege dragged on, the German scientist conceived the idea of adapting the cannons on the ramparts into high-pressure music machines to entertain the troops. To the sounds of this powerful orchestra they danced every evening in the covered trenches, and the soldiers were able to forget the fatigue of the siege in the delight of a rapid polka or a languorous waltz, sheltered from the chloroform bombs." Perhaps XY had so fallen under the spell of the commune that he thought any practical invention must include some form of artistic expression—that "even a common toaster should play the Star Spangled Banner," as XX sarcastically put it.

More useful as inspiration but no less distracting or ultimately useless was an example of what XY interpreted as the potential to adapt an animal form to a machine purpose: "Disdaining henceforth the railway war and banal siege warfare, Farandoul wanted to inaugurate submarine warfare! The fish-rich coasts of Nicaragua had furnished first class auxiliaries: fish of the swordfish family, light, swift-moving and easy to tame, which, once provided with a special harness, became excellent mounts for a corps of submarine cavalry."[2] With Shelley Vaughn's and Mary Lewis's help as metal-workers—they had previously created

---

2 "The Railroad War" text is from Brian Stableford's modern-day translation. We do not know if the Mecha-Ostrich had direct knowledge of the original. – ***The Editors***

Another addition to the main narrative, glued on top of other pages, consisted of this image, with note: "The documents I found among XY's things included this snippet by an unnamed Brazilian member of the artist (initials 'FF'), a kind of early retro-futuristic fiction XY attributed to 'the influence of XX upon him, for I have no time to talk to anyone while being so busy with the Mecha-Ostrich, and she is more in need of conversation than I. She talked briefly of illustrating this man's visions, but then my own project again usurped her efforts.' This is all I can find of FF's work in amongst the papers:

The Cogsmiths had arrived on Dover by 1809, after years of tribulations crossing Europe in the middle of the Napoleonic Wars. It was not of their will to do so. Neither of their master. They had to resort to everything they had learned in years in the Frankenstein Laboratories in Geneva if they wanted to survive. While their master was to be acclaimed worldwide as the Father of the Mechanical Brains, the Cogsmiths would be considered the fathers and mothers of what came to be called then by popular press and workers as the Infernal Devices—nothing more than our modern 'smart machines': contraptions that, if not possessing intellects as the 'descendants' of Frankenstein's automaton—the long-gone Machinekind of sad memory—were at least capable of executing several tasks without the aid of their human owners and handlers. Even with all their expertise, however, the Cogsmiths could not fix their master's greatest creation. The metal, steam-powered automaton, which the former apprentices (now masters themselves, forged in the fires of many conflagrations) had to be dismantle in order to carry with them incognito in their travels, was so battered that they thought it would never work again."

— *The Editors*

ingenious wind-up mechanical rabbits—the weedy backyard became for a time strewn with tiny mechanical catfish that lurched along on their pectoral fins and blew smoke out of the tops of their heads, and opened and closed their mouths as if perpetually hungry.

XY's monomania often allowed for distractions, so long as those distractions somehow seemed pertinent. But work on the main goal was also interrupted by XY's insistence on tracking down the remains of the mechanical elephant that had gone bust, because he felt it would be useful in working out the kinks in the ostrich, whose "mournful cannon" poked out during this period from its "half-assembled but noble chest." Yes, XY had decided to reproduce Electric Bob's creature in its every detail, and XX could do nothing to dissuade him. Of course, in XY's version the "cannon" was actually a telescope with a camera attachment, "for long-distance viewing and memory restoration," as XY put it, perhaps already envisioning an advertisement for his creation.

I can only imagine the scene when the corroded flanks and disembodied head of the mecha-elephant, stinking of rust and mold and fungus, joined the incomplete silhouette of the embryonic Mecha-Ostrich in their large backyard. That backyard had only a pathetically short white picket fence by all accounts—an attempt at normalcy meant to placate the townsfolk that, in this context, only seemed to emphasize the presence of two mechanical monsters, one dead and one about to be born. Certainly, it provided no protection from the prying eyes of the members of the artist commune, who may not have been sympathetic to **_S._**, but who in their often transient comings-and-goings no doubt helped spread a slow contagion of fact and fancy about the couple's exploits that **_S._** couldn't help but notice.

ARMED with new knowledge from examining the elephant's mecha-corpse, XY plunged forward, alternating between welding in the basement (morning) and the backyard (dead of night), along with experiments on the "fluidizing of joints" and the "actualization of movement through interjoined tubes." XX fulfilled what we today would call "project management" and helped talk XY down off of self-created cliffs of nonsense—as when, according to XY's own journal entry, "I was insisting on making it a hundred feet high, with an extra leg for stability, and perhaps replacing the head with a kind of deep sea diver's helmet contraption on top, with but a single red eye."

This mention of a "red eye" disturbed me even on a first reading, let alone the hundredth. Can it be that **_S._**'s influence had already begun to creep into XY's thinking, into his very dreams? That the tentacles of **_S._**'s insurgency of evil had found their mark?

In any event, circumstances would have curtailed XY's vision even if XX's curt appraisal of ballooning costs hadn't soon cut the Mecha-Ostrich prototype down to size. Their entries document a series of setbacks too desperate and complex to recount here, but which in part concerned townsfolk having caught wind of what XX called disparagingly "the golden goose" (to XY's consternation, who kept saying "that is a bird, but not this bird"). At least one reference to an "infernal drumstick" in the town newspaper's humor column during this time supports this theory. Whatever the reasons, business dropped off precipitously, leaving members of the commune, many of them poor, as the main clients.

Even worse for morale, XY reported to XX one day that he had seen "a mysterious figure in what appeared to be a cloak" on a hill overlooking both the house and the commune:

> It—for I would not venture a guess as to its sex—just stood there staring down through the glancing light of the late afternoon sun. When I sent up a hallo—meant much like a blow, to make it stumble from its strange certainty—it made no sign of having heard me. This angered me all out of proportion to the offense, and in a haze of misdirected rage, running all the way, I proceeded up the hill toward the stranger. When I got close enough, I looked up and saw that the animating impulse had left the stranger. All that was left was a cloak mockingly hung upon a large strut of my own devising. But I swear I saw it move before I ascended the hill. And who or what could carry such a large strut up a hill—and why?

This obvious intrusion by _S._ channeled through a kind of "stationary dark rider," conflation of Eye and Old Ones in my opinion, was a warning that XY did not heed—or, as far as is known, even tell XX, for fear, I suppose of it being the last nail, the last bolt, the last nut, that, loosened, would undo their relationship. (Especially as there is evidence in XY's journal that this was not the first sighting; notes in the margin about "shadows" and "uncanny noises.")

Should simply fixing what was broken have gained them the attention of _S._? No, but as I, the modern Mecha-Ostrich know, the brilliant will always call attention to themselves by the very fact of the light that surrounds them, and which they shed, and while this light will attract some, it will blind others and simply piss off those who remain unswayed in a healthier way. Breaking an egg or two, often of enormous size, is unavoidable.

At some point that anonymous donor to the commune known only as "the Prisoner Queen" gave them the money to continue to hobble along. This is where I first heard of the Prisoner Queen, and thought this was XX's way of referring to her rich widow of a mother. Since, I have come to believe that this was another way for _S._ to influence events, as evidenced by the documents I have provided following this account.

The financial stress led inevitably to marital stress. It is clear from the journal entries that XY's many eccentricities, so endearing under other conditions—one can imagine at their most endearing while on vacation in the Bahamas, perhaps, and less so during a knife fight in a Buenos Aires bar—made of him an unbearable monster to XX, and to XY her rebukes sounded like a rejection of his soul. She meant them, of course, out of love and for the preservation of what had begun to be destroyed.

With this image, the Mecha-Ostrich included the following text, glued to the back of a page of the main narrative. "In a later stage of the same comic strip, it became increasingly horrific. Here the inventor, much changed, has added himself to a diabolical steampunk invention that is poised forever between ultimate damnation and eternal good luck. The problem, of course, is that the marker itself, and thus the inventor, must reside in a perpetual form of limbo or purgatory. The official story behind this bleak storyline, as alluded to in an interview for *Comics Journal* in 2001? The artist admitted to 'being stressed from a bad relationship and also depressed by the falling readership for the work.' However, the ways in which XY, admittedly without success, attempted to integrate himself into his sad inventions during his stay in the mental hospital bear an uncanny resemblance to the incredibly black humor in 'American Tinker Under the Influence of Absinthe.'" – *The Editors*

Shaken by the encounter with the thing on the hill, XY even considered, much to XX's dismay, that they should write to the government, asking the Department of the Army to fund the project. XY had at this point taken on board advice about military needs from a former Buffalo Soldier who had gone AWOL and now lived in the commune with his Cherokee wife. Any action alerting the government to their experiment, XX told XY, would just bring unwanted attention down upon them, and the isolation they now felt in their severed relationship with the towns-folk would be compounded by potential scandal in the newspapers.

Ultimately, XY didn't send the letter. But by then XX knew they were too far along to stop, writing in the journal, "We will either complete it or it will utterly ruin us, but it will be over soon." XY's entries manifested the strain in other ways; for example, this passage: "Those horrible brains that come to the fence and stare at me for long minutes while I am in the half-dressed state necessary to continue working on the machine during this incredible heat spell." (Less nonsensical considering later evidence about S&M, but still demonstrating stress.)

Then, a breakthrough, but maddeningly only referenced in either journal with XY's scrawled: "Success! It rode like a beauty, fast and furious!"

Then, some sort of breakdown, with another brief journal entry: "The legs are insufficient to the challenge. Might as well use toothpicks."

Then, what some might call another kind of breakdown, "The red eyes are there on the hill again," and nothing in XX's journal.

Then, ominous silence in both journals for several days, except for something scrawled out in XX's and a few doodles of ostrich legs in XY's, along with a giant eye.

For XY, that eye would be his last entry—he would never, as far as I can tell, write down his thoughts again.

For the next day the end came, in the guise of a raid on the commune by the sheriff's department and several mysterious "tall, strikingly pale men who wore suits, and carried rifles and hammers" (XX) and who seemed "unaffiliated with the local police." Paranoia? Unlikely, for this is the typical modus operandi by which **_S._** carries out **_His_** plans.

Despite protests by XY and a spirited, if ragged, defense by members of the commune, the intruders managed to pull apart and then set fire to much of the yard around the Mecha-Ostrich, while XX tried to drag a distraught XY away.

The twisted remains of the Mecha-Ostrich were quickly loaded onto a cart drawn by draft horses and driven away at a gallop by a "grim-faced giant of a man in a cloak of all things, who was leering at XY and shouting at him in a language neither of us could identify."

In my mind's eye I see the members of the commune who had not been led off to jail for any number of imaginary offenses, from being black to being gay to being artistic, looking on in distress as XX comforts XY, now bawling, as the smoldering Mecha-Ostrich is hauled away. Any time I see something large in a cart, it brings me back to that moment—it could be Stalin's marble head, a buffalo, a heap of pancakes, whatever.

It was all over within an hour, and within two hours no one would have guessed that the Mecha-Ostrich had ever existed there, in the backyard of the house next to the commune.

As it had begun, so it concluded: with XY and XX. Lying in the backyard. Amongst the debris. "Unable to speak, to think, just staring mutely at the sky wondering what we had done to deserve this. We had worked so hard, for so little, for so long, and it hadn't been enough to save us."

WHAT happened in the aftermath, you might ask? Precious little. Less aftermath and more "anti-climax." After all, that's what _S._ prefers, as it is much less messy, less dramatic, and thus draws less attention. The event merited exactly one line in the local newspaper: "Yesterday policemen conducted a raid at ------------- Street to apprehend known criminals."

I think often about who must have been somewhere near the back of the crowd, looking innocuous—a middle-age man with a wiry frame and hunched shoulders, perhaps? A weathered Lithuanian woman in a sun dress? I am sure _S._ was there, in some guise, and _S_'s role in all of this was to burn its red eye into XY's brain and bring an end of sorts to him.

For XY was too delicate, in the end. They had taken too much from him before he had the necessary defenses. He soon went into a kind of catatonic yet gibbering state. XX hugged him to her and yet "I knew he was already gone, that it was all over, and, worse, that I'd known it might happen." Taken to the local sanitarium, the initial fees fronted by the mysterious "Prisoner Queen," XY slid into a state that could only be described as alternating between nonresponsive and manic.

"Practicality is the handmaiden of tragedy," XX wrote during this time, in such distress that I cannot make out most of her handwritten entries.

For she truly loved the fool, and his madness was her burden. XX tried her best to hold onto everything meaningful—to pretend that there would be a return to the old life. But their finances had revolved around the ostrich to such an extent that its absence as sign and symbol of redemption meant the time had come to sell the house and auction off all of their furniture and bits of metal, just to pay debts.

A year passed in a slow agony of dashed hopes. XX received no response to any of her letters to the sheriff's department about the incident, or to the government. The members of the commune had reverted to a polite but distant form of friendship that reflected a sense of blame. XY showed no signs of recovery—indeed, had only become more and more fixated on the shadowy figure on the hill "and its glowing red eye," which XX interpreted as an obsession with the Mecha-Ostrich. XY had gotten no better. XX: "He has little memory of how we met or what we meant to one another—nothing that could bring him back to me." Also, the Prisoner Queen had stopped paying for the treatments.

She couldn't afford to stay, in any sense. "I was losing my own sanity." So she arranged to have XY sent back to his family in Boston, although not before one liaison: "I left hoping that, soon, a microscopic group of cells might cling to the inside of my body."

Accompanied by Ms. Nagalakshmi, who had become a close friend, she made her way into the West, living like a nomad up and down the coast from Los Angeles to Big Sur. She retired from science for art and gained renown, under a different name, for her sculpture and writings. (Let us call her XX-New.) Tagging along, once XX had become visible again in the public eye, was a child she was careful never to let in on her secrets. But she kept as much as she could of papers, pictures, etc., and passed it all down—lost or forgotten until the death of my father a year ago (drinking/bar brawl), whereupon all of the material he found valueless yet had consigned to a safety deposit box became visible to me.

Where the ostrich went, I don't know—there are hints that it was melted down for scrap. It could have been disassembled into its separate parts and reassembled as a Model T or a mortar shell lobbed at the Germans or turned up in a submarine or a skyscraper's girders in Chicago, or in a common bullet that lodged in the brains of two hillbillies simultaneously during an altercation I witnessed near the train tracks just a week ago. It's impossible to tell. Maybe it's lying next to the broken, almost oxidized remains of the mecha-elephant in a pit or quarry, and they tell each other the same decaying stories day after day.

But when I say I am the Mecha-Ostrich, I mean that I *am* the Mecha-Ostrich. Having recovered also now the plans XX and XY left behind, and using money from a series of re-appropriations at various banks, it now *exists*, as my forebears might have imagined it, if in more diminutive, single-person form. *It*, the reality, not the many distortions, the terrible vitiations and the half-truths.

Soon, your dead pixel lives will never be the same. Soon, you will know the power and the glory of the Mecha-Ostrich.

How magnificent it is!

How it mocks **_S_**!

How it shines in the New Jersey sun!

How I inhabit it![3]

---

3 After several inquiries, we discovered that the return address on the Mecha-Ostrich's package was for an apartment complex with the whimsical name of "Roaring Oak Springs," in a New Jersey town that will remain nameless. The specific apartment had been vacant for over two years before the arrival of the current occupants, an unhelpful pair of Brookdale Community College students who appear to have had nothing to do with the sending of the package. Despite the threats of posters and further action in the above text, nothing further has been heard from "the Mecha-Ostrich, Steampunk Heretic." – *The Editors*

A P P E N D I X :
(SUPPRESSED AND SECRET)
EVIDENCE OF ENTRAPMENT
AND COLLUSION, NOW MADE
UNSUPPRESSED, UN-SECRET
(A CONSPIRACY AND HISTORY OF SABOTAGE)
(A RIDDLE OF HALF-TRUTHS)

BEING

(All figure notes by the Mecha-Ostrich)

The Sea of Ingenuity (Mare Ingenii)

There once was an old man who built robots out of driftwood, seashells, and straw. His robots were clever machines, although even their creator wouldn't be able to tell you exactly how they worked. But worked they did, and when they were done with their chores, they went behind the old man's house, and built inventions of their own. To the untrained eyes, their project appeared as one long wing, and people laughed at the robots, for everyone knows that the atmosphere of the Moon is not dense enough to support flight. Even birds have to walk here.

But the robots were not deterred, and their wing grew larger by the day. They polished its surface and inlaid it with mother-of-pearl. The wing was ready, and when the robots held it up to the rising sun, the wing shuddered and took off.

All the people watched in wonderment as the wing shone in the sun and carried off the robots, propelled by the strength of the sunrays. The robots worked in unison, tilting their sail this way and that way to navigate, but nobody knows where they went. Some say, Mars.

Fig 1. Two pages torn from the English translation of *The Russian Book of the Improbable* and credited in the table of contents to an "Ekaterina Sedia," which may be a pen name. In the first instance, the text seems to describe the condition of XY in the mental hospital, for he would spend large amounts of his time using whatever he could find to make inventions, no matter whether or not the materials suited the project. He had no choice. XY would also tell little stories about the inventions, in large part because the stories had to take the place of the inventions' utility. XY's last, rather mournful, journal entry describes making an abacus out of stiff macaroni and celery sticks.

Eclipse of the Sky

At the time of the LZ 129 *Hindenburg* tragedy, many fingers of blame were pointed, but very few of the contemporaries of this extraordinary event remembered a much earlier tragedy that remained even more mysterious and misunderstood than that of the *Hindenburg* in Lakehurst, New Jersey.

It is difficult to believe that the catastrophe that lit up the sky over Europe for days and that caused a seismic wave that could be felt throughout the Russian Empire, the explosion that blotted out the nights over the British isles, eclipsing the moon in its eerie brilliance, remained a mystery for so long—at least, to most of the world.

The gentlemen of scientific persuasion all over Europe speculated on the nature of the explosion, blaming meteorites or asteroids that were known to combust upon entering the atmosphere. While Europe speculated, however, the Emperor of All Russia had dispatched General Chernobelyj, one of his envoys entrusted with all affairs Siberian, east. According to rumors, the expedition headed for the Tunguska region, where the phenomenon had originated. When it came back, weeks later, the general had confirmed the speculations about the meteorite and his report described in great detail the devastation of the taiga and the fallen trees. However, the report had never mentioned that the Imperial Guard had mourned the loss of their mates, brash risk-takers, or the torn fabric and metal debris recovered at the site, some of the twisted aluminum bearing the Imperial Insignia and the letter "L". And the records remained forever silent on the subject of a lone phonograph cylinder, its bronze brilliance hidden under a layer of char, the name "Leviathan" barely discernible under the soot, and how the hands of the Emperor trembled when he picked up the recording. Not even General Chernobelyj was present when the Emperor listened to the last minutes of the flight that never happened.

> The second entry suggests the presence of **S.**, working *His* diabolical destructions out in the wider world. It also hints at further suppression of the gospel of clean technologies, and not just by Soviet authorities. Whether this also indicts the commune abutting XX and XY's house as a breeding ground for Marxist dogma remains unclear to me.

Confessions and Complaints of a True Man, as Related by Himself
by Matthew Alcott Cheney (1823–1893)

EDITOR'S NOTE: This manuscript was found in a tin box in a cellar hole in central New Hampshire in 1975. Few pages had survived the onslaught of time and weather, and those pages that did survive are brittle, stained, and worn. The handwriting is not always decipherable and the ink is often faded. We have reconstructed the manuscript here to the best of our ability, but this should not be considered a definitive transcription. We have also included further evidence from print publications of the period for your pleasure and instruction.

from *The New Hampshire Gazette*, 7 July 1872:

One of the most eminent men of the State of Massachusetts, Mr. James Raymond, was so distraught at the death of his elephant, *Columbus,* which received injuries from which he died, by the breaking of a bridge in South Adams, that Mr. Raymond commissioned the Boston engineer Wallace Tillinghast, Esq., to build for him a Mechanical Elephant that would be impervious to destruction. The creature, *Pizarro,* was immediately proclaimed a true WONDER of our epoch, one of the greatest MARVELS ever to result from the REASON of MAN.

from the Manchester (N.H.) *Union Democrat*, 6 March 1873:

A great tragedy occurred in this city, on the morning of the 4th instant. The particulars, as we understand them, are substantially as follows: The Great Mechanical Wonder known to all the world as the *Elephant Pizarro* suffered a prodigious seizure of its metal viscera, releasing much steam and smoke into the air, until which time the stout pins fastening its armor around the immense skeleton shot from their place like balls from a musket, injuring at least three persons in the crowd that had gathered to gawk at the Wonder. This was not the greatest of the tragedies, however, for the tumult of its intestines continued, and the pressure in the great creature's abdomen was too much to be contained by its structure. *Plates of white-hot metal* burst into the crowd, maiming many a mother and child who, innocent, had come to see what Progress had wrought. The Mechanical Wonder wobbled and tottered and finally fell, and the rumble of the Earth was greater than that of ten cannons or the most terrifying thunder. Three deaths have been confirmed and more are expected, including the death of Miss Lucy Wellington Bishop of Lowell Street, a child of four years, who was crushed in the giant's fall.

from *The Confessions and Complaints of a True Man, As Related By Himself,* by Mr. Cheney, date unknown, handwriting often indecipherable:

Progress! A Lie of the Mind which is buried at the City where it made its *ruinous endeavors.*

The Caravan arrives and you inquire about the Scream, the *Prisoned Demonian* who rides atop the mechanical monstrosity itself, the *Illusionist of Freedom* who shepherds naught but suffering and death. Could but one true person stop amidst the carnage so much greater than ordinary pain and hardship—stop to raise a bloody shard, testament to being the Last True Man Alive—he, possessed suddenly of the Clarity of Extraordinary Strength that is the birthright of He Who Knows Truthfulness—lifts the slab of Human Hubris and, from under the stifling lump, finds the Form that excess of Beauty makes ruinous—and the reflection of all Man's *Misdeeds* lies there, crushed and shattered, destroyed—the Face of Innocence, THE CHILD THAT IS NO MORE.

Such is our allegory. Such is the Tale of the Time in which we live. But to call what we have *Living* is to know not the meaning of that word.

It is glaring to the Innocent Eye, the Light of our long-unlived Life, and in our era of Manufactured Bliss, when the mass of men are quiescent, their greatest Efforts given to the creating of Oblivion for themselves and others—in the world of these seers, it becomes the Blind Person to increase what is known by the sighted, or all Beauty and all Knowledge will die under the weight of an *Elephant of our own making.*

It is weak, the Prisoned Limb; it is faint, the Breath long pent. But oh! The liquid eye, the pring of elastic strength, the reformed blush of *Truth*—I hold still to my Faith in Possibility, because in the heart of man lies the possibility of Rescue. Our time on this Earth is long, and we are not the only Beings upon it, though you would not know this to be the Truth were you to read the statements of the ilk of Tillinghasts. Nature's Music still thrums, however quietly, in our heartchords.

The Rescue Person will rise out of the heart of an Angel, if the individual has accepted the Work. The Scholars of *Life* especially are called, a certain self-culture, a complete development of character within an individual personality. Art, I especially believe, will speak these Efforts and paint Nature's Notes. The person [*missing two lines of text*] this intended, that is presumed, [*missing words*] has indifference completely is not rejoicing, it has not owned excessively this. With private ease and compatibility of the achievement, the World attains worldly good, but the World as World does not need worldly good, for it has that *inherent,* but instead needs a Spiritual Good unknown to charlatans, spiritualists, illusionists, and mechanical engineers. As for the business of self-culture, there is no compromise which can achieve the desired harmony. Compromise is anathema to the Project. One either must do Truthful, Spiritual action, with full clarity of the Goal, or the Project is given up completely, and the Fate of a Child crushed beneath a Mechanical Marvel will be the Fate of us all, and one *richly deserved.*

NOTES, cont'd: ——THE CURIOUS CASE OF PHYSICALLY-MANIFESTED, "BED-SHEET MANIA."

As a doctor responsible for analyzing and inhibiting mental deficiencies, such as those resulting from cranial-facial abnormalities, as well as those caused by excessive consumption of opiates, I would like here to make a note of a relatively unexplored medical mystery. Of late I have been treating a young man (whom the nurses, attempting irony, have nick-named "Dr. Lash" because the frenzied plucking at his face, an unfortunate symptom of his disease, has left his eyelids all but bare) who has fallen prey to an unusual category of mania, the precise psychological cause of which I have yet to pin-point.

Each night, as "Dr Lash" sleeps, he claims to be greeted by the pleasantest of dreams, in which his favorite possessions—an Oriental-style rug, for instance, which boasts a mandala design on a red background—multiply and reproduce until his home is furnished with all the glorious objects any gentleman of worth would consider only proper in domestic décor. So content is he in slumber that, upon waking, his distress is most profound: not only do his lashless eyes easily perceive that he owns no lavishly-equipped home, but, more's the pity, he is destitute and, by all diagnoses, quite delusional. These events, I admit, are no more mysterious than the many works of fiction one might find in a low-brow publication like *Blackwood's Magazine*; however, the curious manner in which his delusions, upon waking, are manifested more universally puts all writers of sensational stories to shame.

Upon the pristine white bed-sheets each morning are transcribed the most unexpected symbols, images and sigils; drawings which seem to spontaneously appear, in green ink, and which "Dr Lash" insists issue full-formed from his left ear, his left nostril, or his left eye—a point which I am in a position to dispute. One can only surmise that these "ink" patterns (of boiling tea kettles; Catherine Wheels spinning; and pistons half-cocked, to name but a few) spring entirely from the confluence of microcosmic bacteria and optical illusion. The left ear of our "Dr Lash" is certainly not the birth-canal for these apparitions. Nevertheless, it is not my intent to dispute the reality of these illustrations, for real they appear to be, but merely to document the course this malady follows. For, the instant they appear, they transmogrify; adapting, to all appearances, to the needs and desires of the viewer—in other words, they gain life independent from the disturbed brain of "Dr Lash." Whereas he might view an oasis on the dunes of his bed-sheets, I might observe a giant penguin, or an antipodean *Cockatoo* (a name given to the parrots of the subfamily *cacatuince*) because I am a keen aviarist and have recently invested in a small flock of exotic songbirds. What one nurse perceives to be an impression of a gardenia, another solemnly declares is a Nanticoke canoe and, further, that this canoe was crafted by a colony of free-thinking artists in Delaware instead, as one would expect, by a tribe of Native Indians. One can easily accept that, like all humans prone to "seeing" logical patterns and shapes where there can be none—soft animals in cumulus clouds, or facial features in the grain of pine-wood boards, for example—we have all, in my modest surgery, discovered pictures which are nothing more than optical illusion paired with overly-stressful circumstances, and a virulent mutation of mould. Yet,

---

FIG. 3. What to make of these pages, featuring a series of notes and queries possibly created, I believe, by the "two brains" from the artists' commune? They are on the one hand quite playful in their attempts to showcase steam power and dirigibles, and on the other their mentions of ostriches and Prisoner Queens seem intent on creating an irritating mystery as to their involvement in the saga of the Mecha-Ostrich. Were they, together, the "Prisoner Queen" who gave money to XX and XY? Did they have further knowledge of *S.*? Did they, in fact, help orchestrate certain events? Were they deported back to Australia, or did they leave willingly? There is no evidence of their existence prior to XX and XY arriving at the house, and no evidence of their existence after the couple left. Regardless, the section on "The Great Air Ferry Disaster" seems taken out of some alternate history novel.*

* It is worth reminding readers of the echoes between this piece, published in the 1800s, and the short story "Dr. Lash Remembers" by Jeffrey Ford, published in the main fiction section of this anthology. When we asked Ford if he had referenced these "Notes & Queries" during his research for "Dr. Lash Remembers," he told us he "could not recall one way or the other." After a day or two, we received a follow-up e-mail in which Ford wrote, "It's possible, but who knows these days where something comes from? Who knows where they got it, either?" Regarding Notes & Queries, this predominantly 18th-century phenomenon found in magazines consisted of notes—the random findings of readers writing in with information considered of interest—and queries or questions, as well as responses to former queries. Thus, Notes & Queries functioned as a primitive version of a modern Internet distribution list or Yahoo! group. – *The Editors*

while this bacterium might be eradicated with a good dose of the laundress's ammonia, a suitable treatment of "Dr Lash's" affliction has yet to be determined, and I can only resort to administering doses of narcotics for his pain.

DR. J.G.F.

THE PRISONER QUEEN: —— References to "The Prisoner Queen" date back to the early fifteenth century, a time-frame confirmed in scholarly circles after years of paleographic research conducted upon illuminated manuscripts found in the derelict convent of the obscure order of *The Nuns of the Empty Name*. This title, first employed in these Tuscan vellums, seems to refer to a phantasm reputed to appear in the dreams of those under the influence of certain berries, *vachimi atatsi*, which are colloquially known as "deathberries." Unwary explorers, not to mention creatures of the wilderness, should only consume these small and black fruits at their own peril, for extreme illness will immediately result upon digestion; however, when brewed, a process which appears to extract the largest part of the poisons contained therein, a rich and heady alcoholic beverage results. Taken in liquid form, the berries will induce an irrepressible desire to climb trees, which is swiftly followed by a most laughable drunken stupor, reputed to endure for up to twelve hours at a time. Bearing all this in mind, it is unlikely there is any factual basis to the "Prisoner Queen"; most probable visions of this fantastical Lady have been the product of overactive imaginations, conjured up by hysterical nuns who have lived for far too long in an isolated location. Several names do, however, continue to appear over a very long period, in connection with this phantasm: the most prominent of these are Millicent Garana and Paulina Sorbilis (sometimes these names are recombined, thus appearing in Church registers alternatively as Millicent Sorbilis and Paulina Garana, amongst a myriad other combinations of letters, initials and anagrams). Inheritance Tax Rolls keep record, every fifty years or so since the late seventeenth century, of property passing from one Millicent or Paulina to the other, or to a son or daughter of one of the aforementioned women, and so on and so forth down to this very day. Recently, the demise of one Milaulina Gorbana has been noted in the English Shire of Warwick, but I cannot testify to the veracity of this information. Are these women manifestations of the so-called "Prisoner Queen"? This writer cannot be sure. Even so, an illness has become associated with her visitations, increasingly referred to as the *Phantom Queen* or *Mab's Wake*, for the sufferer invariably meets with some form of accident—fatal or otherwise—whilst suffering under the effects of her confounding "spell."

A final point of interest in this respect: these hallucinations are accompanied by a rash encircling the roots of the victim's fingers, which sufferers uniformly describe as "ruby rings," or *gifts of the Queen*.

PHYLLIS POSTLETHWAITE

I must object, once and for all: *there is no Prisoner Queen*.
DR. MILLICENT GARANA

QUERIES: ——
THE GREAT AIR FERRY DISASTER:—— I write on behalf of all lovers of the Opera, in the deepest hope that some one of you might come forth to solve a mystery which has vexed me incessantly for nigh on twelve months. I am referring, of course, to the Great Air Ferry Disaster of last June, in which the driver of the magnificent dirigible, *Queen Anne's Lace*, lost his senses, some say under the influence of *Mab's Wake* or, perchance, a tipple one too many of *Margold*, and, shortly thereafter, lost equal control of the vehicle he had been enlisted to commandeer. The consequent crash and conflagration, which cost so many lives of our most prosperous citizenry, has stunned us all; with no offence intended toward the bereaved, I must unravel if, perhaps, it is those of us who love music that are particularly, indeed *acutely*, afflicted as a result of this ill-fated event. Can any of your enlightened subscribers shed light on this query: in truth, was Hieronymus Wensley, noted tenor of the Hot Air Opera, (and who, incidentally, had been forced by recent financial straits to fall back on his experience as Fourth Aviator in the King's own force of zeppelins) responsible for captaining the air ferry at the time of its unfortunate collision with the obelisk in Air Square? Furthermore, is it also true that ostrich feathers floated from the sky like so many flakes of snow in the hours from dusk until dawn after said crash? All enthusiasts of aerial transport are fully aware that the mark of an air ferry captain's cap is three ostrich-feathers crossed; yet how many know that these *grandes plumes* also adorned the dress helm worn by Wensley himself, earlier that very eve, in a performance of *The Prisoner Queen Awakes*? Are we to find credence in the rumors that the man with the exquisite soap-bubble voice is a murderer and a floating suicide, left silenced and impaled on the Queen's Egyptian treasure? I believe I have this information on excellent authority, yet I cannot quite remember from whence it came, and would be most grateful for clarification on this matter.

HERBERT J. FORTESCUE
Equerry to the Prisoner Queen, New York City

LAPIDUS MECHANICUS: —— Have any of your readers encountered small herds of rabbits roaming the fields, quite outside of any warren or burrow, which all at once give off a whirring hum? To what purpose, these creatures?

ANTONINA BEDWATER

GODFREY *FORWARD* OR *FOUERD*?: —— It has come to my attention that a memoir describing the life and times of one Godfrey *Forward* has lately been published in Edinburgh; can it be that the subject of this work is, in actual fact, the renowned Scots Magistrate, Godfrey (also occasionally known as Geoffrey) *Fouerd*, and that the type-setter has made an atrocious mis-spelling in his laying of the frontispiece and title page? This query is of utmost interest to me, as locating one Godfrey *Fouerd* is quite pressing for the successful, and thorough, tracing of ancestral lines in my family.

CUTHBERT B. FOUERD

REPLIES:——
Kandush, or Oyster Rime spores (2nd S. iv. 147)—— Although the inquiry respecting this exotic genus of *spora* appeared in "N. & Q." as far back as June 18--, it has not hitherto elicited an acceptable reply. My object in addressing you this communication is to venture to offer Capt. Madrigal an alternate conjecture as to the application of this particular type of spore, based not upon unfounded chemical analysis, as was so crudely suggested in Vol. v. p.318, but instead upon the ancient wisdom of folk-lore. Previous respondents have pointed Capt. Madrigal toward the *Scientific Register* for 1777 and its subsequent edition of 1778; but evidence of the astringent, not to mention the coagulant, properties of the *Kandush* or *Oyster Rime* spores is simply not there, nor can I find it anywhere but in oral traditions of the Northern Eskimo, or in the sing-songs of their none-too-distant neighbors, the Finnish Lapps. Regarding the first instance, I have been made privy to extensive accounts, related by voyageurs to those parts, that elders of the Eskimo tribes are willing to trade four malamutes for a thimble's-worth of *Kandush*, due to its associations with the legend of injured Orca and His voyage through the eye of a needle; ostensibly, when imbibed, the tissues or canals of the body contract, thus slowing the expulsion of mucus or blood, allowing the victim of gashes or open sores the time he needs to heal. In short, some thing "big" is transformed into some thing "small"; much as was the case with the aforementioned whale. (The Eskimo tale relates Orca's close escape from certain death: upon noticing that Orca has suffered a fatal wound in His wrestling match with long-toothed Walrus, the gentle Aurora releases a shower of *Kandush* which, miraculously landing in Orca's blow-hole, transforms the enormous fish into a minnow, thereby shrinking both his body and also his wound until it is merely a scratch. Orca's ensuing

adventures amongst the more diminutive denizens of the sea need not be narrated here, but the beast's survival—against all odds—seems to be the moral these hardened folk cling to in all versions of this legend.) The value of this story lies not in its charm, nor its aesthetics, but in its practicality: for, I gather, having never ventured so far North my self, casualties resulting from misuse of harpoons and/or the frozen-handed throwing of knives and other sharp objects are rather too common amongst those mysterious peoples; accordingly, any medicines, folkloric or otherwise, which may stem the flow of blood, as does the *Kandush*, are treated with the greatest reverence, and are celebrated in shadow-plays at the solstice and equinox, respectively. Likewise, knowledge of the *Oyster Rime* (so named, I am told, for its salt-like, crumbly texture) is circulated amongst generations of Lapps, those peoples of Arctic Finn-land, in chanted verse for exactly the same purpose. While no translation of the Finnish original is available at this time, its meaning is, roughly:

Crush seeds; chew— Blood becomes glue.

As I have found no other satisfactory account of the *Kandush* spores, I must advise that, unless the inquirer desires a sharpening of his senses, a reduction of his glands, or intends to stopper a bleeding man's abrasions, he would more aptly be directed toward a more prevalent variety of tuber, such as the *Stepmother's Blessing*, for his needs.

S. LE TROUVEUR, ESQ.

27 July 18--, *Monday*

As you will no doubt have noticed, due to the gobbets of ink uncharacteristically spattering too many of your preceding pages, Dear Diary, not to mention the ever-increasingly (and, I might add, uncommonly) illegible nature of the text scrawled thereupon, I have spent much of the interminable week-end working our Brain into a fizz with anticipation of Eudamien Fontenrose's annual review of the Delaware Art Season in *Blackwood's Magazine*. It is to be expected, though many a Creator of Art would deny their subscription to this truism, that an object intended for public consumption inspires in its creator a certain unquantifiable desire to be accepted; acknowledged as *avant-garde;* or, at least, worthy of inspiring future generations to feel inclined to manufacture further works in a similar vein.

In this respect, I must admit, I had fancied our master-works of *papier-mâché* would be lauded by Fontenrose as the Next Big Things. (And, I implore you, explain to me how could they not? We selected only the finest strips of broadsheet-paper, each boasting the ramblings of our greatest Literary minds, to construct the eyes, ears, faces and torsos of our three-headed cats, our long-necked peacocks with their trumpet-feather tails, our exoskeletal *arachnid gigantes;* we fortified their fragile upper parts to iron strength with lashings of the most resilient horse-powder glue; then attached these fabrications to steam-driven lower halves, often with pick-axes or lawn-mowing blades or hedge-clippers for claws or paws, so that our steel-and-*papier* menagerie could simultaneously adorn *and* maintain the garden, proving, as all true Art should inevitably prove, to be both useful *and* beautiful.)

Truth be told, such was my certainty in the commendation of our modest exhibit, and such my excitement to read Fontenrose's acclamations, that the tension threatened to unhinge me; such was my agitation that I was coerced, as early as yesterday noon, into passing our Brain entirely into Mary's care, either until I had managed a few hours' unbroken rest or until my delirium deranged me completely—the former of these options, by the by, to both mine and Mary's relief, occurred first and foremost. Thus, freshly wakened this morning, I paced, with no small amount of irritation, up and down the sycamore-lined drive which connects our commune with the hubbub of plebeian American life as I awaited the arrival of the (ever-tardy) news-paper delivery-man.

The handsome Mr. ---------, our neighbor these past few years, wav'd at me from the landing of his ostentatious house. (You'll remember I had requested his opinion, not too long past, on the most efficient means of powering a herd of mechanical rabbits and we reciprocated in helping him with his mechanical catfish; ever since, he has taken to greeting me as though we were friends, and, if I am honest, I would say he has formed an attachment to me; for whereas his wife is forever imprisoned by the whalebone stays of her corset, both Mary and I have forgone the discomfort of ours in favor of the loose cottons and diaphanous tulles that are much more suited to this country's unpleasantly warm climate. In short, I fear he may fancy me; thus I have vowed to avoid him as much as humanly possible, if nothing else but for decorum's sake.) Luckily, the pubescent, spotty-faced Mercury charged with winging news of our artistic success chose, at that instant, to land, as it were, on our doorstep; in so doing deferring any possibility of my returning Mr. ----------'s dubious greetings.

Would that the bearer of *Blackwood's Magazine* had been waylaid on his journey, thereby preserving me—for a little while longer—from suffering the grotesque effects of reading Fontenrose's vulgar review.

I will be brief, for fear of clouding our Brain with too much that is melancholy before it is once again Mary's turn to wield it independently. Without putting too fine a point on it, our sculptures were pulled to the gutters by the weight of the reviewer's clumsy pen; dubbed as *novelties of conception* where any connoisseur of Mechanical Art would rightly see them as the catalysts of a modern epoch of the craft. (Reluctant as I am to further his acquaintance, Mr. -------- next-door is a fine example of just such a connoisseur, as he has, for more years than I can count, kept a tarpaulin-shielded behemoth in his back-yard which will, no doubt, prove to be a sculpture of immeasurable worth upon its unveiling.) At any rate, the execution of our pieces, to my mind flawless, was, in Fontenrose's crossed-eyes, perceived as *hurried* and, in one instance, *crude*—O! I cannot bear to continue in this vein. How the standards by which Artistic merits are judged have fallen! If we must become bed-fellows with such troglodytes as this reviewer in order to achieve even a modicum of recognition, then sculptors will henceforward have to build not *up* to the heavens, but *down* to the level of *Neanderthal public opinion,* if our creations are to be at all noticed in the broadsheets.

Art criticism has, this season, sunk to such abysmal depths that I am of a mind to turn my hand to challenging the likes of Fontenrose on his own preferred field of battle, namely, the printed page. After long hours studying the blatherings and idiocy of academical writings while laying the foundations of our innovative (*crude!!*) statues, I have become more than adept at counterfeiting the inanities inherent therein—

Indeed, until anon, Dear Diary; I intend to unleash the seeds of a Cultural plague on Fontenrose's publishing House, which, God willing, will bear fruit before his vitriolic pronouncements dissuade our fine Delaware artists from exhibiting next season; or worse, encourage them to adopt the habits of mediocrity he champions.

FIG. 5 – Typical propaganda in fictional form making the production of steam technology synonymous with the necrotic arts—or further evidence, coming from an acclaimed translator of weird and uncanny texts, that the apparitions and strange weather converging on the house of XX and XY meant that the presence of *S*. crossed more boundaries than I might have guessed? Here, in this excerpt of a tale taken from *The Innsmouth Heritage & Other Tales* (1992), Edison has set up a strange invention to connect with the voices of the dead. But might they be something else entirely?

Excerpt from "The Titan Unwrecked" by Brian Stableford

The machine crackled and hummed. The pipes emitted eerie sounds, reminiscent of harp strings stirred by a wayward wind—but then the voices began to come through.

They *were* voices—no one in the saloon could have any doubt about that—but it was quite impossible to distinguish what any one of them might be saying. There were thousands, perhaps millions, all attempting to speak at the same time, in every living language and at least as many that were no longer extant.

None of the voices was shouting, at first; they were all speaking in a conversational tone, as if they did not realize how much competition there was to be heard. As the minutes went by, however, this intelligence seemed to filter back to wherever the dead were lodged. The voices were raised a little—and then more than a little. Fortunately, the volume of their clamor was limited by the power of the amplifiers that Mr. Edison had fitted to his machine, and he immediately reached out to turn the knob that would quiet the chorus—with the result that the voices of the dead became a mere murmurous blur, denied all insistency as well as all coherency.

Edison's own voice was clearly audible over the muted hubbub when he turned to his audience to say: "If you will be patient, gentlemen, I am certain that our friends on the Other Side will begin to sort themselves out, and make arrangements to address us by turns, in order that each of them might make himself heard. It is just a matter...?"

He was interrupted then, by an unexpected event.

Allan Quatermain, who happened to be looking out of one of the portholes, observed four bolts of lightning descend simultaneously from widely disparate parts of the sky, converging upon the funnels of the *Titan*. All four struck at the same instant, each one picking out a funnel with unerring accuracy.... The lightning surged through the hull, possessing every fiber of the vessel's being.

The *Titan*'s wiring burnt out within a fraction of a second and Mr. Edison's machine collapsed in a heap of slag, although it left the man himself miraculously untouched, perched upon his stool. So diffuse was the shock, in fact, that the men standing in the saloon, their womenfolk in their cabins, and even the masses huddled in steerage felt nothing more than a tingling in their nerves, more stimulant than injury.

Allan Quatermain as depicted by Thure de Thulstrup.

Nobody aboard the *Titan* died as a direct result of the multiple lightning strikes, but the flood of electrical energy was by no means inconsequential. Communication between the *Titan* and the world of the dead was cut off almost instantly—but *almost* instantly was still a measurable time, and the interval was enough to permit a considerable effect.

Exactly what that effect was, no one aboard the *Titan* could accurately discern, and the only man aboard with wit enough even to form a hypothesis was Jean Ténèbre, who had briefly borrowed the identity of the elephant-hunter Allan Quatermain.

If the real Quatermain had made any posthumous protest, his voice went unheard.

What the Chevalier Ténèbre hypothesized was that by far the greater portion of the power of the multiple lightning strike, which had so conspicuously failed to blast the *Titan* to smithereens or strike dead its crew and passengers, had actually passed through the ship's telegraph system and Mr. Edison's machine *into* the realm of the dead, where it had wreaked havoc.

What the realm of the dead might be, or where it might be located, the chevalier had no idea—but he supposed that its fabric must be delicate and that the souls of the dead must be electrical phenomena of a far gentler kind than the lightning of Atlantic storms.

Thomas Edison had presumably been correct to dispute William Randolph Hearst's claim that Edison's machine might only enable the *Titan*'s passengers to hear the screams of the damned in Hell—but if the souls of dead humankind had not been in Hell when Edison closed his master-switch, they obtained a taste of it now.

And they screamed.

They screamed inaudibly, for the most part, because the pipes of Edison's machines had melted and their connections had been dissolved—but there was one exception to this rule.

The brothers Ténèbre and Count Lugard's party were not the only individuals on board the *Titan* who might have been classified as "undead." The fragment of the creature that had washed up on the beach at Nettlestone Point, having earlier been found by a fishing-vessel off Madeira and lost again from the *Dunwich*, also had an exotic kind of life left in it. Like many supposedly primitive invertebrates, the part was capable of reproducing the whole, under the right existential conditions and with the appropriate energy intake.

When this seemingly dead creature screamed, its scream had only to wait for a few microseconds before it was translated back from the fragile realm of the dead into the robust land of the living.

It was a strange scream, more sibilant than strident, and it was a strangely powerful scream.

As Edison's machine had briefly demonstrated—confounding all the skeptics who had refused for centuries to believe in spiritualists and necromancers, ghostly visitations and revelatory dreams—the boundary between the human and astral planes was not unbreachable. When the unnamable creature, whose close kin had died by lightning in the Mitumba mountains, was resurrected by lightning, its scream tore a breach in that boundary, opening a way between the worlds—and through that breach, the newly agonized souls of the human dead poured in an unimaginable and irresistible cataract.

FIG. 6 – This fragment of a letter from Mary Lewis writing to Eudamien Fontenrose contains further, independent evidence of _S._'s involvement in the events at the house. Unless, of course, Lewis were in league with _S._, and thus this evidence is presented to throw me off the scent of some still greater mystery. It also provides more information on the "two brains" references. Most importantly, this fragment is the only existing eye-witness account of the trial-run of the Mecha-Ostrich before its tragic destruction.

13th August 18—

Eudamien,

Would that I could still write "My dearest," but both you and I know full well what you have done to lose my regard. What I told you, Eudamien, was meant in strictest confidence. My artist's fears and insecurities were exposed to you in good faith, and in good friendship. My greatest distress is reserved for my poor Shelley, who has contributed in no manner to this situation, and yet has suffered almost as greatly as I; firstly in her avid anticipation of your review of our Art, and then in her terrible despair upon reading the mendacities your execrable scribbling have heaped upon our life's *oeuvre*. Your terrible mocking of our joint desire to create works that are both beautiful and practical was not merely petty, but also inexcusably cruel.

I can only be grateful that you did not reveal our secret to the entire world. Here in Delaware, in our *sanctum sanctorum,* we are at home. We are amongst friends—the family we have chosen for ourselves. We are not accustomed to being subjected to the ridicule and opprobrium we would otherwise garner should our *malady* be discovered by the broader community. We are but victims of a dreadful accident, not entirely of our causing, and the only saving grace, which allows us to continue to exist, is the Cerebral Exchange Compressor, built by my father before his untimely death. In sharing a Brain, one day each, and being able to maintain our own memories and privacy from each other, we preserve each of us a modicum of a normal life. You do not know how difficult it is to communicate with one's best friend and dearest soul, only via the medium of letters and notes left for one another; letters and notes and the pieces of clockwork *mechanic-erie* which we create and leave each for the other to incorporate into our Art. You cannot conceive, Eudamien, what you have done—you have impugned not only our Art, but our fundamental means of communication.

Since your ill-considered criticism, Eudamien, things in our little corner of Delaware have not been quite right. I know you truly believe that the world is ruled and governed by opinion, but you seem unaware or uncaring of the consequences of airing yours.

Our neighbors have become a source of constant concern to me. Shelley does not seem to share my worry, although her main discomfort of late falls at the feet of Mr. ——, who has displayed a rather prurient interest in her. I, on the other hand, may simply see more clearly because of the unconventional hours I am accustomed to keeping. It has been my custom, these past years at the colony, to take an evening stroll, but in recent weeks I have been troubled by a sensation of being…observed; watched by elements unseen and nefarious. As you are well aware, there can be mists around these parts, the river being not so very far away from our settlement. I am a creature of habit and prefer to walk the boundary line between the colony and the land of Mr. and Mrs. ——, but lately…there have been strangers—

Or, rather, things that at once appear human and, at the same time, somehow *incorrect*—they fade from view faster than any mortal should; they move too quickly to be quite…right. I know PQ has acted in the position of guardian for our colony for some time now, but in these latter days I begin to fear that protection may be more dangerous than any threat offered by the outside world.

Why, three nights ago I walked along the hedgerow separating our two lands —there was a most tremendous clanking sound, something I have never associated with the steam art Shelley and I have made our joint life's work; a most terrible grinding like something gnashing its teeth. I froze and waited—for agonizing minutes, it seemed, but good sense tells me it was not more than a few seconds. This thing loomed at me out of the mist and over the hedge, a dreadful specter a full thirty feet in the air, making an awful racket as if to devour me and anything else in its path. Eudamien, I ran…(and we two have known each other long enough for you to recall I do not indulge willingly in such physical exertion).

I threw a single glance over my shoulder as I fled and recognized the thing for what it was—a gigantic metal bird, an ostrich to be precise, black-winged with metallic limbs and steam puffing from its nether parts like a veritable rent torn in the fabric of Hell itself. The contraption was a hideous symphony in wire and steel, hardwood and aluminium. I did not slow my flight, but merely returned to our little cottage shaking like a leaf. I fear Shelley did not receive too excellent a start to her shift, but rather wondered why she felt so nervous and frail upon taking solitary possession of our Brain. Perhaps I should have left her a note, but my hands shook so violently that I couldn't muster the energy to hold the pen. Even now, knowing what it was, that it is nothing truly worse than anything Shelley and I have created over the years, I can no longer bring myself to go out once afternoon borders on its sister, the night.

I fear, I fear, I fear

[fragment ends here]

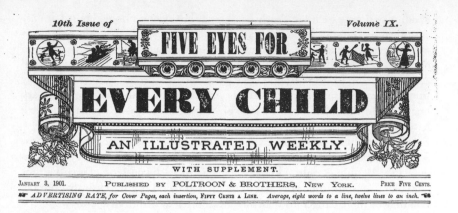

10th Issue of — Volume IX.

FIVE EYES FOR EVERY CHILD

AN ILLUSTRATED WEEKLY.

WITH SUPPLEMENT.

JANUARY 3, 1901. PUBLISHED BY POLTROON & BROTHERS, NEW YORK. PRICE FIVE CENTS.

ADVERTISING RATE, for Cover Pages, each insertion, FIFTY CENTS A LINE. Average, eight words to a line, twelve lines to an inch.

After a while I detected a smell of smoke, which it seemed to me must be a sign of civilization. I imagined perhaps a little woodcutter's hut, as in an old-fashioned fairy-tale—though the noise of clanking & clattering that grew around me as I approached was not such as I could imagine any woodcutter making—and what I found was not *old-fashioned* at all, but rather the beady red eye of the *Future,* glaring at me—but I get ahead of myself.

The woods parted. There was a green & rolling hill. There was a house, & around it a yard with a white fence. The noise had ceased—all was quiet & still. Thinking perhaps to beg for food I looked for a gate.

It was a tall fence—rather taller than I. Over the top of it poked a long stem of metal, which at first I took to be a chimney, or stovepipe. Only slowly did the peculiarity of its shape strike me—the slight spinal curve of the shaft, & that sideways sharpness that can only be described, albeit redundantly, as beak-like, & those two apertures, from which steam puffed gently, which one has little choice but to call *nostrils,* & then—as I pulled myself up to peer over the fence—the red eye that opened!

The lid of that eye was steel, and it opened with a sound like the loading of a revolver. The eye revealed beneath was red as a burning coal. Gentle nostril-puffs of steam became fierce jets. The whole flat metal head lurched, the long shaft of the neck below creaked & clanked, snapped & jerked. I fell.

On my hands & knees I pressed my eye to a crack in the fence, in time to see the thing turn tail and run—& what a magnificent tail!—a fan, a knot, not of feathers but of solid gleaming brass, like the shield of a Spartan!—& rising & falling two wings of good strong battleship steel!—& what <u>legs</u>! Silver and mahogany, rather like two Winchester rifles!—& the telescoping of its neck—& oh, the pistons on its back, up & down & in & out the pistons! Ostrich! Ostrich! —for such a bird it was, yet also—

Understand: I do not speak metaphorically. I shall never speak metaphorically again. When I say that bird was made of brass and battleship steel, I mean precisely that. If I say gears I mean gears, & if I say rivets, then *rivets,* damn it.

Kicking high its legs & swaying mightily from side to side & pouring steam from each of its many vents it began to run, around & around the edges of that little yard. At each step its feet sank in the earth, for there had been rain overnight, & it cannot have weighed less than a grand piano—yet it was indefatigable. Always it seemed it might topple—always it righted itself. The noise was deafening & the heat & steam like that of an African jungle. The wings, I swiftly intuited, worked to fan steam from its delicate internal workings, which might otherwise rust—for like its primitive savannah forbear, that splendid machine was flightless.

If the word *opium* enters your head it reflects poorly on your lack of charity & imagination. Besides it has been devilishly difficult to acquire opium out here in the sticks, as no doubt you knew it would be, damn you.

A vision came to me: one day the streets of New York will throng with these creatures, as men ride to work & women to their appointments on mechanical-ostrichback. & then a further vision: one day the Great Powers of Europe will settle their conflicts with ostrich-mounted riflemen, faster than any cavalry—imagine what mischief the Kaiser might do with a thousand head of mecha-ostrich! & then—

A man stood watching in the window of the house, as around & around his creation ran. I did not, I could not, approach him—not because I was afraid but because I was not worthy—one might as well interrupt God at work in *his* Garden.

Next to this triumph of Engineering, how trivial are the accomplishments of Art! Down all the weary centuries since first Homer sang, what have we artists created to compare—to this splendor, this terror! *Nothing.*

The ostrich lurched to a halt, not three feet from my hiding place. Its wings drooped & its pistons ceased. With one last great grinding of gears it lowered its head & drove it into the earth, as if to command, by example: *SILENCE.* & there it remained, dear children.

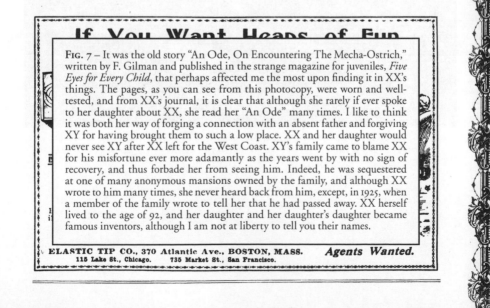

THE FLYING MACHINE OF THE FUTURE WILL PROBABLY BE BASED UPON THE STRUCTURE OF A FLYING BIRD,
THE LOUVRES IN THE WINGS CORRESPONDING TO THE ACTION OF THE BIRD'S FEATHERS.

NONFICTION

Artemisia Absinthe

"**Artemisia's Absinthe**": From the time Anyushka Rutkauska was a young girl, chemistry was all she could think of. While it was difficult for girls to pursue such professions in Poland in those days, it was not impossible, and Anyushka was finishing up her PhD at the University of Warsaw when rumors of the war began bubbling out of lecture halls and cafés like a laboratory concoction gone awry. Perhaps she was prescient, or maybe just restless, but she packed her bags and took off for Paris the day she passed her oral exams. At the time she certainly regretted the decision, as her freshly minted diploma did not translate into French easily, or truth be told, at all. That is how Anyushka found herself tending bar at the Taverne Coeur Noir in the 6th Arrondissement. Despite what she told the proprietor, she had no experience with tending bar, but for a chemist, how difficult could it be? Certainly easier than pronouncing "Anyushka" in French—patrons simply dubbed her "Artemisia" after the potent wormwood-tinged cocktails that were the ruin of many a Coeur Noir customer. Indeed, it became a badly kept secret that Artemisia's cocktails were the best in the City of Lights, and artists, courtesans, poets, academics, and diplomats began to pour into the cramped little bar to sample her potent concoctions. The cocktails proved to be great equalizers, rendering the rogue as well as the statesman a blissful yet blithering mess by the end of the evening. Inevitably, a bombast of German soldiers blundered in, rude and imperious, and with a hard, cold glitter in her heavily kohl-rimmed eyes, Anyushka cooked up something very, very special for the lot of them. No sudden deaths, no, nothing as obvious as that. Permanent impotence, total hair loss, an unshakeable sense of dread, irretrievable madness, the firm conviction that one was really a woman—these were the subtle gifts Anyushka's cocktails imparted to the German occupiers. Where no finger could be pointed, no credit could be given, either. Nonetheless, Artemisia was awarded a Medal of Honor at the end of the war, enjoying heroine status, and best of all, an appointment to the chemistry department at the Sorbonne.

Art & text by Ramona Szczerba.

Which Is Mightier, the Pen or the Parasol?

Gail Carriger

I'M A STEAMPUNK author and I have a shameful confession to make. Long before I discovered Moorcock, when I still thought Jules Verne was destined to remain safely trapped away in the 1800s forever, I wore steampunk. I proudly donned my Victorian silk blouses and little tweed jodhpurs. I twirled my bug-in-resin necklace and clacked about in buckle-topped riding boots. I didn't know there was steampunk to read, I only thought there was steampunk to wear. Finding out about steampunk literature for the first time was a complete revelation. "You can do that?" I thought. "You can marry a love of dressing the past with a love of writing a new version of it?" You could have knocked me down with an aetherogram.

This epiphany pushed me into undertaking a bit of a personal quest. For there I was, noted clotheshorse and proud science-fiction nerd, learning for the first time about a movement that effectively combined the two. Never had such a thing happened to me before. How had a rabid fan-girl such as myself completely missed this revitalized subgenre? How had the fashionista side of my personality happened upon an aspect of sci-fi literature without my inner geek even realizing it? Never before had fashion brought me so firmly into contact with fandom. In the past, I am sad to say, the two almost never met. Twenty years or more bopping about the convention circuit and my obsession with high-heels and pretty dresses was more a dirty little secret than proud bedfellow. Science fiction was getting stylish? How could this be? I felt that something must be wrong with the universe. So, in classic archaeologist fashion, I began to hunt about in history for an explanation as to this mystery.

It seems that, before the dawn of the modern steampunk literary movement, cyberpunk ruled the 1980s. This sparked a memory in my dark high-school soul: cyberpunk too was tied to a fashion movement in its heyday. Perhaps ten years after blue-haired protagonists plugged themselves into computers and battled mafia nanotech, some small pod of the alternative culture types started dressing cyberpunk. While most of America went on to explore the fine art of grunge in the 1990s, cyberpunks donned metallic eye makeup and fabrics that had more in common with red plastic bags than any known fiber. You have only to watch the movie *Hackers* to see the style come to life. Despite its candy-mod meets cyborg appeal, cyberpunk fashion always remained on the sidelines. It never hit mainstream popular dress and rarely walked the catwalks (with the possible exception of Betsey Johnson—who still looks like old-guard cyberpunk). Instead, cyberpunk went off to Japan, had a dirty little affair with the Wicked Witch of the West, and spawned Gothic Lolita. It may also have dropped a couple tabs and flirted with a hippy, if Burner style is to be believed. But essentially, the fashion of cyberpunk vanished.

So how is this tied to steampunk? Well, for one thing, history would seem to indicate that the literature came first and the fashion second. Right around the time of cyberpunk in the early '80s (1980s not 1880s, mind you) aberrant author pens began to deviate from one subgenre to the next, scratching out steampunk instead of cyberpunk. K. W. Jeter, Tim Powers, and James Blaylock led the charge, but with the page, not the pocket-watch, for it would take fashion around two decades to catch up. Not so suddenly, some six to eight years ago, those of us who had been waiting patiently for the Goths to discover color found our wait was over. Brown fabrics began to make a tentative appearance and bronze jewelry instead of silver. Vests were seen displaying their paisley goodness in public, lace blouses came in cream instead of just black, here and there a gratuitous pocket attached itself in patch-like glory, and Cool Things on fobs dangled and jangled. Oh, perhaps not everyone had heard about steampunk fashion, but there it was, and we knew about it. And we started to wear it. We started to turn typewriter keys into earrings. We started to haunt secondhand stores looking for old leather jackets to cut apart and metal cogs and clock parts to sew in rows down the fronts. Finally, in 2008 Ralph Lauren put steampunk down the runway, and there was no question—the style was mainstream. People may still not know the term "steampunk," but if you describe the clothing trend, they've seen someone wear it, or know someone who's into it. It's all around us, the buttoned up brass beauty of old tech and new ideas.

So we now have both steampunk fiction and steampunk fashion, which left me wondering: Was the pen tied to the petticoat, or did they spring up independent of one another? Taking into account the temporal lag between the arrival of *The Difference Engine* and the khaki corset, and combining that with time spent milling about observing both communities, there seems to be very little connecting the fiction and the fashion. Add this to the unfortunate truth that authors tend to have only a nodding acquaintance with decorous attire, and one can only conclude that these disparate aspects of the steampunk movement were separated at birth. The two seemed wholly unaware of each other until relatively recently, when, like long-lost fraternal twins, they were finally reunited. Sure, the authors might have known, in a vague way, that there was some weird thing to do with goggles and top hats going on at the fringes of their universe. The steampunkers might have had some hazy idea that somewhere, somehow, someone was writing something to do with dirigibles and automatons. But that was the sum total of the mutual acknowledgement. I'm inclined to believe it was fate or serendipity or one of those cosmic coincidences that caused the two to coalesce. We all simply found each other in the end: and not just the writers and the fashionistas, but the makers and the musicians and the artists as well. And we formed into a strange little social movement without any real objective, organization, or political agenda.

That said, while we may have arrived at this point together, many of us came by way of the mighty heel of a patent leather spat-cut boot with little buttons up the side. There are still plenty of people out there who are dressing steampunk without realizing it and making steampunk without reading it. Entirely unscientific inquiries suggest that at least 70 percent of steampunkers came to the lifestyle because of the fashion, not the fiction. (Okay, I totally made that up, but it sounds about right.) So, how to explain the basis of the appeal of steampunk style?

It's hard to detail all the threads of steamy fashion that draw us clotheshorses in. It's Edwardian formal wear with industrial trim. It's the lovechild of Hot Topic and a BBC costume drama. It's the gentility and politeness of Victorian manners with free-range cross-dressing options. It's salvaged suits with maker gadgets attached. It's clock parts and candy stripes, and everything in between. It's open to change, it's adaptable, it welcomes invention, innovation, and art. It's personalized and characterized—the ultimate in individuality. It can be worn only in part—a waistcoat here, a vintage military jacket there—or in full-on head-to-toe glory. However, there is more to it than just the look—there are underlying cultural components as well (or so I'm fated by my profession to believe).

It seems to me that a good portion of the lure of the steampunk aesthetic has to do with rebelling against modern design. We are living in an age where technology is trapped inside little silver matchboxes. Functionality has become something shameful, a tiny thing to be hidden away behind plastic and metal. But with steampunk fashion the inner workings of a machine become not just approachable but glorified. We steampunk DIYers force cogs and gears back out into the open. We configure them to spout great gouts of steam (or pretend, using dry ice). We hot-glue-gun them onto top hats. We are sticking our collective tongue out at the teeny tiny tech of an increasingly micro-plasticized world.

Steampunk also has a wonderful cross-gender and cross-generational appeal. Young makers are forming apprenticeships with older and more established artisans, joining tech shops, and hunting down artists and retired engineers for advice and help. Shopping for a stylish outfit tempts some into steamy goodness, while tinkering with gadgetry draws in others. (I won't break that down along gender lines but I certainly have my opinions on the matter.) Steampunk is something couples can engage in together. It has so many different aspects that it can even interest the whole family. It is already bringing fractured groups into semi-harmonious discussion (Burners, sci-fi geeks, tech-heads, cosplayers, rebels, home decorators, DIYers, and, yes, even authors), and best of all, it teaches new artistic skills along the way. We are all forced to be creative and inventive in our effort to personalize and characterize our attire.

There also seems to be psychological components to the appeal of the steampunk aesthetic. It provides us with a nonpartisan means by which we can dress to withstand modern life. There is a pervading feeling of political upheaval and economic chaos right now, a sense that the world is crumbling about us. Steampunk is quietly coping with this impending doom by busily tying itself to the green movement, reusing old parts for new beauty. We are taking things society has thrown away and making them useful again. Also, the connection to the Victorian era ads an element of politeness and order to both the clothing and the people who wear it. In the best of all possible worlds, steampunkers are helpful and kind to one another, we mind our manners, we reinvent etiquette to go along with our reinvented spats. We try to tap into the noblest aspects of 1800s England without the classism or bigotry. This, combined with the afore-mentioned recycling of rejected technology, brings with it a sense of control in chaotic times. Whether acknowledged openly or not, I believe there is a part of the steampunker psyche that believes if we can dress and act the part with integrity and class, making use of society's unwanted inanimate objects, we are exerting control over the crumbling ugliness of the world around us.

Even though I am a steampunk author, I genuinely believe that the attire of steampunk is as vital to the movement as the literature. Fashion is one of the things that sets steampunk apart from other science-fiction and fantasy subgenres. The clothing is a visual representation of the melding of an aesthetic with a sense of creativity and community. It's true that some people are more into the literature and others more into the craftsmanship, but these days almost everyone will nod in the fashion direction with a vest, or a pair of goggles, or a newsboy cap. Fashion has become the social construct that connects the eco-warriors with the threadbangers, the artists with the makers, the scholars with the dilettantes, and the authors with the fans. The power and the potential in steampunk attire is in its community-building effects, in the connections that it fosters and conversations it opens up between people. Steampunk style is not this season's throw-away runway look, nor this year's throw-away cell-phone technology. Steampunk is the opposite of planned obsolescence, which is one of the many reasons the look is still around.

As with any burgeoning social movement, whether we like it or not, the style and the literature have become linked. Whether we are making it, or hearing it, or writing it, or wearing it, we are all steampunk. So I say, "Reach for those top hats and wear them with pride: for goggles, gaiters, glory, and beyond!"

At the Intersection of Technology and Romance

Jake von Slatt

TEAMPUNK MEANS MANY things to many people. That which began as a literary movement has slowly changed into what is colloquially referred to as a "subculture." Throughout that process of change, one element of steampunk that has continually grown in recognition is the idea that the "punk" in steampunk is a direct descendant of the Punk Rock do-it-yourself credo. This rings absolutely true for me, as I grew up during the Punk era and have always been a fanatic do-it-yourselfer or Maker.

When I first started identifying my work, and occasionally myself, as "steampunk," it was not so much that I had discovered a movement to be a part of as that I had discovered the name for the movement to which I had always belonged. This idea that "I've finally found a name for what I am" is something that I have heard countless times from people I've met because of my involvement in the steampunk community, and I think that it's an indication there is a broader phenomenon at work here and that steampunk is just one face of it.

There is currently a resurgence of interest in making things oneself and this is very much a multi-disciplined phenomenon. Whether it be tailoring, textiles, beer, soap, electronics, or bio-hacking, people are starting to get interested again in pursuing hobbies with a technological basis. I have a theory as to why this is happening and particularly why it's happening now. Steampunk is part of this Maker Movement and I am going to walk you through the process of the decline and resurgence of technology-based hobbies using the example of electronics, since it is the one with which I am most familiar.

For many years technology-based hobbies, such as electronics and amateur radio, have been in decline. The magazines that supported the electronic hobbyist are all either out of business or are now purely gadget review rags—and there used to be dozens of them! Many towns had an electronics store packed with kits and components, and national companies like Heathkit and

Eico sold build-it-yourself versions of radios, electric "eyes," amplifiers, and even color television sets. All of this is long gone.

The current resurgence of interest in electronics and other technological hobbies isn't being driven by folks like me who have been involved with these activities for decades. It's being powered by young people, and they are bringing to it their own sensibilities and aesthetics. In the past these were established hobbies. If you had an interest in electronics, you'd usually start with a crystal radio, and then maybe step up to a 100-in-1 Electronic Projects kit. You'd go to Radio Shack or the local hobby center and there would be a whole wall of kits and components and books of things to do. The same was true for other hobbies as well; they each had a progression of standard projects that everyone would do.

However, I think the current resurgence of interest in technological hobbies lacks such defined paths and this means that young people are developing these hobbies later and infusing them with what they are already passionate about. This is what's leading to the development of fascinating hybrids like steampunk.

I've often described steampunk as the intersection of romance and science, and I think romance has a lot to do with steampunk's genesis as a subculture because I believe it's all due to what is essentially a love affair gone wrong.

The Victorian era was the last time that the typical high-school-equivalent education, for those lucky enough to attend school, gave the graduate all of the tools that he or she needed to understand the technology of the time. But more precisely, it was an age where the average educated person was *expected* to have an understanding of how the machines that made modern life possible worked. It helped a great deal that the machines of the time were designed to be appealing and to glorify the technology that made them work. Their inner workings were often exposed and their outer chassis embellished with pin-striping and gold leaf.

A young woman watching a train pull away from the platform could identify all of the parts that made the engine run. The boiler, the firebox, the great steam piston rod that drove the wheels and the smaller rod that worked the valve gear; these components were all visible and their functions obvious.

Technology was handsome, straightforward, and an honest, hard worker. All and all, a very attractive package.

Then along came the excitement of the first date with electricity! Electricity was clean and fast and could do things that used to require incredibly complex mechanisms. But while at first strange and mysterious, once one sat and played with a battery and some wire, electricity was easily understood. If you wrapped the wire around a nail and connected it to a battery, you could pick up another nail with your "electromagnet." When you disconnected the battery, the second nail would drop, and the proverbial light bulb illuminate. "Ah! That's how a telegraph works!" As for light bulbs themselves, the secret behind them was made immediately clear if you short circuited a battery of sufficient power and observed a length of wire grow hot and glow.

Electricity was clearly efficient and helpful, but just a little mysterious. Very sexy indeed!

But it was actually the advent of electronics that initiated the change that drove a wedge between us and technology. With mechanics, action and reaction are clear. In electrics, the action is once removed, but still directly observable. In electronics, instruments are required to convert the electrical impulses within the machines into something that we can sense with our eyes and ears. In the case of the radio, this instrument is the speaker. In the case of television, it's the cathode ray tube. In addition, to troubleshoot and repair any of these things you need meters and specialized testers to detect what's wrong—you can't simply look at it and see the malfunction like you can with something mechanical, such as a steam engine.

Of course, there were still folks who learned to master these tools and build their own radios and televisions, not as part of a profession, but as a hobby, for fun. These were often young people excited about the technology and it would often lead them into technical careers. Most importantly, these concepts were still being introduced to children in schools. Basic electronics was often taught at the middle-school level in the U.S. right up until the late twentieth century.

There were also popular magazines that contained projects for the amateur radio and electronics hobbyist and many folks eagerly awaited the next issue. (Although these same young people were often teased and called names like "Poindexter" after the nerdy character in a popular comic of the time.)

Electronics, and particularly those that relied on vacuum tubes, contained dangerous high-voltage power supplies and thus needed to be enclosed in cabinets. You could no longer view the components that made up your TV, let alone see them working. The television was the first real "black box" appliance in many homes. While commercial radios were equally mysterious, the majority of young people at the time had built or had friends who built crystal sets and understood some of the basics of radio transmission and reception.

Technology was harder and harder to understand for the casual user. It was keeping secrets and refusing to explain itself. Some folks thought it was worth the effort and found that mystery very attractive, but many decided that it wasn't worth the effort.

World War II came along and the rate of technological advancement increased incredibly because it was necessary for our security. We didn't worry that technology had gotten kind of dark—that it was now focused on destruction—we needed it for our very survival.

When the atom bomb ended the shooting war and the cold war began, technology got very scary indeed. It was clearly dangerous and destructive, and in much the same way that societies are always frightened of the veteran returned from war, no matter how grateful they are for what he or she accomplished, we started to truly fear technology ourselves.

The advent of the digital computer during this time further alienated us from our understanding. Now you not only needed special instruments to understand what was going on inside a machine, you needed to learn a new language. As they got smaller and cheaper, computers began to play a greater role in the functioning of everything. Automobiles, once purely mechanical things, now had engine control computers that failed without any obvious sign that something was wrong. People who had been fixing their own cars for years now had to rely on the dealer's "technicians" because not even the local repair shop had the proper tool to diagnose the problem.

Technology now had little connection to the average person. It was just too complicated to understand. And it was dangerous too, and getting more so every day—terms like "artificial intelligence" didn't help in the least, they just fueled the idea that the machines were becoming aware and would one day supplant us as the dominant inhabitants of this planet.

If you were one of those few who were still interested—if you were still seeking out information, mostly online since the electronic hobby magazines are all gone and the guy at Radio Shack no longer knows what a diode is!—you probably got called "nerd" and "geek," sure. But you also got to see names like "hacker" unfairly vilified in the press by reporters who did not understand the origins of the word. And if you brought your electronics project into school to show your friends and teachers, you were as likely to cause a bomb scare as you were to get a compliment for your cleverness, because the average person has no clue how our technological world works.

Many of us have witnessed this progression in our lifetimes. Several years ago, I even found myself saying, "Why should I spend a day figuring out how to fix that when I can just buy another?" In fact, a whole generation made that calculation and decided to stop trying to understand and maintain their own tech. They decided to treat technology as purely consumable, to be bought and discarded as needed.

But a kid growing up will always ask: "Daddy, how does a light bulb work?" and when Daddy can't answer that question, the child is left with a tiny hunger. It is that hunger that's driving the resurgence of electronics as a hobby today. I think that Geek Culture, the Maker Movement, and the reclamation of the pejoratives "nerd" and "hacker" are all a result of a generation of curious kids whose parents had trouble answering that query.

MAKE magazine is one example of a publication that services this interest and has met with fantastic success in the last few years. Now that Radio Shack is simply "The Shack" and no longer serves the electronic hobbyist, providers of kits and components like Adafruit Industries and SparkFun have sprung up online to provide electronic component fodder for a new generation of makers and amateur engineers.

This phenomenon is not limited to electronic hobbyists either. Automotive hackers are reverse engineering the engine control systems on their cars and making open-source trouble-code readers so they can "talk" to their vehicles and once again fix them. One group has even developed its own computer controller fuel-injection system that can be retro-fitted and customized to any vehicle.

Each group has responded to this resurgence of interest in our technological world in its own way. Each has brought to it its own passions, desires, and aesthetics. The steampunks are simply the romantics of this movement. We are as interested in how technology makes us feel as we are in what it does for us and we want technology that makes us feel good.

Steampunk is about taking a breath, starting at the beginning, and understanding the building blocks of technology from the nineteenth century upon which all of today's gadgets are based and realizing that we are the ones in control.

Steampunk is about falling in love again.

The Future of Steampunk: A Roundtable Interview

W E FELT IT would be fitting to conclude this anthology with a short roundtable interview on the future of steampunk, which may be very different than its past. To that end, we invited just a few of the many interesting people who bring wonderful vitality, energy, and vision to steampunk to share their thoughts on the future of the genre and the culture. Here's what they had to say. —The Editors

LIBBY BULLOFF, photographer, maker, creative clairvoyant, anachromancer, WWW.EXOSKELETONCABARET.COM.

I would like to see more steampunk in meatspace, such as additional steampunk spaces akin to the Edison, which capture the mystery, elegance, and whimsy of the aesthetic in three dimensions. I crave more objects that inspire through both their form and function, and more fashion that leans toward style, sustainability, and self-awareness rather than passing trends. I want to view the emergence of a magic-tinged steampunk world that is less hypothetical, less cautious, and totally immersive, a world that doesn't fear political dissonance, or change, or assimilation. I desire steampunk to find its true place outside time and settle into being a classic, respectable style, drawing on a wider variety of vintage and science fiction influences, from periods that aren't specifically Victorian and/or brass-colored in nature.

S. J. CHAMBERS, researcher and assistant editor of *The Steampunk Bible*, as well as writer of various sundries, both fictional and non, WWW.SJCHAMBERS.ORG.

My hope for the next steampunk decade is that its emphasis on sustainability and DIY will continue to inspire and impact how society thinks of consumption.

Sure, I love the clothes and gadgets, but I love more the philosophy behind all aspects of steampunk culture: if you think it, you can make it. We are currently a society of the quick fix: Is something broken? Buy a new one. Can't afford the new model? Here's a loan. We are completely dependent on the Industry of Others, and have no interest in the Industry of Ourselves. Steampunk promotes a self-industry by encouraging within each individual self-reliance, ingenuity, education, perseverance, and transmutation. Things that are quickly fading in our shiny, happy, consumerist iWorld.

JAYMEE GOH, aka Jha, writer, blogger, intersectional theorist, steampunk postcolonialist, WWW.SILVER-GOGGLES.BLOGSPOT.COM.

I, for one, would like to see steampunk grow as a story-telling vehicle that invites diversity and self-awareness, touching all corners of the world. It would be nice to see folks honestly discussing how real-life issues factor into the fantasy, and actively promoting various forms of play, to show there's not just one way to steampunk. With the research into history, steampunk could be an avenue for cultural pride and acceptance of different perspectives, as well as a really entertaining tool for education. I want to see more empires beyond Victoriana, traditionally marginalized identities towering up and above where they have been set, engaging with the self-confidence they would ordinarily be punished for. Being entrenched in history, steampunk is well-placed to examine the hubris of the past and present, to make way for a better future, through the power of stories. More folks should take advantage of that.

MARGARET "MAGPIE" KILLJOY, founder and former editor of *SteamPunk Magazine*, is proud to be a hobo, WWW.BIRDSBEFORETHESTORM.NET.

Steampunk, as a subculture and as an aesthetic, is at its best when it is a way of radically re-addressing the ways that we interact with technology. A way of challenging the assumptions of the industrial revolution. Which is probably more important right now, and over the next ten years, than it has ever been in human history. Top-down approaches to industry have backed our species into a corner (and outright wiped out thousands of others).

I'd love to see steampunks at the forefront of the DIY revolution. We can present people with sustainable approaches to technology and living. We can

help people realize that progress is not necessarily linear: we might have to go back in order to go forward. Perhaps fixed-wing aircraft, while militarily superior to lighter-than-air craft, are not as appropriate for our future. Perhaps what we need are more airships. Run collectively by trade syndicates instead of capitalist corporations, if you ask my opinion. In order to do this, of course, we're going to have to keep the "punk" in steampunk.

JESS NEVINS, librarian and author of *The Encyclopedia of Fantastic Victoriana*, RATMMJESS.LIVEJOURNAL.COM.

Confining myself to fiction: I'd like to see an emphasis on defining steampunk as a subgenre. "Steampunk" is too often used as a sort of catchall term; ungenerously, it is invoked by writers to add cachet and hipness. If the definition of steampunk has changed from what it was in the 1990s—and, clearly, it has—then what the word now means remains unclear. Steampunk is currently a nebulous concept applied to everything from Wild West steam mechas to African zeppelins to the Imperial British colonizing Mars. But we've always had a phrase for those concepts and stories: "science fiction." Steampunk has yet to settle on a set of clearly defined tropes and concepts by which it can be differentiated from historical science fiction. Until those are generally agreed upon, "steampunk" has no utility as a critical term and is best used by marketers rather than writers, critics, and fans. Enthusiasm for steampunk is wonderful; the assumption that "steampunk" is preferable as a term of description to "science fiction," without deciding upon a definition of "steampunk," is not so splendid.

MIKE PERSCHON, the Steampunk Scholar, STEAMPUNKSCHOLAR.BLOGSPOT. COM.

Many have pronounced steampunk dead or no longer having anything original to offer. I feel conflicted about such statements. I agree that steampunk seems to be slouching toward a stagnation of redundancy, but this is because steampunk still sees itself as a subgenre of SF or fantasy. Whatever it was in its nascency, it is no longer a subgenre, or even a genre. Elements from SF and fantasy remain, but current steampunk literature is anything but a coherent genre (and this is assuming steampunk ever was one to begin with). Steampunk is not a narrative structure, but an array of aesthetic elements. It is a visual style that can be imposed upon a genre, as well as multimedia: art, music, fashion, décor. Science fiction and fantasy are still the mainstays of steampunk texts, but we are already seeing steampunk applied to horror (Alan Campbell's *Scar Night)*, romance (Gail Carriger's *Soulless*), and even mainstream fiction (Thomas Pynchon's *Against the Day*). In film, steampunk is used in period pieces (*The Prestige*), as well as contemporary (*Franklyn*). In novels, the steampunk aesthetic is used for whimsical, high-flying adventures, such as Philip Reeve's *Larklight*, as well as serious, politically minded works like Theodore Judson's *Fitzpatrick's War*.

Some might construe derision in my definition of steampunk as visual style, not narrative substance. This definition does not reduce steampunk: it enlarges it. If steampunk is only science fiction or fantasy, it is restricted. Genre is structure, and while structure can be a skeleton, it can also be a straight jacket. If steampunk is an aesthetic employing the conventions of science fiction and fantasy, it can use them in other genres, allowing writers to move beyond homages to Verne, Wells, Reade, or Burroughs into those of Austen, Conrad, Melville, Poe, and Lawrence. It offers the possibility of applying this aesthetic to other forms of fiction, such as medical, political, or philosophical novels. It offers the possibility of being applied to novels as substance, as well as fluff.

So while I have some concern about the current state of steampunk, I disagree that it has reached its expiration date. There are still unexplored horizons for steampunk. And while I have limited my suggestions to the literature of steampunk, I hope they find application in other expressions and media. If steampunk is only a genre, then we can continue rehashing the themes of imaginary voyages and scientific romances. If it is an aesthetic, then the sky in which the airships fly isn't even a limit.

DIANA M. PHO, known in the steampunk world as Ay-leen the Peacemaker, writer, wanderer, wonderer, and the founding editor of BEYONDVICTORIANA. COM.

The definition of steampunk shouldn't limit itself to a "past that never was"; it presents a great opportunity to examine how the past binds us and how we, today, are breaking free from those rusted, time-eaten chains. Currently, steampunk examines the development of modernity in the West. But modernity doesn't end there, and neither should steampunk. I'd like to see steampunk's cultural range broaden in order to decenter its current Western,

Eurocentric framework. I want to hear about steampunk from more folks who aren't white, middle-class, straight, Christian, and male. Most importantly, I want steampunk to foster an open and equal exchange between various sets of global experiences. As other countries become more developed and as the world becomes more interconnected, I'm fully expecting new voices to start celebrating, questioning, and subverting their own pasts. For history's breadth cannot be limited to simple dualities: East versus West, North versus South, industrial versus developing. The face of history is a compass and steampunk is its wandering arrow, pointing out the ways where we can go.

Evelyn Kriete has been actively involved in the steampunk subculture since its development in the early 2000s, www.jaborwhalky.net.

I would like to see steampunk continue to develop as an artist movement. I would like to see the community grow and gather more positive public attention, because an influx of new people is very important to the longevity and vitality of a subculture. And I would definitely like to see steampunk prove to be a viable market to support the numerous artists in the trend. At this point it's pretty much inevitable that steampunk will hit the mainstream, which is fine so long as the increased popularity doesn't drown out the people who have been working in it for years. If the artists, writers, and fashion designers who have been making steampunk art since the mid-2000s and before are able to make a living off their work, steampunk will have been a good thing. On the other hand, if mainstream products and fans who have just gotten into steampunk end up stealing the spotlight from long-established steampunk artists who need to make a living off their work, it will be a terrible thing. And let's not forget that because artists are so busy making their art, there is a very real risk that they will be overlooked in favor of new people who spend more time in the public eye than contributing to the steampunk trend.

That said, I would also like to see people continue to explore the whole range of what steampunk has to offer. There's a lot of potential diversity in steampunk in terms of aesthetics and subject matter, and I really do hope that people will explore the wide range of what they can do in steampunk. And I would also like to see steampunk keep a solid sense of its identity and origins. It's inevitable that people are going to try to capitalize on the word "steampunk" without wanting to stay true to the genre.

At some point, people are going to try and strip steampunk's historical 19th-century-based identity away from it, and I hope that the community is strong enough and dedicated enough to stand fast and maintain steampunk's identity as Victorian sci-fi. Because once steampunk loses its historical grounding, it really has lost itself and the key thing that makes it unique. And I hope we won't see that happen.

-·:[*Art by Eric Orchard*]:·-

Biographies

Nonfiction

GAIL CARRIGER is an archaeologist, self-titled fashionista, and steampunk author who, when not excavating in Peru, lives on a vineyard in Northern California with one cat, three vehicles, and fifty pairs of shoes. She began writing in order to cope with being raised in obscurity by an expatriate Brit and an incurable curmudgeon. Her debut novel, *Soulless*, received a starred review in *Publishers Weekly* and won an Alex Award despite its irreverent, and often facetious, mash-up of several fiction genres. She has two more books in the same series due out in 2010, *Changeless* and *Blameless*.

JAKE VON SLATT is a steampunk contraptor and proprietor of the popular website The Steampunk Workshop (STEAMPUNKWORKSHOP.COM). He has built many of the iconic computer and keyboard "mods" widely circulated on the Internet and has had his projects featured numerous times on Boing Boing, MAKE, and *Wired* magazine's blogs (BLOG.MAKEZINE.COM and WWW.WIRED.COM) as well as countless others. Jake has been interviewed on the subject by the *New York Times*, the journal *Nature, Newsweek*, National Public Radio's *All Things Considered*, PBS's *Wired: Science* television show, and he was the keynote speaker at the *California Steampunk Convention* in Sunnyvale, California, in 2008.

Artists

JOHN COULTHART is an illustrator, graphic designer, and comic artist. His recent work includes CD designs for various record labels; book design for Savoy Books, Tachyon, and Underland; and a cover for Alan Moore's magazine, *Dodgem Logic*. A book collection of his H. P. Lovecraft adaptations, *The Haunter of the Dark and Other Grotesque Visions*, was published in a new edition in 2006. His website is WWW.JOHNCOULTHART.COM. He lives and works in Manchester, England.

ERIC ORCHARD, who contributed the frontispiece and endpiece for this anthology, is an award-winning illustrator and cartoonist living in Canada. He grew up in Halifax, Nova Scotia, where he began illustrating stories in grade school. He studied painting and art history at the Nova Scotia College of Art and Design. Eric has illustrated three children's books. His third children's book, *The Terrible, Horrible, Smelly Pirate*, was released in the spring of 2008 and was nominated for the Lillian Shepherd Memorial Award. In 2008, his work was featured in the Totoro Forest Project charity auction. His work has been recognized in the Spectrum Annual of Fantastic Art and the Society of Illustrators annual exhibit, winning silver in comics in *Spectrum 17*.

When **RAMONA SZCZERBA** (a.k.a. Winona Cookie) is not being a psychologist in private practice in San Diego, she's busy making art, something she has done for as long as she can remember. She enjoys creating whimsical children's illustrations in watercolor, but also loves working with collage and assemblage. She favors the darkest faeries, legendary women, arcane subject matter, and inventors who never were. She is currently obsessed with the steampunk genre and is trying to keep up with the torrent of characters who insist on being depicted and having their stories told. She has illustrated several coloring books, published two calendars, and written a feature article that appeared in Somerset Studios.

About her collages combined with short stories, she writes: "For many years I tried to come up with charming and whimsical children's stories so that I might illustrate them, and hopefully, realize large profits. The stumbling block seemed to be plot—I couldn't think of any. Great characters materialized and meandered about, doing absolutely nothing. When I started creating these collages, something different began to happen: stories come to me as I work on them, usually beginning with the character's name and evolving from there. It's as though their stories really happened, and if they didn't, they should have."

Contributors to "A Secret History of Steampunk"

MATTHEW (ALCOTT) CHENEY ("Mimeographed 1976 *Bulletin of New Hampshire Folklore & Miscellany*, Mecha-Oliphaunt") lives in the town in New Hampshire where Nathaniel Hawthorne died. His fiction and nonfiction have appeared in a wide variety of venues, including *One Story*, *Las Vegas Weekly*, *English Journal*, *Lady Churchill's Rosebud Wristlet*, and elsewhere. He is the former series editor for *Best American Fantasy* and is a columnist for *Strange Horizons*. Of his steampunk researches, Cheney says, "New Hampshire has given the world many things, including one of the all-time worst presidents (Franklin Pierce), the first famous American serial killer (H. H. Holmes), a lurid bestselling novel (*Peyton Place*), one of the most powerful conservative media outlets before the rise of Fox News (the Manchester *Union Leader* newspaper), and refuge for the late J. D. Salinger. Naturally, such a great state has made its share of contributions to the reality and fiction of steampunk. One must simply know under which slab of granite to look."

RIKKI DUCORNET is one of the preeminent surrealists/fantasists of the past three decades, with classic books that include *The Complete Butcher's Tales*, *Phosphor in Dreamland*, and *Gazelle*. The excerpt from her work used in "A Secret History" is from a short story in her collection *The Word "Desire"*.

FÁBIO FERNANDES is a writer living in São Paulo, Brazil. Fernandes is the author of *A Construção do Imaginário Cyber* (2006), *Os Dias da Peste* (2009), and *Os Anos de Silício* (2010). Also a journalist and translator, he is responsible for the Brazilian translations of several prominent SF novels, including *Neuromancer*, *Snow Crash*, and *A Clockwork Orange*. His short stories have been published in Brazil, Portugal, Romania, UK, New Zealand, and USA. In 2008, he created the SFF review blog Post-Weird Thoughts. Fernandes contributed an excerpt from "The Arrival of the Cogsmiths," in the context of inspiring the character XY to complete his mechanical ostrich. The story was "written in the same universe of The Boulton-Watt-Frankenstein Company, both of which were published originally in *Everyday Weirdness* in 2009. The idea was: What if Victor Frankenstein had decided that machines would work better because they would most probably do their master's bidding? The entire story was conceived to be a kind of *tableux vivant* in which I would present the Cogsmiths, apprentices of Frankenstein."

Felix Gilman ("An Ode, On Encountering the Mecha-Ostrich") is the author of the novels *Thunderer* and *Gears of the City*. His new novel, *The Half-Made World*, is forthcoming from Tor in September 2010. For better or worse, it doesn't have any mecha-ostriches. He lives in New York, and his website is www.felixgilman.com. "The spark for the story was that Jeff e-mailed me and said 'would you like to write a few words about seeing a mecha-ostrich in a 19th-century inventor's yard I need it by Friday please' and I said 'ok why not.' That's not a very good story I'm afraid but it's how it was."

L. L. Hannett ("Notes & Queries" and "Excerpts from Shelley Vaughn's journal") lives in Adelaide, South Australia—city of churches, bizarre murders, and pie floaters. She has sold over a dozen stories to venues that include *Clarkesworld Magazine*, *Fantasy Magazine*, *Weird Tales*, *ChiZine*, and *Electric Velocipede*. Her story "On the Lot and in the Air" was on the *Locus* Recommended Reading List for 2009. She is a graduate of the Clarion South Writers Workshop, and hopes to complete her PhD in medieval Icelandic literature before she grows older than her subject matter. She writes of her collaboration with Angela Slatter, "Notes & Queries," which riffs off Jeffrey Ford's "Dr. Lash Remembers" in the Stories section of this anthology: "When Slatter and I were planning our piece, I found myself mentioning the word 'serendipity' way more frequently than is probably acceptable—but I couldn't help it. This was one of those mythical occasions when the universe was out to help us put this mad thing together. Angela had recently been reading some of Ford's other works (and she seems to remember every single line she has ever read in her life), so she quickly came up with really inventive ways to incorporate them into her 'Prisoner Queen' and 'Air Ferry Disaster' sections, thus earning herself the title Queen of Intertextual References. I have always wanted an excuse to write something in a 'N. & Q.' style, and since I've been reading a lot of 19th-century literature lately, the tone and approach we took seemed the natural way to go. We both wanted to play with the ideas in Ford's story without directly translating them into our piece, so we decided to take a couple of concepts that really jumped out at us and mess with them: I was dying to get my hands on 'Dr. Lash' and the mysterious spores, and Angela was instantly attracted to the idea of transforming Millicent and the Prisoner Queen. Our writing styles are different, but complementary, so it's always fun working together. After a few drafts, passing the piece back and forth, it became hard to tell where one Brain ended and the other began—which is just how it should be. All we need now is a Cerebral Exchange Compressor and we'll be set."

MECHA-OSTRICH. The Mecha-Ostrich's fiction has appeared in *Conjunctions*, *Black Clock*, TOR.COM, and many year's best anthologies. After writing the frame story for "A Secret History of Steampunk," the Mecha-Ostrich is a very tired bird.

EKATERINA SEDIA ("Two pages from *The Russian Book of the Improbable*") resides in the Pinelands of New Jersey. Her critically acclaimed novels, *The Secret History of Moscow* and *The Alchemy of Stone*, were published by Prime Books. Her next one, *The House of Discarded Dreams*, is coming out in 2010. Her short stories have sold to *Analog, Baen's Universe, Dark Wisdom*, and *Clarkesworld*, as well as the *Haunted Legends* and *Magic in the Mirrorstone* anthologies. Visit her at WWW.EKATERINASEDIA.COM. As for her contribution, she writes that she has been "working on Russian steampunk for a while now—my agent is currently shopping an alternative history novel in which Russia abolishes serfdom in 1825 instead of 1861, becoming an industrial rather than agrarian power. This setup of course offers itself to all sorts of fun alternative history twists and insane technological developments—and what better place to test airships than Siberia?"

ANGELA SLATTER ("Notes & Queries" and "Mary Lewis' letter to Eudamien Fontenrose") is a Brisbane-based writer of speculative fiction. Her short stories have appeared in such anthologies as *Dreaming Again* (Jack Dann, ed.), Tartarus Press's *Strange Tales II* and *III*, the Twelfth Planet Press's *2012*, and in such journals as *Lady Churchill's Rosebud Wristlet*, *Shimmer*, and *On Spec*. Three of her stories have been shortlisted for the Aurealis Award in the Best Fantasy Short Story category and her work has had several Honourable Mentions in the Datlow, Link, and Grant *Year's Best Fantasy and Horror* anthologies. She has two short story collections out in 2010: *Sourdough & Other Stories* (Tartarus Press) and *The Girl with No Hands and Other Tales* (Ticonderoga Publications). She works part-time at a writers' center. She is also a graduate of Clarion South 2009 and the Tin House Summer Writers Workshop 2006 and she blogs at ANGELASLATTER.COM about writing and random things that catch her attention. Of her collaboration with Lisa Hannett, she writes, "Brain and I at first talked about doing a straight narrative called 'An Audience with the Queen' or 'The Prisoner Queen in Bloom.' However, I am very lucky because Lisa knows everything in the world and mentioned the idea of doing our section in the form of the old Notes & Queries section of an 1800s broadsheet. She even had examples she was able to send me—huzzah for nerdish habits! So we brainstormed to do four main entries and picked four points from Ford's story that we thought could be used. In one of them I wanted to make an oblique reference to Ford's 'The Night Whiskey,' hence the note about the deathberry in the Prisoner Queen, and I also wanted Millicent to be less innocent that she might appear. I also liked the idea of crossing the Hot Air Opera with the Air Ferry Disaster. Lisa had ideas about the spores, Dr. Lash, and the ear-ink that left pictures on the pillows of the sufferers. The other random queries were things we pulled out of the air. I had to read up on the writing style, and luckily Lisa had been reading a surfeit of Oscar Wilde and was able to edit over the worst of my inconsistent and anachronistic phrasings! We did a back-and-forth on the entries about four times before we were happy. I love working with Lisa as we have a similar work ethic, a comparable aesthetic sense, and yet still have very different voices."

BRIAN STABLEFORD ("Excerpt from 'The Titan Unwrecked' and the translation from Albert Robida's "The Railway War") lives in Reading, England. He has published more than 160 books of various sorts, including the recent novels *Prelude to Eternity* and *Alien Abduction: The Wiltshire Revelations*, the recent story collections *The Return of the Djinn and Other Black Melodramas* and *Beyond the Colors of Darkness and Other Exotica*, and the recent nonfiction book *The Devil's Party: A Short History of Satanic Abuse*. He is currently translating classics of French scientific romance, including works by Maurice Renard, J. H. Rosny the Elder, and Albert Robida (from whose *The Adventures of Saturnin Farandoul* "The Railway War" is taken). "The Titan Unwrecked" is a sequel to both Paul Feval's *Knightshade* and Morgan Robertson's "Futility, or, The Wreck of the Titan."

IVICA STEVANOVIC (two images attributed to the comic strip "American Tinker Under the Influence of Absinthe") was born in 1977, in Nis, south of Serbia. He grew up on comic books and old horror movies. In early childhood he began to draw, and is still working. He illustrated a large number of titles for children, and designed the books' covers...He mostly likes to illustrate picture books, and his favorite is Andersen's story *The Emperor's New Clothes*. So far, he has worked mainly with Serbian publishing houses. His specialty is graphic novels and art book projects. To date he has published *Kindly Corpses* (2003), *Lexicon of Art Legions* (2005), *Anatomy of the Sky* (2006), and *Katil* (*Bloodthirsty Man*) (2008). When creating art, Ivica uses different techniques: from ink pen drawing as a basis, through watercolors to digital painting and collage. The results of his work can be seen on WWW.BEHANCE.NET/IvicaStevanovic and EDGE77. CGSOCIETY.ORG/GALLERY. Stevanovic lives in Veternik (northern Serbia) with his wife, Milica, who is also a children's illustrator. Stevanovic currently works as a lecturer at the Academy of Art in Novi Sad (Serbia), the Department of Graphic Communication. He has won several prizes in the fields of design, illustrations, cartoons, and comics.

The Editors

Hugo Award winner ANN VANDERMEER and World Fantasy Award winner JEFF VANDERMEER have recently co-edited such anthologies as *Best American Fantasy #1 & 2*, *Steampunk*, *The New Weird*, *Last Drink Bird Head*, and *Fast Ships, Black Sails*. They are the co-authors of *The Kosher Guide to Imaginary Animals*. Future projects include *The Weird: A Compendium of Strange and Dark Fictions* for Atlantic and *The Thackery T. Lambshead Cabinet of Curiosities* for HarperCollins. Jeff's latest books are the Nebula-nominated novel *Finch* and the writing strategy guide *Booklife*. Ann is the editor-in-chief of *Weird Tales* magazine. Together, they have been profiled by National Public Radio and the *New York Times*' Papercuts blog. They are active teachers, and have taught at Clarion San Diego, Odyssey, and the teen writing camp Shared Worlds, for which Jeff is the assistant director. They live in Tallahassee, Florida, with too many books and four cats. For more information, visit WWW.JEFFVANDERMEER.COM.

THE VICTOR TYPE-WRITER

EXCELS IN SPEED, IN QUALITY OF WORK, IN DURABILITY.

A Perfect Machine.   Very Simple.   Easy to Learn.

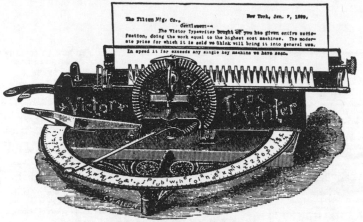

PRICE, $15.00.

The **VICTOR** is now being rapidly introduced throughout the United States, and we offer liberal inducements and exclusive territory to Agents wishing to sell the best Single-Keyed Type-writer made.

WRITE FOR PARTICULARS.

GEORGE D. JOHNSON, GENERAL AGENT FOR NEW ENGLAND.
7 MILK STREET, BOSTON, MASS

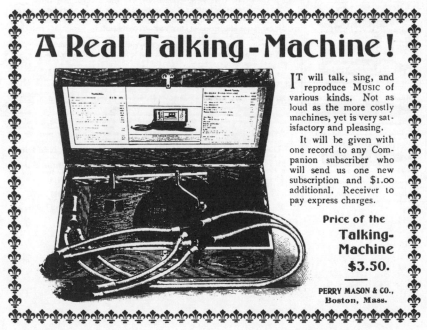

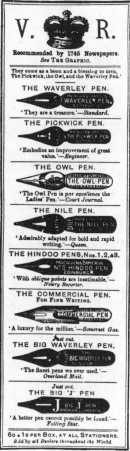
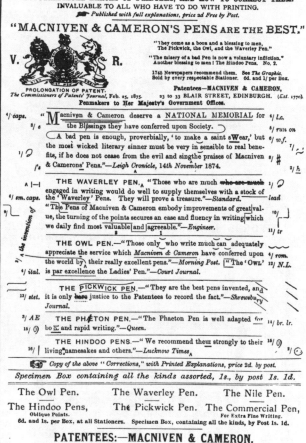